A Different Echo

A Different Echo:

Tiny Words

By: Kimberly Cummings

A Different Echo: Tiny Words

© 2025 The Cozy Scratchpad

Scripture quotations are taken from the King James Version (KJV) of the Bible.

First Edition

Printed in the United States of America

Hardcover ISBN: 979-8-9998730-0-2

Paperback ISBN: 979-8-9998730-1-9

Published by:

The Cozy Scratchpad

Disclaimer

A Different Echo: Tiny Words is a work of fiction. All names, characters, organizations, events, and locations are either products of the author's imagination or are used fictitiously. Any resemblance to actual persons, living or dead, or actual organizations or events is purely coincidental.

Scripture references are quoted from the King James Version KJV of the Holy Scriptures and are used to support the spiritual message of the story.

This book is intended to inspire thoughtful reflection on the spiritual consequences of worldly pursuits and disconnection from faith. It is not intended to diagnose, treat, or offer professional counseling or legal advice.

The brand names, teams, universities, leagues (e.g., Greywood University, Gerry High Hawks, EFL, Titan Bowl), and agents portrayed in this book are fictional and used solely for storytelling purposes.

Any contracts, agreements, or symbolic figures presented in this story, such as the Career Acquisition and Brand Agreement, are literary devices intended to provoke spiritual awareness and are not based on real-world legal practices.

This novel explores deep themes involving morality, temptation, and redemption. Readers are encouraged to seek truth, wisdom, and peace through God's Word.

Dedication

To God
Thank You.

To my family and friends
I love you.

*Ye shall walk in all the ways which the Lord your God hath
commanded you, that ye may live, and that it may be well with you,
and that ye may prolong your days in the land which ye shall possess.*
Deuteronomy 5:33 KJV

Table of Contents

Disclaimer 4

Chapter 1... 6

Echoes from the Table 6

Chapter 2... 15

Taco Tuesday 15

Chapter 3... 24

Eyes on the Field 24

Chapter 4... 34

Film Room Lessons 34

Chapter 5... 44

Aftermath 44

Chapter 6... 53

Just Another School Day 53

Chapter 7... 61

Missing Pieces 61

Chapter 8... 70

Don't Be Dead 70

Chapter 9... 78

Through the Glass 78

Chapter 10 89

A Place to Stand.. 89

Chapter 11 96

Lemon Glaze and Lightness..96

Chapter 12 104

Dust to Dust 104

Chapter 13 112

Back to School..112

Chapter 14 121

A Breath Between Battles 121

Chapter 15 129

Small Town, Big Energy..129

Chapter 16 136

A Feast for the Fight 136

Chapter 17 144

A Breath Between Seasons 144

Chapter 18 151

The Next Play...151

Chapter 19 161

A New Year to Remember 161

Chapter 20 171

Road to Summit 171

Chapter 21 180

Shifting Gears 180

Chapter 22 188

The Road Ahead 188

Chapter 23 196

Between the Whistles 196

Chapter 24 203

Shadows and Summer 203

Chapter 25 213

The Final Drive 213

Chapter 26 222

More Than a Scoreboard 222

Chapter 27 229

Home for the Holidays 229

Chapter 28 238

Miles from Home 238

Chapter 29 246

Unshaken Focus 246

Chapter 30 255

Quiet Before the Whistle 255

Chapter 31 264

When Summer Fades 264

Chapter 32 272

Quiet Influence 272

Chapter 33 284

First Look at the Future 284

Chapter 34 295

The Decision 295

Chapter 35 304

The Final First Day 304

Chapter 36 313

The Sound of Tomorrow 313

Chapter 37 321

Just a Weekend 321

Chapter 38 329

Cabin Weekend 329

Chapter 39 338

Turning Points 338

Chapter 40 347

The Final Walk 347

Chapter 41 355

Day One Drift 355

Chapter 42 364

Just a Little Fun 364

Chapter 43 375

Pulled in Every Direction 375

Chapter 44 385

The Cost of Winning 385

Chapter 45 394

Year Three: No Looking Back 394

Chapter 46 403

The Glare and the Quiet 403

Chapter 47 412

Fame 412

Chapter 48 420

Echo..420

Epilogue..427

The Tiny Words...427

Author's Note 429

About the Author...430

Chapter 1
Echoes from the Table

The cafeteria at Gerry High School buzzed with noise and motion, the clang of lunch trays, the hum of teenage voices, the occasional screech of sneakers across the linoleum floor. It was chili day, and the smell lingered in thick waves that couldn't be masked by cheap air freshener or open windows.

At the corner table near the vending machines, Ethan Phillips sat with his usual crew: Chris Williams, their quarterback; Scott Davis, his best friend since third grade; and Amanda Blackwell, who always wore black nail polish and quoted random facts mid-conversation like a walking encyclopedia page.

Ethan leaned back, his massive frame causing the plastic chair to creak beneath him. At 6'6" and 260 pounds, he was built like a Force Train, even as a freshman. His broad shoulders stretched the seams of his jersey, and when he laughed, which wasn't often lately, it was deep and effortless, the kind that made people look up without knowing why.

"Did y'all see the second quarter?" Chris said, stirring his chocolate milk with a French fry. "Scout from Greyhill College was in the stands, man. Wearing red and everything. I swear he was there for me."

Amanda rolled her eyes. "Or maybe he just… goes to Winslow State and wants a hot dog."

Scott snorted. "Nah, nah. You balled out, bro. That spiral in the third, Textbook."

Ethan nodded along quietly. The table was filled with laughter and trash talk, but his mind wandered.

He remembered the crowd. The band. The moment he bulldozed through two defenders and dropped a lineman like a bowling pin on the way to the end zone.

Everyone had cheered.

But even then, something had felt off.

"So, Ethan," Chris said, nudging him with his elbow. "Are you ready for Friday? Word is a Greywood scout's coming down."

Scott jumped in. "Dude, you're gonna get recruited as a freshman. You're like a tank with legs."

Amanda added, "A thoughtful tank. With the soul of a sad poet."

Ethan cracked a smile. "That's one I haven't heard."

"Seriously," Chris said. "They're saying you're a four-year legend in the making."

Ethan shrugged. "Guess we'll see."

Inside, though, he felt something twist, not pride, not nerves. Something colder. The more they spoke his name, the less it belonged to him.

As the lunch bell rang, Ethan stood, his towering presence casting a shadow over the table. His friends filtered out into the hallway, still laughing. But Ethan paused.

For just a second, the clatter of the cafeteria dulled, and his eyes locked on an empty table near the back. The same table he used to sit at back in middle school. Alone. Before the weight, before the muscle, before football gave him a name.

His chest tightened.

That night, he sat in his room, lights off, curtains drawn. A single trophy glinted from the shelf: "Pop Jump Warm Youth MVP 6th Grade." His mom had cried that day. His uncle George bought him pizza and called him "Little Freight."

But Ethan remembered more than the touchdown.

He remembered the silence in the car when his dad never showed up to watch.

He remembered staring at the stands, scanning for that one face, and pretending he didn't care when it wasn't there.

He picked up his phone. Opened the Voice Memo app.

October 7. Lunch table talk today. Scouts. Praise. Chris says I'm the future. Maybe I am.

However, I sometimes think I reached my peak when I was ten.

Sometimes, I feel like I'm playing someone else's role."

He stopped recording.

Saved it under:

My Future – 02

Then he leaned back in the darkness, listening to the echo of his breath. He finally fell asleep for the night.

The alarm buzzed at 6:15 a.m.

Ethan rolled over, groaning as he swatted at his phone until the noise stopped. The room was dim, lit only by the gray wash of morning peeking through the blinds. Posters of pro athletes hung on the wall, but most were curling at the corners. His cleats sat by the door, still muddy from last Friday.

He sat on the edge of his bed for a moment, rubbing his eyes.

Mornings were always the same…too quiet, too slow, and constantly reminding him of what used to be.

He pulled on his jeans, a black hoodie, and laced up his sneakers. As he slung his backpack over his shoulder, he paused to glance at the shelf near the door. A single photo in a wooden frame: him, about age seven, standing between his mom and dad. All three were smiling, but Ethan could see now what he hadn't then, the strain behind their eyes.

He turned the photo face down.

The smell of bacon drifted upstairs.

Ethan padded down the creaky steps of the old two-story house. The kitchen was small, but it always smelled like comfort, cinnamon, coffee, and something warm. His mom stood by the stove, her curly brown hair pulled into a messy bun, humming softly as she flipped pancakes.

"Morning, baby," she said without turning around.

"Morning," Ethan mumbled, sinking into the chair at the table.

Uncle George sat across from him, already halfway through a crossword, a half-eaten piece of bacon in one hand, pencil in the other. "You sleep alright?"

Ethan shrugged. "Yeah. I guess."

George glanced up. "You've been saying that a lot lately."

His mom turned from the stove and placed a stack of pancakes in front of him. "You sure everything's okay? Not feeling sick or anything?"

"I'm fine," Ethan said quickly, then stabbed at a piece of pancake as it owed him money.

The truth was… he didn't know how to explain it. The heaviness. The fog. The way things felt louder and quieter at the same time.

The house on Birch Street had once belonged to his grandparents. After they passed, five years ago, just months apart, his mom and George moved in together to make ends meet. His mom worked at the town clinic as a registered nurse. Uncle George taught middle school science. Between them, they held things together.

Most days.

Sometimes, on the weekends, Ethan's dad would call, usually drunk, always making empty promises. "Gonna come see you play soon, son," he'd say. "Gonna make things right."

Ethan stopped waiting around in the seventh grade.

He still kept the voicemails, though. Didn't know why.

"Big game this Friday, huh?" George said as he drained the last of his coffee.

"Yeah. A couple of scouts are coming. Chris is hyped."

"You ready for all that?" George asked.

Ethan looked up. "For what?"

"The pressure. The attention. Being the guy."

Ethan nodded slowly, then stood and grabbed his bag. "Yeah… I'm ready."

But inside, he wasn't sure.

Outside, the morning air was cool, biting against his hoodie. He slid into the passenger seat of his mom's car as she locked the front door.

As they pulled out of the driveway, Ethan glanced back at the house.

The porch light still flickered. The gutter still hung loose from the roof.

The house seemed to be trying to stand tall, even as time pulled it down.

Ethan arrived at school, which sat on the edge of town, tucked between an aging strip mall and an overgrown cornfield. The redbrick building looked ordinary from the outside, like any other small-town school. But inside, especially this week, the energy was different.

It was a Friday game week.

As soon as Ethan walked through the double doors, the noise swallowed him: lockers slamming, sneakers squeaking, laughter bouncing off the hallway tiles.

"Yo, Ethan!"

"Beast mode Friday, baby!"

"Gonna carry the whole team again?"

He offered nods and half-smiles as he made his way through the crowd. A couple of first-year students held their phones up, as if they were filming him for a social media sports edit. Someone slapped his shoulder through the hoodie. A girl from the soccer team winked. A teacher in the hallway gave him a fist bump.

He hadn't even reached homeroom yet.

Chris Williams, their quarterback, was already holding court by the vending machines, surrounded by a group of girls and a couple of JV players hanging on every word.

"Recruiter from Cozy University is flying in," Chris was saying. "Coach says if we keep the same momentum, this could be the biggest year in school history."

Beside him stood the other core players:

Lamar Jordan, freshman wide receiver, flashy and fast, always wearing chains he wasn't supposed to.

Steven Gray, the calm senior linebacker who rarely talked unless it was to correct a coach.

Rico Simmons, the senior kicker with a loudmouth and a 4.0 GPA, there was no one who ever saw him coming.

And Trevor Banks, the senior lineman who was as big as Ethan but never tried to outshine anyone.

The "Gerry Five" people had started calling them. Ethan included. Not that he ever asked for it.

"Phillips!" Chris called out. "You got that text from Coach last night?"

"Yeah," Ethan said as he walked up. "He sent the same message to my uncle. Two college reps confirmed for Friday."

Chris grinned. "Let's make 'em regret flying coach."

As the bell rang, students rushed toward their classes. Ethan walked into first-period English and was immediately met by Ms. Daly's enthusiastic clap.

"There he is!" she said. "Our very own Friday Night Force Train!"

The class chuckled. Ethan slid into his seat near the window.

Ms. Daly pulled out a clipboard. "So, I was thinking after your next game, maybe we could do a little feature for the school paper? Something motivational for incoming students next school year? A piece on balance, academics, and athletics? What do you think?"

"Sure," Ethan said, even though he didn't.

Halfway through class, his phone buzzed in his pocket. He didn't check it. Probably another DM request. Lately, they came in hourly — strangers from out of town, old friends from Little League, even a guy claiming to be a youth sports promoter from Texas.

Everybody wanted something.

Everybody saw the spotlight.

But no one saw the shadow it cast behind him.

When the bell rang for the second period, Amanda caught up with him by the lockers.

"You look like you're being swallowed alive," she said, digging through her bag for her sketchbook.

"I'm fine.

"You always say that. But you haven't been you since preseason. It's like you're playing a role."

Ethan didn't respond right away. He looked past her, down the hall where a new bulletin board had been pinned up: "State Title Dreams" in bold letters, with photos of the five boys beneath it.

He was front and center.

Unsmiling.

Unmoving.

Like a statue of someone he wasn't sure he recognized anymore. He and Amanda retreated to their next class.

Later that afternoon, the sun blazed over Gerry High's football field, casting long shadows across the turf. Whistles blew sharply in the air, cleats thundered against the ground, and the sound of helmets colliding echoed like distant thunder.

Ethan tightened the strap on his helmet and took his stance at the line of scrimmage. Sweat already streamed down his back, but his focus was locked in.

"Down! Set, hut!"

Chris dropped back, scanning the field. Ethan burst off the line, his powerful legs cutting through the defense like a blade. He powered through a block, cleared a gap, and bolted toward the end zone. A perfect screen pass hit him in the chest. He caught it in stride, dragging two defenders for another six yards before hitting the pylon.

"Touchdown, baby!" Coach Lanning hollered, tossing his clipboard into the air. "That's what I'm talking about!"

The team exploded in cheers as Ethan jogged back, helmet off, grinning ear to ear.

Chris met him with a shoulder bump. "You're a monster, bro."

Ethan laughed. "Only on game days."

The rest of the practice moved quickly with sprints, red-zone drills, and blocking schemes. Ethan didn't miss a beat. He was quicker than most linebackers, stronger than most linemen, and fast enough to post routes when needed. Coaches loved him. Teammates trusted him. Recruiters were noticing.

But what fueled him most wasn't fame or attention; it was the dream.

Playing football beyond college wasn't a fantasy to Ethan. It was a goal.

And he knew every practice mattered.

After the final whistle, the team circled up at the fifty-yard line. Coach Lanning stepped into the middle, his face flushed and voice gravelly.

"You boys showed up today," he barked. "But tomorrow's film day. No slacking. I want clean blocks, crisp plays, and heads in the game. We've got scouts coming from Greywood and Greyhill. You think this town's quiet now? Win Friday night, and you'll be legends."

The team roared in response.

As they broke the huddle, teammates slapped backs, bumped fists, and tossed their helmets off like warriors coming down from battle.

"Yo," Malik said, jogging beside Ethan. "You think your uncle's bringing that crazy whistle again? Dude nearly busted my eardrum last week."

Ethan smirked. "He says it keeps me humble."

"Man, humble? You stiff-armed two dudes into next week."

Ethan shrugged. "That's just practice."

Malik grinned. "Yeah? Remind me never to stand in your way on game day."

As the sun dipped low over the field, painting the sky in burnt orange and soft violet, Ethan lingered for a moment. Helmet in hand, he looked up at the empty bleachers.

It was easy to imagine the stands filled with the band, the cheerleaders, the roar after a touchdown.

And somewhere in the back row, maybe one day…

His father.

Just once.

But he shook the thought off.

Game first.

Dream second.

Everything else could wait. As Ethan was walking to the locker room to change his clothes to go home, he thought about a summer afternoon, years ago. He must've been around eight, still small for his age, legs all knobby knees and scraped shins.

His father had taken him to the park, a rare day when things felt normal. They tossed a football back and forth for nearly an hour. No yelling. No missed pickups. Just blue sky, grass stains, and the sound of his dad laughing.

Ethan had dropped a deep pass, landing hard on the ground.

"You alright, champ?" his dad asked, jogging over.

"Yeah," Ethan winced, brushing dirt from his elbow.

His dad crouched beside him. "You know why I throw it so far?"

Ethan shook his head.

"Because I already see who you're gonna be. Not just who you are now." He ruffled Ethan's hair and grinned. "Strong arms. Big heart. You're gonna be something special."

Ethan hadn't said anything, just smiled, holding that sentence like a prize.

He still remembered the way his father looked at him that day, as if he genuinely believed it.

Chapter 2
Taco Tuesday

The sky had turned a soft golden gray as cars began lining up in front of Gerry High. Students poured out of the double doors in clusters, laughing, checking phones, tossing backpacks over their shoulders.

Ethan spotted his mom's white sedan idling near the flagpole and jogged toward it. The car door creaked a little as he climbed in.

"Hey, baby," she said, glancing over from the driver's seat.

"Hey, Ma."

She leaned across to push his hoodie back off his head. "How was school?"

"Pretty chill," Ethan said. "Practice went hard, though. Coach made us run extra because Rico forgot his cleats."

She shook her head, laughing. "That boy's gonna lose his feet one day."

They pulled away from the curb. The streets of their small town were quiet, just a few kids on bikes and the smell of someone grilling a few blocks away.

Ethan rested his head against the window, then looked over casually. "What's for dinner?"

"Well…" his mom said, drawing the word out dramatically, "since it's Tuesday…"

Ethan perked up. "Taco Tuesday?"

"You know it."

"Let's gooo!" he grinned. "I love tacos."

"I know you do. You eat seven and act like I didn't cook enough."

They drove a few more blocks in comfortable silence, passing the old library and the corner store where Uncle George always bought those off-brand ginger ales.

Ethan stared out at the sidewalk, watching a father and son toss a football in a yard. The ball bounced once and rolled into the street before the kid ran after it.

He hesitated, then turned down the radio slightly.

"Ma?"

"Yeah?"

"Have you seen Dad lately?"

The question hung in the car like a sudden drop in temperature.

His mom's hands tightened slightly on the steering wheel. "No," she said slowly, eyes still on the road. "Why do you ask?"

Ethan shrugged. "I don't know. I was thinking about him at practice. Just wondering if he might ever... You know... show up to one of my games."

She didn't answer right away.

Instead, she blinked a few times, then took a deep breath through her nose.

"I'll reach out to Aunt Helen," she finally said. "See if she's seen him. He's probably bouncing around again."

Ethan didn't push. "Okay."

His mom turned the corner onto Birch Street, their house now in view. Her voice softened.

"I know you want him there," she said. "I do too. I just... I don't want you sitting around waiting for someone who doesn't know how to show up. That's not on you."

"I know," Ethan said, quieter this time.

She parked in the driveway and turned to look at him. "I mean it, baby. I'll ask around. I'm not ignoring it. I want you to know I'm concerned too, okay?"

He nodded. "Okay."

Her hand reached across the console and gave his arm a gentle squeeze. "Now come on. You can mope later. Get the sour cream out of the fridge. I'm not doing all the work."

Ethan grinned. "Yes, ma'am."

He climbed out of the car, football still on his mind, but tacos first.

Always tacos first.

As Ethan entered the house, it creaked as it always did, the familiar moan of old floorboards and shifting air vents, like the house itself was sighing from age and memory. As soon as Ethan and his mom stepped inside, she dropped her purse on the counter and kicked off her shoes.

"Go ahead and get started on homework," she said, flipping on the kitchen light. "Tacos will be ready in about thirty."

Ethan nodded and headed upstairs, taking the steps two at a time.

His room smelled faintly of peppermint and old cleats. The window was cracked just enough to let in the evening breeze. He tossed his backpack onto the floor, slid into his desk chair, and opened his notebook.

English homework first, a few short responses on character motivation. He answered the questions quickly but thoroughly, his mind half on the page and half on the conversation from the car.

His eyes drifted to the top drawer of his desk.

He opened it slowly and pulled out his journal, a small black notebook with a cracked spine and his initials etched in pencil on the cover.

He flipped to the next blank page and picked up his pen.

October 7 Journal Entry

Today I asked Mom about Dad. I keep thinking about him showing up. Just once.

I imagined him standing in the back row of the bleachers, hands in his pockets, hair slicked back, probably wearing that old brown jacket.

I imagined hearing his voice cheer when I broke the line. I imagined what it would feel like to walk off the field and see him waiting by the gate.

I didn't feel angry at that moment. I felt... proud.

I wrote it all down as it happened. And maybe it still can.

I hope he can stay sober long enough to come. Maybe if he saw me play once, it'd help him stay that way. Perhaps it'd remind him who I am.

Who is he, too?

Ethan paused. His pen hovered over the page, then he added:

But if he doesn't come… It's okay.

I've got Uncle George.

And he's been there the whole time.

He closed the journal gently and tucked it back in the drawer.

A soft knock tapped on the door.

"Yeah?" Ethan called.

Uncle George peeked in. "Food's up, champ."

Ethan stood and stretched. "Smells good."

George gave him a knowing smile. "You know it's your mom's night, but I supervised the seasoning. She was getting reckless."

Ethan chuckled. "You just don't want to admit she's a better cook."

George grinned. "I'll let her have that as long as I get credit for the guac."

As Ethan walked toward the door, he glanced over at his desk.

If his dad didn't show up...

He looked at his uncle again, the man who taught him how to tie a tie, fix a bike chain, throw a tight spiral.

He didn't say anything

He didn't have to.

He just nodded.

And followed him downstairs.

By Friday morning, Gerry High was electric.

The school building had never felt so alive. Lockers were decked out with blue and gold streamers. Posters reading "Crush the Bulldogs!" and "Protect the Home Field" hung above the trophy cases. Even the morning announcements ended with a drumroll from the marching band.

Ethan walked through the front doors, helmet in one hand, cleats slung over his shoulder by their laces. His jersey was crisp and stretched across his broad frame, number 09, bold and sharp.

Chris Williams greeted him at his locker with a crooked grin. "You feel it?"

Ethan raised an eyebrow. "Feel what?"

Chris tapped his chest. "That game day magic. I'm telling you, bro, it's in the air."

Ethan chuckled. "Or it's just the smell of cafeteria waffles."

"Either way," Chris said, "we're winning tonight."

The bell rang, and the football team walked in a loose pack down the hall toward the gym. Teachers stepped out of their classrooms to clap them on the back. Underclassmen whispered and pointed as they passed.

"Go get 'em, boys!" Mr. Ackley, the physics teacher, called out.

Amanda Blackwell leaned out of the yearbook room, camera in hand. "Hey, Force Train! Give me a smolder for the sports page!"

Ethan laughed but kept walking.

Inside the gym, the bleachers were pulled back, and cones were already set up for their walkthrough. The head coach stood at midcourt, whistle in his teeth and clipboard in hand.

"Alright!" Coach Lanning barked. "This ain't a photoshoot. It's a mental check. You play clean in your head, you play clean on the field."

They went through offensive sets, snap counts, formations, and player assignments. It wasn't full contact, but the intensity was absolute. Ethan ran clean routes, blocked as it mattered, and stayed laser-focused, every motion crisp, every read sharp.

During a water break, Ethan stood with Scott and Malik near the bleachers.

"You think the scouts'll talk to us?" Scott asked.

Malik shrugged. "They'll talk to somebody. We gotta make sure they remember the name they write down."

Chris jogged over. "Doesn't matter if they talk or not. All they need is a number and a clip. They'll find us."

Ethan stayed quiet, sipping water.

He was excited, no doubt.

But somewhere, quietly beneath it all, he was also hoping the one person he hadn't seen in the stands all season would finally show up tonight.

Not for an interview.

Not for a highlight reel.

Just for him.

As the walkthrough wrapped up, Coach Lanning gathered the team at midcourt.

"Tonight," he said, "isn't about the scouts. It's not about the crowd. It's about you, doing the job you've trained for all season. Every play, every block, every tackle, do it as if you've already won. Because the only thing standing between you and the next level… is you."

The team clapped in unison. Ethan clapped too, his eyes burning with focus.

The day was only beginning.

But tonight, the lights would come on.

And Ethan would be ready.

Back at home, the house was quieter than usual.

Ethan stood in front of the mirror in his room, adjusting his jersey for the third time. The gold numbers shimmered under the soft ceiling light. His cleats were already tied, his bag packed, and his gloves folded just right inside his helmet.

He'd been dreaming of this kind of night since he was little.

But now that it was here, his stomach fluttered with something he couldn't quite name.

Downstairs, the smell of fabric softener and hot coffee hung in the air. His mom was sitting at the kitchen table, sipping from her favorite mug that said Mama Knows Best. Uncle George leaned against the counter, arms crossed, still in his school slacks, socks, but no shoes.

"You ready, baby?" his mom asked as he walked in.

"Yeah," Ethan said, gripping his helmet. "Mentally and physically."

"Hydrated?"

"Been chugging water since noon."

She smiled, proud. "Good. Don't let nobody take your shine out there."

"Never."

She hesitated a beat, then set her mug down gently. "I spoke to Aunt Helen earlier."

Ethan raised an eyebrow.

"She said… she told your dad about the game tonight. Told him it wouldn't hurt to show his face once in a while."

Uncle George shifted where he stood, lips tightening.

"Don't do that," he said. "Don't get his hopes up."

"I'm just saying what Helen said…"

George cut her off gently but firmly. "He's an alcoholic, Elle. He's inconsistent, irresponsible, and disappears when things get real. Ethan already has a lot on his plate. He doesn't need one more person breaking promises."

Ethan stood quietly for a second, then looked up at both of them.

"It's okay, Uncle George," he said, voice calm but sure. "I'd like for him to show up… I really would. But if he doesn't, I'm not gonna fall apart."

He looked at his mom.

"I got you."

Then he turned to George.

"And I got you."

George stared at him for a moment, then exhaled and gave him a nod of respect.

"Alright," he said. "Well, you've got us on the sidelines loud, embarrassing, and probably crying if you score too early."

His mom chuckled. "And we'll be filming every second like it's the Titan Bowl."

Ethan grinned. "Good. I'll make it worth the tape."

Outside, the sun had just begun to dip behind the trees. The street was quiet, but anticipation buzzed in the air.

As Ethan grabbed his duffel and opened the front door, he paused.

He didn't know if his dad would be in the stands tonight.

But he knew he wasn't alone.

And for now, that was more than enough as they headed out the door.

The street outside Gerry High was packed with cars lined up along the curb, front lawn signs glowing in blue and gold, and students walking shoulder-to-shoulder toward the stadium, jerseys and face paint on full display.

Ethan sat in the back seat, helmet resting on his lap.

"You ready?" his mom asked, glancing at him from the driver's side.

"Yeah," he nodded. "It's time."

"You look good out there, baby. Every time."

He smiled. "Thanks, Ma."

She pulled up to the front entrance circle. Ethan stepped out, straightened his jersey, and gave a small salute to the car before heading toward the locker room.

His mom pulled into a side lot near the visitors' section.

Uncle George reached over from the passenger seat and grabbed the small stadium cushion he always brought. "Let's go, Elle. He's gonna light it up tonight."

"I know," she said, locking the car and grabbing her purse. "I just hope..." she paused, shaking her head. "Never mind. Let's enjoy it."

The line to buy tickets snaked halfway across the sidewalk, filled with chatter, laughter, and the unmistakable scent of nachos and hot dogs. Parents held foam fingers, younger siblings played tag, and volunteers passed out team programs.

Elle and George stepped into line, already recognizing a few familiar faces.

"Y'all here to see the Force Train?" someone asked.

George grinned. "Front row, baby."

Once inside the stadium, the buzz was louder. The band was warming up in the stands, the cheerleaders stretching near the end zone. The smell of kettle corn and grilled sausage filled the night air.

"I'm hitting the concession stand," George said, patting Elle's arm. "Popcorn and a soda. You want anything now, or you waiting 'til halftime?"

Elle glanced at the growing crowd. "I'll wait."

"Alright, I'm gonna find us some good seats after this. Somewhere close."

"Okay," she said. "Close, but not front row, you always end up blocking someone with your big head."

George laughed, already making his way toward the snack counter.

Elle looked toward the field. The stadium lights buzzed overhead, casting a golden glow across the grass. A few players were already warming up, but she hadn't spotted Ethan yet.

She clutched her jacket a little tighter around her, eyes scanning the crowd near the entrance, her heart whispering a quiet question she didn't want to say aloud.

Will he show up tonight?

But she pushed the thought away.

Her son had a game to play. And she would be there, cheering, shouting, and loving him with her whole heart.

Chapter 3
Eyes on the Field

The locker room pulsed with electricity.

Helmets lined the benches. Cleats stomped against the concrete floor. Shoulder pads clicked into place. Inside the walls of Gerry High's varsity locker room, the Gerry Five stood tall and ready.

Ethan paced slowly in front of his locker, rolling out his neck. Chris Williams, their senior quarterback, stood at the whiteboard with Coach Lanning and the offensive coordinator, running over the final routes one more time.

"Trips left, 86 sweep on two," Chris said, tapping the board. "That's your lane, Force Train."

Ethan nodded, locking eyes with him. "I'll blow it open."

Lamar Jordan, fast-talking wide receiver, spun his towel in the air. "Man, I've been waiting all week for this!"

Malik Gray leaned against the bench, quiet as ever. "Play your game. Let 'em chase you."

Trevor Banks, already sweating under his pads, gave a low growl. "No one's taking this from us."

Coach Lanning turned to the group. His voice was low and intense.

"They came to watch you fall apart under pressure. Prove them wrong. Play fast. Play smart. Play as one."

He paused.

"And when you walk off that field tonight, let them know exactly who Gerry High is."

Outside, the stadium roared.

The announcer's voice echoed through the night:

"And now, your Gerry High School Hawks!"

Smoke machines hissed. The tunnel opened.

The team lined up shoulder to shoulder, helmets gleaming under the lights. The five of them, Ethan, Chris, Lamar, Malik, and Trevor, took the front.

Ethan tightened his chinstrap. "Let's eat."

Chris smirked. "Dinner's served."

They exploded out of the tunnel like warriors.

The crowd erupted.

From the press box, scouts leaned forward. Clipboards out. Phones recording.

Representatives from Winslow State University, Briarstone University, Purplestone University, and Impel University watched closely as the game kicked off. Their eyes followed Ethan as he moved, as he hit, as he owned the field.

From the first play, it was clear:

Gerry High came to win.

Ethan opened with a monster block that freed Lamar for a 40-yard run. The very next drive, Ethan took a sweep around the edge and dragged two defenders with him for another 25 yards. He exploded through tackles like they were made of paper.

Chris fired tight spirals down the middle, Malik shut down every major offensive threat on defense, and Trevor protected the backfield like a brick wall.

By halftime, the scoreboard read:

Gerry 21, Bulldogs 7.

Coach Lanning's words rang in their ears:

"It's not over. Make it so loud they have to rewrite the record books."

In the second half, Ethan dominated.

A screen pass on 3rd and 12? Ethan bulldozed down the sideline for 43 yards and a touchdown.

A kickoff return on a surprise onside kick. Ethan caught it on the bounce and ran it back with a stiff-arm that sent a player flying into the turf.

The crowd was on its feet.

Scouts scribbled notes.

One even turned to another and whispered, "He's the real deal."

As the final seconds ticked away, the scoreboard read:

Gerry 38, Bulldogs 14.

The crowd thundered. Fireworks burst in the sky.

The team rushed the field. Helmets in the air. Coaches hugging players. Students are screaming from the stands.

Ethan stood in the end zone, sweat dripping from his brow, chest heaving.

He looked toward the bleachers, not to find a camera or a reporter...

But to see.

Just maybe...

No sign of his dad.

But he didn't let it ruin the moment.

Because his mom was there, arms in the air, shouting his name.

And Uncle George stood beside her, grinning, messy popcorn all over his shirt, recording the whole thing on his camcorder.

Ethan lifted his helmet high.

He played for them.

And tonight, they saw the dream starting to take shape.

After the game, the field was still electric. Coaches from both teams shook hands at the midfield line. The crowd trickled out slowly, reluctant to leave the magic hanging in the Friday night air.

Ethan walked off the field surrounded by teammates, high-fiving fans who leaned over the railing. His jersey was soaked, streaked with dirt and sweat, but his smile stretched wide.

As he reached the sideline, Coach Lanning waved him over.

"You've got company," he said with a grin.

Four men stood near the gate, one in a scarlet pullover with a Paper College lanyard, another in Greyhill blue. The other two wore Cozy University and Winslow State gear.

Ethan jogged over, helmet under his arm.

The man in the Paper College jacket extended a hand. "Ethan Phillips?"

"Yes, sir."

"I'm Coach Villman with Paper College. I have been hearing your name since spring ball. You didn't disappoint tonight."

"Thank you, sir," Ethan said, his voice steady.

The Winslow scout chimed in. "We've been watching the film all season, but seeing it in person? You're special, son. That touchdown in the third quarter was clean footwork and power. That's next-level stuff."

"Appreciate that."

They handed him cards, nodded at Coach Lanning, and made notes on their phones before moving to talk to Chris and Malik.

Ethan turned back toward the field, soaking it in one more time.

The lights. The smell of the grass. The hum of fans still lingered near the gates.

He didn't know what would come next, but he knew it had started.

By the time he stepped back into the locker room, the team was already erupting.

Someone had plugged in a speaker, bass thumping, players jumping and shouting. Cleats stomped, helmets hit lockers in rhythm, and water bottles sprayed into the air like mini-juice showers.

Chris tackled him in a hug. "Let's gooo, Force Train!"

Malik slapped his back. "They were drooling out there."

Trevor flexed both arms. "I told you we were gonna eat tonight!"

Coach Lanning whistled. "Alright, alright! I'm proud of all of you. That's the kind of game scouts remember. That's the kind of game you tell your kids about."

He pointed to Ethan. "And that runs in the fourth? That was a statement."

The team clapped, banging on lockers.

"Speech!" Rico shouted. "Let the man say something!"

Ethan chuckled, then stood on the bench.

"Appreciate all y'all," he said, raising his hands. "That wasn't just me, it was all of us. We blocked, we hit, we hustled. We showed up."

Cheers echoed.

He paused, then added, "And we're just getting started."

The locker room exploded again with laughter, claps, music rising as high as the spirits inside.

Later, as the chaos calmed and players packed up to head home, Ethan sat quietly for a moment, untying his cleats. The excitement hadn't worn off, but something steadier had settled inside him, not pride, but peace.

He pulled out his phone. Opened his journal app. Typed a quick note:

Tonight, I saw it.

The future.

It's real.

And it's mine.

He slipped the phone into his bag and looked up just in time to see Coach Lanning waiting by the door.

"Your mom's outside."

Ethan nodded, stood tall, and walked toward the exit, his heart full, his head clear, and the lights of the field still burning behind him.

The car ride home was filled with excitement.

Ethan sat in the back seat, still wearing his team hoodie, his helmet bag beside him. The night air slipped through a cracked window, cooling the warmth still radiating off his skin from the field.

In the front seat, his mom turned the radio dial as Uncle George talked up a storm.

"I mean, you saw that last run, right?" George said, turning halfway in his seat to look at Ethan. "Boy dropped two defenders like they were made of pillows. Like boom, boom! On the turf!"

Ethan grinned. "I think one of them's still out there."

"I bet scouts are still rewinding the tape," George said. "Greyhill? Cozy? Man, they're gonna be fighting over you like Aunt Helen and her last piece of sweet potato pie."

His mom laughed. "Don't tell her that she might throw something."

They hit a red light. For a moment, the car was quiet except for the soft hum of music and the gentle squeak of the windshield wipers.

Uncle George tapped the dash. "You know what this night needs?"

Ethan raised an eyebrow. "What?

"A victory scoop."

His mom glanced at him. "Kayla's?"

"Kayla's," George said. "It's tradition now. First win, first touchdown, first varsity start... now first game with college scouts in the stands."

Ethan leaned forward. "I'm down for that."

"Good," George said, already flicking on the blinker. "I need two scoops of rocky road and a little moment to reflect on how my nephew embarrassed an entire defensive line."

Elle smiled, shaking her head. "Just make sure you don't embarrass yourself trying to eat that much sugar."

Kayla's Ice Cream Parlor was tucked into the corner of Main and Sycamore, a cozy spot with twinkling string lights and hand-painted windows. The kind of place everyone in town knew by name.

They parked out front, and the bell above the door jingled as they stepped inside. A few other families and classmates were already there, buzzing about the game.

Ethan was met with claps on the back and a couple of "great job tonight!" greetings as he made his way to the counter.

"Same as always?" Kayla asked from behind the register, already scooping up the items.

"You know it," George said.

"Give me cookies and cream," Ethan said. "Double scoop."

"You got it, Force Train."

They sat by the front window, ice cream in hand, the night calm and full of promise.

"I'm proud of you," Elle said, her voice soft but firm.

"Thanks, Ma."

George nodded. "You've got talent, Ethan. But more than that, you've got heart. That's what makes people watch."

Ethan took a bite of his ice cream and looked out at the quiet street. The stadium lights dimmed in the distance now, but the glow was still inside him.

Tonight wasn't just a win.

It was a memory.

And it tasted like cookies and cream. As they finished their ice cream, they headed back to the car to drive home. The house on Birch Street was dark when they pulled into the driveway. Porch light glowing. Wind chimes barely swaying in the night breeze.

"Thanks again, Ma," Ethan said as he stepped out of the car.

"You earned it, baby," she replied.

Uncle George stretched and groaned. "My back ain't built for bleachers, but I'd sit through it again in a heartbeat."

Inside, the house creaked with its usual welcome. Ethan kicked off his shoes, hung his hoodie by the door, and gave both his mom and uncle a quick goodnight before heading upstairs.

His room was quiet.

No music. No notifications. Just the sound of the ceiling fan spinning above.

Ethan set his helmet on the shelf. Took a long breath.

The adrenaline from the game had faded, but something else lingered, not anger, not even sadness. Just a quiet space where a small hope used to be.

He sat down at his desk, pulled open the drawer, and reached for his journal.

He flipped to a new page.

The ink bled slightly as he pressed the pen to paper.

He didn't show. And I don't care. He stared at the words for a moment.

Then, he closed the journal and tucked it away.

Climbing into bed, Ethan turned off the lamp and let the darkness settle.

The stadium lights were off.

The crowd was gone. The dream remained.

And whether his dad showed up or not…

Ethan wasn't done. Not even close.

Sleep found him fast, peaceful, quiet, and undefeated.

Saturday morning brought a quiet calm to the neighborhood. The sky was overcast, soft gray clouds rolling low, as if the town itself was still resting from the night before.

Ethan tossed his duffel into the backseat and climbed into the car, helmet in hand.

"You good?" his mom asked, adjusting the rearview mirror.

"Yeah," Ethan said, still a little groggy. "Just ready to see the film. Coach said we might get clips sent out this week."

Elle smiled. "Just make sure they spell your name right."

Ethan smirked. "They will."

She dropped him off at Gerry High's side entrance, watched him disappear inside the building, then turned the car toward home, her fingers tapping the steering wheel.

By the time Elle pulled into the driveway, she noticed someone walking up the front steps of the house.

Her stomach dropped.

Even from a distance, she recognized the unsteady sway, the slouched shoulders, the half-buttoned shirt.

Michael.

Her ex-husband.

"Michael!" she shouted, slamming the door and stepping out. "What are you doing here?"

He turned, squinting, his words already slurring before they even left his mouth.

"I'm… I'm here for the football game," he said, swaying slightly. "Where's Ethan?"

Uncle George had heard the shouting from inside. He opened the door just as Elle stepped between Michael and the porch.

"You're what?" George said, his voice rising. "Oh, my goodness, the game was yesterday, Michael."

Michael blinked. "I… I overslept."

George stepped out onto the porch, chest broad, voice booming. "You overslept a varsity game? After years of no-shows and radio silence, have you decided to drag your drunk behind up here today?"

"I just wanna see my son," Michael said, his voice cracking slightly. "I missed it, okay? But I'm here now."

Elle's eyes welled with tears, but her tone was fierce. "No. You're not here for Ethan. You're here for yourself. He's not home, and even if he were, I wouldn't let you near him like this."

Michael stumbled forward, trying to move past them into the house.

Uncle George stepped into his path. "You need to go. Now."

Michael's breath reeked of whiskey. "I'm his father. You don't get to tell me…"

"I get to protect him," George snapped. "And you don't get to blow in here after everything you've done, or haven't done, just because you feel something in the moment."

Michael shoved him.

George stood firm.

Elle shouted, "Michael, stop!"

Michael tried again to push past, more desperate than angry now, but George held the line. Just then, a voice called from across the yard.

"Everything okay over there?"

Mr. Jennings, their neighbor, was walking toward the porch, concerned.

George nodded. "Just handling it. Appreciate you."

Mr. Jennings narrowed his eyes at Michael. "You need to go, man."

Elle stepped forward, voice trembling now. "Michael… please. Just go. Ethan's not here. He's watching a film at school. If… if you want to see him, come back later. Sober."

She knew he wouldn't.

He never did.

Michael backed away slowly, still muttering under his breath, stumbling off the porch and toward the sidewalk.

Elle turned to George, wiping her eyes. "Thank you."

"You don't have to thank me," he said, his voice low. "That boy's already got a future. We're not letting Michael tear that down again."

They both stood on the porch in silence, watching the street return to stillness.

Neither of them said it out loud, but they knew:

Ethan couldn't know.

Not today.

Not after the night he just had.

They would protect his peace even if it meant hiding the storm from him altogether.

Chapter 4
Film Room Lessons

Inside Gerry High's film room, the morning sunlight cast golden streaks across the worn carpet and the whiteboard.

The room smelled faintly of dry-erase markers and gym socks. A stack of folded chairs leaned in the corner, but the core of the team, the Gerry Five, were spread across the first two rows of plastic seats, eyes locked on the glowing screen up front.

Coach Lanning stood near the projector, remote in one hand, laser pointer in the other.

"Pause right here," he said.

The screen froze on a wide shot of the third quarter, Ethan cutting left behind a block, two defenders diving helplessly behind him.

"Now look at this lane," the coach said, circling the gap on the screen. "Trevor sealed the edge. Malik picked up the blitz. But Ethan saw this before the snap."

Ethan nodded. "The linebacker was leaning too hard inside."

"Exactly," Coach Lanning said. "You read it. That's the difference between a highlight and a habit. Start seeing the game like it's happening in slow motion."

Chris leaned over and whispered, "That's why they're calling him Freight Vision now."

Ethan smirked but kept his focus forward.

After an hour of breakdowns, praise, and corrections, Coach turned off the projector and tossed the remote onto the desk.

He folded his arms and looked around the room.

"You boys played your hearts out last night. But this next chapter, the recruiting, the scouts, the interviews, it's not just about football anymore."

Everyone leaned in a little closer.

Coach's voice dropped just enough to pull them in.

"Some of you are gonna get offers. Some of you are gonna meet agents. People with smiles and promises. They'll say you're the next big thing. And maybe you are, but don't get blinded by hype."

He looked straight at Ethan.

"You've got something special, son. But special doesn't mean safe."

Ethan's eyebrows lifted slightly.

Coach continued. "When the time comes, and it will come, read every word before you sign anything. Don't let dollar signs cloud your vision. Don't be afraid to say no. And if it sounds too good to be true?"

"It probably is," Lamar finished.

Coach nodded. "Facts. Talk to people you trust. Keep your circle tight. No matter how far you go, stay grounded."

Ethan absorbed it all, every word, every warning. Not just for himself, but for the dream. The real dream. The one that extended beyond the field.

"Understood," Ethan said. "Thank you, Coach."

Lanning cracked a rare smile. "We're building more than athletes here. We're building men."

As the team packed up, Chris clapped Ethan on the shoulder. "Looks like you just got the 'future star' talk."

"Guess that means I'm on somebody's radar," Ethan replied.

Chris grinned. "You're on everybody's radar."

Ethan chuckled, but he tucked the advice deep in his chest like armor.

The field had always been his stage.

Now, it was becoming his future.

And he planned to step into it wide-eyed and ready. The sun was high when Ethan stepped out of Lamar's dad's car, duffel bag over his shoulder, still feeling the fire of Coach Lanning's words in his chest.

He was smiling.

Until he heard it.

"Ethan!" a voice called across the street.

Mr. Jennings, their long-term neighbor, stood by his mailbox, holding a small bag of groceries.

"Your dad was here this morning! Showed up drunk, stumbling all over the place. Uncle George nearly had to knock him flat!"

Ethan froze mid-step.

His heart skipped, then thudded hard against his ribs. He turned sharply toward the porch where his mom was sweeping the steps, and George sat with a cup of coffee.

"Is that true?" Ethan asked.

Elle's head jerked up.

George set his mug down. "Ethan, now…"

"Why didn't you tell me?" he demanded, walking quickly up the steps. "Why did I have to hear it from a neighbor?"

"You just got here."

His mom looked stricken. "We didn't want to ruin your morning. You just had the biggest game of your life."

Ethan dropped his bag with a thud. "That's not your decision to make! He finally shows up, and I didn't even know?"

"Ethan, listen to me," George said, standing up. "Your father wasn't just late. He wasn't just confused. He was drunk. He came up here shouting, shoving, trying to push his way in."

Ethan blinked, jaw tightening.

"He shoved you?" he asked, voice lower now, but firmer.

George nodded. "I kept him out. But it wasn't some peaceful reunion moment. It was chaos. And we decided to protect you from it."

Ethan looked at his mom.

Her eyes welled with tears. "I told him to come back when he was sober, Ethan. I wanted him to see you. But not like that."

Ethan backed away slightly, hands on his hips, head down.

He didn't speak for a long moment.

Then, finally: "You should've told me. I had the right to know."

He didn't yell. He didn't cry. But the sting in his voice cut deep.

George opened his mouth to speak again, but Ethan turned toward the door, picked up his bag, and stepped inside without another word.

Inside his room, he sat on the edge of his bed.

He didn't pull out his journal.

He didn't turn on the music.

He just sat there, staring at the wall, jaw clenched, the weight of knowing sitting heavier than the pain of wondering ever had. The sun had dipped behind the trees, casting long shadows across the backyard. Crickets chirped in the bushes. A porch light buzzed softly overhead.

Ethan sat on the back steps alone, hoodie pulled over his head, the night breeze brushing against his face. The anger had faded, but the ache remained.

He heard the screen door creak behind him.

Uncle George stepped out, carrying two bottles of root beer.

"I figured it's not ice cream," George said, handing one over, "but it's a peace offering."

Ethan took it without looking up. "Thanks."

George sat down beside him, exhaling slowly. "You wanna be mad at me? Go ahead. I can take it."

Ethan shrugged. "I'm not mad anymore."

"You were."

"Yeah," Ethan admitted. "I just... I don't like being protected from things I have to live with anyway."

George nodded slowly, understanding in his eyes. "Fair."

They sat in silence for a moment, sipping root beer and watching the stars peek through the treetops.

"I wanted him to come," Ethan said finally. "I mean, not drunk. Not stumbling. But just... there. Just once."

"I know," George said gently. "And part of me wanted to believe he might show up the right way. But when he didn't, when he showed up the wrong way, I wasn't about to let you hear about that, but Mr. Jennings spoke too soon. Not after the night you had."

Ethan looked over at him. "You think I can't handle it?"

George shook his head. "No, I think you've handled more than most kids your age ever will. But sometimes even strong people need protection, especially from the people who were supposed to protect them."

Ethan leaned back against the porch railing, processing that.

"You think he'll ever come around?"

George was quiet for a moment. Then he said, "I think your dad has a lot of battles going on, some you can see, and some you can't. But it's not your job to fix him."

"I know," Ethan whispered. "I just thought... maybe football would pull him back."

George placed a hand on Ethan's shoulder. "You can't control who shows up, son. But you can control who you become."

Ethan nodded slowly, the words sinking deep.

"I'm proud of you," George added. "Not just because you're killing it on the field. But because you're figuring out how to handle life off it."

Ethan gave a faint smile. "That means more than you know."

"I mean every word."

They sat there a while longer, two men, one younger, one older, saying very little, but understanding everything. It's Sunday morning, and Ethan is still rolling over in his bed. He heard his mother calling him from downstairs to get up and eat breakfast before church. After 10 minutes of drifting in and out of sleep, Ethan finally got up to head downstairs to eat.

By 11:00 AM, the pews of the local community church were full that Sunday morning, the sanctuary humming with quiet anticipation. Sunlight filtered in through the tall stained-glass windows, painting soft blues and golds across the congregation's faces.

Ethan sat beside his mother and Uncle George near the middle aisle, dressed in a button-up shirt and dark jeans. His football jacket hung over the back of the pew, the only visible sign of the night he'd had two days earlier.

He wasn't thinking about stats, scouts, or headlines this morning.

He was listening.

Up at the pulpit, Pastor Williams held his Holy scriptures high, his voice steady but full of fire.

"Psalm 108:1 KJV," he read aloud.

"O God, my heart is fixed; I will sing and give praise, even with my glory."

He paused, eyes sweeping the congregation.

"Church, we live in a world that'll try to shake your foundation. Fame, fortune, failure, pressure, disappointment — but when your heart is fixed on God, you'll still praise Him through it all."

Murmurs of amen rippled through the sanctuary.

Pastor Williams took a step forward. "We're rising in this season financially, emotionally, spiritually, and physically. But not because of who we are, because of who He is. When you make God your source, when you keep Him first, you don't need to chase what this world offers."

He flipped to another scripture.

"Matthew 6:33 KJV But seek ye first the kingdom of God, and his righteousness; and all these things shall be added unto you."

"See," he said, his voice lifting with passion, "too many people are seeking deals, validation, money, attention. Young people, hear me today: not all sources are from God. Some of those offers. They might shine, but they'll lead you into darkness."

Ethan leaned forward slightly, the verse sinking deep into his heart.

Pastor Williams pointed upward.

"God is the source. Not the scouts. Not the headlines. Not the likes, the contracts, or the social media buzz. He gives the talent. He opens the doors. And if you want to walk in real success, seek Him first."

Elle wiped a tear from the corner of her eye.

George gave a firm nod, quiet but full of conviction.

And Ethan sat back, eyes steady on the pulpit, the message echoing through his spirit like a drumbeat.

Fix your heart and give Him praise even with your glory.

He didn't fully understand it all.

But something inside him stirred not fear, not pressure…

Alignment. After church, the house was peaceful. Elle had changed into her lounge clothes and started a load of laundry. Uncle George was in the kitchen fixing his famous lemon tea and humming a hymn from service. The afternoon sun warmed the hardwood floors, casting slow-moving shadows across the living room.

Upstairs, Ethan sat at his desk with the window cracked open and a gentle breeze curling through the room. His holy scriptures lay open on the corner, Psalm 108 KJV still marked with the church bulletin.

He opened his journal, the same one he used to record thoughts after games and practices, but this entry wasn't about football. This was about something more profound. He pressed a pen to paper.

Today's sermon hit me differently. O God, my heart is fixed.

The pastor said we're rising in every way, but only if we keep God first. I don't want to chase things that look good but aren't from Him.

When I grow up, if I make it to play professionally, I'm gonna buy my mom a house. I'm gonna get Uncle George a truck with leather seats and big tires like he always talks about.

But more than that… I never want to forget to praise God.

To sing to Him. To thank Him. He gave me this gift. So, I'll put Him first.

In every deal. Every game. Every win. I'll give Him my glory. Because without Him, I'm just noise. Ethan paused, stared at the page, then slowly closed the journal. He looked out the window.

The world outside was wide open. But his heart was fixed. Three hours later, Ethan heard his mother yelling his name for dinner. Dinner was warm, quiet, and filled with laughter.

Ethan sat at the table with his mom and Uncle George, still chewing on his third helping of macaroni and baked chicken. Elle was mid-story about a patient who'd accidentally scheduled her physical during a dental cleaning. George was already shaking his head, chuckling, when…

BANG. BANG. BANG.

The knock at the door wasn't casual; it was violent, urgent. Everyone froze.

Then they heard the voice.

"I want to see my son!"

Elle's smile dropped. Her hand reached instinctively for Ethan's wrist.

Uncle George stood quickly, pushing back from the table. "Stay here," he said.

But before he could reach the front door, it burst open with a crack, the old wood splintering as the door slammed against the wall.

Michael.

He was heavily intoxicated, eyes glassy, face blotchy, and swaying where he stood.

"I WANT TO SEE MY SON!" he screamed again.

"Michael, calm down!" Elle said, standing now, her voice trembling but firm.

George moved fast, trying to block his path as Michael stumbled toward the kitchen.

"Back off, man!" Michael shouted, pushing George.

The two men crashed to the floor, knocking over a chair in the process. Ethan stood frozen, watching in disbelief as the man who'd once held his hand at the park now rolled drunkenly across their kitchen.

Michael tried to push himself up using the stove. His hand knocked a pan of macaroni to the floor, and the noodles spilled across the tile.

Elle gasped, covering her mouth, eyes already wet with tears.

Michael finally stood, breath ragged, eyes darting around until they locked on Ethan.

"Son," he slurred, reaching out, "I just… I wanted to see you…"

He stumbled forward and tried to hug him, but he tripped over the fallen chair and collapsed into Ethan, sending them both back into the wall.

Ethan caught his balance just in time to see his father turn pale. Then vomit.

Right across the dinner table. Right on the food. Right in the middle of the table.

Elle cried out, backing into the corner of the room.

George stood, livid now. "You've got to GO, Michael. You've crossed the line."

Ethan, stunned, with eyes wide and his chest pounding, found his voice.

"Get out."

Michael froze, blinking.

"I said get out," Ethan repeated, voice firm, low, and shaking. "Leave."

Those words stung not because they were shouted, but because they were true.

Michael looked at him like he'd been struck.

"I just… I just wanted to see my son, see you."

Elle, through quiet sobs, said softly, "Not like this, Michael. Not like this. You've got to change."

Michael looked around at the mess, at the faces of the people who used to be his family, and then slowly turned and walked out the door, stumbling into the night.

The door hung half-broken behind him.

Ethan stood silent for a moment longer, then turned and bolted up the stairs.

He slammed his bedroom door behind him and sank onto the floor, chest heaving, hands gripping his knees. It wasn't supposed to happen like that. Not a hug. Not the first visit. Not him. And now, the picture of the man he once hoped would cheer in the stands was shattered, replaced by someone he barely recognized.

Someone he didn't want to know.

Chapter 5
Aftermath

The kitchen was quiet now.

No shouting. No chaos. No crashing dishes. Just the soft clatter of broken plates being swept into a dustpan and the steady hum of the ceiling light above the dinner table, the same table that just hours ago was covered in laughter, food, and family. Elle knelt near the stove, wiping up what remained of the spilled macaroni, tears still drying on her cheeks.

George stood over the trash can, shaking his head as he tossed in crumpled napkins, ruined food, and the final broken glass.

Neither of them spoke at first. The silence between them wasn't cold; it was heavy. Worn. Familiar.

After the kitchen was clean, George grabbed the toolbox and started working on the front door. The frame had cracked when Michael kicked it in. Elle followed behind him with a flashlight, holding it steady as he drilled in a new brace.

Finally, she broke the silence.

"George… I think I'm going to call the local crisis center. Maybe they can help… maybe they can get him into an inpatient facility."

George paused, leaning against the doorframe, drill still in his hand.

He let out a long breath. "I think you should leave it alone." Elle looked at him, surprised. "Leave it?"

"I'm still furious, El," he said, voice low. "You saw what he did. He came into our home… where Ethan lives. Where we raised him after everything, and he nearly destroyed all of that in five minutes."

"I know," she whispered. "But he's still his father. And he's still your brother-in-law."

"Ex-brother-in-law"

George sat down on the bottom step, elbows on his knees. "Yeah… and we've been fighting for him since Ethan was five years old. And now Ethan's almost grown, and it's only gotten worse. You think I want to give up?"

He looked up at her, pain raw in his eyes.

"He stole from our parents. Took the flat screen from Helen's living room and pawned it for booze. Took money right out of her wallet. Helen hasn't spoken to him in a month. Everyone is tired, Elle. I'm tired."

Elle sat beside him. Her hand found his.

And for a moment, they were just two siblings grieving the ex-brother-in-law and ex-husband they once knew and praying for the man he'd become.

"I don't know what else to do," George said, voice cracking.

"I don't either," Elle whispered, leaning against his shoulder.

They sat in silence, hugging gently, as their grief filled the hallway.

Upstairs, Ethan stood quietly in the hallway just out of view.

He had heard it all. He hadn't meant to eavesdrop, but once he caught the tone of their voices, he couldn't walk away. And now, he knew more than he ever had before.

He had seen the frustration in his uncle's eyes.

The tears in his mother's eyes.

The truth hit harder than anything his father had done. Back in his room, Ethan lay across his bed, staring at the ceiling, his heart thudding with emotion.

He didn't cry. Not now. Instead, he folded his hands and whispered into the silence:

"God… fix him.

Please. Fix my dad. I don't know what's wrong inside him, but you do.

Take away the alcohol. Take away the anger.

Let him be whole again. I forgive him.

But I need you to heal him."

He didn't know what else to say. But maybe that was enough. He closed his eyes, his soul was still heavy…But his faith is fixed. Monday morning came too soon.

The alarm buzzed at 6:30 sharp, and Ethan groaned as he rolled over and slapped at the snooze button. For a moment, he just lay there, staring at the ceiling, letting the memory of the weekend creep back into his mind.

The shouting. The crashing pan. The vomit.

The look in his father's eyes was like he knew he'd already lost something he'd never be able to win back.

Ethan sat up slowly and let out a long breath. "God… just give me peace today."

He got dressed in silence, grabbed his hoodie and cleats, and headed out the door with a quick goodbye to his mom and Uncle George, who were both moving a little slower than usual themselves.

At school, the building buzzed with the usual Monday morning mix of exhaustion and weekend gossip. Posters for Spirit Week lined the walls, and the front hallway was decorated with blue and gold streamers.

Ethan walked toward his locker, earbuds in until he saw Chris, Lamar, and Scott waving him down from across the hall.

"There he is!" Chris shouted. "The silent superstar!"

"Force Train rolls in like a ghost," Lamar added. "What, you forgot how to talk over the weekend?"

Ethan chuckled. "Nah. Just a lot on my mind."

Scott gave him a friendly nudge. "Well, forget whatever it was. Spirit Week just kicked off, and you're about to be challenged to the student vs. faculty dodgeball game."

"Oh no," Ethan said, raising an eyebrow. "Not dodgeball. Coach Lanning still has that wicked curve throw."

Lamar leaned in. "We got a plan. You play like you're dodging scouts on game film. Boom untouchable."

Chris grinned. "By the way, Coach said recruiters are asking for your full tape. He thinks Greyhill College might come back next week."

Ethan gave a slight nod. "That's cool."

But his voice lacked the usual spark.

Amanda walked up from the side hall, balancing her sketchbook and binder.

"You look like you need a laugh," she said.

Ethan looked at her. "You got one?"

She flipped open her sketchbook.

It was a cartoon of the five of them, drawn as medieval knights in armor, Chris holding a golden football, Scott riding a chicken instead of a horse, and Ethan towering over them with a giant '08' shield.

Ethan laughed out loud. "Where do you even come up with this stuff?"

Amanda shrugged. "It's either this or do actual homework."

By the time the bell rang, Ethan had relaxed. For the first time since Friday night, he smiled, not the polite kind, but the real kind.

His friends didn't ask about the weekend.

They didn't need to.

They showed up.

And for now, that was enough. The third period felt like it would never end.

Coach Lanning's study hall wasn't technically a class, but it was filled with athletes: half pretending to do homework and half waiting for lunch. Ethan had his geometry book open in front of him, but hadn't turned the page in ten minutes.

"Bro," came a voice from two seats over, "do you know what a 'CPU bottleneck' is?"

Ethan looked up.

A tall, skinny kid with big glasses and a hoodie that read "I paused my game for this" was hunched over his laptop with three different snack wrappers poking out of his backpack.

Ethan blinked. "Jordan?"

Jordan looked up. "Sup, Force Train."

"You're not even in this class."

"I am now," Jordan said casually. "Ms. D'Angelo said I was distracting the robotics team. Yelling 'Boom! Headshot!' during their circuit exam wasn't encouraged."

Ethan smirked. "Sounds about right."

Jordan spun his laptop around. On the screen was a spreadsheet of computer parts and a note labeled Ethan Gaming Rig Build: v5.1.

"Building you a PC," he said. "For post-professional, of course. You're gonna need something chill when you're not being famous and stuff."

"I didn't ask for that," Ethan said, amused.

"You didn't have to. Friendship includes unsolicited tech gifts and snack offerings."

He tossed Ethan a bag of mini-chocolate chip cookies. Ethan caught it midair.

"I accept," he said.

Jordan leaned back, arms folded behind his head like he owned the place. "You've been tense lately. Like, M. Black-down-by-ten tense. I figured cookies and nerd energy might help."

Ethan raised an eyebrow. "That obvious?"

Jordan shrugged. "Not to most people. But I see stuff. I observe. Like a lion. Except with worse posture and more caffeine."

They both laughed.

By the time the bell rang, Ethan felt a sense of relief. Not because the pressure was gone, but because someone had made space for normalcy.

As they walked out of the classroom, Jordan added, "By the way, if you ever need to rage-quit life for a minute, my basement has a VR headset, surround sound, and my grandma makes legendary grilled cheese."

Ethan grinned. "I'll keep that in mind."

Jordan held up a finger. "Just don't tell anyone I said something sincere. It'll ruin my brand."

After sixth-period class, it was lunchtime, finally. The lunchroom was buzzing, trays clattering, sneakers squeaking, and the faint beat of a student-made playlist bumping from a phone in someone's backpack.

The athlete table smack in the middle of the room was crowded with varsity jackets, football bags, and stories about Friday night lights.

Ethan slid into his usual spot between Chris and Scott, just as Amanda joined them with her sketchbook and an apple.

"Dodgeball tomorrow," Chris announced. "Y'all better be ready. I've been watching a film."

"You mean that one social media video called 'Dodgeball K.O.s'?" Amanda asked.

Chris grinned. "It's research."

Just then, Jordan appeared at the edge of the table, tray in hand, balancing a chocolate milk, a bowl of nachos, and a portable gaming console clipped to his jeans.

He moved to sit down.

Chris looked up. "What are you doing?"

Jordan froze. "Uh… sitting?"

Chris laughed. "At this table?"

"Yeah. I mean, unless I accidentally stumbled into a tryout," Jordan replied, only half-joking.

"You're not an athlete, bro," Chris said. "We're not playing video games during lunch."

There was a pause just enough to feel sharp.

Jordan's eyes flicked to Ethan.

But before Jordan could speak, Ethan said, "It's fine. He can sit."

The whole table looked at Ethan

"He's my friend," Ethan added. "That's all that matters."

Chris raised an eyebrow but didn't say more. He went back to eating.

Jordan eased into the seat beside Amanda and popped open his chocolate milk like nothing had happened.

Amanda leaned over and whispered, "Guess you're varsity by association now."

Jordan whispered back, "I'm just here for the milk and the moral support."

They went back to laughing, trading fries, and debating who would win in a dodgeball match: Coach Lanning or the gym teacher with the headband and the knee brace.

But underneath the chatter, Jordan gave Ethan a quiet glance, a nod of thanks.

And Ethan returned it without saying a word.

Because he knew what it felt like to be left out. And he wasn't about to become someone who forgot that.

The final bell echoed down the hallways of Gerry High School, and students poured out of classrooms like a slow-moving river. Backpacks slung over shoulders, lockers slammed shut, sneakers squeaked on tile floors.

Ethan made his way toward the gym, his duffel bag bouncing against his side.

"Yo, Force Train!"

He turned to see Jordan jogging up beside him, one strap of his overstuffed backpack dangling loose, a comic book wedged awkwardly between two notebooks.

"Football time, huh?" Jordan asked, slightly out of breath.

"Yeah," Ethan said, adjusting his bag. "Film, drills, and probably extra laps. Coach said we need to be sharper on defense."

Jordan nodded, then slowed his pace a little, falling into step beside him.

"Hey… random question," he said. "Do you like movies?"

Ethan raised an eyebrow. "Who doesn't like movies?"

"Exactly!" Jordan said, pointing at him like that, proved something. "So, listen, Amanda and I were talking at lunch, and she said there's a midnight showing of The Last Exit on Saturday. A big psychological thriller-action flick. Total nerd overload. I already got our tickets, but she told me I had to make it social."

Ethan laughed. "Wait, so this is a mission?"

Jordan shrugged. "More like a suggestion disguised as a mission. But I figured you could use a break. You've been in beast mode since camp. And besides…" He paused. "You deserve to hang out with people who don't only care about how fast you run a forty."

Ethan looked ahead toward the field doors.

"Saturday night?"

"Yup. Amanda's driving. I'll bring snacks that aren't entirely legal by theater standards."

Ethan smiled to himself.

For a long time, his weekends had been just football, journaling, family, and pressure. But a movie? With people who liked him even without a jersey on?

That didn't sound bad at all. "Alright," Ethan said. "I'm in."

Jordan grinned. "Nice! I'll make sure Amanda doesn't pick some weird organic kale popcorn again. She says it's good for your chakras or something."

Ethan laughed, shaking his head. "See you after practice?"

Jordan gave him a mock salute. "Go make the crowd scream."

As Jordan disappeared down the hallway, Ethan pushed through the doors to the locker room, still thinking about what it meant to be seen not just as an athlete, but as a person.

The locker room smelled like turf, sweat, and that lemony floor cleaner the janitors used when they were mad at the football team. Cleats clattered across the tiles, and Coach Lanning's voice echoed off the cinderblock walls.

"Pads on, mouths closed, minds sharp! We're not here to jog through drills like it's gym class!"

Ethan laced up his cleats in silence. His teammates were hyped, still riding the high from last week Friday night win and the whispers about scouts in the stands. Everyone had something to prove. Ethan did too. He always did.

But as he tugged his jersey over his shoulder pads, his thoughts drifted… to the movie plans, to how Jordan cracked jokes like life didn't weigh a thousand pounds, and to Amanda's sarcastic smirk that somehow made everything feel lighter.

Something inside him tugged a subtle ache for a different kind of life. Not one without football, but one where football wasn't the only thing.

Out on the field, the sky was smeared with orange and gold as the sun dipped toward the horizon. Coach Lanning had them running plays over and over again.

"Again! Tighten that formation! Ethan, you're leading too far left! Set your eyes downfield!"

"Yes, Coach!" Ethan shouted, refocusing.

He dropped into position. The quarterback called the snap. Ethan exploded off the line, bulldozing past two blockers like a force train. The coaches clapped. Teammates hollered.

He loved this. The power. The respect. The clarity of it all.

And yet…

A part of him still wondered what it would feel like to sit in a movie theater, no pads, no pressure, just popcorn and friends?

They broke for water. Ethan bent over, catching his breath.

Scott slapped him on the back. "Yo, you good? You looked distracted."

"Just tired," Ethan lied.

Scott nodded. "Gotta stay locked in. Especially now. You know the scouts from Winslow State are coming back."

Ethan nodded, sipping water. He looked out at the field, then past it, toward the world that didn't revolve around yard lines and playbooks.

The tug-of-war had started.

And he didn't know yet which side would win.

Chapter 6
Just Another School Day

The morning bell blared across Gerry High, and Ethan hustled into first period just before the final ring. He wasn't late, but he wasn't early either, just on time. Just like always.

"Mr. Phillips," said Mr. Carter, his math teacher, with an arched eyebrow. "Gracing us with your athletic presence."

"Always a pleasure," Ethan grinned, sliding into his seat.

He sat near the window, not because he liked the view, but because it gave him enough room to stretch his long legs. At six-foot-six and two hundred-sixty pounds, Ethan wasn't exactly built for desk chairs.

Scott tossed a crumpled piece of notebook paper at him from across the aisle. Ethan opened it.

Dodgeball MVP = me. Change my mind.

Ethan smirked and scribbled back:

You trip over cones during warmups. Sit down.

The second period was English. Mrs. Walters was on a poetry kick again, handing out printed lyrics from a '90s song like it was poetic.

"Who can tell me what this line means: 'The quietness isn't so bad, 'til I look in a mirror and see my eyes, sadness'?"

Amanda raised her hand without looking up. "Regret. Reflection. It's emo and beautiful."

Jordan muttered from behind Ethan, "I just regret not bringing headphones."

Mrs. Walters heard him. "Mr. Rivers, care to elaborate?"

Jordan sat up straighter. "Uh… I think it's about someone staring at their hands because they're… sad?"

Laughter broke out, and even Mrs. Walters chuckled.

"Not wrong, Jordan. Not profound, but not wrong."

Third period, History. Ethan barely stayed awake through a documentary on ancient trade routes. He took notes anyway, just like his mom always said. "No slacking in school, I don't care how many touchdowns you score."

At lunch, he sat at the same table, this time joined again by Jordan, Amanda, Scott, and Chris.

"Movie's still on for Saturday, right?" Jordan asked, pulling a candy bar out of his backpack like it was contraband.

"Yup," Amanda said. "And I'm picking the seats. I don't want to sit behind someone tall again."

They all looked at Ethan.

He held up his hands. "Hey, I can't help being blessed."

"Blessed?" Jordan said. "Try oversized."

The day continued with Spanish, followed by weight training and study hall. The familiar rhythm of high school life. Not easy, but predictable.

Still, Ethan felt it again: that subtle tug toward something else. Not to give up football, but to breathe a little outside of it.

To be… normal.

Just a kid.

That afternoon, as he changed in the locker room before practice, he stared at his cleats a little longer than usual.

The season was moving fast. Expectations were rising. Recruiters were watching.

But Saturday night?

That was for him. The late afternoon sun cast long shadows over the Gerry High football field, baking the turf just enough to make every sprint feel like it was happening in a sauna. Whistles blew. Coaches barked. Helmets clashed.

Ethan wiped the sweat from his forehead as he got into position.

"Alright!" Coach Lanning shouted. "Defense, line up! You know the drill, ten-yard reads, breakdown on the ball!"

Ethan dug his cleats in, eyes forward. The ball snapped.

He surged forward with a fast, powerful, controlled movement.

Too fast.

"Ethan! Pull up!" Coach barked as he blew his whistle. "You overran the gap again!"

Ethan skidded to a stop, frustrated. His technique had been off all week. His mind was drifting to the movie, to Jordan and Amanda laughing at lunch, to anything but formations and gap control.

He jogged back to the line, silent.

"Phillips," Coach Lanning called out. "Walk with me."

Ethan peeled off from the group and jogged over.

"You alright?" the coach asked, his voice quieter now. "You've been a step off since Monday."

Ethan hesitated. "Just tired. A lot on my mind."

Coach nodded slowly. "Listen, I get it. You're young, but the spotlight's already on you. I heard from Cozy University's scout again. Winslow's reaching out. You've got talent, Ethan. But talent without focus? That's wasted potential."

Ethan nodded, staring down at his cleats.

Coach Lanning's voice lowered. "You've got a gift, son. But don't let distractions, even good ones, loosen your grip on them. There's a time for friends, movies, all that. But you've gotta know when to lock in. Especially if you want that next level."

"Yes, sir."

"I'm not saying don't live your life. Just remember, not everyone gets this shot. Don't fumble it."

Ethan looked up and met his coach's eyes. "I won't."

"Good. Now get back out there."

As Ethan returned to the huddle, his chest was tight.

He wasn't mad at Coach. Everything he said was true.

But part of him, the part that wasn't wearing shoulder pads or chasing stats, just wanted to laugh without pressure. Sit in a movie theater. Be a first-year student.

He got back into position.

The ball snapped.

This time, he hit his mark. The last whistle of football practice blew, and a collective groan of relief echoed across the field.

"Pads off, hit the showers!" Coach Lanning shouted. "Weight room tomorrow, no excuses!"

Ethan unlaced his cleats and peeled off his jersey, the evening breeze cooling the sweat on his skin. Most of the team headed toward the locker room, but a few guys lingered on the gym side of the building.

Jordan was one of them, standing near the open double doors with a dodgeball tucked under his arm like a football.

"Oh no," Ethan muttered, chuckling as he walked by.

"Oh yes," Jordan said with a grin. "Gym's free. Coach Harper left early. That means it's dodgeball time, gentlemen."

Chris raised an eyebrow. "Aren't we a little old for dodgeball?"

"You're never too old to humble yourself with a rubber ball to the face," Jordan replied. "Come on. Ten minutes. No tackling. No helmets. Just glory."

Ethan shrugged. "Why not?"

They filed into the gym, where a few kids from the track team and basketball squad had already claimed a side of the court. Amanda was there too, tying her shoes.

"Didn't peg you for the dodgeball type," Ethan said.

"I'm here to win," she replied coolly. "Or at least to watch Jordan embarrass himself."

"I'm the dark horse," Jordan whispered. "They never see me coming."

"Because you're crouching behind Ethan," Scott said.

Coach Harper's bins of dodgeballs were already set up. Within minutes, teams were formed, and the air was buzzing with adrenaline, laughter, and light-hearted trash talk.

Ethan hadn't smiled this much all week.

He ducked, dodged, caught a ball one-handed, and whipped it across the gym, knocking out a junior who'd been taunting Jordan the whole time.

"Force Train!" someone yelled from the sidelines.

Ethan laughed, catching his breath.

He felt… normal.

Not the face of Gerry High football.

Not the scout magnet.

Just a kid in a gym, playing a game that didn't come with scholarships or expectations.

The game ended when Amanda caught Jordan's throw mid-air and launched it back at him, a direct hit.

"That's not even legal!" Jordan shouted.

"That's reflexes," Amanda grinned.

They sat on the bleachers afterward, sweaty but happy.

Ethan leaned back, arms draped over the bench behind him.

He didn't say it out loud, but he thought it: I needed this. After Ethan had finished playing with his friends in the gym, he waited for his mother to arrive.

While sitting alone in front of the school's entrance, he thought about what happened with his father. He could not believe that he had come to their home extremely intoxicated. A tear formed in his eyes as his mother pulled up. He quickly wiped his eyes and headed towards the car. He did not want his mother to notice. Ethan tossed his backpack into the back seat and climbed into the passenger side, still buzzing with leftover adrenaline from practice. His uniform clung to him, sweat-drenched and dusty, but his thoughts weren't on football.

"Hey, Mom," he said, glancing over as she buckled her seatbelt. "Did you hear anything yet? About Dad?"

His mother hesitated, put the car in drive, and slowly pulled away from the school. "Not yet," she said. "But I was just about to call your Aunt Helen."

Ethan didn't respond immediately. He stared out the window, chewing the inside of his cheek.

They pulled into the driveway a few minutes later. The house looked the same as it always did, with a worn porch swing, a garden that was somehow still alive, and front steps that creaked, but something felt different. Heavy.

"I'll go change," Ethan said, heading inside first.

"Give me a minute. I want to try Helen," his mother replied, pulling her phone from her purse and stepping onto the porch.

Inside, Ethan peeled off his uniform and threw on some gym shorts and a T-shirt before slumping onto the couch. He could hear his mother's voice from the front porch, low and concerned.

Then the front door creaked open behind him.

Uncle George walked in, carrying a bag of groceries and a look that said he'd heard too much already.

"You alright, kid?" George asked, setting the bag on the counter.

Ethan nodded, but it wasn't convincing. "Mom's calling Aunt Helen," he muttered. "I just wanna know if he's okay."

George sighed and walked to the fridge, placing a carton of milk inside before closing the door slowly. "He's still your dad. I get it. You wanna know he's alive, not lying somewhere alone."

Ethan swallowed hard. "Is that too much to ask?"

"No," George said, folding his arms. "But you know your dad. Sometimes silence is his way of saying he's not ready to be found."

His mom reentered the room, phone still in hand. Her face was unreadable.

"Did she answer?" Ethan asked, sitting up straighter.

"She did," she said carefully. "She said he was... in the downtown area last week. But no one's seen him in a few days. He didn't come by like he usually does. She's worried too."

George rubbed the back of his neck. "That's not good."

Ethan leaned forward, hands clasped between his knees. "What if something's happened to him?"

His mother sat beside him, wrapping an arm around his shoulders. "We don't know that. Your dad has his patterns. He disappears, then reappears as if nothing happened. It's not healthy, I know. But that's been his rhythm since the divorce."

Ethan shook his head slowly. "I just want him to show up one time... for me. One game. One birthday. Something."

George sat across from them now, more serious. "Let me drive around tonight after dinner, see if I can find him. He tends to hang out in the same places when things get tough. Liquor store off 4th Street, the shelter on Maple Rd..."

Ethan looked up. "You think he's at the shelter?"

George shrugged. "Could be. Could be nowhere. But I'll try."

"Thanks, Uncle George."

His mother rubbed Ethan's back. "No matter what happens, Ethan, you are not responsible for your father's choices. You hear me?"

Ethan nodded but didn't respond. It didn't feel that simple. His father's absence still echoed in the corners of every accomplishment. No matter how loud the crowd cheered, one silence always stood out.

Later that evening, after dinner, Ethan sat at the window, watching the sun set over the street. Uncle George's car pulled away from the house and disappeared down the road. The neon "OPEN" sign flickered against the cracked windows of the mini liquor mart, casting a faint red glow across the pavement. Uncle George pulled his car into a side space and stepped out, glancing toward the front of the store. Two men stood near the entrance, one leaning against the wall, sipping from a brown paper bag, the other lighting a cigarette with hands that looked too worn for his age.

George approached, his boots crunching over loose gravel. "Evenin'," he said calmly, nodding in greeting.

The man with the cigarette sized him up. "Evenin'."

"I'm lookin' for someone," George said. "Michael Phillips. Tall guy, thin, beard's probably a little unkempt. Kinda talks like he's got something stuck in his throat." He forced a small smile. "Drinks a lot."

The two men exchanged a glance.

The one with the paper bag squinted. "You said Michael Phillips?"

"Yeah. He's my brother-in-law."

"Can't say I've seen him," the smoker said, blowing a stream of smoke into the air. "He used to come through here, but not lately. Not in a couple of weeks."

"He still breathing?" the man with the bag asked with a dry chuckle, then quickly added, "No disrespect."

George kept his tone even. "That's what I'm trying to find out."

The smoker took another drag, then nodded down the street. "You might wanna try the shelter. Maple Road. Last time I saw him, that's where he was headin' after dark. Said he needed to get warm."

George sighed. "Alright. Thanks."

He turned to leave, then paused. "If you do see him… tell him George is lookin'. And that Ethan is asking about him."

The smoker gave a slight nod, his expression softening just a little. "Will do."

As George got back into his car, he gripped the steering wheel and stared out into the night. The liquor store was fading in the rearview mirror, but the ache in his gut stayed sharp. He knew too well the pattern: the breadcrumbs they lost always led to the quiet corners of town that most people ignored.

He turned the ignition and headed for Maple Road, praying this wasn't another dead end.

Chapter 7
Missing Pieces

The parking lot of the Maple Road Shelter was nearly empty, except for a dented bike chained to a sign and a lone streetlamp flickering overhead. Uncle George stepped out of his car and adjusted his coat collar against the breeze. The air smelled faintly of damp concrete and stale coffee.

Inside the shelter, fluorescent lights buzzed overhead. The front desk attendant, a weary-looking woman in a maroon cardigan, looked up as he entered.

"Evening," George greeted with a polite nod. "I'm looking for someone who might've stayed here. Name's Michael Phillips."

She clicked her mouse, then turned to a clipboard resting beside her. "Michael... haven't seen him in a while," she said, flipping a few pages. "He was here off and on last month, but it's been over two weeks now."

George's face tensed. "So, he hasn't checked in at all?"

"Nope." She sighed. "But tell him if you see him, he needs to report in by the end of next week, or he loses his bed. We've got a long waiting list, and policy is policy."

He nodded slowly. "Thanks."

As George stepped back outside, frustration curled in his chest like a clenched fist. The sky above was now charcoal gray, blanketing the city in a stillness that felt heavier than usual. He sat in the car for a moment, the engine off, the silence ringing louder than the street noise around him.

He pulled out his phone and called his sister. She picked up on the second ring.

"Hey, George," Elle said, her voice hushed, probably trying not to worry Ethan.

"I stopped by the shelter. Another dead end," he said flatly. "They haven't seen him in over two weeks." A pause.

"I figured," she murmured. "He's really gone off the grid this time."

George sighed and leaned his head back against the seat. "Yeah. Listen, I think we should stop by the police station in the morning. Just in case something's happened. You know how this city is if he's lying in a hospital bed somewhere or worse... they'd be the ones to know."

Elle's silence on the other end said everything she couldn't bring herself to speak aloud.

"Alright," she finally said. "I'll go with you."

"I'm gonna check under the bridge on Mason Avenue before I head home," George added. "That's where a lot of the guys go when they don't want to be found."

"I hate that you even know that," Elle whispered.

"I hate that I have to," he said, and hung up gently.

The keys jingled in his hand as he started the car and pulled away from the shelter. He turned toward Mason Avenue, headlights slicing through the darkness, heart heavy with the weight of too many nights like this chasing ghosts who didn't want to be caught. The bridge on Mason Avenue loomed overhead like a sleeping beast, massive, cold, and indifferent. Beneath it, life clung to the shadows in the form of tents patched with duct tape, cardboard shelters, plastic tarps, and blankets layered thick against the night air. Smoke from a small fire pit drifted upward, the only sign of warmth in a place forgotten by most.

Uncle George pulled his car to the curb and rolled down the window.

The stench hit first, sour with damp clothes, old food, and desperation. He leaned slightly over the steering wheel, peering into the darkness, the beam from his headlights cutting across the encampment.

"Michael!" he called out, voice firm but not hostile. "Michael Phillips! You out here?"

At first, there was only silence. Then came the groans.

"Yo, shut up!" "Go on, man! Ain't nobody wanna hear all that!" "I'm tryna sleep!"

The bitter murmurs echoed from under blankets and tents, tired voices annoyed by another stranger who had pierced the fragile calm.

George started to roll up his window when a gravelly voice drifted up from somewhere near a broken shopping cart.

"Try Edison Avenue," the voice said, muffled and low. Whoever said it didn't bother sitting up. "He was headed that way last week."

George leaned out the window a little. "You see him for sure?"

But there was no answer. The man was already back in his slumber or pretending to be.

George stared into the shadows a moment longer, then slowly shook his head. "Edison Avenue…" he muttered. "That's across town."

He let out a slow sigh, gripping the steering wheel.

"I'm goin' home," he said out loud as if to confirm the decision to himself. "We'll look for him in the daylight."

With one last glance under the bridge, he rolled the window up and pulled away from the curb, the beams of his headlights retreating from the makeshift shelters and the people inside them. He headed home.

The city blurred past his window as he drove, but his mind wasn't on the traffic or the streetlights. It was on the boy at home, Ethan, and how every passing hour chipped away at hope. The next morning, the sun filtered through streaked windows as George pulled out of the driveway with Elle in the passenger seat. The weight of exhaustion clung to both of them, he from searching half the city last night, and she from years of worry that stretched across too many years.

Neither spoke for the first few minutes of the drive.

Then Elle pulled out her phone. "I'm gonna call Helen. Just to be sure he didn't show up before we file this."

George nodded, keeping his eyes on the road.

Elle tapped the screen and put the phone on speaker. It rang twice before Helen picked up, her voice slightly raspy, like she hadn't slept well.

"Hey, Elle," she answered. "Everything okay?"

"We're on the way to the police department now," Elle said gently. "But before we file the report, I just wanted to check in… Did Michael show up last night?"

Helen sighed heavily on the other end. "No. Still no sign of him. His bed hasn't been slept in. His wallet's still here. I even checked the fridge to see if he snuck in and ate something, but…nothing."

Elle looked out the window, and her jaw clenched. "Alright. I didn't want to jump the gun."

"I'm gonna start calling around today," Helen added, her voice a bit shaky. "I'll check with the hospital again. Maybe the coroner's office, too, just in case…"

"No," Elle said quickly, her hand pressing against her chest. "Don't talk like that yet. Let's not go there unless we have to."

"I know. I… need to do something," Helen said. "Not knowing is worse than knowing."

Elle's eyes welled slightly, but she blinked the tears back. "After we file the report, why don't you come over for dinner tonight? George is making spaghetti. Ethan's been asking about you."

Helen chuckled softly. "You still let that man cook?"

George grinned from the driver's seat. "Better than you think."

"Alright," Helen said, her tone softening. "I'll come by. Thanks, Elle. I know we're not technically family anymore, but…"

"We are," Elle interrupted. "Always will be."

The line was quiet for a beat before Helen cleared her throat. "Alright. I'll see you both tonight."

Elle ended the call and looked over at George. "You really making spaghetti?"

George smirked. "Better start boiling the water when we get back."

They pulled into the lot of the local police department, the building standing stoic and sun-worn. Elle took a breath before opening the door.

"Let's find him," she whispered. Together, they stepped inside. The lobby of the police station smelled faintly of coffee and stale paperwork. A uniformed officer sat behind a thick glass partition, typing something into a computer. George stepped up to the counter first.

"Good morning," he said. "We need to file a missing person report."

The officer looked up, gave a brief nod, and pulled a clipboard from a drawer. "Names?"

"George Jenkins. This is my sister, Elle Phillips."

The officer scribbled quickly, then handed George a form. "Have a seat. Someone will be with you shortly."

George and Elle took a seat on a row of plastic chairs near the wall. A muted television in the corner played the local morning news. Ten minutes passed. Then fifteen.

George checked the wall clock and muttered, "What is taking so long?"

Elle shrugged lightly. "I don't know. Maybe they're backed up. Policing is busy."

"Yeah, you're right," George replied, though the impatience in his voice still lingered.

Just then, a female officer in plainclothes stepped into the waiting area. Her badge was clipped to her belt, and her expression was calm if slightly worn.

"Mr. Jenkins? Ms. Phillips? Sorry for the wait," she said. "I'm Officer Riley. Come with me."

They followed her down a short hallway and into a quiet room with two chairs and a desk. A file folder and a police tablet rested on the surface.

"Alright," Officer Riley said, settling in. "Tell me everything you can about the person you're trying to locate."

Elle leaned forward, folding her hands in her lap. "His name is Michael Phillips. He's my ex-husband. He's struggled with alcohol for years. Sometimes he's on the streets… other times he stays with his sister, my former sister-in-law, Helen."

George nodded beside her. "We're still close with Helen. She hasn't seen him in over two weeks."

Riley typed as they spoke. "When was the last time you saw him?"

"Not in person for about three weeks," Elle answered. "But he usually calls Ethan, our son… well, my son, his son too, but nothing. He didn't come around for the last few games or even leave a voicemail."

"I went out looking for him last night," George chimed in. "Checked the liquor store on Harlan, the shelter on Maple Road, the lady there said he hasn't checked in, and he's about to lose his bed, and I stopped by the bridge on Mason Ave. Lots of tents, cardboard setups under there."

Officer Riley looked up. "Did you speak to anyone there?"

George nodded. "Yeah. Got cursed out mostly. But one guy said to check Edison Ave. I didn't go; it was too late and on the other side of town."

He sighed, rubbing the back of his neck. "Michael… he disappears sometimes. Goes on binges. But he always turns up after a few days. Never this long. Never without at least leaving a trail."

Elle added, "We're not here to cause drama. We need to know he's okay. If he wants to be left alone, fine. But if something's happened…"

Officer Riley's expression softened. "You did the right thing coming in. I'll submit the report and alert nearby patrol units to keep an eye out. We'll also notify hospitals and jails under his name, just in case something recent got logged that hasn't been flagged in the system yet."

"Thank you," Elle said softly.

"I'll also pass the note about Edison Avenue," Riley continued. "It's a rough area, but we'll send a unit through sometime today."

She stood and offered a business card across the desk. "Here's my direct line. I'll keep you updated with anything we find."

George took the card. "Appreciate it, Officer."

As they left the station and walked back to the car, Elle sighed deeply.

"At least something's being done," she murmured, sliding into the passenger seat.

George started the engine. "Now we wait." Back in the car, the silence between George and Elle wasn't uncomfortable; it was heavy. Thoughtful. The kind of silence that follows helplessness.

"Are we still stopping at the store?" George asked, glancing over.

Elle nodded. "Yeah. If Helen's coming for dinner, I need garlic bread. And more sauce. You used the last of it last week and never replaced it."

George smirked. "You keep track of sauce?"

"I keep track of everything," she said with a tired smile. They pulled into the parking lot of Gerry Market, a small local grocery store with creaky carts and dim lights. The moment they stepped out, Elle paused near the entrance, squinting.

"Is that..." she whispered. A man with graying hair, a weathered face, and a slight limp leaned against the newspaper stand, sipping a cup of coffee. His jacket was torn at the sleeve, and his eyes were sunken but familiar.

"Burt?" Elle called out, walking closer. He looked up, surprised. "Elle? Wow... been a long time." She smiled gently. "Too long. You doing okay?"

Burt gave a slow shrug. "Getting by. Things haven't been easy."

George nodded respectfully beside her. "Good to see you, man." Elle hesitated, then asked, "Have you seen Michael lately?"

Burt's brow creased, and he looked down at his coffee. "No... not in weeks. Maybe more. Last time I saw him, we talked about football. He was hyped about Ethan making varsity as a freshman. Said he was gonna get clean."

Elle exhaled sharply, her shoulders dropping.

"If I see him," Burt added, "I'll tell him you're looking."

"Thanks, Burt," she said quietly.

They parted ways and stepped into the store. The aisles were familiar rows of boxed pasta, garlic knots in the freezer section, salad kits that George claimed made him "feel healthy."

They quickly filled the cart, grabbing what they needed for spaghetti night: pasta, sauce, Parmesan, and a loaf of Italian bread.

But Elle was distracted. Her face tight, her steps slower.

"You okay?" George asked, picking up a jar of crushed garlic.

"No," she admitted. "Ethan's gonna ask again today. He's already asked three times in the past week. And I keep saying, 'We're trying to find him.' What happens when that answer isn't good enough anymore?"

George didn't respond right away.

"He came by the house a few weeks ago," Elle added, lowering her voice. "Drunk. Loud. Scared Ethan. He yelled at me for not answering his calls. He was a mess."

George sighed, placing the garlic in the cart. "You think Ethan remembers?"

"I know he does," she said. "And as much as I hated that night... I don't want that to be the last memory my son has of his father."

They stood quietly in the checkout line as the cashier scanned their items. The beep of each barcode echoed against Elle's thoughts.

Once the bags were packed and loaded into the trunk, they climbed back into the car. The ride home was quiet again, this time filled with anticipation, frustration, and a desperate hope that the next knock at the door wouldn't bring more regret.

They pulled into the driveway just past noon, ready to start dinner preparations and brace for the conversation they knew was coming.

Chapter 8

Don't Be Dead

George and Elle pulled into the driveway just as the afternoon sun began to warm the edge of the porch. The quietness of the neighborhood was almost jarring compared to the emotional weight they carried through the police station and grocery store.

George unlocked the front door while Elle grabbed the bags from the trunk.

"Spaghetti night's still on," George said, trying to lighten the mood as they stepped into the kitchen.

Elle cracked a small smile. "If you don't burn the garlic bread this time."

"I make no promises."

They moved around the kitchen together with a familiar rhythm of putting away groceries, stacking cans, and setting the sauce on the counter. The light hum of the refrigerator filled the room with a dull background noise. Footsteps thumped softly down the stairs. Ethan appeared in the hallway, wearing basketball shorts and an oversized hoodie. His eyes were alert, focused, and hopeful.

"Did you find my dad?" he asked, voice direct.

Elle froze mid-motion, still holding a box of pasta. George turned first.

"No, kiddo," George said gently, wiping his hands on a towel. "But we're still working on it."

Elle added, "Aunt Helen's coming for dinner tonight. We thought it would be good to all be together."

Ethan looked at her, searching her face. "Is something wrong?"

Elle took a breath and set the box on the counter. "We went to the police station this morning. We filed a missing person report. Just as a precaution, it's been a while since anyone's seen your dad."

Ethan's expression didn't change, but his shoulders dropped slightly.

"We just want to make sure he's okay," she added. "It doesn't mean something bad happened. Just means we're doing everything we can."

He nodded slowly. "Okay." But she could see the worry that clung to his eyes.

"I'm not worried," she said with a soft smile. "So, you don't have to be either."

Ethan offered a nod, but it was stiff and automatic.

He crossed the kitchen quietly, opened the fridge, and grabbed a cold apple juice. Then he pulled a bag of pretzels from the cabinet and made his way back toward the stairs.

"Let us know if you want to help with dinner," George called after him.

"Okay," Ethan mumbled, already halfway up.

He shut the door behind him once inside his room. The walls, covered in sports posters and high school banners, suddenly felt too loud. Too full. He sat on his bed, his snacks untouched.

He's probably dead somewhere, Ethan thought bitterly, staring at the apple juice in his hand.

He didn't want to think it, but the thought kept coming back.

Don't be dead. He squeezed his eyes shut.

Despite all the chaos, all the yelling, all the nights his mom cried after a phone call, Ethan still wanted him to be okay. He still wanted him to get clean. To show up. To sit in the bleachers again like he used to, shout too loud, and call him "champ."

But that was a long time ago. And even the strongest memories had started to fade. Time passed quickly, slipping away between the simmering sauce and the scent of garlic bread warming in the oven. The kitchen was filled with the gentle clatter of preparation, and the house, though still heavy with worry, carried the faint rhythm of normalcy.

Then came the knock, three gentle taps.

Elle dried her hands and moved toward the door with a familiar smile already forming. "Right on time," she said, opening it.

Aunt Helen stood on the porch in her neatly pressed coat, a warm smile on her face, and a covered dessert dish in her arms.

"Hope someone saved room for sweets," she chirped.

Ethan appeared at the top of the stairs, eyes immediately locking onto the treat in her hands.

"Strawberry shortcake?" he asked, descending with sudden urgency.

Helen laughed. "Of course. Still your favorite, right?" "Yes, ma'am."

She handed the dish to Elle, then leaned forward and wrapped Ethan in a hug. "You're so tall," she whispered.

"I've been drinking chocolate milk," Ethan replied seriously.

George chuckled from the kitchen.

Moments later, everyone gathered around the table. The lights were low, the air warm with the aroma of pasta, spices, and toasted bread. For a while, there was only the sound of forks clinking against plates and the soft hum of small conversation.

After a few bites, Helen turned to Ethan, her expression gentle. "So, tell me how school is?"

"It's good," Ethan said between forkfuls of spaghetti. "I've got all A's except for English. I think she grades too hard."

George snorted. "Or maybe you need to study harder."

"Maybe both," Ethan said with a grin.

"And football?" Helen asked. "How's it feel to be a freshman on varsity?"

Ethan shrugged, but the pride in his eyes gave him away. "It's amazing. I'm learning a lot. Coach says I've got potential, and a recruiter from Cozy State already asked about me."

Helen's eyes sparkled. "That's wonderful, baby. But listen…promise me something?"

He paused, mid-bite. "Okay?"

"If you make it, beyond high school, beyond college, wherever this life takes you… Don't ever think you did it alone. Don't play just for yourself. Remember to acknowledge God for everything He's given you."

Ethan nodded slowly, listening closely.

Helen reached over and gently touched his wrist. "Psalms 118:1 KJV says, 'O give thanks unto the Lord; for he is good: because his mercy endureth forever.' His mercy… not just once. Not just when we ask. But forever."

Ethan looked down at his plate, then up again. "I'll remember."

"I know you will," she said, her voice tender. "Because even when people disappear, God doesn't."

Elle quietly placed her hand over Helen's, a silent thank-you for saying what her heart couldn't.

For a while, they sat there…three adults and one growing boy, each of them clinging to something unseen, hoping that gratitude and faith might fill the gap where certainty was missing. After dinner, the house settled into a quiet hum of conversation. The dishes were mostly done, except for a few in the sink. Ethan offered to finish cleaning something he rarely volunteered for, but tonight felt different. Maybe it was the shortcake. Perhaps it was Aunt Helen's words. Maybe it was the silence that always came after people tried their best to be normal.

In the living room, George leaned back in the recliner while Helen and Elle sat across from each other on the couch, murmuring about old times and familiar places. Then came the knock.

Three sharp, unexpected raps at the door.

Elle's smile faded. She exchanged a glance with George. He stood up slowly.

When he opened the door, two uniformed officers stood on the porch, their expressions heavy.

"Mr. Jenkins? Ms. Phillips?" the taller officer asked. "May we come in?"

Elle's breath caught in her throat. "Of course," she said, standing.

The officers stepped into the living room, removing their hats. Helen rose to her feet as well, her hands instantly clasping together.

"I'm Officer Kellis. This is Officer Morales," the taller one said. "I'm sorry to bring this news... but earlier this evening, we received a call from a citizen who discovered a body in an alley off 12th Street."

Elle's knees buckled slightly. George stepped behind her instinctively.

"We've identified the deceased as Michael Phillips. He had no ID on him, but a bus card with his name and address helped us locate you. He was found with an open bottle of alcohol in his hand."

Helen gasped, her hand flying to her mouth. "Oh God... oh no..."

Officer Morales added gently, "While it appears the cause of death may be related to alcohol, possibly poisoning or exposure, we won't know for certain until the coroner completes the examination."

Ethan, still in the kitchen, heard everything. The crash of ceramic against tile cut through the room. The officers paused. "Ethan..." Elle whispered.

He stood frozen near the sink, a broken container in pieces around his feet, apple juice soaking into his socks. His eyes were wide, stunned, hollow.

Then he turned and bolted up the stairs.

"Ethan!" Elle called after him, rushing toward the hallway.

But the door slammed before she reached it.

Inside his room, Ethan collapsed onto his bed, fists gripping his blanket, chest heaving with the kind of grief he didn't know how to name. The image burned into his mind a bottle in his father's hand, alone in an alley sliced deeper than words could ever reach.

You couldn't even say goodbye. You were just gone.

Downstairs, George stood stone-still, jaw clenched, pain flickering behind his eyes. He took a step toward the officers. "We'll come to identify the body. … give us a minute."

"Take your time," Officer Kellis said gently, leaving a card on the entry table. "When you're ready, call that number."

The officers gave their condolences and stepped out into the night, closing the door behind them.

Elle sank to the floor in the hallway, hands shaking, her back pressed to the wall.

Helen knelt beside her, tears slipping down her cheeks. "He was troubled… but he was ours," she whispered. "He was ours."

George sat on the arm of the couch, burying his face in his hands.

The house, so full of warmth just an hour ago, now pulsed with silence, heartbreak, and the sharp ache of what would never be said. The house was quiet again, but this time the silence wasn't peaceful; it throbbed with grief.

George stood at the bottom of the stairs for a moment before nodding to Elle and Helen. Without a word, they ascended together, each step heavier than the last.

At the top, Elle gently knocked.

"Ethan?" she said softly. "Honey, we're coming in." The door creaked open.

He was sitting on the floor near his bed, knees pulled to his chest, head buried in his arms. His shoulders shook with silent sobs. The broken pieces of the container he dropped earlier still lingered in all their minds, shattered glass mirroring his broken heart.

Elle knelt beside him first, placing a hand on his back. George crouched opposite her. Helen sat on the edge of the bed, her hands folded tightly in her lap.

"Ethan…" Elle whispered, brushing back the curls from his forehead. "You don't have to hold it in, baby. You can be mad. Say whatever you need to say."

Ethan lifted his head, eyes red, lips trembling. "Why didn't anyone help him?" he said through gritted teeth. "He was out there… dying. And nobody saw him. Nobody helped."

His voice cracked into a sob.

"I hate that bottle," he choked. "I hate it more than I hate him… but I don't want him to be dead."

George blinked hard, trying to hold it together. "You're allowed to be angry, son. Believe me, I've been there. I still am."

Ethan's voice trembled again. "He was supposed to come back. He was supposed to get clean. He said he would!"

Aunt Helen moved to the floor beside him now, her arms slowly wrapping around his back. Her voice was gentle but firm, woven with scripture and grace.

"Psalm 30:5 KJV says, 'For his anger endureth but a moment; in his favour is life: weeping may endure for a night, but joy cometh in the morning.'"

Ethan sniffed, his breathing jagged.

"There's a time to cry, Ethan," she continued. "There's a time to mourn. But there's also a time to heal, a time to laugh again. You will smile again, just not tonight. And that's okay."

She paused, stroking his shoulder. "We're going to get through this. All of us. Together."

Elle nodded, tears falling freely now. "You are not alone, Ethan. Not ever."

George wiped at his face with the sleeve of his shirt. "We need to go to the coroner's office to identify his body. I think it's time."

Elle looked to her son. "You don't have to come. I'd rather you stay home."

But Ethan's eyes were firm now, even though there was pain. "I want to go."

Aunt Helen gently touched his cheek. "You don't have to see your father like this, sweetheart. You can remember him from before."

"I have to see him," Ethan said. "Even if it hurts. He was my dad."

There was silence again, this time filled with respect.

George stood and offered his hand. "Okay then. Let's go."

As the family rose from the floor together, a shared resolve began to take shape between them, not one of perfect strength, but of collective courage. In their grief, they leaned on one another.

And together, they walked out the door to face what came next.

Chapter 9
Through the Glass

The ride to the coroner's office was painfully silent.

No music. No conversation. Just the hum of the engine and the rhythm of tires over pavement, carrying the weight of four people bound by blood, love, and loss.

George drove. His hands gripped the steering wheel a little too tightly, his knuckles pale against the leather. Elle sat in the passenger seat, her fingers tangled together in her lap, her lips moving in a silent prayer she couldn't finish. In the back seat, Aunt Helen stared out the window, her mind drifting somewhere between memory and regret.

Ethan sat beside her, still and pale, his heart pounding so loudly it drowned out the world.

When they arrived, the receptionist greeted them with a solemn nod and led them down a cold, narrow hallway. The air smelled of disinfectant and loss. Every step felt heavier than the last.

"In here," the attendant said, stopping at a viewing room with a large glass window. "We'll bring him out shortly."

The room was silent, with sterile walls, two rows of chairs, and a table with tissues already placed at the center.

Moments later, the curtain on the other side of the glass was drawn back, revealing a metal gurney. The body was wheeled into view, a white sheet covering everything but the face.

George took a breath and stepped forward first. "It's him," he said hoarsely.

Elle's knees buckled, but Helen caught her.

"It's Michael," Helen whispered, voice breaking. "Oh God… It's really him."

His hair was matted. His skin looked gray. The peacefulness of his expression only made it worse.

Because there was no peace in how he left.

Ethan stood back, still in the corner, fists clenched at his sides. He stared at the figure through the thick glass window, not blinking, not breathing.

Then something inside him snapped.

He rushed forward, pressing both hands against the glass, his breath fogging it up.

"Why didn't you come back?" he shouted, his voice cracking. "You promised!"

He slammed his hand against the glass, hard.

George moved toward him, but Elle held him back.

"Let him," she whispered. "Let him feel it."

Ethan pounded his palm again, leaving a print. "You said you were gonna try. I believed you!"

The echo of his fists hitting the glass filled the room like thunder in a chapel.

Tears streamed down his cheeks.

"I was gonna make it to the league, Dad. I was gonna give you tickets. You were supposed to be there!"

He pressed his forehead to the glass now, sobbing.

"I wanted you to see me."

Behind him, Helen cried softly into a tissue, her heart breaking all over again.

George placed a hand on Ethan's back. "He would've been proud of you," he whispered. "Even like this... he would've been proud."

Ethan didn't respond.

He just stood there, fists pressed against the cold window, tears slipping down his face as he stared at the man he loved and lost. A man trapped in a life he couldn't escape.

And though Ethan couldn't reach him, not through the glass, not through death, he whispered one last thing under his breath.

"Don't be dead... but you are."

The room remained quiet, except for the sounds of grief. After 20 minutes of viewing the body, the drive home from the coroner's office was even more peaceful than the one before. No one spoke.

There were no words that could carry the weight of what they had just witnessed.

Ethan stared out the window, his reflection barely visible against the fading daylight. His hand rested on the door handle, his mind still pressed against the glass in that cold viewing room, screaming for a father who could no longer answer.

When they pulled into the driveway, Aunt Helen turned slightly in her seat. "I'm going to head home," she said gently. "Elle, I'll call you tomorrow morning. We can go to the funeral home together… figure out what comes next." Elle nodded. "Thanks for everything, Helen."

Helen leaned across the seat and gave Ethan's shoulder a soft squeeze. "You're stronger than you think," she whispered.

He didn't reply. He opened the car door and walked inside.

Elle and George watched him disappear up the stairs without saying a word.

Inside his room, Ethan closed the door behind him, kicked off his shoes, and lay across his bed. He didn't cry. He didn't move. He just stared at the ceiling, empty, as if his body had spent everything it had left.

Downstairs, the house was still. George poured a glass of water and leaned against the counter. "Elle," he said after a long pause, "I don't think Ethan should go to school tomorrow. It's Friday. Let him stay home. He needs to breathe."

Elle nodded, arms folded tightly across her chest. "I'll call the office in the morning. Let them know he's excused."

George took a sip. "He's holding it in now, but it's going to come back up. When it does, we need to be ready." "I know," she whispered. "I just don't know how."

George placed a hand gently on her back. "You're not doing this alone." Upstairs, Ethan finally moved.

He reached for the leather-bound journal on his nightstand. It was worn at the edges, filled with half-finished entries, stats from football practice, Holy scriptures verses Coach Lanning made them memorize, and the occasional scribbled sketch of a helmet or cleats.

He opened to a blank page and began to write slowly:

Dear Dad,

I wish you had stayed. I wish you could've seen me play. I wish the bottle hadn't won.

I don't know if I'm supposed to hate you right now or miss you. But I do both.

I thought you had more time. We all did. I'll try to forgive you. I'll try to remember the good parts. I'll try to become the kind of man who never runs. Even though you're gone, I still want to make you proud. Somehow.

Love,

Ethan

He closed the journal, slid it under his pillow, and lay back down. The darkness wrapped around him like a heavy blanket.

And finally, after everything, he slept. The house was still cloaked in morning quiet when Elle rose from bed.

The sun had barely touched the horizon, casting a soft gray light through the kitchen windows. The silence felt heavier today, not peaceful, but solemn, like the calm after a storm that never truly ended.

She padded gently down the hallway and paused outside Ethan's room. She knocked lightly, then pushed the door open a crack.

He was still curled beneath the blankets, his journal peeking from under his pillow.

Elle stepped inside quietly and leaned over, brushing her hand over his hair. "Baby," she whispered, "you don't have school today. I already called it in. Just rest, alright?"

Ethan stirred but didn't open his eyes. He nodded slowly and turned to face the wall.

Elle closed the door gently behind her and walked downstairs, each step echoing in the silence of the house. In the kitchen, she set a mug under the coffee maker but didn't bother pressing the button. Instead, she sat down at the table alone.

The same table where Michael once slammed his fist down, drunk and bitter, yelling about coming home to no dinner, as if she hadn't cooked and waited, as if sitting at a bar for four hours was an acceptable exchange for being a husband and father.

Her mind drifted.

The image of him stumbling through the front door, eyes glassy, voice loud, blaming everyone but the bottle.

But then just as quickly came the softer memories.

The times he brought home roses, unwrapped and clumsily held behind his back. The sober days when he washed dishes and danced with Ethan in the living room, humming an upbeat song under his breath. The mornings he'd leave notes by the coffeepot that said, "Trying again. Love you."

Elle pressed her hand to her heart.

Why? she thought bitterly. Why wouldn't you stay clean?

She clenched her jaw. "Why couldn't you fight harder?" she whispered out loud.

She pushed back from the table and grabbed her Holy scriptures from the windowsill, flipping through them until her eyes landed on the verse she didn't even know she was looking for:

Matthew 10:28 KJV

"And fear not them which kill the body but are not able to kill the soul: but rather fear him which is able to destroy both soul and body in hell."

She stared at it. Long and hard. Her lips parted. Her eyes welled.

He allowed the enemy to kill the body…

Elle closed the Holy scriptures and pressed them to her chest, shaking as the grief broke through again. Her tears fell freely, soaking into the pages still warm from her hands.

"Lord," she sobbed, her voice cracking under the weight of it all, "please, please don't let Ethan take the same road. Please don't let bitterness make him numb… don't let pain pull him away from You."

She bowed her head lower.

"I pray that Ethan remains aligned with Your Word. Let him walk the path his father couldn't finish. Let him rise."

The prayer hung in the kitchen like incense, curling toward heaven as Elle rocked slowly in her seat, clinging not to answers but to hope. By late morning, the house felt like a waiting room for grief.

Elle stood in front of her bedroom mirror, fastening the small gold cross necklace Michael once gave her during one of his sober stretches. She hesitated when she clasped it, fingers trembling at the memory.

Her outfit was modest black slacks, a soft gray blouse, and low heels. But it wasn't the clothes that made her feel heavy. It was everything else.

Downstairs, Ethan emerged just long enough to grab toast and a bottle of water. His eyes were swollen from sleep or maybe from crying, Elle couldn't tell. He didn't say a word. Just nodded when she told him she'd be back in a few hours and disappeared back upstairs.

George had already left for work. "I hate to go," he had said before stepping out, "but my students have a major test on Monday. I can't cancel today.

Elle understood. Grief doesn't always pause the world around it.

She grabbed her purse and quietly closed the front door behind her.

At Helen's house, the mood was subdued but determined. The two women embraced briefly, then drove together to the local funeral home—a red-brick building with white columns and flower beds that felt too cheerful for such a sorrowful task.

Inside, the air was cool and still. Classical music hummed faintly through the speakers, and the lighting was just dim enough to feel respectful without being dark.

A man in a navy suit approached them with a gentle smile. He was tall, with silver at his temples and a voice like soft cloth.

"Good morning," he said kindly. "You must be the family of Mr. Michael Phillips."

"Yes," Elle said, her voice catching in her throat. "I'm Elle… his ex-wife. This is Helen, his sister."

"I'm Derrick Townsend," he said, extending his hand. "I'll be helping you with the arrangements today. I knew Michael… not well, but enough to know he had a kind heart beneath the struggle."

Helen nodded, eyes glistening. "He really did."

They followed him to a private conference room where warm tea and tissues had already been placed on the table. Derrick opened a simple black folder containing paperwork.

"I want first to say how sorry I am for your loss," he said sincerely. "I know Michael battled alcoholism for many years. I was hoping… well, we all were hoping he'd pull through."

Elle looked down. "We were, too."

Derrick continued gently. "We'll walk through this step by step. You don't need to rush anything."

Helen cleared her throat softly. "He didn't have life insurance. But we'll figure out how to cover the basics."

"We'll work with you," Derrick assured her. "Let's focus first on how you want to honor his life. Burial or cremation?"

Elle exhaled deeply. "He always said if anything happened, he wanted to be buried. Something about 'not leaving the world the way he lived in it scattered.'"

Derrick nodded, making a note. "We'll start there."

As the conversation unfolded, with each detail of a casket and a date, the question of music and flowers felt like another small goodbye. But both women remained composed, holding on not to who Michael was in his addiction, but who he was underneath it.

And though the room was filled with decisions, the silence between them spoke louder than words. Back at home, the afternoon sun filtered softly through the upstairs windows, casting long shadows along the hallway walls. The house was still. Ethan's footsteps echoed faintly as he climbed the narrow staircase that led to the attic.

He hadn't been up there in years.

The door creaked open, the familiar scent of dust, wood, and time greeting him like a forgotten memory. He switched on the overhead bulb, its dim light flickering to life.

Boxes were stacked against the walls with holiday decorations, old baby clothes, and random tools, but one trunk near the back caught his eye. It was old and scratched; the leather handle was worn down from years of use.

Ethan knelt in front of it and slowly flipped the latch open.

Inside were the pieces of a life he barely knew.

On top sat a worn high school yearbook. Taped inside the back cover was a photo of Michael. He was young, strong, and smiling, dressed in a red-and-white football jersey. Number 7. His arms were raised in celebration, and a crowd blurred behind him.

Ethan touched the image, fingers lingering over the edges. He used to be somebody.

Underneath the yearbook was a small stack of framed photos. One was of Michael and Ethan sitting on a park bench. Ethan was maybe four years old, mid-laugh, and Michael had his arm around him, half-turned to say something that looked like a joke. Both were smiling genuinely.

The next photo was harder to look at: a family portrait taken when Ethan was just a baby. Elle held him in her arms, Michael behind them, resting a hand on her shoulder. He didn't look drunk. He didn't look bitter. He looked… present.

When was the last time he was like that? Ethan thought, his stomach tightening.

He closed his eyes, trying to remember his father watching sports without a beer in his hand, coming home before dinner, or sitting with them at the table instead of staggering through the door after midnight, smelling like smoke and whiskey.

But those memories were harder to find.

Instead, his mind filled with the shouting matches voices rising late at night, his mother's firm tone trying to hold the line, his father's slurred words crashing over it. Ethan could still hear the tension in the walls, still remember creeping to the door to listen.

He used to press his ear against the wood, trying to understand, trying to prepare, then sprinting back to bed at the sound of footsteps down the hall, pretending to be asleep before the door opened to check on him.

He clenched his fists.

The anger returned.

Why didn't you stop drinking?

Why didn't you fight for us?

Why weren't we enough?

Tears burned his eyes, but he wiped them away. He didn't want to cry anymore. He tried to rise from the ashes of his father's failure. He wanted to break the pattern.

"I'll be better than you," he whispered to the attic air. "I swear it."

He sat on the old futon near the window, journal beside him, the family photo still clutched in his hand. The silence wrapped around him like a blanket, and without realizing it, he drifted into sleep, his mind caught between memory and promise, past and future.

And for the first time since the knock at the door, he slept without tears. The front door creaked open as Elle stepped into the house, her purse still slung over her shoulder, and her heart weighed down by the emotional toll of the funeral arrangements. The quiet was immediate, pressing.

"Ethan?" she called out, locking the door behind her.

No response.

She kicked off her shoes and moved through the living room, peeking into the kitchen, his usual hiding spot when he didn't want to talk.

"Ethan?" she said again, her voice rising slightly.

Nothing.

She hurried upstairs and opened his bedroom door. His bed was still made. The water bottle and potato chips from earlier were untouched. Panic rose in her chest.

She moved quickly to the back patio door, unlocking it and stepping out barefoot onto the wood planks. The sun was beginning to dip toward the trees, casting long shadows across the yard.

"Ethan?" she called again, her voice breaking this time.

No answer.

She stood still for a moment, scanning the yard. Where would he go? Would he…? No. No, he wouldn't.

Her hand flew to her chest as the worst thoughts began to creep in. Please God, no. Don't let him do anything to himself.

She rushed back inside, her heart pounding in her ears. As she turned toward the stairs again, something caught her eye.

The attic door. It was cracked.

She hadn't noticed it earlier, but now the open sliver of darkness felt like a light of hope. She took a breath and slowly climbed the narrow steps, the wood creaking under her feet.

At the top, she pushed the door open all the way and stepped inside.

And there he was.

Ethan lay on the old futon, curled toward the window, one arm draped over a framed photo, his chest rising and falling in deep, even breaths.

Elle let out a long, shaking sigh… part relief, part heartbreak.

She didn't want to wake him. Not yet.

She quietly stepped closer and noticed the trunk beside him, its contents open, pictures scattered like memories laid bare. His journal sat on the floor. His face, even in sleep, looked worn.

She sat on the edge of the futon and gently brushed a curl from his forehead, whispering, "You scared me, baby."

His fingers twitched, but he didn't stir.

Elle looked around the attic at the photos, the mementos, the life that Michael had lived before it fell apart, and she understood why Ethan had come up here. He wasn't running away. He was searching.

Searching for pieces of the father he wanted to remember. The man behind the bottle. The man who once smiled in a football jersey held his son at the park and brought roses home.

She rested her hand on Ethan's shoulder and closed her eyes.

"Lord," she whispered again, "please protect his heart. Let this grief shape him, not destroy him."

And with that, she sat quietly beside him, watching the golden light spill across the attic floor as the day slipped gently toward night.

Chapter 10
A Place to Stand

The scent of rosemary and simmering onions drifted through the house, wrapping itself around the corners of the hallway and pulling Ethan gently from sleep.

He blinked awake, still lying on the futon in the attic, the family photo clutched loosely in his hand. For a moment, he didn't move. The dust, the quiet, the memory, it all felt like a cocoon he didn't want to break. But eventually, he rose, stretched, and made his way downstairs.

The house was warmer now. Lived in. Real.

He found his mother in the kitchen, standing at the stove with her sleeves rolled up and her apron tied at the waist. She was spreading a thick layer of ketchup glaze across a pan of meatloaf. On the counter behind her sat a bowl of loaded mashed potatoes, creamy and buttery, speckled with shredded cheese. Green beans sizzled in the skillet, seasoned just the way Ethan liked.

At the kitchen island, Uncle George nursed a cup of black coffee, flipping through the folded corner of a funeral home pamphlet.

Ethan didn't speak at first. He just pulled out the stool beside his uncle and sat down.

George looked over and gave him a slight nod. "Hey, kid."

Ethan nodded back. "Hey."

Elle turned slightly, smiling softly over her shoulder. "You hungry?"

"A little."

"I'll fix your plate when it's done. Just a few more minutes."

George gently set the pamphlet down. "We were just going over some of the funeral arrangements," he said. "Figuring out the little things."

Ethan glanced at the papers. "When is it?"

"Next Wednesday," Elle replied, still stirring the green beans. "Gives us time to prepare. Helen's coming by this weekend to help go over everything." Ethan nodded.

George took another sip of coffee, then added, "I also reached out to Coach Lanning, let him know what's going on. He understood why you missed practice today. Said there's no pressure."

Ethan looked up. "We don't play until Saturday, right?"

"Right. Tomorrow's a walk-through. Coach did ask if you could come an hour early, though," George said. "He wants to talk with you before the team meeting. Said the two of you can decide if you're up to playing."

Ethan leaned on the counter with his elbows and stared at the steam rising from the mashed potatoes. For a moment, no one said anything. Then he spoke.

"I'll play," he said quietly. "I need to clear my mind. I'll be fine."

Elle turned off the burner and looked over, gently drying her hands on a towel. "Ethan, take your time," she said softly. "There's no need to rush back into anything."

"I know," he replied, eyes still down. "But I'd rather be on the field than in my head."

George nodded slowly. "Then we'll be there tomorrow. Just say the word if anything changes.

Ethan didn't say anything else. He just sat quietly as the comfort food finished cooking, the house filled with warmth and the smell of home, even in the shadow of loss.

And for that brief moment, sitting between his mother and his uncle, he found a place to breathe. Later that night, Ethan sat on the edge of his bed while Elle stood in the doorway, arms folded, her expression soft.

"You sure you're up for this?" she asked.

He nodded. "Yeah. I think it'll help."

She took a step into the room, pausing beside his dresser, where a framed photo of him and Michael sat, taken after a junior league game three years ago. They both had helmets in hand, grass stains on their pants, and half-sincere smiles stretched across their faces.

"I know you want to push through," Elle said gently, "but don't carry everything out there with you. Let the field be what it's always been for you, a place to breathe."

Ethan looked up at her. "I'll try."

She kissed the top of his head, as she used to when he was little. "I'm proud of you, Ethan. Not because you're playing. Just… because you're still standing."

He gave a small smile, the kind that didn't quite reach his eyes

"Goodnight, baby," she whispered.

"Night, Mom."

They both went to bed, the weight of the week curling around them like a shadow, but this time, thinner. Bearable.

The next morning, Ethan woke up just after nine. For the first time all week, the weight in his chest felt a little lighter. Not gone. But different.

He stretched, got dressed, and opened his journal:

October 14

Game day. Still hurts. Still heavy. But I need this.

When I hit the field, I'm not Ethan-the-son-of-an-alcoholic. I'm just Ethan. Number 9. Running. Catching. Leading. I miss you, Dad. But tonight, I'm doing this without you. I'm doing this for me.

He closed the journal and tucked it into his drawer, then headed downstairs where the scent of seasoned chicken and cornbread filled the air. Elle had cooked a late lunch early enough to eat, but not too close to game time.

They sat together at the table in a peaceful silence, the clink of silverware the only sound between them.

After eating, Ethan excused himself and went back upstairs. He didn't play music. Didn't check his phone. He just lay on his bed for a while, visualizing the field, the scoreboard, the first snap. His body buzzed with anticipation. He wasn't playing for glory tonight; he was playing to remember who he was before everything changed.

Time slipped by faster than expected.

"Ethan! Let's go, baby!" Elle's voice called from downstairs. "We've got to leave!"

Uncle George added, "Don't forget Coach wants to see you an hour early!"

Ethan grabbed his duffel bag, double-checked for his cleats and gloves, then took a breath in front of the mirror. He didn't look like a kid grieving anymore.

He looked like a player ready to reclaim something.

"Coming!" he called back, bolting down the stairs.

As they loaded into the car and pulled out of the driveway, Ethan stared out the window, watching the houses and trees roll past. For the first time in days, he felt movement not just around him, but within him. Tonight, it wouldn't erase the pain. But it might just give him a reason to keep going. The field lights buzzed overhead as the team gathered in clusters for warmups, the scent of cut grass and chalky sports drink powder floating through the air. Cleats scraped against the turf. Helmets clinked softly. But Ethan wasn't with them yet.

He stood just outside the locker room tunnel, his duffel slung over one shoulder, watching the early crowd trickle into the bleachers. Nerves rolled through his stomach, not the kind from competition, but the kind that comes when you're trying not to break in front of people.

A hand clapped gently on his shoulder.

"Ethan," Coach Lanning said, nodding toward the hallway. "Walk with me."

They moved away from the noise, down a quiet corridor lined with framed photographs of past championship teams and all-star players. The smell of leather pads and athletic tape clung to the walls.

"I'm glad you came early," Coach said. "Wanted a minute with you.

Ethan nodded, his throat dry.

Coach stopped near an empty bench and sat down. Ethan sat beside him, staring at the floor.

"I know you weren't at this school yet," Coach began, his voice low and steady, "but three years ago, I lost my mom." Ethan turned his head slightly, surprised.

Coach nodded slowly. "Breast cancer. It happened fast. One minute, we were planning her treatment; the next, I was speaking at her funeral. I remember coming into work the day after. Everyone was trying to be normal… but I wasn't. He paused, eyes fixed on a distant memory.

"I didn't tell many of the guys. I was not seeking sympathy. But I do want you to know…I get it. I get the silence. The weight. The need to do something familiar so that you don't fall apart."

Ethan blinked back the moisture threatening his eyes.

"I'm here for you," Coach said. "Whether you suit up tonight or sit it out, that's your call. You don't have to prove anything."

Ethan took a deep breath. "I want to play. If I get too distracted or my head's not in it… I'll tell you. But I need this."

Coach nodded. "Then suit up, Number 9. You've got a team behind you. And a coach who believes in you."

They stood up. Coach clapped a firm hand on Ethan's shoulder. "You don't have to carry it all tonight. Just play."

Meanwhile, across the street, George and Elle sat in the car outside a small local bakery. Elle held a white box in her lap, a surprise Bundt cake Ethan had always liked after games, glazed with lemon icing.

"Even if he's not hungry after, it might still make him smile," Elle said softly.

George nodded. "He's stronger than I thought."

"I just don't want that strength to become silence.

They sat quietly for a moment before Elle reached for her phone. "I need to call Helen, let her know we won't be available to speak with the funeral director tonight."

She dialed.

Helen picked up on the first ring. "Hey, how's Ethan?"

"Getting ready to play. He had a moment with Coach Lanning. I think it helped."

"I'm glad," Helen said gently.

"We were going to check in with the funeral home tonight, but… I'd rather be fully present for Ethan."

"I can call them," Helen said without hesitation. "I'll let them know we're pushing our final walkthrough to tomorrow. No problem."

"Thank you," Elle said, exhaling with relief. "You've been amazing through all of this."

There was a brief pause before Helen added, "I also posted something in the paper this morning. Just a short piece. Obituary section. A few words about who Michael was before the struggle."

Elle blinked away sudden tears. "Thank you for that."

"I thought maybe Ethan could clip it out one day when he's ready."

They said their goodbyes, and Elle closed her phone.

George looked over. "You okay?"

She nodded. "I think tonight… might be good for all of us."

They started the car and headed toward the stadium, Bundt cake in the back seat and quiet hope riding with them. The stadium lights beamed down like stars, illuminating every inch of the turf with electric brilliance. The stands were packed parents, classmates, alums, and even local news buzzing with anticipation as the announcer's voice echoed through the speakers.

"Coming onto the field, your Gerry Hawks!"

Ethan jogged out with his teammates through the tunnel, his helmet in one hand, his heart pounding in his chest. The cheers exploded around him, but they barely registered. His focus tunneled in on the field, the end zones, and the quiet calm of being back—back in the one place that still made sense.

He strapped on his helmet, adjusted his gloves, and lined up for the first play.

From the moment the whistle blew, Ethan was on fire.

His footwork was sharp, clean. His routes were crisp. On the second drive, he broke through two defenders and made a 40-yard catch, dragging a safety with him down to the 10-yard line. The crowd roared as his name echoed through the speakers:

"Ethan Phillips with the catch, first and goal!"

By halftime, he had already racked up over 100 receiving yards, with a touchdown under his belt.

Coaches along the sideline exchanged impressed glances. One assistant from the opposing team leaned over to their head coach and muttered, "Where'd this kid come from?"

Even Coach Lanning couldn't hide his pride. He clapped Ethan on the helmet after each drive, shouting above the noise, "That's how you play with purpose!"

But it wasn't about numbers tonight, not for Ethan.

Every step, every catch, every juke, it was him proving to himself that his father's death wouldn't be the end of his story. It was him reclaiming something.

In the fourth quarter, with the score tied and only two minutes on the clock, Ethan returned a punt that changed the game.

He caught the ball clean, scanned the field, and then took off…dodging one defender, spinning past another, stiff-arming a third. The stadium shook with every cut he made.

He sprinted down the sideline like the pain was at his heels and crossed into the end zone like he was running straight out of grief.

Touchdown.

The crowd erupted.

Final score: Hawks 31, Visitors 24.

Ethan stood in the end zone, hands on his hips, chest heaving. His teammates rushed him, shouting and slapping his helmet, but he kept his eyes on the sky for a moment longer.

Then he whispered to himself, barely audible under the noise:

"This is for you, Dad." He pointed his finger at the sky.

Chapter 11
Lemon Glaze and Lightness

The locker room buzzed with laughter, shoulder bumps, and the clatter of cleats against tile. The air was thick with sweat and sports energy drinks, but it was also filled with something more profound: relief, victory, and the kind of joy that only comes after carrying a heavy burden and still outrunning it.

Ethan sat at his locker, helmet in his lap, sweat dripping from his forehead. He had played with fire in his veins and purpose in his heart. But now, as the adrenaline faded, what remained was a strange, quiet peace.

He glanced down at the towel draped around his neck, then at the text lighting up his phone from his mom:

We're waiting outside. Got a little something for you.

Love you.

Ethan smiled, slipped on his hoodie, and grabbed his bag.

Outside the stadium, the night air was cool and crisp. The crowd had mostly dispersed, but Elle and George stood near the car, parked just under the lamplight. The trunk was open, and Elle held a white bakery box in her hands.

"There he is!" George grinned, clapping as Ethan approached.

Elle beamed and held the box out toward him. "Game MVP deserves his favorite."

Ethan raised an eyebrow. "Is that what I think it is?"

She opened the lid slightly with a flourish.

A perfectly round lemon Bundt cake, its glossy glaze catching the light, waited inside like a quiet trophy.

"Say less," Ethan said with a grin, tossing his duffel into the trunk and reaching for a plastic fork from the glovebox like it was a golden utensil.

George laughed. "We figured you wouldn't want a party, so we went old-school. Bundt cake in the car. Some things don't change." Ethan sat on the hood, took a bite, and let the lemony sweetness melt on his tongue

"You did well tonight, son," George said, leaning against the car beside him.

"More than good," Elle added. "You lit up that field."

Ethan chewed slowly, then swallowed. "Thanks. I needed it."

They stood there together, sharing bites of cake, letting the joy linger. The parking lot lights hummed above, and the stars peeked through a clear sky.

For the first time in days, Ethan felt light.

Not because the pain had vanished, but because he'd proven to himself that he could still rise. Still run. Still smile. And in that moment, under a lamppost with his family and a half-eaten Bundt cake, Ethan didn't feel like the boy who lost his father. He felt like the young man who had just begun to find himself.

Back in the stadium tunnel was nearly empty now, echoing only with the soft scrape of cleats on concrete and the distant hum of field lights powering down. Coach Lanning walked alone, reviewing notes in his hand, replaying moments from the game with quiet pride. Ethan's performance had been nothing short of phenomenal, focused, driven, almost otherworldly.

He was halfway to the parking lot when a voice spoke from the shadows behind him.

"Impressive game tonight, Coach."

Coach Lanning stopped, startled. He turned sharply, his hand instinctively tightening around his clipboard. A tall figure stood just outside the reach of the tunnel light, leaning against the brick wall where the shadows swallowed half his body.

The coach squinted. "Who's there?"

The man took a step forward, but his features remained oddly blurred.

Coach Lanning stiffened. "I said, 'Who is it?'" Another step.

Still, there is no clear view of the man's face, just the outline of a tailored coat and something unsettling in his stillness.

Finally, the man moved closer, and, like a mask dropping, his features appeared perfectly ordinary. Smooth, professional, even warm.

"Oh, I'm sorry," the man said with a pleasant voice, flashing a smile that felt too practiced. "Must've been the dim lighting. Didn't mean to scare you."

Coach Lanning exhaled slowly, still unsettled. "It's alright. You just… caught me off guard."

The man stepped fully into the light now, his presence polished, his gaze sharp. "I was watching a few of your players tonight, talented roster. Very talented. One of them in particular stood out. Number 9."

Coach Lanning nodded. "Ethan Phillips."

"Yes," the man said, the corner of his mouth twitching. "That one."

He reached into his coat, pulled out a sleek black card with silver embossing, and handed it to the coach.

"I represent certain interests… sponsorships, media exposure, things that open doors before college even begins. Nothing official yet, of course. Just a conversation for the future."

Coach Lanning took the card and glanced down. There was no company name.

Just a name, Devon Kaye, and a phone number that seemed to shimmer for a second under the tunnel light.

"Thanks," Coach said, still cautious. "I'll hold onto it." The man smiled wider. "You'll be hearing from me." Just then, the Coach's assistant called from outside. "Lanning! You heading out?"

Coach turned his head for a split second. "Yeah, coming!"

But when he turned back toward the man, he was gone.

The tunnel was empty. No sound of footsteps. No fading echo. Nothing. Coach Lanning stared down the corridor, a chill running up his spine. He looked again at the business card. It felt colder than paper should be. Coach Lanning gave the empty tunnel one last glance, his brows still furrowed as he slipped the mysterious card into his jacket pocket. A chill lingered in the air, one that had nothing to do with the weather. He turned and walked briskly toward the parking lot, where his assistant coach stood waiting by the gate.

"You good, Coach?" his assistant asked, noticing his distracted look.

Lanning gave a slow nod. "Yeah… yeah. Just tired. Let's get out of here."

They left the stadium under the fading lights, but a flicker of unease followed quietly behind.

Across the lot, Ethan smiled, not just from pride, but from something deeper, a relief. "Thanks for the cake."

They loaded into the car and drove home, the windows cracked, the late-night breeze washing away the crowd's noise and replacing it with something still and sacred.

The next morning, the house filled with the smell of sausage and cinnamon as Elle moved through the kitchen with purpose, flipping pancakes and warming syrup. Ethan came downstairs dressed in a navy button-up shirt, his Holy scriptures tucked under his arm.

George sat at the table, sipping coffee, already in his Sunday best. "Look at that," he said with a smirk. "Number 9 all cleaned up."

Ethan rolled his eyes playfully. "Gotta be presentable for church."

Elle turned from the stove. "You want cheese in your eggs?"

"Always."

They ate together in quiet unity, then headed out into the morning sun, the church steeple just visible in the distance as they pulled onto the main road.

The sanctuary was packed. Warm light poured through stained glass windows, casting soft hues across the pews. Ethan sat between Elle and George, his Holy scriptures open on his lap as Pastor Williams stepped up to the pulpit, his voice strong, but his eyes full of compassion.

He began reading from James 1:27 KJV:

"Pure religion and undefiled before God and the Father is this, To visit the fatherless and widows in their affliction, and to keep himself unspotted from the world."

Pastor paused, then looked out over the congregation.

"Church, it's not enough to wear the name of Christ. We must walk it out. We must live it."

He stepped down from the pulpit and walked slowly along the front row.

"People are hurting, young men growing up without fathers, women carrying grief alone. As believers in the true gospel of Jesus Christ, we are called to visit them… to sit with them… to bring food, drink, compassion, presence."

He looked upward, then added, "Don't forget those in need. Not if you say you follow Him."

Ethan sat still, but the words sank into him as an anchor dropped deep into water.

He thought of his pain. His father's absence. The food was left untouched on the table, the quiet in his mother's eyes.

And then he thought about other kids, ones who never got to say goodbye… who didn't even have an Uncle George… or a Coach Lanning… or a Bundt cake in the car.

One day, he told himself, when I make it, when I play pro…I'm going to help them.

He looked at his mom and uncle and smiled.

Not just you all, he thought with quiet fire. But everyone who needs it. The fatherless. The forgotten. I'm going to help them all.

The pastor was still preaching, his voice rising like a tide. But Ethan had already received the Word. After church had ended. The sky was a soft canvas of pale blue as the family stepped out of the church. A light breeze swept across the parking lot, stirring the leaves that had just started to turn golden. Birds chirped lazily in the distance, and the world felt still like God had carved out a few hours of peace just for them.

Elle walked with her Holy scriptures clutched to her side, smiling quietly. George held the door for a few elderly members before joining them near the car.

Ethan followed slowly, the words of Pastor Williams still echoing in his heart.

Visit the fatherless... sit with them... don't forget those in need.

The message stirred something in him, not just guilt, but purpose. He wasn't sure what it would look like yet, but he knew one thing:

He didn't want to live a life only for himself.

The ride home was calm. Windows cracked, gospel music playing low on the radio. No one said much, but no one needed to. It was the kind of silence that wrapped around you like a blanket instead of a burden.

Once home, Elle warmed up leftovers and placed a peach cobbler in the oven. George slipped out onto the back porch with a glass of iced tea and a newspaper. Ethan grabbed his phone and went up to his room.

He tossed himself onto his bed and stared at the ceiling for a moment before calling Scott.

The phone rang twice.

"Yo!" Scott answered. "You alive, man? You straight-up ghosted me since Saturday night."

Ethan smiled. "Yeah… sorry. Just needed to breathe."

"You good though? We saw the highlights online. Bro, you were a monster. That second-half return? Man…"

"I know," Ethan laughed softly. "It felt good. I needed it."

"Everyone on social media has been talking about it. Ethan sat up, surprised. "Seriously?"

"Dead serious. You're blowing up, man."

As Scott talked, another call beeped in, Amanda.

Ethan clicked over. "Hold on, Amanda's calling me too."

He merged the calls.

"About time!" Amanda said when she joined. "Tried texting you all weekend. I even baked muffins to cheer you up. You know how much I hate baking."

Scott laughed. "Lies. You burned the last batch."

"I still tried!"

Ethan grinned, lying back on his pillow. "I appreciate you both. For real."

A short pause followed…gentle, respectful.

"How are you doing, E?" Amanda finally asked. "Really?"

Ethan's voice softened. "It still hurts. But I'm not folding. Just… trying to keep my head on straight. Church helped today. Pastor said something that stuck."

"Like what?" Scott asked.

Ethan looked out the window, watching a squirrel scurry across the fence.

"That real religion is taking care of the fatherless and the widows. Not just believing but doing something about it."

Amanda was quiet for a moment. Then she said, "Sounds like something you were made to do."

Scott added, "Yeah, man. That's who you are."

Ethan didn't respond right away. But he smiled again, this time more deeply.

"Thanks. I needed to hear that."

They stayed on the phone for another hour, laughing, reminiscing, and even making plans to meet up next weekend. It wasn't a loud day. Or a dramatic one.

But it was healing. And for Ethan, that was enough.

Later that Monday, the school building felt louder than usual.

Lockers slammed. Sneakers squeaked against tile floors. Someone was shouting about cafeteria nachos down the hall. But to Ethan, everything felt muted, like he was watching the day unfold from behind a sheet of glass.

He walked through the halls with his hoodie up, backpack slung low. His teammates offered fist bumps and nods, a few of them whispering, "Great game, man," or "You lit it up Saturday."

But their smiles faded slightly when they looked him in the eye.

The news had spread. He could feel it. Some teachers offered concerned, lingering glances. Others gave him soft, slow smiles that said I'm sorry without speaking. Even Mr. Gilmore, the strict English teacher who rarely showed emotion, touched Ethan's shoulder as he passed his desk and said, "I lost my dad at sixteen. If you need time, take it."

Ethan appreciated the kindness, but it all felt… off. Too gentle. Too cautious. He didn't want to be handled. He didn't want pity. He wanted space to breathe.

At lunch, he sat with Amanda and Scott near the windows, pushing a half-eaten sandwich around his tray. His other football friends were at the far table, probably waiting for him to join them, but he didn't move.

He reached into his backpack and pulled out his journal. It felt heavier than usual.

He flipped past the pages where he had written about the funeral planning, the attic, and the night before the game. He stopped on a fresh page and uncapped his pen.

October 16

Lunch.

Everyone's looking at me like I'm either fragile or untouchable. Like they don't know whether to cheer or apologize.

I still played hard Saturday night… but now I know I wasn't playing for him.

I was playing to remember who I am.

Ethan closed the journal and slid it back into his bag.

The bell rang, and students started to file back into the halls. He stood up slowly, tossed his tray, and made his way toward class. As he passed one of the trophy cases near the stairwell, he caught his own reflection… tired eyes, a steady posture. Still standing.

Chapter 12

Dust to Dust

The sky hung gray over Chelsea Memorial Park, as if the heavens themselves had paused to mourn.

A thin mist clung to the air, not quite rain, not quite fog, just enough to make the grass feel soft beneath their feet. Rows of black folding chairs lined the burial site, facing a polished wooden casket nestled above the open earth. A canopy had been set up to shield the immediate family, though the weather had held just long enough.

Ethan stood beside his mother and Uncle George, his black suit neatly pressed, a white rose pinned to his lapel. His fingers fidgeted at his side, gripping the edge of the funeral program. The photo on the front was one he hadn't seen in years…his father smiling, eyes clear, holding baby Ethan in his arms. He didn't remember that day. But he remembered the man.

And he remembered the absence that followed.

The chairs slowly filled with family, old friends, and faces Ethan barely recognized. Helen sat near the front, her shoulders trembling beneath a black shawl as she dabbed her eyes with a handkerchief. A few of Michael's old coworkers from the plant had shown up, nodding solemnly at Elle and George as they arrived. Some of the mourners looked uncomfortable, unsure how to grieve a man whose life had unraveled so publicly.

But still, they came.

Pastor Williams stood near the head of the casket, Holy scriptures in hand, his voice calm and reverent as he welcomed the small gathering.

"We're not here because life was perfect," he began. "We're here because life was real. Because Michael was someone's son.

Someone's brother. A father. A man who fought more battles than most of us ever knew."

Ethan kept his eyes on the closed casket, his jaw tight.

Pastor Williams continued, "Psalm 34:18 KJV says, 'The Lord is nigh unto them that are of a broken heart.' And I believe that God was near to Michael even in his darkest moments."

A soft sniffle came from the row behind.

Pastor paused, then turned slightly toward the family. "We do not come to this place to bury a man and walk away unchanged. We come to remember, to reflect, and to release."

Ethan's heart pounded in his chest.

"Sometimes," Pastor added, "people ask me, 'How do you honor someone who didn't always get it right?' And I tell them: You honor them by living better. By choosing differently. By walking forward when they could not."

Elle reached over and gently took Ethan's hand.

He looked down at their joined fingers, then back at the polished wood in front of him. The casket gleamed, its stillness echoing all the words left unsaid.

When the pastor opened the floor for reflections, there was silence at first.

Then Helen stood. Her voice was soft, cracked by grief, but steady.

"He wasn't perfect," she said, looking at the casket. "But he was my brother. And I never stopped hoping for him."

She sat down without saying another word. Then Pastor Williams offered a gentle nod, his eyes sweeping over the group.

"Anyone else who would like to share a few words about Michael… now is the time."

There was a long pause.

Then a man from the back slowly stood.

His clothes were modest with dark jeans, a clean black hoodie, and worn sneakers. He looked out of place among the suits and dresses, but his voice was steady.

"My name's Reggie," he said, nodding toward the family. "I knew Mike from the streets."

Ethan's gaze lifted.

"I know people didn't always see the best parts of him… but I did. Even out there under bridges, behind shelters, outside gas stations, Michael was always talking about his boy. You." Reggie looked directly at Ethan. "Said you played ball. Said you had a gift. Man used to tell folks that his son was gonna go pro and do something real with his life."

A few murmurs rolled through the crowd.

Reggie shook his head, blinking back tears. "He didn't always get it right. But he loved you. Every chance he got, he reminded us that he had a reason to keep fighting. Some days, that reason kept him going. Other days… it just hurt too much."

He swallowed hard, gave a respectful nod to Elle and George, and sat down.

Another man stood next at the podium. He was thinner and older, with a name tag clipped to his coat that read "Shelter Volunteer." He clasped his hands as he stepped forward.

"My name is Harold. I work at the Maple Road Shelter. Michael came through many times over the years."

He paused, collecting his words.

"Most folks don't see what happens when the world forgets you. But I do. I saw Michael when he was broken, yes… but I also saw him when he was whole. When he wasn't drinking, he was loud—in the good way. Full of energy. Always cracking jokes, always asking if we needed anything. He'd give away his extra blanket if someone showed up cold."

He looked toward Elle. "I hope it's not out of place to say this… but when Michael was clear-headed, he was kind. Deep down, he was one of the good ones. He just got lost."

He nodded solemnly and sat back down.

Then, from the side row, a man in his mid-fifties stood, holding a small Holy Scripture in his hand. He walked with quiet reverence to the front.

"My name is Thomas. I was Michael's sponsor for three years. I met him at a recovery meeting down on 8th Street. We laughed a lot. We cried more. We relapsed, restarted, relapsed again."

He opened the Holy scriptures and flipped to a bookmarked page.

"Michael used to beat himself up for not being strong enough," Thomas said, voice cracking. "He thought his story couldn't be redeemed."

His expression darkened just slightly, more somber.

"Addiction is a brutal fight. Michael didn't always win… but he never stopped swinging. He struggled with his demons, yes. But he also encouraged many people to keep going. He reminded us that shame isn't stronger than grace."

He opened his Holy scriptures slowly and said, "This verse always reminded me of the battle Michael was in and honestly, one we're all in, whether we know it or not."

Then he read:

'Be sober, be vigilant; because your adversary the devil, as a roaring lion, walketh about, seeking whom he may devour.'

1 Peter 5:8 KJV

Thomas's voice softened. "Michael knew that lion. He felt the breath of it behind him. But he also believed that the Lord could still rescue him. I believe he cried out more times than we knew… and I believe God heard him."

He looked directly at Ethan.

"Your father loved you. He didn't always know how to show it. But he talked about you, bragging about you. Said he'd be front row when you made it to the pros."

Thomas closed the Holy scriptures. "Let's not remember just how Michael left. Let's remember what he kept trying to return to: his family, his faith, his fight."

He bowed his head and returned to his seat. As the final speaker stepped away from the podium, a reverent hush fell over the room. Pastor Williams rose slowly and stepped forward, his Holy scriptures open in his hands, his eyes gentle as he scanned the grieving faces seated before him.

He cleared his throat softly.

"Today, we lay to rest a man many knew in different ways. Some knew Michael Phillips as a friend. Some knew him as a brother, a father, an uncle. Some knew him in his struggles and others, in his strength. But I want us to remember that in all of that, Michael was a man who loved his family.

He paused, letting the weight of his words settle.

"I know grief weighs heavily, and I know some of you are left with questions. But our comfort comes not from understanding… but from trusting. Trusting in a God who sees what we cannot."

He turned a page in his Holy scriptures.

"In 1 Thessalonians 4:13 KJV, the Word tells us: 'But I would not have you to be ignorant, brethren, concerning them which are asleep, that ye sorrow not, even as others which have no hope.' We do grieve, but not without hope."

He looked over at Ethan for a brief moment, offering a reassuring nod.

"Let this be a moment that binds us together, a moment to extend compassion, to seek healing, and to walk in grace. Michael's journey has come to a close here on earth. He closed his Holy scriptures gently and looked out at the room one last time.

"May the Lord bless you and keep you. May He make His face to shine upon you and give you peace, even in the midst of sorrow. Let us prepare now to follow the family to the burial site."

Soft organ music filled the room as Pastor Williams stepped aside.

The wind rustled softly through the trees as the long line of cars pulled into the cemetery. A sea of black moved in silence as friends and family stepped out onto the gravel path and followed behind the hearse. The sky was overcast, gentle clouds casting muted shadows across the rows of stone.

The graveside service was short. The pastor spoke a few final prayers. Then, one by one, people stepped forward to lay roses on the closed casket.

Elle approached slowly, the crunch of gravel beneath her heels the only sound. She looked down at the polished wood, her fingers trembling as she held a single white rose.

"I loved Michael," she said quietly, "through the pain, the tears… and the happy times. I hope that he now rests easy."

She placed the rose gently on the casket and stepped back

Ethan stood beside her, but he didn't say anything. Not at first. His hands were clenched tightly at his sides, his jaw set, his eyes glassy. As the crowd slowly dispersed, leaving the family alone near the open grave, Ethan finally stepped forward.

He knelt beside the casket, resting his hand on the edge. A tear traced down his cheek as he whispered, just loud enough for those nearest to hear:

"I will continue to stay sober… because I don't want the adversary to devour me."

His voice cracked, and the tears came freely.

Elle wrapped her arms around him from one side. Aunt Helen joined from the other, her hand gently on his back. Uncle George stepped in and pulled them all into an embrace.

He leaned close to Ethan's ear and said softly, "Don't be afraid to live, Ethan. Just don't forget about God on your life's journey, even when you're at a high point, don't forget about God."

Ethan nodded, eyes still fixed on the rose resting on his father's casket. As the last shovel of earth hit the top of the casket, a stillness fell over the small crowd. The wind slowed. The trees stood motionless.

Uncle George stepped back from the gravesite and scanned the crowd as they were leaving one last time, his eyes paused.

There.

At the edge of the cemetery, just beyond the old wrought-iron fence, stood a figure dressed in black, perfectly still. Watching.

George squinted, trying to make out his face.

"Do you…?" he murmured to Elle beside him. But when he looked back again, the figure was gone.

Vanished.

No movement. No footprints. No sign of anyone.

George's chest tightened. He didn't say anything more, not yet. Just slipped his hand into his coat pocket and whispered under his breath, "The enemy is always nearby."

He looked over at Ethan, who stood with his head bowed in silence.

And somewhere deep in George's spirit, he knew: the battle was only beginning. Uncle George directed everyone to the family car to head to the repast, which Elle was hosting at their home. After a 30-minute drive back home, the scent of collard greens, baked macaroni, and fried and baked chicken filled the house as friends and extended family brought in dishes and condolences. The clatter of dishes, the hum of conversation, and the quiet sobs of guests created a soft background to a day already soaked in emotion.

Ethan sat on the edge of the couch, still dressed in his funeral attire. He watched as people came and went, each carrying their version of grief. Some hugged his mother. Others shook Uncle George's hand and offered words like "He's in a better place" or "He's at peace now." Words that were meant to soothe, but Ethan wasn't sure they helped.

Plates clinked. Laughter tried to fill the awkward silences. But Ethan mainly stayed quiet. Numb. Listening. Observing. Enduring.

He felt far away from it all.

Eventually, the crowd thinned. A final couple of visitors offered their goodbyes, and the door shook shut. The house, once full of voices and motion, became still again.

Ethan stood slowly, stretched, and quietly headed upstairs. The weight of the day pulled at his legs like ankle chains. He didn't say anything as he passed his mother in the hallway; he just nodded, and she understood.

He slipped into his room, closed the door behind him, and sank into his bed without changing. A long exhale left his lungs as the quiet wrapped around him.

A few minutes later, Elle peeked in, her soft knock barely breaking the silence.

"You okay, baby?" she asked gently, stepping into the room.

Ethan nodded, barely meeting her eyes. "I'm just tired."

She walked over and brushed her hand through his hair.

"You don't have to go to school tomorrow," she said. "I already called them."

"I want to go," he replied. "I think I need to."

She nodded, understanding without needing explanation. "Alright then. Try to get some sleep."

"Night, Mom."

"Goodnight, son." She paused at the door. "I'm proud of you."

Ethan didn't respond right away. But just before she stepped out, he said softly, "Thanks."

The door clicked gently shut behind her.

In the quiet, Ethan stared at the ceiling. The room felt darker tonight—not just because the lights were off, but because something had shifted inside of him. A sadness. A promise. A question about what comes next.

He didn't write in his journal.

He just closed his eyes and drifted into a heavy, dreamless sleep.

Chapter 13
Back to School

The morning air was crisp, the kind that hinted fall was settling in for good. Ethan stepped out of the car in his team hoodie and backpack slung low, greeting the familiar buzz of students spilling into the building.

It felt strange.

He hadn't walked these halls yesterday because of the funeral. Faces turned toward him, some with soft eyes of pity, others with nods of quiet respect. A few classmates gave him space. Others tried too hard. But Ethan? He kept moving.

He laughed a little louder than usual at Chris's jokes in homeroom. He gave Amanda a quick side hug in the hallway. He joked with Marcus at his locker about missing Tuesday's science quiz… "I hope Ms. Givens got amnesia," he teased, earning a snort.

But behind the charm, the jokes, the easy smile… something was cracked just beneath the surface. He was trying not to show it.

At lunch, Ethan picked at his sandwich while his friends talked about upcoming Friday's game. Amanda nudged him playfully, "You ready to shut down East Cal Good again?"

He forced a grin. "They're gonna wish they stayed on the bus."

But deep inside, his thoughts weren't on touchdowns. They kept wandering back to the casket… the white rose… the silence after everyone left.

He didn't open his journal during lunch. The final bell rang, and school was dismissed until tomorrow morning.

Later that day at football practice, the scent of fresh-cut grass and sweat filled the air. Pads clanked, whistles blew, and cleats dug into the turf. Ethan was in his zone. His helmet on, chin strap tight, legs moving like he never missed a beat.

Coach Lanning stood on the sidelines, watching closely. During water break, he finally walked over.

"Ethan," he said in a calm, fatherly tone.

Ethan pulled off his helmet, wiping sweat from his brow.

"I just wanted to say… You played with heart last week. I know it wasn't easy." Ethan nodded, swallowing hard. "Thanks, Coach."

"I know everyone grieves differently. Just wanted you to know I see you. And I'm proud of you."

Ethan gave a quiet, grateful smile. "Thanks, Coach. Really."

Coach Lanning patted his shoulder and walked off, not lingering too long. He knew when to give space.

As the assistant coaches passed by, they each offered a nod or a handshake.

"Sorry for your loss, kid," one of them said.

"Your dad would've been proud of that last game," another added.

Ethan nodded again. Said very little. But the weight in his chest felt just a bit lighter.

For the next hour, he ran drills like he had something to prove. Not to the coaches. Not even to himself.

But maybe to the version of his dad who once watched from the shadows of the bleachers with a beer in hand, yelling, "That's my boy!"

Ethan wasn't playing for pity.

He was playing for legacy. After practice, Ethan walked to the car, gym bag slung over his shoulder, his hair still damp with sweat. His mother was waiting in the usual spot. He gave her a tired but genuine smile as he slid into the passenger seat.

"How was practice?" Elle asked gently.

Ethan shrugged. "Good. Coach said I don't have to start tomorrow, but I want to."

She nodded, keeping her eyes on the road. "I'm proud of you."

"Thanks, Mom."

Back at home, the familiar smell of garlic and tomato sauce wafted through the air. Elle had made one of Ethan's favorite meals…Chicken Parmesan over creamy pasta. It was warm. Comforting.

After showering and finishing his homework at the kitchen table, Ethan ate quietly. The food was good, but he barely tasted it. He was just tired…physically and emotionally.

Later, he sat on his bed with his journal balanced on his knee. The pen hovered for a while before he finally scribbled:

"I believe in myself. Keep going strong."

It wasn't much. But it was something.

He closed the journal, slid it back under his pillow, and turned off the lamp.

Sleep came quickly.

However, downstairs, Uncle George and Elle sat in the dim light of the living room. A small lamp cast a golden glow over the coffee table, scattered with the day's mail and leftover tea mugs.

Neither spoke at first.

"I keep hearing his voice," Elle said finally. "Even in the silence."

George sighed deeply, rubbing his hands together. "Grief has echoes. Sometimes they fade. Sometimes they don't."

Elle looked at her brother. "You think Ethan's really okay?"

"He's trying. That's all he can do." George paused. "He's a strong kid. But strong doesn't mean untouched."

Just then, Elle's phone buzzed.

Aunt Helen.

Elle answered. "Hey."

"Just checking in on everybody," Helen said. "Especially Ethan."

"He's resting now. Long day."

"I was thinking of coming to his game tomorrow night. I want to be there if that's okay."

"Of course. It's an away game. I'll text you the address and kickoff time."

"I'll be there," Helen said softly. "Let him know someone extra is cheering."

"I will."

After they hung up, Elle looked toward the staircase.

"He has so much ahead of him," she whispered.

George nodded. "And we'll help make sure he doesn't lose sight of who he is, especially when the world starts noticing him."

The living room fell into a comfortable silence again, broken only by the sound of the old clock ticking steadily on the wall.

Tomorrow was game day. Ethan woke up before his alarm. For once, his body didn't feel heavy. The ache in his chest, the one that had haunted him all week, had dulled just enough for him to breathe a little easier.

The game was tonight. But this morning… it was school.

After a hot shower and a quick bite of scrambled eggs and toast, Ethan packed his bag and headed downstairs. His mom was already up, sipping coffee at the table.

"You slept okay?" she asked.

"Yeah," he said, grabbing his jacket. "I feel… good."

Elle gave a small smile. "Have a great day. And enjoy the pep rally."

He nodded and walked out the door with a little more bounce in his step.

At school, it was Pep Rally Fever. Everyone was dressed in their school colors.

By midday, the school was buzzing with energy. Lockers were wrapped in streamers, kids painted their faces in school colors, and handmade posters with players' names were taped to the gym walls. Ethan's said "#9 Go E!" with stars drawn around it.

In the final class before the rally, his friends Chris and Amanda passed notes back and forth.

"You ready to destroy tonight?" Chris whispered.

Ethan smiled. "Born ready."

The bell rang.

Students flooded into the gym. The cheerleaders performed a high-energy routine. The marching band blared the fight song. Teachers joined in with goofy dances and chants. Then the football team was introduced.

"Ethan Phillips, tight end, #9!"

He jogged out with his team, waving as the crowd roared. The gym echoed with stomps, claps, and school pride.

For the first time in a long while, Ethan felt like a kid again. Not the boy grieving his father. Not the one journaling in pain.

Just Ethan, 15 years old, alive in the moment.

The pep rally ended with a chant led by Coach Lanning and the cheer squad:

"Whose house?"

"Our house!"

"Who's going to win?"

"We are!"

After the rally, as students filtered out, Amanda caught up with Ethan.

"You okay?" she asked gently.

He nodded, adjusting his backpack. "Yeah. Today… felt good."

She gave him a quick fist bump. "Crush it tonight." The stadium lights pierced through the night sky like beacons, casting long shadows across the field. The stands were full of students screaming, cheerleaders dancing, parents clapping, and cowbells clanging. It was small-town high school football at its best.

Ethan jogged onto the field, helmet in hand, soaking in the energy of the night. The pep rally from earlier still echoed in his mind. For the first time in days, he felt something that almost resembled joy.

In the crowd, Elle stood wrapped in her warm jacket. George had brought a thermos of hot cider. And Aunt Helen, draped in her team hoodie and a scarf with the school's colors, waved proudly at Ethan as he stretched on the sidelines.

"That boy is something special," Helen said softly, her eyes brimming.

Elle smiled. "He needed this tonight."

From the first whistle, Ethan was explosive.

He returned the kickoff to the 45-yard line, dodging defenders like poetry in motion. The crowd roared. On offense, he caught two first-down passes and later broke free down the left sideline, juking one, stiff-arming another, and flying into the end zone.

Touchdown.

Cheers erupted. George jumped to his feet. Helen clapped with tears in her eyes.

"That one was for his dad," Elle whispered, blinking hard.

Coach Lanning gave Ethan a firm nod as he came off the field. "You're leading tonight, son."

Ethan breathed heavily, sweat glistening on his forehead, but he nodded.

"I needed this, Coach."

At halftime, the score was tied. The band played in the background. Ethan sat with his team, towel around his neck, listening to the Coach's strategy. Then he closed his eyes for a moment.

He whispered under his breath:

"Stay focused. Do it right. Don't let him down."

Ethan dominated.

On defense, he tipped a crucial pass. On offense, he caught two more passes, including one that set up the winning touchdown.

With two minutes left on the clock and the score tied, the quarterback launched a high spiral downfield.

Ethan sprinted full force, leapt in the air, and came down hard at the 10-yard line. The crowd gasped.

He stood up. Ball in hand. First down. Two plays later, the team scored. Game over. Victory.

Final score: 28–21

Students stormed the field. Parents leaned over the railings, calling their kids' names. Aunt Helen hugged Elle tightly.

"He did it," she said. George stood tall. "Michael would've been proud."

Ethan took it in, his heart pounding not just from the game, but something else. Something deeper. His mind flashed to his father, and then... to something strange.

He turned toward the tunnel. A figure stood watching him. A man in a long, sleek coat. Still. Too still.

Coach Lanning walked past him, heading toward the tunnel to grab his bag. The figure didn't move. Coach slowed, squinting.

"Can I help you?" Coach called.

No response.

Coach stepped forward again. "Who's there?"

The man took a step forward.

Coach stopped.

The closer the man got, the more ordinary he looked—but Coach's heart pounded anyway. There was something… wrong. Something he couldn't explain. "I…I was admiring your player. Ethan, right?" the man said with a polite tone. "I represent athletes with long-term potential. You'll be seeing more of me. I left my card with one of your assistants."

Coach nodded slowly. "Alright then." The man smiled, stepped back into the shadows, and was gone. Coach turned when someone shouted his name from the field. He looked back.

No one was there. He headed to the locker room.

The locker room was alive.

Shoulder pads slammed lockers, cleats scraped against the concrete, and loud music blasted from someone's portable speaker. The team danced and shouted, high on adrenaline and the thrill of a hard-fought win.

Coach Lanning walked in, blowing his whistle. "Alright! Good win tonight, gentlemen!"

Cheers erupted again.

"But remember, one win doesn't define you. Character does. How you show up on and off the field is what lasts. You made us proud tonight, especially you, Ethan."

The room burst into applause.

Ethan smiled, wiping sweat from his brow. For the first time in days, he felt weightless.

After the game, outside, under the stadium lights, Aunt Helen pulled Ethan into a hug.

"You were incredible tonight, sweetheart. Your dad would've cried watching you out there."

"Thanks, Aunt Helen," he said, his voice catching.

"I'll be over in the morning," she added with a wink. "I've got a surprise for you.

Ethan raised a curious brow, but she gave nothing away.

"You'll see."

Elle and George joined them, offering tired smiles. The four of them walked to the car, warm cups of cider in hand, laughter dancing around them like fireflies.

Back at the house, the night had settled into a peaceful hush.

Ethan went upstairs to his room, kicked off his shoes, and flopped on his bed. The cheers still rang in his ears. He reached for his journal, scribbled a few words, then his phone buzzed.

It was Scott and Amanda.

"Yo! E, that play in the third quarter?! You broke ankles, man!" Scott shouted through the speaker.

Amanda chimed in, "Tell him about that dude from East Cal Good, who was talking trash all day and then got smoked on the field!"

Ethan continued laughing; he wanted to feel laughter and friendship without thinking about his father's death.

"I saw him trip over his cleats," he said, chuckling. "That man talked himself right into a loss."

They laughed, joked, and replayed their favorite moments. The call lasted nearly an hour. For a moment, life felt normal.

When he finally hung up, Ethan leaned back on his pillows and whispered, "Thank you, God... for this moment."

Then he closed his eyes and drifted off to sleep, the scent of victory still in the air.

Chapter 14
A Breath Between Battles

The morning sun poured through the kitchen window, casting soft golden rays across the breakfast table. Ethan shuffled into the kitchen wearing athletic shorts and a hoodie, the smell of turkey bacon and cinnamon toast already drifting through the house.

"Morning, sweetheart," Elle greeted, her eyes still slightly tired but smiling.

"Hey, Mom," he said, sitting down at the table just as Uncle George placed a glass of orange juice in front of him.

"Sleep okay?" George asked, sipping coffee and scanning the newspaper.

Ethan shrugged, then nodded. "Yeah… I guess. Kinda still thinking about the game last night. It felt good."

"You played like you had fire in your veins," George said with a grin. "That hit in the third quarter. I thought that quarterback was going to crawl off the field."

Ethan cracked a small smile. "It felt good to move again… like I could finally breathe."

Elle reached over and rubbed his shoulder gently. "We're proud of you. But you don't always have to be strong. Take it one moment at a time."

They finished breakfast in quiet conversation, the kind that didn't need to be heavy. For once, the house felt light. Peaceful.

Later that afternoon, just after one o'clock, the doorbell rang. Ethan jumped up from the couch, expecting Scott or maybe Amanda, but instead, he found Aunt Helen standing on the porch, holding a small white envelope and wearing a wide grin.

"Aunt Helen!" he said, opening the door.

"Hey, baby," she said, pulling him into a tight hug. "You didn't think I'd forget about my favorite nephew after a big win, did you?"

She handed him the envelope. Inside, there was a $250.00 gift card to the mall.

"I figured you might need a little wardrobe refresh. You've got school and games coming up. Might as well get yourself something that makes you feel good."

Ethan's eyes lit up. "This is too much…"

"You've been through too much," she interrupted softly. "Let me do this. Besides, I wanted some one-on-one time with you. Let's grab some lunch too, my treat."

They drove to a local diner just off Main Street, nothing fancy, just the kind of place with the best burgers and milkshakes in town. Aunt Helen and Ethan talked about everything and nothing. She asked about his classes, his teammates, and even cracked a few jokes about Coach Lanning's bald spot.

"I don't care what anyone says," she said, dipping her fries in ranch. "You've got the heart of a lion, Ethan. And even when things go dark, you keep moving forward. That's rare in this world."

He smiled, cheeks full of burger. "Thanks, Auntie."

"I mean it. And whenever the world tries to pull you away from who you are, remember whose name you carry, and more importantly, who you are."

Ethan nodded. He didn't say much after that, but her words nestled somewhere deep inside. They left the diner, and Aunt Helen dropped him back at home.

Later that evening, Ethan was back in his room, headset on, controller in hand, yelling into his mic.

"Chris…pass it! Bro, what are you doing?!"

Chris's voice laughed through the speakers. "I'm giving the other team a chance!"

Scott chimed in. "Y'all better chill before I turn into a football video game and school you both."

The screen lit up as they played, voices full of joy. For a while, Ethan forgot about everything: the grief, the weight, the expectations.

Just boys. Just laughter. Just life.

And for now, that was enough. Later that evening, Ethan stood in the kitchen, pouring a glass of orange soda, when Uncle George came in holding his phone. "Guess what I just got off the phone about?" George asked, grinning. Ethan raised a brow. "We're getting a puppy?"

George chuckled. "Close. Playoffs. Gerry High made the playoffs, and your name came up more than once in the call with Coach Lanning."

Ethan's eyes lit up. "For real?"

George nodded. "First time in five years the school's made it this far. And let's say, there's a lot of buzz about a freshman player with poise under pressure."

Ethan tried to play it cool, but a shy smile tugged at the corners of his mouth. "That's crazy. I mean... good crazy." Elle, who had just walked in from the backyard, caught the tail end of the conversation. "Playoffs? Ethan, that's wonderful!" She kissed the top of his head. "Your father would be proud. We all are." Ethan lowered his gaze, and for a moment, the joy on his face dimmed just slightly. "Yeah... I hope so."

Aunt Helen texted Elle shortly after, letting her know how much she enjoyed their afternoon together. "Tell Ethan he's growing into a fine young man," she wrote. "Michael would be proud of him, too."

That night, Ethan lay in bed, his mind buzzing. He opened his journal but stared at the blank page for several minutes before finally writing:

"We're in the playoffs. I can feel something big coming. I want to make everyone proud, Mom, Uncle George, and even Dad. I'm going to go all the way."

The following Monday, Gerry High buzzed with playoff fever. Posters lined the hallways, the gym had been decorated with the team colors, and chants of "Let's go G-H!" echoed through the lunchroom like an anthem.

Chris slapped Ethan on the back as they walked to class. "Dude, you're like... a celebrity now. My sister even posted about you on her blog story. She hates football."

Amanda, walking beside them, laughed. "My grandma said she saw your game highlights on TV and called you a 'handsome young man.' You're officially multigenerational now."

Ethan rolled his eyes but grinned. "Tell her I said thanks."

In between the playful teasing and bursts of excitement, Ethan couldn't help but feel the growing pressure. He was still grieving, still trying to make sense of the loss, but on the field, none of that seemed to matter. There, he had purpose. Direction. Control.

Practice that afternoon was intense. Coach Lanning had the team running drills under the fading sun, emphasizing discipline, communication, and focus.

During water break, one of the seniors, Tyrell, clapped Ethan on the shoulder. "You've been solid all season, Fresh. Don't go Hollywood on us now."

Ethan laughed. "Not a chance."

Coach Lanning approached as they were wrapping up, his clipboard tucked under his arm. "Ethan, got a minute?"

They stepped aside, the field clearing behind them as the team hit the showers.

"You've done well leading this team," the coach said. "But playoffs are different. Higher stakes. Bigger lights. More eyes. I need to know if you're mentally ready."

Ethan hesitated. "I think so. I'm trying."

Coach nodded. "Trying is honest. And that's good. Just remember, you don't have to carry everything alone. Football is a team sport. So is life."

Ethan swallowed hard. "Thanks, Coach. I needed that."

As he walked toward the locker room, Ethan noticed someone watching from just beyond the stadium fence, a man in a crisp black coat, face obscured by a baseball cap and the shadow of a tree. When Ethan blinked, the figure was gone.

Later that evening at home, the living room smelled of baked ziti and garlic bread. Elle had cooked to celebrate the playoff announcement.

"You've got two more weeks of practice before the big game," she said, scooping pasta onto their plates. "And we're going to be at everyone. Right, George?"

Uncle George looked up from his phone. "Wouldn't miss it for the world. Besides, I gotta be there to make sure none of those scouts take my nephew before he graduates."

"Scouts?" Ethan's eyes widened.

George smiled. "You didn't hear this from me, but I got a call from a coach at Diversity Tech asking about you. Just inquiries. Nothing official."

Ethan felt like the room spun for a second. Everything was happening so fast.

After dinner, he excused himself and went up to his room. He opened his window and sat on the ledge, feeling the cool night breeze brush against his face.

Below, the backyard was peaceful, no shouting, no chaos, just the sound of wind through the trees.

He closed his eyes and whispered a simple prayer.

"God, I don't want to mess this up. I want to stay focused. Help me not lose my way."

Then he opened his journal and scribbled:

"So much is changing. I don't want to drift. I want to be grounded. I don't know how to hold it all."

The rest of the week flew by.

Each day brought more attention, more media interest, and more intense practices. At school, teachers excused him from some homework because they knew the spotlight was on him.

By Friday, Gerry High was electric. Students wore jerseys and face paint. Teachers cheered in the hallways. A full-on pep rally was planned for next week.

At home, Uncle George built a mock playbook with Ethan to help him mentally prep.

"You've got the skills, kid," he said. "But it's the mind that separates stars from champions."

Saturday morning came like a soft drumroll.

Ethan dressed early and headed downstairs, finding Elle in the kitchen scrambling eggs and frying turkey bacon. Uncle George poured orange juice while reading the sports section of the paper, which unsurprisingly featured Ethan and Gerry High. The family was proud of him.

The cold November wind swept across the field like a warning. Breath curled from mouths like smoke. The bleachers were packed with students wrapped in blankets, parents bundled up in coats, and the marching band's drums echoing in the night air like thunder.

Gerry High had made it to the playoffs.

Ethan stood on the sidelines, his helmet tucked under his arm, his heart thudding like a war drum. He took a slow breath and scanned the crowd. He could see his mother, Elle, waving from the middle row, Aunt Helen beside her, bundled in a thick scarf. Uncle George stood with arms folded, eyes locked on the field with the intensity of a scout.

This was it.

"Let's go, number 9!" someone shouted behind him.

He turned and grinned. His teammates slapped his back as the defense huddled together for the first series.

Coach Lanning called out the defensive set. "Let's start strong. Ethan, you're rushing the left edge. Watch the quarterback, he scrambles under pressure."

"Yes, Coach."

When the whistle blew, Ethan stepped onto the field as he belonged there.

First snap, Ethan exploded off the line, low and fast. He bent around the tackle with speed and force and nearly took the quarterback's arm off as he grabbed for the sack. The ball flew wild into the air, intercepted by Gerry's cornerback. The crowd erupted.

Second quarter, offense time. Ethan lined up as a tight end. The snap came, and he charged forward, blocking with ferocity, then peeled off for a post route. The quarterback saw him just as he broke the coverage.

Twenty-five yards. Touchdown.

The student section roared. People jumped to their feet. Someone in the crowd rang a cowbell over and over.

By halftime, Gerry High was up 21–7.

In the locker room, the team sat on the benches, sweaty, breathing hard, energized. Coach Lanning stood in the middle, gripping a whiteboard.

"You boys have come a long way. Don't let up. Don't get comfortable. This team is good, but you're better when you play together."

He looked directly at Ethan.

"You've got a gift, son. But stay humble. Remember why you play."

Ethan gave a slight nod.

Inside, he thought of his father.

He thought of the promise he made not just to stay sober, but to keep going. To keep faith. To keep fighting.

Second half, fourth quarter. The score was 28–21. The other team was driving.

On third down, they called a run sweep to Ethan's side. The guard came barreling toward him. Ethan planted his feet, threw his shoulder low, and shed the block like a paper towel.

He met the running back head-on and dropped him with a textbook tackle behind the line.

The stadium exploded again. A wave of sound rolled over the field like thunder.

On the final play of the game, Ethan sealed the win with one last defensive stand, crashing into the quarterback as he tried to scramble. The ball popped loose. Gerry High recovered.

Game over.

Victory.

The team piled on each other in celebration. Coaches threw fists in the air. The announcer shouted over the loudspeaker, "Gerry High advances to the semi-finals!"

Ethan dropped to one knee on the sideline, not out of exhaustion, but out of reverence.

He whispered to himself, "Thank you, God. I'm not doing this without You."

When he rose to his feet, Coach Lanning was there.

"You're on fire out there," he said with a grin. "Proud of you."

"Thanks, Coach."

Ethan turned and saw his family rushing to the edge of the fence, Elle, Helen, and George smiling like they hadn't in weeks.

He jogged over, still catching his breath. Elle hugged him tight, tears in her eyes.

"You're doing it," she whispered. "You're really doing it."

Uncle George gave him a nod of approval. "One game at a time, champ. You keep that spirit, and you'll go far."

Aunt Helen leaned over the rail. "You've got half the city talking about you now. Don't let it change you."

"I won't," Ethan said.

Chapter 15
Small Town, Big Energy

The buzz around Gerry High School was electric. For the first time in nearly a decade, the Gerry Hawks were heading into the state semi-finals. The excitement spilled far beyond the football field and into the heart of the entire town. From the local coffee shop on Pine Street to the grocery mart near the edge of town, everyone was talking about Friday night's game.

Signs that read "Go Hawks!" and "State Bound!" were posted in shop windows, on telephone poles, and even painted on the windows of cars driving down Main Street. Kids wore their team colors proudly, gold and blue, with temporary Hawks claw tattoos pressed to their cheeks. The local ice cream shop ran a Friday special: 50% off if you wore anything with the school logo. The hot dog cart near the high school dropped their prices by half, too. But the biggest hit was Tacos, a small taco shop two blocks from the school. When the news hit that Gerry High had advanced, the owner shouted across the lunch crowd, "Free tacos, from 2 to 5! One per student! Let's go, Hawks!"

By Monday morning, the energy had shifted from hopeful to unstoppable. The principal's voice came over the loudspeaker at 8:15 sharp.

"Good morning, students and faculty of Gerry High. Let me be the first to say what I know many of you are already thinking our Hawks are making history. Congratulations to the football team for advancing to the semi-finals! As a celebration, tomorrow will be a dress-down day, but school colors only! Let's flood this building with gold and blue pride."

Cheers erupted in classrooms, and the hallways echoed with claps and high-fives. Even students who didn't know the rules of football were caught up in the energy. School was still in session, tests still needed to be taken, and projects still needed to be turned in, but there was something different in the air. Teachers loosened up, just a bit. Homework was still given, but deadlines felt gentler. Everyone was riding the same wave.

In the middle of it all was Ethan, walking through the halls with a quiet confidence. He wasn't boastful, but the students and teachers alike gave him nods and fist bumps. He carried his backpack slung over one shoulder and his team jacket slightly unzipped, revealing his "Gerry Hawks" shirt underneath.

"Ethan!" someone shouted from behind.

He turned to see Amanda and Chris jogging up beside him.

"You ready for Friday?" Amanda grinned.

Ethan smiled. "Always.

"I heard Coach is having practice indoors today because of the rain," Chris said. "You still doing weights before school?"

"Yup. Uncle George's idea," Ethan said with a half-smirk. "Man wakes me up at 5:15."

"Dedicated," Amanda laughed. "If we win Friday, the whole town might explode."

Ethan chuckled, but deep down, he felt the weight of it all. The town, the team, the expectations, it was a lot. But it was also a gift. For the first time since the funeral, life was moving forward again. And football was his way through it.

The final bell of the day echoed through the halls, followed by the steady shuffle of sneakers and the creak of lockers opening and slamming shut. Students poured into the corridors, buzzing with anticipation for Friday night's semi-final game.

Ethan slung his backpack over his shoulder and gave a quick nod to a few classmates who offered waves or pats on the back. The atmosphere was electric. Posters with the team colors blue and gold lined the hallways, and someone had chalked "STATE OR BUST" on the pavement outside the front entrance.

He made his way to the athletic wing, where players were already beginning to gather for practice. As he turned the corner, Tyrell caught up to him, slightly out of breath and nervous.

"Yo, Ethan," Tyrell said, adjusting his duffel bag strap.

"What's up?" Ethan replied, opening the locker door and holding it for him.

Tyrell hesitated, then said quickly, "I was thinking… for the game tomorrow… maybe I could get in during the first quarter? Just a few snaps at tight end?"

Ethan slowed his pace, considering the request. Tyrell had come a long way this season. He worked hard, rarely complained, and had made the most of every opportunity. Ethan respected that.

"You want to start in the first?" Ethan asked, eyes narrowing slightly.

Tyrell nodded, trying to hold back his nerves. "Yeah. I feel like I can help set the tone early, you know? Been watching tape and everything."

Ethan gave him a long look, then offered a slight nod. "Alright. I'll talk to Coach. We'll see what he says."

Tyrell broke into a grin, his shoulders visibly relaxing. "Thanks, man. I appreciate it."

They walked the rest of the way together, their cleats echoing on the tiled floor as they entered the locker room.

Inside, the room was already humming, shoulder pads clinking, music thumping low from a speaker in the corner, and the voices of teammates getting in the zone. Ethan headed to his locker, nodding to a few guys on the way. He pulled off his hoodie and began suiting up for practice, his mind already shifting to game mode.

Coach shouted from the doorway, "Let's take the field, it's sloppy, but we will be ok." One of the assistant coaches said, "Let's head out."

The field, damp from last night's rain, was spongy under the players' cleats. But the mud didn't matter. Spirits were high.

"Let's get moving!" Coach Lanning shouted as the players jogged out onto the turf. "Semi-finals aren't going to win themselves!"

Ethan led the charge, helmet under his arm, chin up, mind focused. They ran through warm-ups, followed by agility drills, and then straight into position work.

"Phillips," the Coach called. "You're lining up on defense first."

"Yes, Coach."

Ethan sprinted over to the defensive group and dropped into his stance at the end of the line. The whistle blew, and like a shot, he exploded off the line, pushing through two blockers before reaching the dummy in the backfield.

"Clean!" the assistant coach barked. "Great take-off!"

They rotated through drills, switching to offense next. Ethan strapped his helmet back on and looked across the line to Tyrell, a senior who had worked hard all season but spent most games warming the bench.

Ethan jogged over to Coach Lanning. "Coach," he said quietly, "let Tyrell take reps at tight end today. I want to stay on defense. I've been thinking…he's ready."

Coach Lanning raised an eyebrow, surprised. "You sure about that?"

Ethan nodded. "Yeah. He needs the game time. I'll lock it down on D."

Lanning gave him a rare grin. "Alright, Phillips. I respect that."

The rest of the practice went by fast, with Tyrell showing promise and Ethan wreaking havoc on defense. As they ran their final sprint drills, Ethan could hear his mom's car pull into the lot. Practice wrapped up with claps and shouts. Everyone knew this team was exceptional.

He waved goodbye to his teammates and jogged over to Elle's car. The passenger door creaked open, and Ethan climbed in, tossing his gear bag into the back.

"You looked good out there," Elle said, pulling onto the road.

"Thanks," Ethan replied, leaning back against the headrest.

They rode in silence for a minute, the low hum of the heater filling the space.

"You know," Elle began gently, "you don't have to carry the whole team."

Ethan glanced out the window. "That's what the coaches keep saying."

She kept her eyes on the road but softened her voice. "They're right. You've got a team for a reason. You've been through a lot, Ethan. It's okay to share the weight."

He hesitated, then turned toward her. "I told Coach to let Tyrell start at tight end. I'll stick to defensive end."

Elle's face lit up with a proud smile. "You did?"

"Yeah. He's good. He just needed a chance."

"That's leadership, Ethan. That's real strength."

He looked down at his hands, calloused from weightlifting and practices. "I just want to win the right way. We all worked for this."

Elle reached over and squeezed his shoulder. "And you're doing just that. I'm proud of you."

They pulled into the driveway as the sun dipped low behind the trees, casting long shadows over the porch. Inside, the smell of slow-cooked stew filled the air. Ethan grabbed his bag and followed his mom inside the house.

The next day, the bleachers were full long before kickoff.

It felt like the whole town had turned out to watch Gerry High's semi-final playoff game. Cars lined the street outside the stadium, parents wore gold and blue scarves, and local news cameras panned the crowd, catching the signs that read: "Finish the Fight!" and "Go Gerry! One More to STATE!" The air buzzed with excitement, fried food, and the raw anticipation of small-town pride.

Ethan stood on the sideline in full pads, bouncing on his heels. The field lights cut across the early evening sky as the announcer introduced the team. When his name rang through the speakers, "Number 9, Ethan Phillips!" the crowd roared. He spotted his mom and Uncle George in the stands beside Aunt Helen, all three waving wildly, bundled in winter jackets.

The game kicked off fast. Gerry High scored on their first drive. Tyrell, starting at tight end just like he and Ethan had agreed, caught a 15-yard pass that helped move the chains early in the game. Ethan focused on defense, disrupting plays, rushing the quarterback, and keeping their momentum strong.

Midway through the second quarter, it happened.

Tyrell went up for a slant route and was mid-air when a linebacker from the other team, late on the play, and clearly frustrated, hit him low and dirty. The sound of the impact silenced the crowd in an instant. Tyrell collapsed to the turf, clutching his leg, screaming.

Coach Lanning and the medical team rushed to him. Players from both sidelines knelt. Ethan ripped off his helmet and sprinted across the field, kneeling beside his friend, heart pounding.

Tyrell gritted his teeth in pain, sweat mixing with tears. "It's my leg… I heard it pop," he choked out.

The trainers stabilized him, and the ambulance arrived within minutes. As they loaded Tyrell in, he gripped Ethan's forearm. "Go win this, man. For me."

Ethan nodded, jaw clenched. "We got you."

Coach Lanning turned to Ethan. "You up for playing both sides the rest of the game?"

Ethan didn't hesitate. "Yes, sir."

What followed was something only the crowd would later describe as legendary. Ethan was relentless, blocking, tackling, catching passes, and even recovering a fumble. It wasn't just talent, it was purpose. He played like the whole town was on his shoulders, like Tyrell's hopes were tied to every snap.

When the final whistle blew, Gerry High had won by two touchdowns.

They were going to the state championship.

As confetti and shouts filled the air, Coach Lanning gathered the team in a huddle and said, "Before we celebrate, we've got one more place to be. Let's go see our brother."

Later that night, at the county medical center, the team loaded into a caravan of cars and vans, and one by one, players entered the hospital waiting room still in full gear, helmets tucked under their arms. Nurses and doctors smiled at the unexpected wave of teenagers piling into the lobby.

Tyrell was sitting up in a hospital bed, leg wrapped and elevated. He grinned when the team filed in, led by Coach Lanning and his coaching staff.

"You look like you're headed to war," Tyrell joked.

Coach approached, holding the game ball. "We did. We won. For you."

Tyrell laughed and shook his head. "Coach, you'd better win State now."

Someone handed him a Gerry High hoodie signed by all the players. A few moms from the community had even dropped off baked goods for the hospital staff as a gesture of gratitude. One nurse wiped her eyes as she watched the team surround Tyrell's bed.

At that moment, it wasn't just about football. It was about community. Loyalty. Brotherhood.

And the entire team knew something deeper; this was the kind of support they needed the most. Maybe, just maybe, this town is different from most.

Chapter 16
A Feast for the Fight

Two weeks had passed since the semi-final game, and though the buzz of victory still lingered, the Phillips family was focused on something else today: Thanksgiving.

Ethan, Elle, and Uncle George drove through the quiet streets of Gerry early that morning, carrying foil-wrapped dishes, folding chairs, and a container of peach tea. The air was crisp, and the trees had nearly shed all their leaves. Aunt Helen's small bungalow on the corner of Maple and 2nd Street already had steam fogging the windows and laughter spilling out the door.

Inside, cousins darted between adults. Uncles debated football stats over dominoes. The TV blared the local Thanksgiving Day Parade while the sweet potato pie cooled near the window.

Aunt Helen, standing proud in her sunflower apron, waved them in with a wooden spoon.

"Make room! The champions have arrived!" she teased, hugging Ethan first.

"You'd better save me some pie," Ethan smirked.

"No promises," Helen grinned.

Later that afternoon, Ethan was on the covered porch with three of his younger cousins, all under 13. They sat cross-legged in a circle, eating cookies from paper plates.

"You're lying," little Malik pouted. "You did not eat the last slice."

"I did," Ethan said with mock seriousness. "And it was the best sweet potato pie of my life. So sweet. So fluffy. It almost brought tears to my eyes."

"Nooooo!" they shouted in unison.

"Should've gotten your plate faster," Ethan shrugged, leaning back in the patio chair, proud of his fake confession.

Inside, Elle watched from the kitchen window. Her son was laughing again. Not just smiling but laughing, shoulders loose, eyes lit up. For the first time in weeks, she saw a glimpse of the little boy who used to climb into her bed at night with his toy football.

She smiled and returned to stirring the candied yams.

As the evening went on, the house filled with stories and memories. Uncle George made a toast, nothing fancy, just heartfelt words about family, strength, and staying together through the hard seasons. Ethan stood beside him, nodding quietly, grateful for the safe harbor his family had found through the storm of grief.

One week later, the energy shifted again. The Gerry High team loaded their duffel bags onto two charter buses. They were heading to the state championship game, which would be held at a local university stadium just over an hour away. The ride was full of music, jokes, and boys stretching their necks as they imagined the size of the crowd waiting for them.

At the university stadium, the bleachers were massive. The field looked like it belonged on TV. But the boys of Gerry High didn't flinch. They had come too far.

Ethan suited up in the locker room, helmet tucked under his arm. Tyrell, in a team hoodie and crutches, tapped him on the shoulder.

"You know what to do, right?" Tyrell grinned. "Win it. Bring it home."

"I got you," Ethan said, bumping fists with him.

Up in the stands, Elle held her phone tightly in both hands, recording as the team ran out onto the field. Aunt Helen was already yelling. Uncle George stood with his arms crossed, pride carved into every crease of his face.

The small town of Gerry had come alive again.

They weren't just chasing a trophy.

They were chasing history.

The Gerry Hawks stood on one sideline in their gold-and-blue uniforms, eyes focused, helmets polished, hearts pounding. Across the field, the Chelsea City Tigers roared in orange and black, known for their speed, discipline, and the kind of aggression that made state titles possible.

Banners waved. School bands battled for volume. The small town of Gerry had shown up in full force, clapping, shouting, stomping their feet in bleachers that shook under the excitement. The Hawks were the underdogs, but tonight they felt different. They had grit. They had unity. And they had something more, something personal.

Ethan stood quietly during the national anthem, eyes closed. His breath steamed in the cold air, and his gloves tightened around his hands. For once, he wasn't carrying the team on his shoulders. He wasn't the star in his mind. Not tonight. This was about more than football.

The first quarter was intense; both teams scored early, neither giving ground. Ethan, now focused mainly on defense with Tyrell out, had a few decent tackles but felt... off. A step behind. His mind drifted more than once to his dad's face, to the funeral, to the promise he made to stay strong.

By halftime, the Hawks were up by 3.

Inside the locker room, Coach Lanning wasn't yelling or throwing clipboards. He slowly walked around, making eye contact with each player, his hand on their shoulder, nodding with pride.

"You're playing with heart. That's how we win, not just with skill, but with unity. I saw the block Marcus gave to free Ethan on that blitz. I saw Isaiah cover for Tyrell's zone. I see each of you showing up for one another. Keep that energy."

He paused, then locked eyes with Ethan.

"Are you alright, son?"

Ethan nodded, forcing a small smile. "Yeah, Coach."

Coach didn't press it. He just nodded and continued. "We've got two more quarters. Let's bring the heat."

The second half was magic.

Tyrell, though limping on crutches on the sideline, was shouting louder than anyone. "Let's go, Hawks!" He yelled, waving his towel like a flag. His energy spread through the team like wildfire.

Ethan shook off the fog and dialed in. He exploded through the line on a key third-down stop. He forced a fumble in the fourth. And on the final play of the game, with Chelsea on fourth-and-goal and two seconds left, Ethan deflected a pass in the end zone.

The clock hit zero, the final score: Gerry Hawks – 27, Chelsea City Tigers – 20.

The crowd erupted. The players threw helmets into the air. Some cried. Some hugged. Coach Lanning lifted his arms to the sky, shaking with joy. Uncle George had Elle in a side hug, both shouting and laughing. Aunt Helen waved her rally towel with tears in her eyes.

The Hawks had done it…state champions. The moment the final whistle blew, the field transformed into a sea of joy. Students rushed the turf, screaming and waving homemade signs. Parents poured from the stands, phones in hand, recording every moment as the scoreboard glowed: Gerry Hawks – State Champions.

Ethan stood frozen for a second, overwhelmed. He scanned the field, teammates tackling each other in joy, Coach Lanning hugging his assistant coaches, confetti cannons from the boosters shooting gold and blue paper into the sky.

Tyrell, hobbling as fast as his crutches would allow, made his way to Ethan. "Yo! We did it, bro!" he yelled, pulling Ethan into a one-armed hug.

"We did," Ethan said, the weight of the season finally lifting. "We really did."

Uncle George reached him next. He grinned, sweat on his brow like he'd played every down. "Proud of you, champ." He pulled Ethan into a hug, patting him firmly on the back.

Elle followed with Aunt Helen, tears streaming down their cheeks. Elle wrapped her arms tightly around her son. "Your father would be proud," she whispered.

Ethan nodded, eyes glistening. "I thought about him a lot today."

"Then you gave him the ending he always dreamed of," Aunt Helen said, handing him a bottle of water. "Now go enjoy the spotlight, Mr. MVP."

Photographers snapped pictures. Local news reporters circled the field. Someone from the student media shouted, "Ethan! Quick interview?"

He stepped over, still dazed but smiling.

"How does it feel to win the state championship as a freshman?"

Ethan looked at the camera, then at his team around him. "It feels like... like family did it. We didn't win because of one player. We played for each other. And for our town."

"Any words to your community?"

"Thanks for showing up. For believing in us. And for all the free tacos."

Laughter erupted around him. Scott and Amanda found him next, pushing through the crowd.

"Man, you were a beast out there!" Scott shouted.

"Superstar!" Amanda added, flicking a piece of confetti off his shoulder.

They posed for a photo, arms slung over each other's shoulders, smiles wide, the trophy glinting in the background.

As the team gathered near the end zone for the official photo with the trophy, Ethan found a quiet second to look up at the stadium lights and the sky above. In the blur of victory, his heart whispered a prayer of thanks. Not just for the win, but for strength, for his mom, for healing.

For hope.

The picture was snapped. After the celebration on the field, the team headed back to Gerry. By the time Ethan walked through the double doors of Gerry High on Monday morning, the energy in the hallways felt electric. Banners still hung from Friday's pep rally, and a makeshift posterboard outside the main office read in bold letters:

STATE CHAMPS: CONGRATS, GERRY HAWKS!

Students clapped him on the back as he passed. Some gave high-fives, others just pointed and grinned. Teachers paused mid-lesson to acknowledge team members. Even the usually grumpy janitor gave him a nod of approval.

"Alright, superstar," Amanda teased as she caught up with him at his locker. "You still humble, or should we start calling you Mr. Football?"

Ethan laughed. "Let's just stick with Ethan."

By lunch, it felt like the entire cafeteria was buzzing about the game. More than once, someone walked past Ethan's table to say, "Congrats!" or "That fourth-quarter sack was wild!"

After the final bell, the football team met in Coach Lanning's room. The whiteboard still had diagrams from their last practice, but someone had written in blue marker across the top:

CHAMPIONS MEETING

Coach Lanning entered with a rare full smile. "Alright, gentlemen. Still basking in the glory?"

Cheers erupted.

He raised his hands to calm them. "You earned it. Every drop of sweat, every late practice, every hit you took on the field, it paid off. But before we close out the season, we've got one last team event."

He stepped to his desk and pulled out a mockup of a flyer. "Football Banquet. Next week, on Wednesday evening, before Christmas break starts. I'm reserving a few tables at Font's, the local Italian spot off Main Street. It'll be casual parents, players, maybe a few teachers. You'll get your awards, and we'll celebrate as a team one more time."

"Coach, can we bring guests?" one player asked.

"Limit it to three per player. I'll email your parents tonight. Let them know. I need a headcount by Friday so Fonts can set everything up."

Ethan thought of inviting Aunt Helen along with his mom and Uncle George. He knew she'd love it.

Coach continued, "One last thing, I'm proud of all of you. But remember, championships aren't the finish line. They're just the beginning. Some of you will go further than you ever imagined. Some of you may not. But we'll always be part of this legacy. Don't take it for granted."

As the team began to leave, Ethan lingered. Coach Lanning caught his eye and nodded.

"You okay, son?"

"Yeah," Ethan said quietly. "Just still taking it all in."

Coach patted his shoulder. "You did well out there. On and off the field."

Ethan smiled. "Thanks, Coach."

Outside, the winter wind was crisp, but Ethan didn't feel the cold. He had a championship ring coming, a banquet to look forward to, and a town that now knew his name. The afternoon sky had shifted to a mild winter gray by the time Elle pulled up to the front of Gerry High. Students were still scattered near the front steps, sharing stories from the weekend and reliving the championship win.

Ethan opened the passenger door and dropped his gym bag in the back seat before settling in.

"Hey, baby," Elle said with a warm smile. "How was school? Still flying high?"

Ethan chuckled. "It was cool. Everyone's still talking about the game. Coach Lanning met with us after school. He said we're having a team banquet next Wednesday."

Elle looked over quickly before pulling out of the parking lot. "A banquet? Oh, how fancy! Where at?"

"At Font's," Ethan said. "Coach said each player can bring up to three guests."

"Ooh, Font's! That's the good pasta," she grinned. "You already know I'm there. Uncle George, too. And we'd better call your Aunt Helen before she hears about it from someone else."

Ethan nodded, knowing exactly how that would go.

Elle tapped her steering wheel controls and called Helen's number. Within seconds, the car's speaker lit up.

"Heyyyy y'all!" Aunt Helen's voice rang through the car like sunshine. "I was just thinking about you. My football champion nephew!"

Ethan grinned and looked out the window, hiding a small smile.

"We're calling with an official invitation," Elle teased. "Banquet next Wednesday for the team. It's at Font's, and we're allowed to bring three guests."

"You'd better stop!" Helen squealed. "I am not missing that for anything. I'm wearing my good boots, too. The suede ones!"

Ethan chuckled in the passenger seat.

"Well, make sure you bring your appetite, too. You know Font's doesn't play with the portion sizes," Elle said.

"Oh, honey, you know I'm ready. Let me mark my calendar now," Helen said as the sound of scribbling echoed faintly. "I'm so proud of you, Ethan. You hear me? You earned this."

"Thanks, Auntie," Ethan said sincerely, his voice soft but grateful.

The car ride home was filled with light chatter and the warmth of family. No trophy or banner could compare to moments like these, where love was loud, and support filled every space.

As they pulled into the driveway, Elle ended the call, promising to text the banquet details. Ethan grabbed his bag, still smiling.

This was more than a win. It was a memory.

Chapter 17
A Breath Between Seasons

The days following the championship buzzed with excitement throughout the hallways. Students who barely paid attention to football were now wearing Hawks hoodies, replaying highlight clips on their phones between classes, and congratulating players in the halls like they were local celebrities. Ethan didn't mind it. For once, the attention didn't feel like pressure…it felt earned.

The week went by in a blur of regular classes, group projects, and hallway laughter. Teachers did their best to keep students focused, but they occasionally brought up the win. Mr. Ward, Ethan's history teacher, opened Thursday's lesson with, "Before we talk about the French Revolution, let's give another round of applause to the Gerry Hawks for making this town proud."

Ethan stayed grounded, though. He met up with Amanda, Chris, and Scott a few times during the week at lunch, where they talked about everything from upcoming finals to who might win MVP at the banquet. But when Saturday rolled around, it was time to unwind.

"Don't go spending it all on sneakers," Aunt Helen had warned with a wink when she handed Ethan the $250 gift card a few weeks ago. But today, with the weight of grief still lingering beneath the surface, he was ready for something light, something fun.

That afternoon, Uncle George pulled up to the entrance of Gerry Mall, dropping the four teens off with a simple, "Be safe, don't act up, and call me when you're ready."

"Thanks, Uncle G!" Ethan called as the car pulled away.

The mall glowed with early holiday decorations—twinkling lights, garlands wrapped around columns, and a massive tree near the center court that reached the second floor. The scent of cinnamon pretzels and popcorn filled the air.

Ethan led the way to one of the athletic stores first. "I've had my eye on these since last month," he said, holding up a pair of limited-edition cleats.

Scott nodded in approval. "Man, those are fire. You getting 'em?"

"Yup," Ethan said, grinning.

The afternoon flew by in a comfortable rhythm of laughter, food-court fries, and fitting-room selfies. Amanda tried on a hoodie that was three sizes too big and modeled it like a fashion runway star, while Chris tried to talk Ethan into buying matching joggers "for team chemistry."

Three hours later, bags in hand and stomachs half full of soft pretzels and slushies, they piled into Uncle George's car.

Back at the house, Elle had dinner waiting. She made chicken fajitas, warm tortillas, and fruit salad. Amanda's dad arrived just as dessert was being served, waving at the group from the porch while Amanda slipped on her boots.

"Thanks for having me, Mrs. Phillips!" Amanda said as she left.

The night stretched long and cozy as Chris and Scott stayed over. The boys piled into Ethan's room with their snacks, soda cans, and loud banter, launching a video game tournament that lasted for hours. Somewhere around midnight, they threw on hoodies and snuck outside to sit on the porch.

The December air bit at their fingers, but the sky above was clear, painted with stars.

"Crazy how fast this year's gone," Scott said, sipping from a bottle of grape soda.

Ethan leaned back in his chair. "Yeah... feels like we just started high school, and now it's almost Christmas break."

Chris nodded. "You ready for next season?"

Ethan didn't answer right away. He stared at the stars, then whispered, "I think so."

The silence that followed wasn't awkward; it was understood. There were things each of them was still carrying fears, dreams, and questions, but for now, friendship and fresh air were enough.

Eventually, they all drifted back inside, closing the door behind them as the cold wind whistled softly through the trees. The next morning, the smell of crispy bacon and warm cinnamon toast wafted through the house. Elle stood in the kitchen, flipping pancakes on the griddle and humming to herself. It was nearing 11 a.m., and she knew three teenage boys with bottomless stomachs would be emerging any moment.

Sure enough, the sounds of shuffling feet and groggy voices trickled down the hallway.

"Something smells fire!" Scott said as he plopped onto a chair at the kitchen table, rubbing his eyes.

Chris followed behind him, sniffing the air like a bloodhound. "Is that sausage gravy too? Yo, Mrs. Elle, you didn't have to go all out."

Elle smiled. "You boys earned it. Champs get a champ's breakfast."

Ethan brought up the rear, still stretching and yawning. "You didn't have to make all this, Mom."

"Don't be silly," she said, setting a large plate in front of each of them. "Eat up. Y'all ran all over that field last week; your bodies need fuel."

The boys didn't need any more encouragement. Conversation slowed as chewing increased, but now and then, one of them would toss out a line about the game, the crowd, or how Amanda's dad looked like he was ready to run onto the field when she screamed Ethan's name after his second sack.

By 1 p.m., Scott's mom rang the doorbell. Chris's older sister pulled into the driveway just minutes later.

"Tell your mom thanks for the cupcakes!" Chris shouted as he grabbed his jacket.

"See you Monday, E!" Scott called over his shoulder.

When the door finally closed, peace settled over the house.

Elle let out a slow breath and turned on soft gospel music while she wiped down the counters and started loading the dishwasher. The living room still had snack wrappers and gaming controllers scattered across the floor. She chuckled to herself. Teenagers.

Not long after the quiet settled in, Ethan and Uncle George emerged, jackets zipped and ready to go.

"We're headed to the barbershop," Uncle George said, grabbing the keys.

"Don't let them mess up my son's edge-up!" Elle teased.

At the barbershop, the energy was buzzing just like it had been since the championship win. The shop was full of laughter, clippers buzzing, the faint scent of aftershave in the air. Nearly every barber chair was filled, and every man in the room had something to say about Gerry High.

One of the barbers, a tall man with a full beard and a proud glint in his eye, paused mid-convo to greet George. "Yo, George! Look who you brought with you, the Hawk himself."

Ethan smiled, dapping him up. "Hey, Mr. Roland."

Roland, who was also Tyrell's father, pulled out his phone. "Been showing off these clips to everyone. Even at work. Y'all boys brought the city together. Tyrell was crying at the house, mad he couldn't be out there with you, but he's healing. He'll be out of the cast by the New Year. Doc said his leg is setting really well."

"Tell him we all missed him on the field," Ethan said, hopping up into the chair. "That game felt different without him."

"He knows," Roland nodded. "But seeing you boys finish what y'all started? He said he felt like a champ, too."

Uncle George smiled from across the room. "Proud of you, kid."

As the clippers buzzed and conversation flowed, Ethan sat still, eyes on his reflection in the mirror. Life was moving forward. And so was he. After receiving fresh cuts, they walked toward George's newer sedan, parked just down the block. The sidewalks were lined with Christmas decorations, storefront windows displaying string lights, inflatable reindeer wobbling in front yards, and a few early-bird carolers setting up outside the café.

"Looks like everyone's already in holiday mode," George commented as he opened the car door.

Ethan climbed in and pulled on his seatbelt. "Yeah. It feels… different this year, though."

George turned the key in the ignition, letting the heater roar to life. "Different how?"

"I don't know," Ethan said, watching the neighborhood roll by through the frosty window. "Maybe it's just everything that's happened lately. Feels like I'm seeing stuff for real now, not just football or school. Like… life, I guess."

George glanced over and nodded. "That's not a bad thing, son. Pain will open your eyes like nothing else."

Ethan was quiet for a moment. "You think it'll ever stop hurting?"

George's voice softened. "No… not completely. But it won't always feel like a fresh cut. Time doesn't erase love, it just teaches you how to carry it."

Ethan looked down at his hands. "Thanks, Unc."

They drove the rest of the way in thoughtful silence, the only sound the hum of the heater and the occasional flick of the blinker. When they turned onto their street, the porch light was already glowing, and the smell of something delicious greeted them the moment they opened the front door.

Elle peeked her head from the kitchen, wiping her hands on a dish towel. "Perfect timing. Dinner's almost done!"

"What's cooking?" George asked, pulling off his coat.

"Roasted chicken, herb potatoes, and cornbread," she grinned. "And I made apple pie too, since I know how much y'all tore up the apple pie on Thanksgiving."

George rubbed his belly dramatically. "Now that's what I'm talking about."

Ethan dropped his jacket over the couch and headed toward the table, finally smiling with both his mouth and his eyes.

"Smells good, Mom."

"Wash up," Elle said, swatting his shoulder gently with the towel. "We're eating in five."

Upstairs, Ethan splashed water on his face and looked at himself in the mirror. For a fleeting second, he thought about his dad, how proud he might've been watching him play, or hearing about his grades, or just sitting at the table with them.

"Still hurts," he whispered. "But I'm okay."

And with that, he dried his face, walked back down the stairs, and joined his family at the table.

After dinner, Ethan settled in his bed for a while scrolling on social media before drifting off to sleep. The next morning, Ethan woke up and got dressed for church. A few hours later, they arrived in the church's parking lot.

Sunday morning, sunlight filtered through the church's frosted windows. The sanctuary was full of families in coats and scarves peeling off layers, warm smiles exchanged, and Holy scriptures opened to mark the day's text. The choir had just finished singing "Amazing Grace," and the atmosphere settled into reverent anticipation.

Pastor Williams stepped forward, holding the Holy Scriptures, and smiled gently at the congregation. He cleared his throat and began:

"Today, I want to speak from Philippians 4:4-7 KJV. Turn there with me."

Ethan sat beside his mother and Uncle George, flipping to the verse in his own Holy scriptures.

Pastor Williams read aloud:

'Rejoice in the Lord alway: and again I say, Rejoice. Let your moderation be known unto all men. The Lord is at hand. Be careful for nothing; but in everything by prayer and supplication with thanksgiving let your requests be made known unto God. And the peace of God, which passeth all understanding, shall keep your hearts and minds through Christ Jesus.'

He closed the Holy scriptures and looked across the crowd.

"Family," he began slowly, "don't let your circumstances blind you to the blessings still flowing in your life. Whether it's grief, uncertainty, joy, or success, rejoice in the Lord always, not just when it's easy. Not just when you win championships, get promoted, or feel good. But always. In your sorrow. In your struggle. In your silence. In your waiting."

Ethan's chest tightened. He leaned forward slightly in the pew, eyes fixed on the pulpit. His heart whispered:

I gave Him praise when we won. I felt it. I meant it. And I want to keep doing what's right. I want to live the right way in God's sight.

Pastor Williams continued, his voice rising gently.

"You see, when we rejoice, we shift our posture from inward to upward. That's where peace is found. Not in the scoreboard, not in the applause, not even in the comfort of routine, but in Christ."

Elle reached over and gently placed her hand over Ethan's. He didn't look at her, but he gave a slight squeeze in return.

"Some of you may feel forgotten or burdened," Pastor Williams said. "But I'm here to remind you today that the Lord is at hand. He's near. He's closer to the struggle. And when you offer up your needs with thanksgiving, that peace… that unshakable peace… it guards your heart."

Ethan felt a quiet stillness rise inside him. No words. Just a subtle clarity.

He didn't fully understand what God had in store for his life, but he was beginning to feel that he wanted it. And not just for the victories on the field. But for something bigger. Something deeper.

He looked toward the front of the church again and whispered in his heart:

Please help me to live right… even when nobody's watching.

Chapter 18
The Next Play

Monday morning rolled in brisk and cold. Ethan stepped out of Uncle George's car and zipped up his jacket as he walked toward the main entrance of Gerry High. The usual buzz of student chatter filled the halls, but this time it carried the weight of pride and victory. Championship weekend still hung in the air like the scent of fresh-cut turf.

Throughout the day, Ethan was greeted with fist bumps and back claps. Even a few teachers paused mid-lesson to congratulate him and the team. His math teacher wrote "STATE CHAMPS!" in bold red marker across the top of the whiteboard. Despite the celebratory mood, classes were in full swing. Ethan took notes, turned in a history paper, and tried to focus, though his mind occasionally drifted to Wednesday night's banquet.

After the final bell rang, he walked outside to find Elle already waiting in the car.

"Hey, honey," she smiled as he climbed in. "We've got to stop by the grocery store, just need a few things for the week."

Ethan nodded, pulling out his phone and scrolling through texts from teammates. "Cool, I'll walk with you."

They made their way through the aisles of the grocery store, gathering pasta, chicken, a loaf of bread, and a new bottle of Elle's favorite peach tea. A few people recognized Ethan and congratulated him again, which made Elle beam with quiet joy.

By the time Wednesday night came, Ethan stood in front of the mirror fixing the collar of his dress shirt. "You look great, baby," Elle said as she adjusted his jacket sleeve. Uncle George walked in behind them with a proud smirk. "Let's go celebrate," he said.

Font's Italian Eatery was already buzzing when they arrived. The entire coaching staff, players, and their families filled the reserved dining space. Candle-lit tables were set with red-and-white cloths and dinner rolls at each setting. Laughter and chatter filled the room, blending with the aroma of garlic bread and pasta.

Coach Lanning stood to speak midway through the meal. "This team," he said, pausing as the room fell silent, "has not only made history, but you've shown what commitment and unity can do. I'm proud of each one of you."

Applause echoed as plaques were handed out, state championship rings were opened in velvet boxes, and parents took photos like it was prom night.

Then came the surprise.

Coach held up a small stack of envelopes. "I've been in touch with a few elite programs' summer football camps. Some of you have been invited to attend. These aren't just any camps; these are the ones that matter if you're thinking D1."

Gasps and murmurs swept the room. Ethan's heart pounded as Coach handed him one of the envelopes.

After dessert and hugs, Ethan leaned over to Marcus, who had also received an envelope. "I'll call you when I get home. Let's figure out which one we're hitting."

"Bet," Marcus nodded, gripping the envelope like it was gold. Once home, Ethan kicked off his dress shoes and sank into the edge of his bed, the envelope still in his hand. The house was quiet, Elle had gone to her room, and Uncle George was watching TV in the living room. The soft hum of the dishwasher was the only sound as Ethan pulled out his phone and tapped Marcus's name.

It rang twice.

"Yo!" Marcus answered, clearly still hyped. "Man, can you believe tonight? Coach really came through!"

Ethan laughed, dropping back against his pillows. "I know. That speech... and the rings? Bro, I can't stop looking at mine."

"Same," Marcus chuckled. "I'm wearing mine to school tomorrow. You think we can?"

"Why not?" Ethan grinned. "We earned it."

They were silent for a moment before Ethan brought it up. "So… you got the same envelope I got?"

"Elite players, rising stars, and every regional academy," Marcus listed off. "You?"

"Same. Plus, a handwritten note from Coach about the regional camp. Said it's an invitation-only and we'd both be good fits."

Marcus let out a low whistle. "That's big. Like… national recruit big."

"Yeah," Ethan said, voice softer now. "Coach said scouts from top schools will be there."

"So, which one are you thinking?" Marcus asked.

"I don't know yet. The regional is the obvious pick for top exposure, but I want to go where we can both go together," Ethan admitted. "It's been a crazy year. I want to enjoy the summer and work."

"I feel that. I'll talk to my mom. If she's down, let's go to the regional camp. If we ball out, we could both be getting real offers by junior year."

"Yeah…" Ethan paused. "Let's do it. Let's start something that matters."

Marcus was quiet for a second. "Are you good, though? Like, with everything going on?"

Ethan hesitated, then nodded even though Marcus couldn't see. "Some days I'm not. But tonight helped. Winning helped. You guys helped."

"You helped us, too, E. You aren't just a player…you're a leader. Don't forget that."

Ethan smiled faintly. "I'll see you in the morning."

"Cool. And hey…bring your ring to school."

"You know it."

They hung up.

Ethan rolled over and reached for his journal on the nightstand. He flipped to a blank page and scribbled:

"Tonight felt right. Not because of the lights, or the cheers, or the awards, but because I didn't feel alone. I know what I want now. And I'm going to get there."

He closed the book, turned off the lamp, and lay in the quiet. A whisper of gratitude escaped his lips before sleep pulled him under. The school day flew by faster than Ethan expected. Hallways were lined with locker tinsel and taped-up Santa hats. Teachers wore goofy Christmas sweaters, and students passed candy canes and handwritten cards like trading cards. Ethan turned in his last exam, dapped up his teammates in the hall, and gave Ms. Blackwood a thank-you for her encouragement this semester. When the dismissal bell rang at 1:00 p.m., students poured out like a wave of relief and excitement.

Aunt Helen was already waiting in her silver SUV out front. She leaned on the horn twice with a broad smile as Ethan approached.

"School's out!" she cheered as he climbed into the passenger seat. "You made it through your first high school semester, champ."

He chuckled. "Yeah, it was wild. But it's over."

"You hungry?" she asked.

"Nah, I'll eat later," Ethan said. "Just ready to crash on the couch."

When they pulled into the driveway, Ethan jumped out, jogged up the steps, and let himself in. The house was still and quiet. He dropped his bag by the door and made a beeline for the living room. With a satisfied sigh, he flopped on the couch and flipped on the TV, settling into a marathon of holiday movies.

He hadn't even changed out of his school clothes when Elle and Uncle George walked through the door just after 4:00 p.m., bags in hand, faces lit up like they were carrying a secret.

"Hey, champ!" Uncle George greeted, tossing his keys into the ceramic bowl on the entry table.

"Hey," Ethan replied, half-looking up from the screen. "No school till next year."

Elle smiled and walked over to sit next to him. "Well, since you're officially on break, we thought it was time for a little surprise."

Ethan sat up. "Surprise?"

Uncle George grinned and handed him a large envelope. "Open it."

Ethan tore the flap open and pulled out several colorful brochures and a printed itinerary. His eyes widened. "Wait… the Bahamas?"

Elle nodded. "Yup. Seven days. White sands, palm trees, sunshine instead of snow."

"For real?" Ethan gasped, flipping through the pages. "Like… this Christmas?"

"Your Aunt Helen and I were talking on Thanksgiving, and well… one thing led to another," Elle said, chuckling. "Your uncles pitched in. A bunch of us planned a last-minute family getaway to celebrate the season and the big championship."

"Your cousins don't know yet either," Uncle George added. "We're telling everyone tonight. We fly out Saturday morning."

Ethan's jaw dropped. "This is insane."

"You deserve it," Elle said, pulling him into a hug. "This year's been a lot. Time to make some happy memories."

Ethan hugged her back. "This is the best surprise ever."

Later that night, Ethan stood in his room surrounded by open drawers, an empty duffel bag, and clothes scattered like a whirlwind. He held up two swim trunks and yelled toward the hallway, "Mom! Blue or red?"

Elle peeked in, holding her own packing list. "Take both. You're gonna want options."

Ethan grinned. "I'm bringing my phone charger, headphones, and extra socks. Oh, and I'm taking that shirt that says Beach Vibes Only."

"Perfect," Elle said. "And don't forget your dress shirt. We're doing one fancy dinner."

Uncle George walked by with a suitcase in one hand and a neck pillow around his shoulders. "Make sure you pack light. We don't need airport security pulling you over for carrying the whole house."

Ethan laughed. "I'm good. I'm just excited."

The house was buzzing with energy. Aunt Helen called twice to make sure everyone had their boarding passes. Cousins were texting in the group chat about hotel pools and excursions. By 10:00 p.m., everything was zipped, charged, and stacked by the front door.

Saturday morning, the family met just after sunrise at the local airport. Ethan's eyes lit up when he spotted the crowd gathered near the check-in line.

"Whoa…" he whispered, slowing his steps. "There's like… thirty of us."

Cousins, uncles, aunts, and a few close friends were gathered in matching shirts that read "Bahama Family Getaway 2008." The mood was electric—laughter, selfies, rolling suitcases, and coffee cups in hand.

"Look who finally made it!" someone shouted as Ethan approached.

He was immediately swarmed with high-fives and shoulder bumps. Aunt Jan hugged him tight and said, "You better not leave me behind at customs, champ."

Ethan grinned. "This is gonna be epic."

As they passed through security and made their way to the gate, Ethan turned to his mom and said, "I'm gonna take so many pictures. When we get back, I'm going to show everyone at school. They won't believe this trip."

Elle smiled. "Make the memories count."

Boarding was called. Ethan stood in line, his heart thumping with anticipation. As the plane door opened, he looked back at his family…. laughing, smiling, buzzing with excitement, and then ahead at the tunnel leading to the plane.

The journey was beginning. The moment Ethan stepped off the plane, he was hit with a wave of warm tropical air and the scent of salt and sunscreen. Palm trees swayed lazily in the distance, and the sky stretched out in endless blue.

"We're not in Gerry anymore," Ethan whispered to himself, squinting up at the sun.

The resort was like something out of a postcard: turquoise pools, white sand, colorful beach umbrellas, and the steady rhythm of steel drums in the background. Ethan couldn't believe this was real.

By day two, the family was fully immersed in vacation mode.

Thursday morning, the family decided to go parasailing. Ethan found himself strapped into a harness beside his cousin Dionte, their legs dangling freely as the boat below tugged them into the sky. The parasail lifted higher and higher until the resort looked like a miniature model beneath them.

"This is insane!" Ethan shouted over the wind.

"I can see the whole island!" Dionte yelled back.

They soared above the ocean, the water below glimmering like crushed glass. Ethan felt something in his chest he hadn't felt in a long time, which was pure joy. Free and weightless, just a boy suspended in the clouds. By the afternoon, back on solid ground, Uncle George, Uncle Melvin, and Uncle Terry geared up for jet skiing. Ethan watched them rev their engines and cut across the waves like teenagers again. They laughed loudly, racing each other in the open water.

Meanwhile, Ethan suited up for scuba diving with his mom, Aunt Helen, Aunt Renee, Aunt Tricia, and a few older cousins. After the instructor's briefing, they descended beneath the surface into a new world. Fish of every color swam around coral reefs. Ethan spotted a sea turtle gliding effortlessly past him.

Elle gave him a thumbs-up underwater, her eyes wide with wonder behind her goggles.

When they surfaced, everyone was talking at once.

"I saw a barracuda!"

"That turtle was HUGE."

"Someone better have this on video!"

That night, the family dressed in their best. The restaurant had glowing lanterns, ocean views, and a live band playing soft island jazz. Ethan sat between his mom and Aunt Helen, his plate filled with buttery lobster tail, grilled shrimp, filet mignon, and garlic mashed potatoes.

"This is the best food I've ever had," he mumbled between bites.

Uncle George raised his glass. "To family, to freedom, and to creating stories we'll laugh about forever."

They all clinked glasses of water, wine, juice, whatever was in hand, and the night continued with laughter, dancing, and photo ops near the tiki torches.

On Saturday, they explored the local shops with vibrant, colorful stands with handmade jewelry, art, spices, and clothing.

Ethan picked up a small, beaded bracelet woven with green and silver. "Amanda would like this," he said, turning it over.

"She'll love it," Elle nodded.

He also found T-shirts that read "Bahamas Vibes" and "Chill Mode Activated"…one for Chris, one for Marcus, and one for Scott.

"These are perfect," Ethan said, folding them neatly.

As they left the marketplace, Ethan paused to take a picture of the alley full of hanging lanterns and locals dancing in the street.

He smiled. "They're never going to believe how awesome this was." Sunday morning greeted the family with a breeze that smelled like salt and sweet island flowers. The sun had barely peeked over the ocean when Aunt Helen came knocking on every villa door.

"Rise and shine! This is our last full day, we're doing the island tour!"

Ethan groaned into his pillow but couldn't hide his excitement. The thought of seeing even more of the island stirred something adventurous in him. By 9 a.m., the whole group, over 30 family members deep, piled into four open-air safari tour trucks with a local guide named Javi, who wore a straw hat and smiled like he hadn't stopped smiling in years.

They began at an old pirate fort nestled high on a hill. From the top, Ethan could see the entire bay, cruise ships anchored like floating cities, and colorful rooftops dotting the coastline.

"Back in the day," Javi explained, "this fort protected the island from invaders. Now it protects memories."

Ethan took a picture with his mom and cousins in front of a rusted cannon.

Next, they visited a rum cake factory where the adults sampled small bites of various flavors, and the kids devoured warm vanilla and coconut slices fresh from the oven. Ethan stuffed a box into his souvenir bag.

The final stop was Blue Hole Lagoon, a natural swimming spot surrounded by thick palms and limestone cliffs. The water was calm and crystal clear, and Ethan and a few brave cousins jumped off the smaller ledge into the deep water below.

"On three!" someone yelled.

Ethan soared through the air and crashed into the water with a grin so wide it almost hurt. He came up laughing and gasping, "Let's do that again!"

That evening, just before dinner, Elle and Uncle George took a walk down the beach with Ethan. The sun was melting into the sea, painting the sky in pinks and golds.

"I'm glad you got to enjoy this," Elle said, looping her arm through Ethan's. "You deserve moments like this."

"I wish it didn't have to end," Ethan said softly, watching the waves lap the shore.

Uncle George smiled. "That's how you know it was a good memory. It makes you want to hold on."

They walked a little farther in silence, the only sound was the sea gently whispering its secrets.

That night, the family had one last buffet-style dinner together under the outdoor terrace. Laughter echoed under string lights, and Ethan took a moment to sit back and soak it all in with his family, the joy, the peace.

As he lay in bed later that night, he wrote in his journal:

"This trip was more than just fun. It reminded me that family is everything. I want to be the kind of man who never forgets where he came from, even when life changes."

He closed the journal, turned off the lamp, and whispered, "Thank You, God.

The sun hadn't even stretched over the Bahamian horizon when suitcases began zipping shut, and flip-flops were exchanged for sneakers. The family lined up at the resort lobby with sleepy smiles, passports in hand, and matching island t-shirts Ethan's Aunt Tricia had insisted they all wear. The shirts read: "Phillips Family Bahamas 2008" in bright blue across the chest.

As they loaded into vans headed to the airport, Ethan turned back to the ocean one last time and snapped a final photo.

"Back to snow," he joked to Marcus, who groaned dramatically, pulling his hoodie over his head.

After a smooth flight, the family landed back in Gerry, where the chilly air greeted them like an old friend. Still glowing from their trip, they parted ways at baggage claim just for a day.

By 6:00 p.m. on New Year's Eve, Aunt Tricia's large craftsman-style home was glowing with string lights and the smell of baked ham, jerk chicken, mac and cheese, collard greens, and peach cobbler. Her expansive living room had been transformed, tables pushed against walls to make space for dancing, karaoke gear set up in the corner, and a "2009" banner stretched above the fireplace.

Uncle George handled the grill on the back porch, wearing an apron that read "Smokin' Good Time." The kids gathered in the finished basement, where Ethan and his cousins started a ping-pong tournament while Leon and James set up the karaoke machine.

Elle walked around with sparkling cider in flutes, hugging relatives and greeting old church friends. She looked happier than she had in months, her laughter easy and bright.

The living room came alive when Aunt Renee sang "Paper, Paper, I love Paper," pulling Ethan's mom on stage with her. The two danced like teenagers while the whole family clapped and cheered.

Later, Ethan and Alyssa teamed up for a goofy duet of "I Love You" by the K. K. Cee Boys, earning them thunderous applause and playful boos from the uncles.

Terrance beat everyone in charades, acting out "a stranded pirate" so dramatically that Aunt Tricia spilled her punch from laughing.

Kids ran back and forth between the snack table and the board game corner. Matching games, Spades, and checkers were all in rotation.

As the final seconds of the year ticked down, Aunt Tricia turned off the music and turned up the TV volume. Everyone gathered in the living room, standing together in the glow of Christmas lights still up around the house.

"Ten... nine... eight..." they counted.

Ethan stood between his mom and Uncle George, holding a sparkling cider in one hand and his phone in the other, ready to record the moment.

"Three... two... one...Happy New Year!"

Cheers erupted. Glasses clinked. Hugs were exchanged. Aunt Helen shouted, "Let this be the year of peace and progress!" as the room exploded into joy. They all shouted.

Around 1:30 a.m., the crowd thinned. Blankets were passed out for cousins sleeping over. Ethan sat on the couch scrolling through photos from the Bahamas and smiling to himself.

He opened his journal one last time that night and wrote:

"This year, I'll play harder. Pray stronger. Help more. And never forget where I came from."

As he closed the journal and tucked it under his arm, his mom kissed him on the forehead and whispered, "Happy New Year, baby."

"Happy New Year, Mom," he said with a sleepy grin. The next morning, the sun peeked through the car windows as Ethan rode home from Aunt Tricia's house, slouched comfortably in the back seat. His stomach was still full from the night before with stuffed mushrooms, wings, peach cobbler, and way too many frozen cranberry slushies.

Elle and Uncle George chatted animatedly in the front.

"That karaoke battle between your mother and Aunt Renee was something else," Uncle George said, shaking his head with a chuckle. "I still can't believe she hit those high notes."

Elle laughed. "That's because I had backup dancers," she said, glancing at Ethan through the rearview mirror.

Ethan smirked. "More like backup comedians."

They all laughed.

"Tricia's addition to the house really made a difference, though," George added, settling into a nostalgic tone. "That sunroom? Perfect for board games. I could see us hosting something like that in the future."

Elle nodded. "Yeah, she made it cozy. Spacious but warm. Everyone had a seat, no one was crammed, and those sliding doors let all the sound drift outside."

"Even the neighbors came over to join the dancing," George said.

Ethan was quiet but smiling. The night had been perfect, one of those family memories that felt like a warm blanket you'd carry with you for years.

As the car turned down their street, Ethan glanced out at the melting snowbanks, the gray slush at the curbs, and the faint shimmer of a new year stretching ahead. He didn't know what the next few months would bring: football camps, school, maybe even new friendships, but for now, he was grateful.

He was home. Ethan's room was dim and quiet, the curtains slightly drawn to keep the late morning sun from heating the space. Without bothering to unpack his suitcase, he flopped down onto his bed, letting out a satisfied sigh. The warm comforter and stillness of his room invited him into a quick nap, and within minutes, he was fast asleep.

Downstairs, Elle and Uncle George worked together unpacking their luggage and sorting through souvenirs. A few T-shirts, shells from the beach, and a bottle of spicy Bahamian hot sauce made it to the counter before Elle declared, "I'm done for today."

George chuckled. "Same here. Let's leave the rest for tomorrow and catch up on that crime drama we missed."

They collapsed onto the couch, the hum of the television soon blending with their relaxed conversation. The house, full of laughter and chatter only weeks earlier, was now peaceful.

Upstairs, Ethan stirred awake a little after two in the afternoon. He rubbed his eyes, stretched, and padded down the hallway and stairs. The smell of laundry detergent and comfort food from the night before still lingered faintly.

"Hey, Mom," he said, entering the living room.

Elle looked over and smiled. "Hey, sleepyhead."

"Yeah," he nodded. "You two unpack everything?"

"Mostly. You hungry?"

"I'll make something." Ethan walked into the kitchen, pulled out the loaf of bread, some turkey slices, and cheese, and began assembling a sandwich. He grabbed a bag of chips from the cabinet and poured a handful onto his plate.

As he took the first bite, his phone buzzed on the counter. He quickly picked it up and saw Amanda's name flashing on the screen. A smile crept across his face.

"Hey!" he answered, his voice suddenly lighter.

"Hey, Ethan!" Amanda chirped on the other end. "Back from your island life yet?"

He laughed. "Yeah, just got in a couple of days ago. I took a nap and barely unpacked. I missed my bed."

"I bet. I want to hear everything. Did you bring me back anything?"

"I did actually. Got you something from a little outdoor market on the island. I saw it and thought of you."

"Ooooh, now I'm excited," she said. "You know I love surprises."

Ethan chuckled. "Yeah, you'll like this one. It's handmade."

Amanda giggled. "Meanwhile, my family's big holiday adventure was… staying at home."

They both cracked up.

"I'm serious," she said. "We watched movies, played board games, and I think my dad grilled hot dogs one night in the snow."

"That actually sounds nice," Ethan said sincerely. "Sometimes quiet breaks are the best."

Amanda asked, "Have you talked to Chris or Scott yet?"

"Not yet. I just woke up like twenty minutes ago," he said. "But I'm gonna hit them up later."

"Well," Amanda said after a short pause, "if you're not busy later, want to hang out before school starts back Monday?"

Ethan leaned back in his chair, a grin spreading across his face. "Yeah, I'd like that."

Later that afternoon, Ethan rang the doorbell to Amanda's house, a small two-story brick home on a quiet street just a few blocks from his own. Her mom opened the door with a warm smile.

"Hi, Ethan! Come on in. The others are already downstairs."

"Thanks, Mrs. Blackwell," he said politely, stepping inside with a small gift bag in hand.

He made his way down to the finished basement, where soft lighting, a comfy sectional, and the scent of buttery popcorn welcomed him. Amanda was curled up in a blanket on the couch, while Scott and Chris were fighting over who picked the last movie.

"You're late!" Amanda teased.

Ethan grinned. "Island time, remember?"

They laughed as he handed Amanda the small gift bag. "Brought you something."

She gasped dramatically and opened it. "A bracelet! It's beautiful, thank you!" She put it on immediately. "Now I have something to remember your vacation."

"Don't worry, I got you guys too," he said, turning to Scott and Chris and pulling two folded T-shirts out of his hoodie pocket. "One for each of you."

"Yo! Bahama Strong?" Scott said, reading the shirt. "This is dope."

Chris chuckled. "Thanks, little bro. Appreciate it."

They all settled in with snacks: popcorn, chips, soda, and started a movie. Halfway through, conversation took over.

"So," Amanda said, stretching her legs out. "We've only got a few months left of the school year. What's everyone doing this summer?"

"I'm working," Amanda said. "Need to start saving up. I want a car by next year."

"Same," Scott nodded. "My uncle's getting me a job at the rec center. Not glamorous, but it's money."

Chris leaned forward. "I'm working part-time at the dealership with my dad until August. Then I'm out."

"College life," Amanda said with a hint of pride. "You're really doing it."

Chris gave a humble shrug. "Trying."

Amanda turned to Ethan. "What about you?"

"Elite football camps," Ethan said. "Coach Lanning recommended a few, and I'm going with Marcus to a couple. They're supposed to be big."

"That's crazy, bro," Scott said. "Freshman year and you're already being looked at."

Ethan rubbed the back of his neck. "Still a long way to go."

Chris nodded. "Just stay grounded. The attention can mess with your head if you're not careful."

Amanda leaned in. "You're not going to change on us, are you?"

Ethan smirked. "Nah. Same Ethan. Just with a couple more bruises and hopefully a better 40-yard dash."

They all laughed.

The evening faded into more movies, more snacks, and quiet moments of friendship that they didn't yet realize they'd miss once summer hit, and their lives started to go in different directions.

The weekend had passed in a blur of laughter, leftovers, and catching up with friends. After hanging out at Amanda's, Ethan spent Sunday lounging around the house, helping his mother with laundry, and watching a movie with Uncle George. The Bahamas already felt like a dream, tucked between the memories of sea breezes and late-night board games. But now, Monday had arrived, and with it came the return to school, routines, and the countdown to spring break. As Ethan packed his backpack and laced up his sneakers, he knew break was over, but the excitement from winter still lingered like a quiet echo in his heart.

The halls of Gerry High buzzed with energy as students returned from winter break. Backpacks were a little heavier, eyes slightly groggy, but the chatter was lively, filled with tales of family vacations, new clothes, and awkward Christmas dinners. Ethan walked through the front doors, greeted by the scent of floor polish and freshly brewed teacher's lounge coffee.

Study hall was the first class on his schedule, and he was glad for the slow start. He sat down at his usual table, dropping his backpack with a thud, and was soon joined by Amanda, Scott, and Marcus.

"Back to reality," Amanda muttered, unzipping her binder.

"Yeah, but at least it's a short week," Marcus said, flipping through a football magazine. "Friday's a teacher workday."

Ethan leaned back in his chair, glancing around the room. "Everyone's got stories today."

"No kidding," Scott chuckled. "Some kid in gym said he saw a dolphin on his cruise. In December."

Ethan smirked. "I saw a whole reef while snorkeling. So, beat that."

They all laughed quietly, trying not to draw attention from the monitor at the front of the room.

Later that day, the cafeteria was buzzing even more. Kids jostled trays, hugged friends, and slid back into their favorite lunch tables like nothing had changed. Ethan grabbed his tray with chicken nuggets, mashed potatoes, and chocolate milk. He found his spot with Amanda, Scott, Chris, and a few of the junior varsity players.

Across the room, at the staff lunch table near the vending machines, Ethan caught snippets of a conversation between two teachers, Mr. Clarke, the history teacher, and Ms. Vaughn, who taught Spanish.

"The parade was beautiful this year," Ms. Vaughn said. "Even with the snow."

Mr. Clarke nodded, peeling an orange. "The fire department had a whole float this time. Tossed out peppermints and everything."

"They had the little kids from Main Street Academy singing, too. It was freezing, but the crowd stayed. That's small-town pride for you."

Ethan smiled to himself, picturing it all. He hadn't gone; he'd still been in the Bahamas, but he could almost hear the laughter and see the glowing lights on Main Street. He thought of Uncle George, who would've loved the homemade hot chocolate vendors, and Aunt Helen, who probably cheered the loudest when the marching band passed by.

"It's always a good time," Amanda said, breaking into his thoughts. She had followed his gaze. "You missed it, though. The hot cocoa was fire this year."

Ethan shrugged. "Guess I'll catch it next Christmas."

Scott elbowed him. "You'd better be here. Unless you're already off at some college camp in Cali by then."

Ethan grinned. "Only if you're coming with me."

They laughed, the kind of carefree, youthful laughter that echoed off the cafeteria walls and made winter feel a little less cold. One week later, Ethan's phone lit up with a group call from Amanda.

"Hey, guess what?" Amanda said, barely able to hold her excitement. "My mom's taking me to Summit Thrills Amusement Park over spring break, and I asked if I could bring some friends. She said yes!"

Scott and Chris chimed in immediately with questions about the rides, the food, and what days they'd go. Ethan, who had just finished his homework, darted downstairs with his phone in hand.

"Moooom!" he called, finding her folding towels in the laundry room. "Amanda's family is going to Summit Thrills for spring break, and she invited us…Can I go?"

Elle looked up, surprised by the sudden burst of energy. "Slow down, baby. Let me talk to Mrs. Blackwell first, okay? I want to make sure there's proper supervision, hotel details, the whole itinerary."

"Okay," Ethan said, bouncing slightly. "But can you talk to her soon? Everyone else is already asking their parents."

Back upstairs, the group continued planning in their usual chaotic way, Amanda talking fast, Chris cracking jokes, Scott asking about bringing snacks, and Ethan crossing his fingers that the answer would be yes.

Later that night, the scent of lemon dish soap still lingered in the air as Ethan finished drying the last plate and handed it to his mom. She nodded her thanks and set it in the cabinet. He started to head upstairs when he heard her voice drift into the hallway. She was on the phone in the living room, and something in her tone made him pause just outside the doorway.

"Yes, I just wanted to go over the details about the spring break trip," Elle said, her voice warm and polite.

Ethan stayed quiet, pretending to scroll through his phone while his ears tuned in like radar.

"Oh, you're leaving Friday morning?" Elle asked. "Got it. So, school lets out Thursday… and you're staying until Sunday?"

"That's right," came Mrs. Blackwell's voice on speaker. "We've got three rooms booked. One for me and my husband, one for the girls, Amanda, her sister, and two of their close friends, and one for the boys: Ethan, Scott, and Chris. They'll all be supervised, of course."

Ethan's heart jumped a little at the sound of his name.

"My husband's renting a twelve-passenger van," Mrs. Blackwell continued. "It should be comfortable, and we'll stop for food on the way. We're just asking each family to send $100 to help with the room costs. That'll cover his spot. He'll need spending money for park admission, meals, and whatever games or souvenirs he wants."

Elle smiled, glancing up as Ethan finally stepped into the room with wide, hopeful eyes.

"Well," she said, locking eyes with her son, "it sounds like a safe and fun trip. Ethan could use the time to relax and celebrate a great school year with his friends."

Ethan's face lit up as he tried to stay cool, nodding casually like it wasn't the most exciting thing he'd heard all week.

"I'll send the money first thing in the morning," Elle confirmed. "Thank you again for inviting him."

As she hung up the call, Ethan leaned on the edge of the couch. "So… I can go?"

Elle gave him a mock-serious look. "You'd better keep your room clean this week and stay on top of your homework."

He grinned. "Deal!"

"Go on and start thinking about what you'll pack. And make sure your laundry is done by Thursday."

Ethan nodded, already mentally picking out his favorite shirts and gym shoes. His first big weekend trip with friends…this was going to be epic.

Chapter 20
Road to Summit

The energy inside Gerry High School was electric. Students bounced from class to class, their minds already halfway into spring break. Teachers tried to keep order, assigning final worksheets, reminding students of due dates, but the building practically hummed with excitement.

Ethan strolled into his last period of the day, backpack slung low and hoodie half-zipped. Chris and Scott were already seated, grinning ear to ear.

"You packed yet?" Chris asked, nudging Ethan with his elbow.

"Almost," Ethan said with a smirk. "Mom made me clean my room first."

They all laughed.

Down the hall, Amanda waved to them before disappearing into her class, mouthing, "See y'all tomorrow!"

After the final bell rang at 1:45 PM, the school exploded with cheers, slamming lockers, and chatter about travel plans, sleepovers, and family time. Ethan met his mom in the parking lot, buzzing with the kind of joy that only comes when you know adventure is right around the corner.

That night, Ethan triple-checked his bag: hoodies, extra socks, snacks, phone charger, and laid out his favorite outfit for the next day. He drifted off to sleep with a smile, dreaming of roller coasters and arcade tickets.

The next morning, Ethan stood by the living room window, suitcase in hand, dressed in athletic shorts and a Summit Amusement Park T-shirt that Uncle George had surprised him with the night before.

At exactly 9:00 a.m., a white 12-passenger van pulled into the driveway. The side door slid open, revealing Amanda, her sister Kiera, and two of her friends waving wildly. Chris and Scott were seated behind them, already snacking on mixed nuts and chips.

"Bye, Mom! Love you!" Ethan called, giving her a quick hug.

"Be safe, baby!" she said, straightening the strap on his duffel bag. "And listen to the adults."

"Yes, ma'am," Ethan grinned and bounded down the steps.

Mr. Blackwell helped load his bag while Mrs. Blackwell checked off names from her clipboard.

"Alright, that's everyone," she said. "We've got snacks, water, first aid, and backup chargers. Let's hit the road!"

The van rumbled to life, pulling away from the neighborhood with music playing and windows cracked to let in the spring breeze.

Inside, the teens laughed and joked as they shared memes, debated which rides they'd go on first, and dared each other to try the tallest coaster at Summit, The Hurricane Drop.

From the front seat, Mr. Blackwell looked over at his wife and smiled. "You know," he said, "we've got some pretty amazing kids."

Mrs. Blackwell nodded, watching Amanda and Ethan laugh over something Chris had just said. "We really do."

Three hours later, the van pulled up to the grand entrance of Summit Amusement Park, with the sound of screams from nearby coasters echoing in the background and the smell of funnel cake wafting through the air.

"This," Ethan said, stepping out of the van, "is going to be the best weekend ever."

Later that morning, the group stood just inside the gates of Summit Amusement Park, their eyes vast with anticipation. Colorful banners waved overhead, cheerful music pulsed from hidden speakers, and the smell of sizzling onions, sweet funnel cakes, and buttery popcorn filled the air.

"Alright," Mrs. Blackwell said, handing out brightly colored wristbands. "You all stick together. Check in with us every two hours. And Ethan," she added with a smirk, "don't go trying to conquer every ride on your own."

Ethan laughed. "Got it."

As soon as the parents walked off to find a shady bench near the food court, the teens bolted toward the first ride they saw, The Vortex Viper, a towering, green steel coaster that twisted through multiple loops and corkscrews.

"I dare someone to keep their eyes open the whole time!" Scott shouted as they raced up the ramp.

"I double dare you not to scream," Amanda added, nudging Ethan.

"Easy," Ethan grinned.

They climbed into the coaster, locked in, and with a sudden lurch, the Vortex Viper roared to life. Screams echoed in every direction as the train hurtled through the loops, dipped into a tunnel, and emerged into sunlight before slamming on the brakes back at the starting point.

Amanda stumbled off laughing, her hair wild. "Okay, maybe I screamed once."

"Once?" Chris teased. "You sounded like a fire alarm."

Next, they ran toward Iron Fang, a drop coaster known for its nearly vertical first fall.

"This is the one," Ethan said, eyes sparkling.

They braved more coasters, The Cyclone Rush, Sky Climber, and The Inferno Plunge, each one more thrilling than the last. At one point, Scott nearly lost his sunglasses on a twist, and Amanda dropped her hat trying to fix her ponytail mid-ride.

After the rush of adrenaline wore off, they headed to the boardwalk area of the park and spent the next hour playing midway games. Chris won a giant red gorilla from a ring toss, while Ethan spent twenty-five dollars trying to win a football plush from the Spin Shot game.

"This thing is rigged," Ethan muttered, missing again.

"No excuses," Amanda teased, tossing her ball perfectly into the bucket and winning a small stuffed bear. "Some of us just have the gift."

They wandered toward the food court, deciding on a round of pizza slices from Tony's Firebrick Grill, followed by hot dogs from Benny's Cart, and finished it off with funnel cakes drenched in powdered sugar.

"Don't forget ice cream!" Kiera shouted, leading them to Chill Swirling, where Ethan devoured a triple scoop of vanilla with rainbow sprinkles.

By late afternoon, their feet were tired, their voices hoarse from screaming, and their pockets lighter from arcade games, but no one cared.

As they rested on a bench near the wave ride Blue Surge, Ethan leaned back and sighed contentedly. "This is what spring break should feel like."

Scott nodded. "Yeah, good friends, no homework, and stomachs full of junk food."

"Best day ever," Amanda agreed, biting into her second funnel cake.

They still had the whole weekend ahead of them.

That night, as the sun dipped below the tree line, Summit Amusement Park transformed. Twinkling lights illuminated the paths, casting a soft glow on the evening crowd. The group gathered near the central fountain, just in time for the fireworks show.

A hush fell over the park as the first firework exploded overhead in brilliant gold. Moments later, bursts of crimson, blue, and green followed dancing across the night sky in perfect rhythm to the music playing through the loudspeakers.

Ethan stood between Amanda and Chris, his face lifted in awe. "Man, they really went all out," he said.

Amanda nodded. "It's perfect."

As the grand finale lit up the sky with thunderous color and crackling light, the teens clapped and cheered along with the crowd, hearts still racing from the day's excitement.

After the show, they made their way to the hotel, a cozy mid-range place called The Horizon Inn, just ten minutes from the park.

Mr. Blackwell checked them in while the rest of the group lounged in the lobby, still buzzing from the day.

Once upstairs, Ethan tossed his bag on one of the beds in the boys' suite, his legs sore and his voice almost gone.

"I don't know about y'all, but I'm done," Scott mumbled, flopping onto the other bed.

Chris nodded, already kicking off his shoes. "Same. That last coaster nearly took me out."

They barely managed to brush their teeth and change before collapsing under the covers. From across the room, Ethan muttered, "Good day."

The room was silent within minutes.

The next morning, sunlight filtered through the curtains as the new day began. In a few short hours, they'd be slipping down giant water slides, floating on lazy rivers, and splashing their way through Summit Splash Island, the connected water park next door. The smell of sunscreen, chlorine, and sizzling food carts filled the air as the group walked through the colorful archway of Summit Splash Island. Giant palm tree statues lined the entrance, misting cool water over passing guests. Music pulsed through hidden speakers, and the splash of water echoed everywhere.

"Alright," Mr. Blackwell called out, raising his voice above the noise, "we meet back at the cabana at 1:00 for lunch. Stay in groups. Stay safe!"

"Yes, sir!" the teens shouted back in unison, then broke out in laughter and excitement.

Ethan, Chris, Scott, and Amanda led the charge toward a towering blue-and-green slide structure called The Vortex Drop, a multi-story thrill ride that twisted like a corkscrew before sending riders into a pool with a massive splash.

"This is it!" Ethan grinned, handing his towel to Amanda. "First ride of the day."

He climbed the winding stairs with Scott right behind him, both of them shouting "Let's go!" to pump themselves up. From the top, the whole park stretched out below them: wave pools, lazy rivers, mini slides, and a giant bucket overhead that tipped every few minutes, drenching everyone beneath it.

When it was his turn, Ethan sat back, crossed his arms, and launched down the chute. The force pushed him through loops, walls of rushing water, and then…whoosh! He shot out of the bottom into the pool, sending up a massive wave.

Scott popped up seconds later, laughing hysterically. "I thought I lost my trunks, man!"

They high-fived before running off to the next attraction, Rip Curly Canyon, a four-person raft ride with twists and sudden drops through pitch-black tunnels and unexpected waterfalls. Amanda and Chris joined them, piling into the inflatable raft and screaming the entire way through. At one turn, Amanda's laughter turned into a surprised shriek as cold water poured down from above.

"Why didn't anyone warn me?" she laughed, wiping her face.

"That's the best part!" Ethan said, grinning.

Later, they floated lazily through Lagoon Loop, the park's winding river attraction. They linked their inner tubes together, letting the current pull them under bridges, past waterfalls, and through gentle sprays.

"This is the life," Chris sighed, arms behind his head. "No school. No pressure. Just water and sun."

Ethan nodded, letting his fingers trail in the cool water. "Yeah… It's perfect."

After a few rounds around the loop, they dried off and headed to Tidal Reef, a massive wave pool that mimicked the rhythm of the ocean. The waves started small, then built into rolling crests. Ethan and Scott tried body surfing while Amanda stood in waist-high water, dodging the splashes and cheering them on.

Around 12:45, they made their way to the cabana for lunch, sunburnt, soaked, and smiling. Mrs. Blackwell had lunch ready: burgers, fruit cups, and frozen lemonades.

As they ate, Ethan glanced around the park, families laughing, kids running with water guns, lifeguards whistling from towers, and something settled in his heart. Pure joy. A moment of youth and peace. A time before things would get more complicated.

They still had one more night at the hotel, but for now, Summit Splash Island had given them something better than thrills.

It gave them memories. That evening, after long showers and short naps, the group met in the hotel lobby dressed in their nicest outfits. The marble floors reflected the glow from elegant chandeliers above, and a soft melody from a live pianist echoed from the far end of the dining room. Mr. Blackwell adjusted his collar, chuckling at the group of teenagers attempting to look grown-up in collared shirts, loafers, and dresses.

"Y'all clean up nice," he teased, patting Ethan on the back.

Ethan smirked. "Don't get used to it."

They walked together into The Coral Bay Room, a reserved banquet space inside the hotel that overlooked the ocean. Floor-to-ceiling windows displayed the last golden rays of sunset as waves rolled calmly beyond the terrace.

Servers in white jackets escorted the group to two long tables, already set with menus printed in gold script. Amanda's eyes widened as she sat beside Ethan. "This place is beautiful."

"It looks expensive," Scott whispered, eyeing the silverware.

Mr. Blackwell chuckled from the head of the table. "Just enjoy it, kids. You earned it."

The menu was filled with options none of them had ever tried before: grilled swordfish with pineapple glaze, stuffed lobster tail, herb-roasted chicken, and filet mignon with garlic butter. Ethan chose the filet, while Amanda opted for the lobster tail. They sipped sparkling lemonade from champagne glasses and laughed like grown-ups.

As the food arrived, their laughter quieted to awe.

"This is the best steak I've ever had," Ethan mumbled between bites.

"You've only had, like, two steaks in your life," Chris shot back, grinning.

Mrs. Blackwell stood to toast. "I just want to say how proud I am of all of you, Amanda, Kiera, and all of your friends. You were respectful, responsible, and a joy to travel with. Thank you for making this trip fun for us, too."

They all raised their glasses of lemonade and clinked them gently across the table.

"To spring break," Amanda smiled.

"To memories," Ethan added.

Later, they took photos on the terrace as the stars blinked above the water. Amanda pulled out her phone for selfies, while Scott tried to photobomb each one. Chris stood with Mr. Blackwell, deep in a debate about which roller coaster was scarier.

When they finally returned to their rooms, bellies full and spirits high, the teens fell into their beds with tired smiles. It had been more than just a getaway. It had been unforgettable.

Tomorrow, they would head home.

But tonight… tonight was golden. Sunday morning, the sun peeked through the hotel curtains, casting a soft amber hue across the carpet as alarms buzzed throughout the rooms. By 8:00 a.m., sleepy teenagers were rolling suitcases into the hallway, rubbing their eyes, and yawning mid-sentence. Ethan tossed his backpack over his shoulder and met Amanda, Chris, and Scott at the elevator.

"You guys ready for three hours of pure excitement?" Scott said with mock energy, his hair still tousled from sleep.

"Only if that excitement includes sleeping," Chris replied, slouching against the wall.

Once everyone gathered in the hotel lobby, Mr. Blackwell did a quick headcount. "Seven teenagers, two adults. We're good."

They piled back into the 12-passenger van, backpacks stuffed between seats, souvenir bags tucked at their feet. As soon as the engine hummed to life and the wheels pulled away from the hotel curb, the teens came alive.

Scott immediately fired up a playlist on his phone. "Let's make this van ride legendary!"

Songs from all decades filled the van as voices rose in off-key harmony. Amanda belted out the lyrics while snapping pictures of everyone mid-laugh. Ethan chimed in for the choruses, his voice cracking with exhaustion but joyfully unbothered.

There were jokes about roller coaster screams, water park wipeouts, and who had the worst sunburn. Chris had clearly lost that competition. Mrs. Blackwell passed back granola bars and juice boxes like a mom on a mission, smiling as the van rocked with teenage energy.

Halfway through the ride, the music faded, and a peaceful stillness settled over the group. Heads leaned against windows, conversations softened, and one by one, the teens drifted to sleep. Ethan rested his head back, watching the clouds move lazily outside. His heart was whole. The memories, the laughter, the friendships, he knew this trip would live in his mind forever.

By the time the van rolled into their neighborhood three hours later, voices were slowly waking back up. Hair was messy, voices raspy, but the mood remained light.

Ethan smiled as they passed familiar landmarks. Home.

When his mother opened the van door, Ethan stepped out with a quiet "thank you" to the Blackwells and a sleepy smile on his face.

"I'll never forget this," he whispered to Amanda before they waved goodbye.

And just like that, spring break came to a close not with a bang, but with laughter, full hearts, and the glow of friendship that didn't fade with the sunset.

Chapter 21
Shifting Gears

Later that Sunday afternoon, sunlight streamed gently through Ethan's window, casting warm rays across his neatly made bed. His suitcase sat unzipped at the foot, half-unpacked, a reminder of the whirlwind weekend at Summit Amusement and Splash Island. He sat cross-legged on the carpet, pulling souvenirs from the side pockets: his winning token from the "Dragon Wing" ride, a Summit Splash Island towel, and a silly photo booth strip of him, Chris, Scott, and Amanda making goofy faces.

Downstairs, the house was quiet. Elle was folding laundry while Uncle George watched a vintage-car documentary at low volume. The peace was refreshing after two days of roller coasters, water slides, neon lights, and teenage energy.

Ethan grabbed his journal, leaned back on his bed, and began to write:

Spring break was crazy fun. We laughed so much it hurt. Amanda screamed like a baby on The Sidewinder. I'll never forget that. The water park was next level. I'm grateful for friends like them. I'm blessed even to get the chance to go. Time to finish the school year strong. Bigger things are coming… I can feel it.

He paused for a moment and added:

"God, help me stay focused. I don't want to lose sight of what matters."

By evening, the house smelled like lemon-pepper chicken and roasted potatoes. They ate dinner as a family, and Ethan shared stories from the weekend, especially how Mr. Blackwell almost dropped his sunglasses in the wave pool and blamed it on Scott.

Laughter filled the room.

Elle smiled, leaning back in her chair. "Sounds like a great break, baby. I'm proud of you for having fun but being responsible too."

Uncle George nodded. "Yeah, and I heard Amanda's dad say you looked out for your friends, too. That's character, Ethan."

Ethan smiled. "Thanks, Uncle G. I was just trying to make sure everybody had fun." The Monday after returning from Summit Amusement Park, Ethan woke up later than usual, stretching under the weight of soft sunlight and the leftover thrill of the weekend still buzzing in his chest. The house was quiet, still wrapped in that mid-spring calm, and the scent of cinnamon toast drifted up from the kitchen. It felt good to be home.

That afternoon, Scott and Chris came over with a backpack full of snacks and a brand-new multiplayer video game they were eager to test. The three boys posted up in the living room, controllers in hand, laughter echoing through the walls as they yelled over scores and missions. Uncle George popped in once or twice, shaking her head with a smile and dropping off a tray of pepperoni pizza rolls and lemonade.

Amanda came by a few hours later. The four of them sat outside on the porch, bundled in hoodies, sharing stories and music. Amanda brought over a shoebox filled with friendship bracelets she had started making. She tossed one to Ethan; it was blue and gold with a white stripe in the middle.

"Those are team colors, right?" she said with a grin.

"Gerry Hawks forever," Ethan replied, tying it loosely around his wrist.

Later that evening, they walked to the corner ice cream shack, Breezy Scoops, a tiny family-run place that opened early every spring. Ethan got cookies and cream, Amanda ordered mint chocolate chip, and Scott and Chris argued about which flavor was superior. They sat on the curb, swinging their legs and watching the sky shift to lavender.

Wednesday rolled in with a surprise knock at the door. Uncle George had picked up movie tickets for the early afternoon showing of Love Only Me. Ethan, Scott, and Amanda loaded into the sedan and spent the next two hours with popcorn fingers and wide eyes, totally immersed in the cinematic world of Love Only Me.

"Love Only Me" is a heartwarming story that follows the Carter family as they navigate the joys and challenges of life. The narrative begins with the birth of Mya Rose Carter, the long-awaited daughter of Jenna and Noah Carter, and the youngest sibling to Theo, Levi, and Owen. As Mya grows, her natural talent for singing becomes evident, leading her to perform at church and eventually enroll in the Gregory Performing Arts Center. Throughout the story, Mya faces jealousy and adversity, particularly from a fellow student named Brittany, yet remains resilient with the support of her loving family and unwavering faith.

The cinematography was soul-stirring. The dialogue was raw. By the time the credits rolled, the theater was dead silent.

Ethan sat in his seat, unusually quiet, the popcorn bowl still half full in his lap.

"That ending though," Chris muttered. "I didn't see that coming."

"Me neither," Amanda whispered. "It felt... real."

Scott nodded slowly. "That one's gonna stay with me for a while."

On the ride home, the car buzzed with debate about what each scene meant. Ethan didn't say much, but one line from the movie echoed in his mind:

"You can keep running, but eventually... you'll reach your last chance to do something great."

Thursday was chill. Ethan stayed home, cleaned his room per mom's request, and helped Uncle George reorganize the garage. Later that night, Amanda hosted a "game night" at her house. They played chess, charades, and even a few rounds of karaoke using a phone and a wireless mic her dad bought years ago. Ethan got teased relentlessly for his off-key version of a made-up love song called "Heart on the 50-Yard Line."

"I should've recorded that," Amanda giggled, wiping tears of laughter from her cheeks.

"No, you shouldn't have," Ethan said, half-embarrassed but secretly pleased with the moment.

By Friday morning, spring break was winding down. Ethan sat at the kitchen table with a bowl of cereal and a notepad beside him, jotting down a few goals. Work out. Stretch. Watch a film. Read at least one chapter from Coach Lanning's recommended book. He didn't want to waste the momentum from the season or the camps ahead.

Saturday brought one last hangout. They all met at Timber Park, where kids played tag near the playground, and older folks barbecued under the pavilion. Ethan and his friends tossed a football around, lounged under trees, and talked about the upcoming schoolwork, summer jobs, and, of course, college dreams.

Chris was still quarterbacking plans for his last few months before college.

Amanda was thinking of applying for a job at Breezy Scoops.

Scott talked about shadowing his cousin, who worked in landscaping.

And Ethan?

"Elite camps," he said, tossing the ball in the air. "And hopefully, more doors opening."

That night, Ethan lay out his clothes for Monday, checked his backpack, and set his alarm. Sunday came and went peacefully, filled with church, a late brunch, and some light yardwork. By the time the sun dipped behind the trees, he was ready for the final stretch of his first year.

The alarm buzzed at 6:15 a.m., and Ethan rolled over, surprisingly energized. Spring air filtered through his open window, fresh and cool. He dressed quickly, grabbed his backpack, and joined Elle and Uncle George for breakfast. A plate of scrambled eggs and toast waited for him.

"You ready to finish strong?" Elle asked.

"Yes, ma'am," Ethan replied with a grin. "Let's get it."

By the time he reached school, the hallways were buzzing with students trading stories about their spring break. Some went to cabins, others stayed local, and a few hit the beaches.

In the study hall, Chris slapped Ethan's shoulder. "Back to reality, huh?"

"Unfortunately," said Ethan as they moved to the study hall.

Study hall moved at a snail's pace, with students half-focused on their worksheets and half-lost in conversations about spring break. Ethan tapped his pencil against the desk while Amanda recapped her family's last-minute cookout. Chris leaned back in his chair, arms crossed behind his head, and Scott scrolled through photos from the amusement park. The room buzzed with the soft rustle of papers and quiet laughter. As the bell rang, they all stood and grabbed their bags. They were still talking about their trip. Ethan chuckled. "Barely. I still got sand in my shoes."

"From Splash Island?" Amanda asked, raising a brow.

"Yeah, and that fake beach near the wave pool? Still in my socks."

They walked out together, blending into the current of students heading toward the cafeteria. The smell of pizza and tater tots floated in the air, and the noise grew louder as doors swung open and lunch hour officially began. When lunch was over, the hallways buzzed with renewed energy as students filed back into classes for the remainder of the day. The final bell rang, echoing through the hallways like a sigh of relief. Backpacks zipped, lockers slammed shut, and a wave of students spilled out onto the school's front steps. Ethan walked alongside Amanda, Chris, and Scott, the sun casting long shadows on the pavement as they talked about how weird it felt to be back. His mind drifted briefly to the rides, the beach, and the laughter from the week before, but now it was time to focus again. As his mom's car pulled up, he waved goodbye to his friends and slid into the passenger seat, letting the rhythm of routine settle back in. It was only Monday, but he could already feel the countdown to summer beginning in the air.

First year had flown by, and now the final weeks of April were packed with projects, final spring sport practices, and year-end review packets.

By the second week of May, bulletin boards had shifted from spring themes to summer countdowns. Teachers reminded students of finals and make-up assignments. College banners lined the hallways for the seniors, and whispers about graduation hung in the air like pollen.

Ethan kept his head in the game both on the field during spring workouts and in the classroom. Football camp dates had been confirmed, and he was already thinking about drills and conditioning. But for now, school wasn't over yet.

Lunchroom conversations shifted from weekend plans to what everyone was doing this summer. Amanda talked about her new part-time job at a smoothie shop. Chris mentioned shadowing his uncle at an auto shop before college. Ethan stayed focused; he was determined to finish the year with solid grades and make the most of every opportunity ahead.

The morning announcements were filled with reminders: end-of-year band concerts, art showcases, field day sign-ups, and final exam schedules. Everyone could feel it; summer was almost here. At home, Elle was already ahead of the game. She sat at the kitchen table surrounded by hotel brochures, camp schedules, and a color-coded calendar that mapped out Ethan's entire summer. "You're going to six camps," she told him, flipping her planner toward him. "No excuses. No slacking. One week on, one week off. Marcus' mom and I already talked. We'll take tag-team rides. Uncle George is booking the hotels tonight."

Uncle George, hunched over his laptop, nodded. "We're set for the first one near Lexington. Got a good deal on a two-night stay. You boys better be ready to impress."

Ethan glanced between them, overwhelmed and a little excited. His summer was already spoken for: drills, film, sweat, and a shot at something bigger. Elle smiled knowingly as she packed up the last of the school-year clutter. "This is it," she said softly. "No more echoing potential. Let's show them who you really are."

The next morning, the sun filtered through Ethan's window as his alarm buzzed softly, nudging him awake for one final time. "Today was the last day of school," shouted Ethan from his bedroom. When he arrived at school, the hallways buzzed with energy that felt different from any other day, lighter, louder, full of anticipation. Students shuffled between classes with yearbooks in hand, stopping to scribble quick notes and inside jokes before the final bell. Teachers wore relaxed smiles, some showing movies, others letting students talk freely as long as they cleaned out their desks. In the study hall, Ethan leaned back in his chair, soaking it all in: the laughter, the whispered summer plans, the last-minute attempts to trade snacks and stories. The countdown to freedom echoed in every classroom. By lunchtime, the cafeteria felt more like a celebration than a meal. Music played from someone's speaker, and the usual lines were replaced with groups posing for pictures and exchanging hugs.

The final bell of the school year rang with a tone that echoed longer than usual, or at least it felt that way. It wasn't just a signal to pack up and leave, but a soft chime that marked the end of an era, the close of Ethan's first year of high school. He stood by his locker for a moment, hand on the door, just taking it in. The noise in the hallway had a different energy today, more laughter, tighter hugs, heartfelt goodbyes. A few seniors walked past in their caps and gowns for rehearsal, reminding everyone how quickly time could fly.

Chris bumped him on the shoulder. "I survived, man. Senior year…done. You're next."

Ethan smiled. "Feels like we just got here."

Amanda and Scott joined them, arms full of yearbooks and last-minute papers. Amanda had scribbled 'HAGS' Have A Great Summer, on nearly every page of her yearbook, while Scott was still chasing their biology teacher down for a final signature. They took one last walk through the hallways together, passing familiar classrooms, open lockers, and teachers who offered waves and well-wishes.

When they stepped outside, the sun greeted them like an old friend. Students filled the front lawn, tossing backpacks into cars and taking group selfies. Ethan spotted Mrs. Farley, his English teacher, standing near the flagpole with a tissue in her hand. She had taught seniors, and the weight of their departure showed in her eyes.

"Promise me you'll keep writing," she called out to Ethan as he passed.

He nodded. "I will."

At the edge of the parking lot, Elle stood leaning against her car, sunglasses on, her smile steady. Uncle George was in the passenger seat, waving them over.

"You made it," she said as Ethan slid into the back seat.

"Yeah," he breathed, glancing back at the school building. "I really did."

As they pulled away, Ethan rolled down his window and let the warm air rush in. The school building shrank behind him, but something inside him expanded purpose, anticipation, maybe even hope.

He didn't know exactly what the summer would hold, but he knew it wouldn't be ordinary. The last bell had rung. And now, he was ready to chase the next echo.

Chapter 22
The Road Ahead

The sun beamed through the car windows as Ethan leaned his head back, letting the wind from the cracked window brush across his face. The weight of finals, early mornings, and crowded hallways lifted with each mile closer to home. His backpack sat at his feet, lighter than ever, not just because it was nearly empty, but because the first year was officially behind him.

His mother's car rolled into its usual spot in the driveway. Ethan was all smiles as he swung the passenger door open and jumped out. Moments later, his mother followed him inside, carrying a tall glass of lemonade.

"Welcome to summer," she said, handing it to him.

Ethan grinned. "Feels like freedom.

But rest wouldn't last long.

Elle pulled a printed itinerary from a kitchen drawer and slid it across the table. Enjoy the weekend. Because Monday, your summer officially begins," said Uncle George.

Ethan looked down. Six camps. Six different cities. The first one was just three hours away, and Marcus was already texting him about hotel check-ins and the elite coaches rumored to attend.

"Think you're ready?" Uncle George asked from the living room.

Ethan didn't hesitate. "Born ready."

That night, as fireflies blinked outside the window and the neighborhood settled into a quiet hush, Ethan lay in bed thinking about what lay ahead. This summer wasn't just about football. It was about proving something to himself, to the coaches, to anyone who had ever doubted what a kid from a small town could do.

He turned off the lamp, letting the darkness wrap around him like a challenge.

The road ahead was waiting. And Ethan was ready to run it. The alarm buzzed at 5:30 a.m., breaking through the silence with urgency. Ethan slapped it off and sat up, rubbing his eyes. Sunlight hadn't even touched the sky yet, but he could already feel the energy in his chest. Today wasn't just the start of summer break; it was the beginning of a journey that might shape his future.

Downstairs, the scent of cinnamon toast and scrambled eggs greeted him. His mom stood by the stove, flipping the last of the eggs while Uncle George filled two travel mugs with coffee.

"Got everything?" Elle asked, placing a small baggie of snacks into Ethan's duffel.

"Cleats, gloves, towel, extra socks," Ethan ticked off on his fingers, pulling on a hoodie. "Yeah, I'm good."

By 6:15, they were on the road. Marcus and his dad were already waiting at the gas station off Route 17, their SUV loaded up. Marcus hopped out as they pulled in, dapping Ethan up with excitement in his voice.

"First camp of the summer! You ready?" Marcus asked.

"I was born ready," Ethan grinned, throwing his bag into Uncle George's trunk. "Let's eat."

The drive to the camp location, Desktop University, was quiet at first, but eventually filled with football talk, camp rumors, and playlists full of hype songs. Marcus was eager to show off his arm. Ethan was anxious to see how he'd measure up against some of the best in the region.

As they pulled into the campus, the field complex stretched out in all directions. Tents were set up for registration. Kids were everywhere, some were already running warm-ups, others posing for photos in their team gear.

Ethan stepped out and took it all in.

This wasn't high school. This was elite.

The boys signed in, grabbed their numbered jerseys, and made their way to the turf fields. Coaches in polos and sunglasses barked out drills, ran stopwatch timers, and sized up talent from the sidelines. Ethan and Marcus were assigned to Field 3.

By noon, sweat clung to Ethan's shirt, and his arms burned from drill after drill. He wasn't the biggest player on the field, but he was fast. Agile. Focused. Every tackle, every block, every pass rush was a chance to show what he had.

During a water break, a coach from one of the state's top schools pulled Ethan aside.

"You play both ways?" the coach asked.

"Yes, sir. Tight end and defensive end."

The coach nodded, jotting something in his clipboard. "Keep that intensity. I'll be watching."

Ethan swallowed his water and smiled.

It was only day one, and someone was already taking notes. By the end of the first day, Ethan's legs ached, and his cleats felt like bricks. But he didn't complain. Uncle George gave him a fist bump as they left the field.

"You held your own out there," he said. "Real proud of you, kid."

Ethan nodded, breathing heavily as he dropped into the passenger seat. "Thanks, Unc. I'm trying to leave a mark."

Back at the hotel, he and Marcus reviewed clips they recorded on their phones, pointing out good plays and mistakes.

"You blew past that linebacker like he was stuck in sand," Marcus said, rewinding one video.

"Yeah, but I missed the seal block right after," Ethan admitted.

"You'll get it tomorrow."

The next morning, they were up early again. The camp opened with film breakdowns of proper footwork, stance discipline, and how to read offenses. Ethan soaked it all in. He wasn't just relying on raw talent anymore. He wanted to be brighter, sharper, faster.

By Wednesday, things started to click.

Ethan's name was getting called out more in the drills.

"Good containment, Phillips!"

"Way to explode off the edge!"

He chased down running backs, broke through blocks, and even swatted a pass during a scrimmage. His confidence grew, but his humility stayed grounded. Every night before bed, he'd quietly thank God, praying the exact words:

"Let my work speak louder than my mouth. Let me give you the glory in everything."

Thursday brought the one-on-one challenge drills.

Linemen versus linemen. Receivers versus corners. Tight ends versus linebackers.

Ethan lined up across from a thick, 6'2" linebacker from the city. The coach blew the whistle.

Bam.

Ethan lowered his shoulders and executed a perfect inside swim move, spinning around the linebacker and catching the pass over the middle.

"Again!" the coach called.

They reset.

This time, Ethan faked the same move, then cut the opposite way and left the defender reaching for air.

"Nice footwork, 43," the coach barked, checking his roster list. "Ethan Phillips, right?"

"Yes, sir."

The coach smiled slightly. "We'll be in touch."

By Friday morning, the energy on the field shifted. College scouts showed up with notebooks, cameras, and shaded eyes. Players stood taller. Every rep meant something.

During a scrimmage, Ethan recovered a fumble and ran it back for a touchdown. His teammates mobbed him, slapping his helmet.

After the game, one of the assistant coaches approached Ethan and Marcus.

"You two work well together," he said. "Keep that bond. You both got something special."

That evening, the camp ended with a small awards ceremony. Players received participation medals, and a few stood out enough to earn MVP nods.

Ethan didn't win MVP, but he didn't need to.

He walked away with something better.

A mention from two college coaches.

And a deeper hunger to keep going. On Saturday afternoon, it brought a much-needed breather.

The sun was high, the grill was smoking, and laughter danced across the backyard as Ethan, Marcus, Elle, and Uncle George relaxed on the patio. Uncle George was wearing his signature apron… "Grill Sergeant" flipping burgers and ribs while singing off-key to old soul music blaring from the speaker.

"Y'all don't know nothin' about this!" he shouted, shimmying his shoulders as smoke rose from the grill.

Marcus laughed, kicking his feet up on the cooler. "Unc, you're gonna scare the neighbors with those moves!"

"I'm just seasoning the air with joy," Uncle George said proudly.

Elle sat nearby, sipping sweet tea and watching the boys with pride in her eyes. "You two earned this weekend. That first camp was no joke."

Ethan nodded, stretching out on the grass with a paper plate in his lap. "I didn't think I'd be this tired."

"You looked great out there," Marcus said. "Especially during the one-on-ones. That move you pulled, I still don't know how you didn't trip."

"It was all God," Ethan said, not joking at all.

Elle smiled at that. "I'm glad to hear that, son. Keep giving Him the credit, no matter how high you climb."

After dinner, the group moved to the front porch. Fireflies began to glow in the yard, and the air grew cooler.

"So, where's the next camp again?" Marcus asked, licking barbecue sauce off his thumb.

"Briarstone," Ethan answered. "Unc said it's about four hours from here. Smaller school, but solid coaching staff. He thinks it'll help us develop more technique."

Uncle George nodded. "That one's more technical. Less flash, more grind."

"You ready?" Elle asked, glancing at Ethan.

He took a breath and looked up at the darkening sky. "I think so. I'm not chasing stars…I'm just trying to be better than I was yesterday."

Uncle George let out a proud grunt. "That's what I like to hear."

Later that night, as the stars blinked awake overhead, the four sat around a small fire pit roasting marshmallows. Stories were shared, jokes exchanged, and for a moment, time slowed.

It was just a summer evening.

But for Ethan, it felt like a chapter one worth remembering before life picked up speed again. The early morning sun stretched across the sky as Uncle George's truck rolled through the winding roads of West Virginia. Pine trees lined both sides of the two-lane highway leading toward Briarstone University, a small private college tucked away in a sleepy town known more for its football tradition than its population. Ethan stared out the window, earbuds in, mentally preparing for the second leg of his summer journey.

"Briarstone ain't like Oak Pines," Uncle George said, breaking the silence. "They're tougher on technique here. Old-school coaches, some of them played pro back in the day."

Ethan nodded. "I'm ready. Coach said they focus a lot on the mental part, too, like reading the line and learning how to adjust on the fly."

Uncle George glanced over with a proud smile. "That's the next level right there."

When they pulled up to the dorm-style lodging assigned to campers, Ethan spotted a long banner stretched across the practice field: Briarstone University Summer Gridiron Camp: Respect the

Craft. Marcus had already arrived and was sitting on the dorm steps, tossing a football into the air.

"Man, you're late," Marcus called out. "I've already scoped out the lunch menu."

They bumped fists, and Ethan grabbed his duffel from the backseat. Uncle George lingered for a moment, then said, "Y'all make us proud. And don't forget to stretch this time."

Inside the dorms, the setup was basic: two beds, two desks, and a bathroom they shared with the room next door. But Ethan didn't care. This was about grinding, proving himself, and learning something new every day.

The first practice opened with a bang.

Coach Redding, a wiry man with a booming voice and a stopwatch always hanging from his neck, gathered everyone on the field. "This camp ain't about just showing off your speed. This is where football IQ meets grit. You show me who can think and move."

They jumped straight into three-point stance drills, line recognition, and release timing. Unlike Oak Pines, the coaches here pushed more film analysis between sessions. In the evenings, the players studied real college footage in breakout rooms, breaking down route trees and defensive shifts.

Ethan thrived.

During a scrimmage, he read the linebacker's shift and altered his route mid-play, catching a bullet pass and splitting two defenders for a touchdown.

Coach Redding clapped hard from the sideline. "That's how you read and react! Number 87, what's your name again?"

"Ethan Phillips," he said, catching his breath.

"You've got good instincts, son. Keep your head in the game."

Later that night, Ethan called home from the hallway phone, his voice buzzing with excitement.

"We're running college-level plays out here, Ma," he said. "It's crazy. I think I impressed one of the coaches today."

Elle laughed softly through the phone. "I'm proud of you, baby. Stay humble and stay prayed up. That's what matters most."

"I am. I promise."

As the week went on, Briarstone's challenges intensified: early wake-ups, mental exhaustion, and pressure to perform in front of visiting scouts. Ethan had one rough day where he missed a key block during a red-zone drill and got chewed out in front of everyone.

But Marcus clapped him on the back afterward. "Shake it off. Even pros mess up. Tomorrow's a reset."

By Friday, Ethan rebounded with one of his best performances. He played both sides of the ball for a full scrimmage, grabbing an interception and recording a sack, then rotating to offense and catching two passes over the middle.

Coach Redding pulled him aside afterward. "You're coachable, you've got the heart, and I like the way you carry yourself. Don't lose that."

That night, as he packed up his gear, Ethan scribbled something in his notebook:

"Respect the craft. Give God the glory. Stay focused. Stay hungry."

Chapter 23
Between the Whistles

Two camps down. Four more to go.

And with each one, Ethan felt himself inching closer to something bigger, something that demanded more than talent. It required faith, discipline, and a heart that could withstand both praise and pressure.

By Friday afternoon, the final scrimmage at Briarstone University Football Prospect Camp had come to a close. Ethan stood on the edge of the practice field, sweat glistening on his forehead beneath the summer sun. The past five days had pushed him harder than ever, with grueling two-a-days, drills against some of the fastest players he'd ever faced, and intense film sessions that stretched late into the evenings.

Coach Parnell, the defensive coordinator at Briarstone, approached him as players began packing up their gear.

"You've got quick instincts, Phillips," he said, clapping Ethan on the shoulder. "You don't just react, you calculate. That's rare in a rising sophomore."

Ethan thanked him, trying to keep his grin from stretching too wide. He glanced at Marcus, who stood nearby grinning and mouthing, "Big time, baby!"

Later that evening, at the farewell dinner in the campus dining hall, the camp directors handed out informal awards. Ethan earned recognition for "Most Explosive Defensive Playmaker," while Marcus got "Leadership in the Huddle." They high-fived like little kids and stuffed themselves with BBQ chicken, mac and cheese, and sweet tea.

On the drive home, Ethan dozed off in the passenger seat. Uncle George was behind the wheel, Marcus in the backseat, humming along to some R&B soul music.

"Two down, four to go," Uncle George whispered with a chuckle, watching Ethan sleep. "This boy's growing."

Saturday morning at home felt like a gift. Ethan slept in until nearly ten, his muscles grateful for the rest. The house smelled like pancakes and sausage, Elle's signature Saturday breakfast. He joined her and Uncle George at the table, groggy but smiling.

"Next week's Langston Hills Camp," Elle said, passing him syrup. "We're leaving Tuesday morning. Got the hotel booked. Marcus's parents are staying next door to us again."

Ethan nodded, already thinking about what gear he'd need. "I'm ready."

"Well," Uncle George said, grabbing his keys, "I'm headed to Parkway Market. We're out of lemonade and water bottles, and I think y'all drank all the root beer last night."

"Want me to come?" Ethan offered.

"Nah, stay and relax. Be back in a few."

Uncle George had just passed through an intersection on Easton Avenue when a delivery van ran the light. George had just turned on the radio when he felt the impact of a truck that struck the driver's side of his car hard enough to send it skidding into a light pole. Airbags deployed, glass shattered, and for a moment, just a moment, everything was still.

When Uncle George opened his eyes, pain seared through his left leg. He couldn't move it. But he was conscious, breathing, and could see flashing red and blue lights already pulling up behind the wreck. The wail of sirens pierced the summer air as paramedics rushed toward the wreckage. Smoke curled from the crumpled hood of Uncle George's sedan, now lodged against a leaning streetlight. Shards of glass glittered like fallen stars across the pavement. The pain was sharp like fire pulsing from the bone.

One of the paramedics, a young man named Devon, crouched at the driver's side door. "Sir, can you hear me?"

Uncle George nodded, wincing. "Leg's... busted. I think."

"We've got you," Devon assured him. Another paramedic opened the passenger door and carefully unbuckled the seatbelt. "On three, we're going to lift you onto the stretcher. Try not to move your leg."

Traffic had backed up for nearly a block. Onlookers stood frozen on the sidewalks, watching as the medics braced Uncle George's neck, carefully pulled him from the car, and lowered him onto a stretcher.

"Vitals are good. Blood pressure's a little high—probably from the pain," Devon noted as they loaded him into the back of the ambulance.

Uncle George gritted his teeth, trying to stay alert. "Call... call my sister, Elle Phillips. Tell her I'm okay."

"We'll have the hospital reach out as soon as we get there," Devon promised, sliding into the back with him. The other medic shut the doors and gave the driver the signal.

As the ambulance pulled into traffic, Uncle George glanced out the window. The city blurred past. His mind spun with a mix of relief and confusion…he was alive. He could've been gone.

He closed his eyes for a moment and whispered, "Thank You, Lord."

The paramedic rechecked his pulse. "You're lucky. That was a pretty nasty hit."

Uncle George tried to smile, but couldn't because of the pain. The ambulance doors swung open the moment they backed into the bay at Gerry General. Nurses and ER staff moved swiftly as the paramedics rolled Uncle George inside.

"Fifty-seven-year-old male, motor vehicle collision. Broken left tibia, minor abrasions on the forearms and temple. Alert and responsive," Devon recited as they wheeled him in.

The fluorescent lights overhead buzzed faintly as they rushed him into Trauma Room 3. Uncle George grimaced as the gurney jolted slightly to a stop.

"You're safe now, sir," the nurse said gently. "We're going to get X-rays and start some pain medication."

Uncle George gave a weary smile. "Appreciate it. Tell Elle, my sister, that I'm alright. She'll be worried."

Within the hour, he was cleaned up, X-rayed, and his leg had been immobilized with a temporary cast and elevated on a support pillow. Scratches on his face and arms had been treated and bandaged. He looked worn but stable.

Then the door opened.

In walked a tall, sharply dressed doctor with a clipboard. His coat was crisp, and his eyes held a peculiar, intense, unreadable sheen.

"Mr. Jenkins," he said, glancing briefly at the chart. "I'm Dr. Langham. You're fortunate. Tibial fracture, but no internal bleeding, no concussion, and no damage to surrounding arteries. You'll need a full cast for a few weeks, but you'll walk again."

Uncle George nodded. "Thank God. I was tellin' the EMTs earlier... felt like an angel had to be riding with me."

Dr. Langham didn't respond at first. His pen scratched something onto the clipboard before he finally looked up.

"Sometimes... people survive what should have taken them out. It's rare, but not unheard of."

Uncle George chuckled softly, shifting slightly in the bed. "Yeah, but this, this was more than luck."

The doctor didn't acknowledge the comment. He checked the IV line, straightened the blanket, and said, "A nurse will come in to talk to you about discharge protocol and follow-up appointments. Try to stay off that leg."

He turned toward the door and began to exit.

But just before he crossed the threshold, Uncle George heard something...barely above a whisper.

"They're always getting in the way."

George blinked. "What'd you say?"

Dr. Langham paused for a half-second. Then, without turning around or repeating himself, he walked out the door and disappeared into the hallway.

Uncle George stared after him, a chill creeping down his spine that had nothing to do with the hospital air conditioning.

He whispered to himself, "What in the world…"

Back at home, Elle was sitting in the kitchen when the phone rang. She almost didn't answer, but something told her to pick up. The voice on the other end was calm but firm, "This is Nurse Delaney from Gerry Medical. Your brother, George Jenkins, was brought in after a car accident. He's stable, but you may want to come right away." The kitchen spoon dropped to the floor. "What?" Elle's voice cracked as panic rushed in. "My brother? Oh God… okay…we're on our way."

She grabbed her keys and called out to Ethan, who had just come down the stairs. "Uncle George's been in an accident, we have to go now." The fear in her voice made Ethan freeze. His heart thudded wildly as they raced to the car. The drive felt like an eternity. Elle's hands gripped the steering wheel so tightly her knuckles turned white. Ethan stared out the window, his mind spiraling. Images of his father's funeral a few months ago crept in. The casket. The crying. The aching silence that followed. "Please don't let it be the same," he whispered under his breath, fists clenched. He couldn't lose Uncle George, too. The man who taught him how to throw a football, who always showed up, who never left. The hospital sign finally appeared in the distance, but the air in the car remained thick with unspoken prayers.

The automatic doors of Gerry Medical slid open as Elle and Ethan rushed inside, the fluorescent lights almost blinding after the tension-filled ride. Elle marched straight to the front desk, her voice slightly trembling. "I'm here for George Jenkins. He was brought in after a car accident; he's my brother."

The nurse behind the counter nodded. "Yes, ma'am. He's in Room 312 on the third floor. Take the elevators to your left. He's stable, but the doctor may still be running tests."

Elle grabbed Ethan's hand and didn't let go. The elevator ride was silent, every ding stretching the nerves between them. When the doors opened, they followed the hallway signs, hearts pounding louder with every step.

Outside Room 312, a nurse greeted them with a gentle smile. "You're his family?"

Elle nodded, eyes misting. "Yes, I'm his sister. This is my son."

"He's awake. A little banged up, but alert," the nurse said kindly, stepping aside. "You can go in."

Elle slowly pushed open the door.

There he was, Uncle George, lying in a hospital bed with his leg in a cast and a few scratches on his face, but alive. His eyes lit up when he saw them.

Ethan exhaled the breath he hadn't realized he was holding. "Uncle G…"

George gave them a half-smile, his voice rough but steady. "Hey, I'm alright. Don't cry, y'all. I just wanted a break from driving y'all around."

Elle rushed to his side and took his hand. "You scared us, George. You really scared us."

Ethan stood at the foot of the bed, the knot in his chest finally loosening. For a moment, the fear faded, replaced with quiet relief. Uncle George was still here.

Later that evening, Elle and Ethan sat beside Uncle George's hospital bed. The hospital grew quieter with each passing hour. Machines hummed softly, and the glow from George's heart monitor cast faint green lines across the room. Elle sat in a chair beside her brother, nodding off now and then, while Ethan shifted on the pullout cot near the window.

Around 10 p.m., Ethan's throat was dry, and the small paper cup of water from earlier didn't cut it anymore. He stood quietly, not wanting to wake his mom or uncle, and slipped out the door in his socks.

The hallway was darker than he expected. Most of the overhead lights were off, leaving only a few glowing exit signs and the buzz of a single vending machine halfway down the corridor. Its flickering light cast long shadows on the tile floor.

Ethan hesitated, the eerie silence stretching around him like a blanket. He rubbed his eyes and muttered, "Come on, man… It's just a drink."

He padded forward, pressed a few buttons, and grabbed a bottle of orange juice from the tray. As he turned to leave, something caught his eye.

A shadow.

Just at the corner of the hallway.

Still.

Watching?

He didn't wait to find out.

Ethan hurried back to the room, his heart hammering in his chest. When he closed the door softly behind him, his mom stirred. "Everything okay?"

He sat down beside her and unscrewed the bottle cap with trembling fingers. "The lights were off in the hallway," he whispered. "I don't know… I started seeing things that probably weren't there."

Elle looked at him, her voice low but firm. "Sometimes darkness does that, baby. That's why you always need to stay vigilant. Not everything you see is real, but not everything invisible is harmless either."

Ethan didn't reply. He just stared at the glowing monitor by his uncle's bedside, the quiet beeping steady and reassuring in the thick silence.

Chapter 24
Shadows and Summer

The wheels of the car crunched over the gravel as Elle carefully pulled into the driveway. Uncle George, with one leg braced in a cast and his face still carrying faint scratches, winced slightly as Ethan helped him out of the car and onto the porch. The warm afternoon sun blanketed the house, but the mood was still subdued. The hospital discharge papers rustled in Elle's purse, and her voice was firm but caring.

"You're staying put, George," she said, unlocking the front door. "There's no way I'm letting you travel like this. I'll call Aunt Helen to come stay with you until we're back."

"I'll be fine," George protested gently, but Elle gave him that look, the one he knew not to argue with.

Inside, Ethan trailed behind quietly, his mind still stuck in the sterile brightness of the hospital and the shadowy hallway that sent a chill through him the night before. He set his uncle's overnight bag on the floor and helped him get settled on the couch.

A long silence lingered between them before Uncle George finally spoke. "I know you're shaken up, Ethan."

Ethan glanced away, then slowly nodded. "I keep thinking... what if it was worse? What if I lost you, too?"

George's eyes softened. "You didn't. And I'm not going anywhere, kid." He leaned forward slightly, wincing from the movement but not backing down from the conversation. "You've got to keep moving forward. Life doesn't pause, even when things shake us up. You've got another camp coming, and I want you to go."

Ethan shifted uncomfortably in the chair. "But I don't want to go without you there."

"You won't be alone," George said firmly. "Coach Tiller, and your mom will be there, and Marcus too. I'll be cheering you on from right here and probably sending annoying check-in texts every day."

A small smile tugged at Ethan's lips, but it didn't quite reach his eyes. "It just feels...different now."

George nodded slowly. "It is different. But different doesn't mean bad. It means you're growing, and growth isn't supposed to be easy." He placed a hand on Ethan's shoulder. "This isn't just about football anymore, Ethan. It's about who you're becoming."

Ethan didn't respond right away, but his heart felt lighter just enough to breathe again. He looked at his uncle, then down at the camp schedule Elle had left on the table.

"Okay," Ethan said quietly. "I'll go."

George smiled, proud and relieved. "That's my boy." Uncle George took a nap on the couch while Ethan went upstairs to his room.

Ethan sat on the edge of his bed, the late afternoon sun casting golden light through the blinds. His duffel bag sat half-zipped on the floor, with cleats freshly cleaned and shirts neatly folded. But his thoughts were anything but organized. He stared at his phone for a long moment before finally tapping Marcus' name.

"Yo, E!" Marcus answered, his usual upbeat tone spilling through the speaker. "You ready for the next camp? I got my gear packed already."

Ethan hesitated. "Hey, I need to tell you something."

There was a pause on the other end. "What's up?"

"My uncle..." Ethan swallowed. "He got into a car accident two days ago when we got back from camp."

Marcus's voice dropped. "Whoa, man. Is he okay?"

"Yeah," Ethan nodded, even though Marcus couldn't see it. "Broken leg, some scratches. It could've been worse, but he's home now. Just... shook me up, you know?"

"Dang, man. I'm really sorry. That's scary."

Ethan leaned back against the headboard, the tension finally pushing past the lump in his chest. "He's the one who got me into football. Every camp, every practice, he's been there. It's weird thinking about going without him."

"I get it," Marcus said. "But you know what? He'd want you to go. Still grind, still show up."

"He told me that," Ethan said quietly. "And I'm gonna try. It's just… it feels different this time."

"You're not alone, though," Marcus said firmly. "I got your back, E. We're in this together."

"Thanks, man," Ethan said, a small smile tugging at the edge of his mouth. "I needed to hear that."

After they hung up, Ethan stood and walked over to the mirror. He stared at his reflection, the same face, but something deeper had changed. The weight of the summer had settled on his shoulders, but so had a deeper sense of purpose.

He dropped to the floor and began a set of push-ups. Then sit-ups. Then lunges. He moved through the motions with quiet determination, not just because of the game but for the man who had believed in him from day one.

When the workout ended, he stood in front of the mirror again, sweat lining his brow and chest rising with deep breaths.

"You've got this," he said to himself. That night, after a hot shower and a quiet dinner, Ethan sat cross-legged on his bed with his journal in his lap. The house was mostly silent, except for the faint sound of a TV show playing in the living room. Uncle George had fallen asleep in the recliner with a pillow under his elevated leg. Elle had turned in early, emotionally drained from the week.

Ethan opened to a fresh page, the pen in his hand feeling heavier than usual. He wrote:

July 8th

Tomorrow's Greywood. Another camp. Another week. Another shot to prove I belong.

He paused, tapping the pen against the page.

This one feels different, though. Not just because of the training or the competition, but because I'm going without Uncle George for the first time.

He told me I was strong. Told me I could handle it. But the truth is, I'm still shaken. I keep replaying the call, the car, and the drive to the hospital. I thought I was going to lose him just like Dad.

He closed his eyes for a second before continuing.

But I didn't. God kept him here. I don't know why or what's coming next, but I feel something is shifting. This isn't just about football anymore. It's about faith, resilience, and trusting God even when the lights feel low.

I'm going to Greywood with my whole heart. For Uncle George. For myself. For every time I doubted, I could push through.

He set the pen down, quietly shut the journal, and whispered, "Lord, just go with me."

Then he slipped under the covers, his duffel bag already by the door, packed not just with cleats and gloves but with purpose. The next morning arrived with a golden hue stretching across the neighborhood rooftops. The air was warm and still, with only the gentle rustling of the trees outside to greet the day. Ethan zipped up his final duffel bag and slung it over his shoulder, trying to shake the heaviness still sitting in his chest.

Downstairs, Aunt Helen was already in the kitchen, humming while she stirred a pot of oatmeal. She gave Ethan a warm, motherly smile.

"I packed a few extra snacks for the ride. And don't worry about your Uncle, I'll be right here," she said, her voice as steady as her presence.

In the living room, Uncle George sat with his leg propped up, a travel pillow behind his back. He looked better tired, but sharper. "Come here, champ," he said, motioning Ethan over.

Ethan dropped his bag and walked over, kneeling beside his uncle's chair.

"You good?" Uncle George asked.

Ethan nodded slowly. "Yeah. I just… wish you were coming."

"I know. Me too," George replied, placing a hand on Ethan's shoulder. "But this is where you step up. This is your time, son. Just keep doing what you've been doing, stay focused, stay humble, and don't forget to look up now and then."

Ethan offered a half-smile, then hugged him tight. "I'll make you proud."

"You already do."

Moments later, Elle appeared at the front door with Marcus beside her. The SUV was packed and ready. Marcus gave Ethan a fist bump as he opened the back seat.

"Greywood's waiting, bro," Marcus grinned.

Elle glanced back at the house. "Helen, call me if you need anything. George, rest. We'll be back before you know it."

As they loaded in and pulled away from the house, Ethan looked back at the front steps where Aunt Helen stood with one arm wrapped around George's shoulder. He waved from the passenger window.

It didn't feel the same, but he knew he had to keep moving forward. New camp, new week. This time, he carried the weight of experience, loss, and faith in every step.

Greywood State was calling. Three hours later, the SUV rolled into the main entrance of Greywood State University, a sprawling campus tucked between pine-covered hills and modern athletic complexes. A large banner read:

"Welcome Athletes – Greywood State Elite Football Camp 2009"

The fieldhouse buzzed with life: athletes checking in, parents lugging suitcases, coaches barking directions, and clipboards flying. Ethan stepped out of the car, staring up at the turf stadium just behind the trees.

Marcus nudged him. "New field, same grind."

Ethan smirked. "Let's get it."

After checking in, they were handed their camp gear, navy shorts, and gray shirts with the Greywood Wolf logo and assigned to Dormitory C, third floor. Ethan and Marcus shared a room with two beds, a desk, and a window overlooking the practice field.

Once unpacked, they were ushered to the welcome orientation inside the indoor practice dome. Coach Hughes, a former Division I standout, took the mic.

"You're here because you're hungry," he said. "You're not the best just because you showed up. You become the best because you do what others won't: train harder, listen more, sacrifice sleep, and push past pain."

Ethan's heart pounded. The words hit harder this time, especially after all he had just been through.

That evening, their first session began intense sprints, route-running drills, footwork ladders, and 7-on-7 simulations. The competition was fierce. Ethan found himself matched against a tall receiver from New Jersey and a lightning-fast DB from Texas.

But something clicked. He was sharper, stronger, and more focused than before. Even the coaches started taking note.

"Phillips! Nice cut! You've been coached well!" one shouted.

Ethan just nodded, sweat dripping, lungs burning. He glanced to the sky briefly and whispered, "This one's for you, Uncle G."

That night in the dorm, as lights flickered off, Marcus tossed a football up and down from his bed.

"Day one's always the toughest," Marcus said.

"Yeah," Ethan replied, staring at the ceiling. "But it's worth it."

Day Two began just after sunrise. A loud whistle echoed through the dorm halls at 6:15 a.m. sharp.

"Let's go! Greywood Wolves don't sleep in!" Coach Hughes hollered from the hallway.

Ethan groaned as he sat up, shoulders stiff from yesterday's drills. Marcus tossed him a towel. "We asked for it."

By 6:45, they were out on the track for warm-up laps. The dew still clung to the grass, and the air was crisp with a light mist rolling off the hills. Coaches barked instructions while the players jogged, stretched, and were mentally prepared for another grueling day.

That morning's training focused on mental toughness. Players rotated through circuits that tested agility, speed, and reaction time, then had to memorize play combinations and run them on tired legs. Ethan slipped once on a cut but corrected and finished strong.

In the film room after breakfast, Coach Hughes introduced a new drill: Shadow Reads.

"Quarterbacks, you're going to fake out ghosts. Linebackers, you'd better read the shadows. If you can react without hesitation, you win the game before the ball's snapped."

Ethan loved it. It was fast, cerebral, and forced him to trust his instincts. He even beat Marcus in two of the rounds, and Marcus was still fuming by lunch.

"Man, you guessed that route," Marcus said, nudging him.

"I read you like a book, bro."

That afternoon, 7-on-7 scrimmages again. Ethan rotated in as a starter, holding the defensive edge against two explosive offenses. On one play, he tracked a tight end across the field and deflected what would've been a touchdown pass.

Coaches huddled near the sideline and scribbled his name into their notes.

That night, Marcus and Ethan sat on the dorm steps, eating protein bars and talking about the future.

"You think we'll still be doing this in college?" Marcus asked.

"Yeah," Ethan said. "But not just playing. I want to lead."

Day Three brought challenges of a different kind…rain.

A thunderstorm rolled in just before breakfast, forcing all drills indoors. The turf dome turned into a chaotic warzone of whistles, cones, soaked cleats, and padded collisions.

During a live contact drill, Ethan took a hit that knocked him to the turf. He rolled to his feet quickly, shaking it off, but the wind had been knocked from his lungs.

"You good?" Marcus asked.

Ethan nodded. "I'm not quitting."

Later that afternoon, they worked on leadership and communication drills. Ethan stood out again. He called defensive shifts, aligned the secondary, and encouraged younger campers when they messed up. One coach pulled him aside.

"You've got natural leadership in you, son. Keep sharpening it. You'll be a captain somewhere."

Ethan smiled, the words sinking deep.

That night, the lights went out earlier than usual. Everyone was worn out.

Ethan lay in bed, staring at the ceiling fan as it spun slowly overhead.

He whispered a prayer: "God, thank You. I miss Uncle George being here, but I know he's proud. Help me stay focused. Help me do this the right way."

Day four brought clear skies and rising temperatures. The morning began with a sunrise hike and motivational talk on the ridge above the practice fields. Coach Hughes gathered the team beneath the open sky, letting the golden morning light fall on their tired faces.

"You can have talent," he said, "but grit is what takes you to the finish line. Leadership is not just about calling plays; it's about who you are when no one's looking. That's who coaches recruit. That's who teammates follow."

Ethan nodded, soaking in every word. His shoulders still ached from the indoor scrimmages the day before, but he welcomed the pain; it meant he was growing.

The remainder of the day focused on technique refinement and review. Coaches spent extra time reviewing footage from drills, correcting foot placement, hand position, and zone drops. Ethan sat at the edge of his seat in the film room, eyes locked on the screen, scribbling notes furiously. His game awareness was sharpening by the hour.

By Day Five, energy was running low, but adrenaline kept the boys going. The final camp scrimmage, a full-pads exhibition game, was the highlight of the week.

Ethan was assigned as the defensive captain.

Standing in the huddle, helmet tucked under his arm, he looked around at the other boys and called out confidently, "Let's show 'em what we've learned. No regrets, all heart. Play smart, let's go!"

The game was intense, but Ethan's defense held strong. He made two tackles for loss, nearly snagged an interception, and rallied the team with discipline and fire. By the end of the game, the coaches were nodding in approval. One even walked up to him after the final whistle.

"You've got something special, Phillips. Don't lose it."

Ethan smiled and nodded. He left this camp feeling more confident than before.

When Saturday morning arrived, Elle and Marcus' parents were already waiting in the parking lot. Ethan climbed into the car, sweaty and sore, but with a gleam in his eye.

"I'm proud of you, baby," Elle said, hugging him at the car. "You pushed through."

Back at home, Aunt Helen greeted him with a warm smile, and Uncle George, still in a brace but moving better, was seated on the porch with a lemonade.

"Look at that, the star returns," Uncle George teased.

Ethan laughed, hugged him carefully, and sat beside him on the steps.

"I made you proud?"

George grinned. "Always."

That weekend was slow and peaceful. No whistles. No pads. No drills. Just grilled burgers, a fruit bowl, and laughter on the porch.

Ethan and Marcus hung out Sunday afternoon, tossing a football in the yard while Aunt Helen and Elle sat nearby chatting. The sun dipped behind the trees, casting golden light across the grass.

"Monday starts another one," Marcus said, catching a pass.

"Yeah," Ethan replied, "but I needed this weekend. Bad."

He glanced at his uncle, who gave him a thumbs-up from the porch.

"Feels like everything's changing," Ethan whispered.

"It is," Marcus said. "And we're ready."

Chapter 25
The Final Drive

The early morning sun poured through the curtains like a gentle nudge from heaven, waking Ethan from a restless sleep. The house felt different today. It wasn't just the lingering scent of Aunt Helen's pancakes or the faint hum of the ceiling fan above him; it was the anticipation of what lay ahead. Today marked the beginning of the last leg of summer camps, and this time, Uncle George would be joining him again.

"Mom!" Ethan called from the stairs, lugging his duffel bag over his shoulder. "Is Uncle George ready?"

"He's waiting outside," Elle said, sipping her coffee by the window. "And behaving like he didn't just get his cast removed a day ago."

Outside, George stood by the car, leaning on his good leg with the pride of a man who refused to be sidelined. The pain in his leg had mainly subsided, though he moved with caution. But nothing, not even a broken bone, would keep him from supporting Ethan in these final three camps.

They loaded up the car, made a quick stop at Marcus's house, and headed toward Header-Dreener Gridiron Academy, their third camp of the summer.

Header-Dreener was intense. Tucked in the foothills of a small college town, it was known for conditioning athletes not just physically, but mentally. The training facility boasted state-of-the-art equipment, padded turf fields, and a staff of former professional coaches who didn't tolerate sloppiness.

The first drill was brutal.

"Again!" Coach Brighton barked. "Get low and drive!"

Ethan and Marcus dropped into their stances for the fourth rep in a row. Sweat soaked their shirts, their cleats digging into the turf like claws. Still, Ethan kept pushing. He could hear Uncle George yelling from the sideline, encouraging him, cheering him on.

"Let's go, Ethan! Get angry!"

By the end of the first day, the players had ice packs taped to their knees, and the cafeteria was nearly silent from exhaustion. That night, in the dorms, Ethan sprawled across his bunk, muscles aching and heart full.

"You alive?" Marcus teased from across the room.

"Barely. I think my soul is still on the field," Ethan replied with a smirk.

Header-Dreener taught Ethan control and precision. It wasn't just about being the fastest; it was about reading plays, anticipating gaps, and knowing when to strike. By the end of the week, Coach Brighton pulled Ethan aside.

"You've got something rare," he said. "Not just talent but heart. Don't let that go."

As they drove away from Janville, Ethan leaned his head against the window, proud but exhausted. Uncle George gave him a fist bump from the front seat. "Four down, two to go."

The next stop was Winslow State Elite Football Institute, a camp renowned for its scouting connections. It was held on a sprawling campus near a significant city and packed with recruiters who watched every move like hawks.

The first day felt different. Sharper. More competitive.

"Don't get cocky," Uncle George warned as they arrived. "Play your game. Let them see who you are, not just what you can do."

Ethan nodded. Winslow wasn't just about technique it was a mental battlefield. The drills were fast-paced, the scrimmages aggressive. Every player was there for one reason: to get noticed.

During one-on-ones, Ethan went up against a five-star recruit from Texas. The boy was taller, bulkier, but Ethan had speed. He juked left, spun through a tackle, and dove into the end zone.

The crowd watching erupted.

Recruiters scribbled in their notebooks.

Afterward, a scout in a charcoal suit handed him a card. "We'll be in touch. Keep working."

That night, Ethan couldn't sleep. He stared at the card on the nightstand, wondering what this could mean. Uncle George found him in the lounge and sat beside him.

"You did well, son," he said. "But don't let a card define you. Remember why you started."

Ethan nodded. "It's not about being famous. I want to do something that matters."

Winslow sharpened Ethan like a blade. It wasn't just about power or plays; it was about poise. And by the time they left, he felt more prepared than ever.

The final camp of the summer was at Rockdale University's Rising Star Showcase, held on a mountaintop campus with picturesque views and brutal workouts. Uncle George, now fully mobile, walked the sidelines like a coach himself.

Rockdale was designed to mimic a college football environment: two-a-day practices, classroom sessions on football IQ, film reviews, and even press conferences.

"This feels like real college ball," Marcus said on the first night.

"Because it is," Ethan replied, flipping through his binder of playbooks.

The highlight of the week came during the final scrimmage. Ethan was selected as team captain, and under his leadership, his squad won 24-17. Marcus threw a touchdown pass on a trick play, rushed for another, and recorded two sacks on defense.

As he walked off the field, Uncle George met him at the gate.

"You left it all out there," he said, wrapping his arm around Ethan's shoulder. "That's how champions are made."

On the drive home, the car buzzed with energy. The mountains rolled by as Uncle George played his favorite jazz station, and Ethan and Marcus shared memories from each camp, inside jokes, challenging drills, and new techniques.

"Out of the three," Marcus said, "Rockdale was my favorite."

"Same," Ethan agreed. "Felt like we were already living the dream."

Elle greeted them at home with open arms and a spread of grilled food in the backyard. Aunt Helen had stopped by, and together they made a celebratory dinner to close out the summer.

Ethan sat by the fire pit later that night, journal in hand.

"This summer changed me. I feel stronger, not just in body but in spirit. I faced the pressure. I faced the fear. And I didn't back down. I don't know what's next, but I know this: I'm ready for it."

As the embers crackled and the stars stretched wide above, Ethan looked over at Uncle George and his mom, laughing over sweet tea. That weekend, he permitted himself to relax. He slept in Saturday morning, something he hadn't done in weeks, and spent most of the day lounging on the back porch with a cold sports drink, reviewing his camp notes and sketching plays in a notebook. Uncle George sat beside him with a folded newspaper, occasionally chiming in with coaching tips and questions about the different camp styles.

"Greywood's staff really pushed you," Uncle George said, tapping his finger against the edge of the paper. "But I think Winslow gave you that edge. You looked sharp this week."

Ethan smiled. "Yeah, I feel more ready than ever. Like I actually belong out there now."

***

Sunday was reserved for errands. Elle had circled the date on the calendar two weeks ago: Back-to-School Shopping Day. Ethan groaned as they pulled into the parking lot of the Gerry Shopping Plaza, but he secretly enjoyed spending time with his mom. They sifted through jeans, athletic wear, and notebooks, debating whether high-top cleats were worth the extra forty dollars and what color backpack best matched his sneakers.

"Don't look at me like that," Elle said, holding up a bright green hoodie with the tag still attached. "This is stylish."

Ethan smirked. "For you, maybe. I'm trying to make varsity, not get roasted."

She tossed the hoodie back with a chuckle and pulled out her phone to check her list. "Alright, Mr. Fashionable. We still need socks, a calculator, and deodorant that lasts longer than two hours."

They laughed together all the way to the checkout, filling their bags with supplies and fast-food wrappers. It was a simple outing, but it reminded Ethan of what mattered: being grounded, being loved, and staying humble.

That evening, Ethan laid everything out in his room: new gear on one side, playbooks and handwritten notes on the other. The camps had pushed him physically, but it was the quiet in-between moments watching film with Uncle George, walking through drills with Marcus, and talking life with his mom that gave him the confidence to believe he could rise.

With just under two weeks left before the first day of school, Ethan had his focus set. Football tryouts. Preseason conditioning. Balancing academics. He was ready. Later that evening, after dinner and some light stretching, Ethan lay across his bed with the ceiling fan spinning above him. His phone buzzed with an incoming group call from Amanda and Scott.

He smiled as he swiped to answer. "Yo, what's up?"

"Finally! Took you long enough," Amanda teased. "You done traveling the world and being an all-star athlete of the year?"

Ethan laughed. "Something like that. Just finished the last camp a few days ago. I'm finally breathing again."

Scott chimed in. "Bro, we've been bored without you. Amanda's been trying to get us all to do karaoke again."

"You're just mad I beat you with my version of 'Huddles in My Heart' last time," she fired back.

Ethan chuckled. "Please tell me someone recorded that."

"Nope," Scott replied quickly. "We swore to leave those memories in the basement where they belong."

They all laughed, the kind of laugh that only happens between real friends. Ethan hadn't realized how much he missed just... talking. No drills, no reps, no pressure. Just them.

Amanda asked about the different camps, and Ethan gave a quick rundown…Briarstone's insane heat, Greywood's tough love coaching, and how Winslow's final showcase gave him a real sense of his own growth. But then he paused.

"What's wrong?" Amanda asked.

Ethan exhaled. "It was just… a lot. I mean, don't get me wrong, I learned a ton. But after Uncle George's accident, something shifted. Like, I started seeing everything a little clearer. I'm not just doing this for football anymore."

Scott went quietly for a second. "Doing it for what then?"

Ethan hesitated. "Purpose, I guess. I don't fully know yet. But I've got this feeling that something bigger is at stake."

Amanda didn't respond right away. Then softly, "You've changed. But in a good way."

"Yeah," Ethan replied. "Just trying to stay grounded. I've seen too many dudes lose themselves before they even make it."

They stayed on the phone another hour, talking about summer reading lists, which teachers they hoped they wouldn't get again, and whether their favorite lunch lady still worked the same line.

Before they hung up, Amanda added, "We're meeting at Gerry Shopping Mall next Saturday. Last hurrah before school starts."

Ethan smiled. "Wouldn't miss it."

That night, as the sun dipped below the treetops and the cicadas hummed outside, Ethan lay back in bed, staring at the ceiling again. He felt tired but not from the workouts. From growing. From knowing he wasn't the same boy who'd started summer with dreams of professional stardom and nothing else.

Now, he was stepping into something deeper.

He didn't know exactly what was ahead, but for the first time, he wasn't afraid of the unknown. Ethan drifted off to sleep. The Saturday before school started, Ethan met up with Amanda and Scott at the Gerry Shopping Mall. The weather outside was warm and breezy, the kind of day that made you forget school was right around the corner. Inside the mall, families bustled between stores, students picked through racks of clothes, and the smell of pretzels and cinnamon rolls filled the air.

Ethan spotted Amanda waving near the central fountain, holding two iced lemonades. Scott leaned against the railing, scrolling on his phone.

"There's the future professional football star," Amanda teased as Ethan walked up.

"Future professional," Ethan corrected with a smirk. "No lawsuits."

Scott laughed. "Yeah, yeah, just don't forget us when you're famous."

They wandered into their usual spots, Retro Threads, Kicks Station, and the upstairs arcade, where they still battled for bragging rights on air hockey. Ethan beat Amanda by one point, and Scott claimed victory in the basketball shootout.

Afterward, they grabbed lunch at the food court, piling up trays with burgers, fries, and smoothies.

"I still can't believe summer's basically over," Amanda said, sipping her mango smoothie. "It flew by."

"I'm just glad I don't have to run 40-yard dashes this week," Ethan said. "My legs need time to forgive me."

Scott laughed. "You going out for captain this year?"

Ethan shrugged. "Coach hinted at it. We'll see."

They walked a few more laps through the mall, stopping at a bookstore to flip through comics and college prep books. Amanda found a leather journal and handed it to Ethan.

"You should write in this like, for real," she said. "You always have something to say. Might as well put it somewhere."

Ethan took it with a small smile. "I might."

As the afternoon wound down, the three of them sat on the bench near the exit, watching the carousel spin and talking about classes, teachers, and their last two years of high school.

"Promise me," Amanda said, standing up, "we'll stay close no matter what. Even after we graduate."

Scott threw an arm around both of them. "Deal."

Ethan nodded, feeling the weight of the moment. "Deal."

As the late afternoon sun dipped behind the clouds, Ethan's mom pulled up outside the Gerry Shopping Mall. He said goodbye to Amanda and Scott, tossing his shopping bags into the back seat before sliding into the car. The ride home was quiet, the kind of stillness that made everything feel final: summer, laughter, freedom. By the time they pulled into the driveway, Ethan was settling into the fact that school was tomorrow. A new year, new goals, and a fresh chapter waiting to be written.

The alarm buzzed at 6:00 a.m., jolting Ethan from a deep sleep. He blinked against the early morning light seeping through his curtains. For a split second, he thought he was still at Greywood Camp, with Marcus snoring in the bunk below him and cleats resting by the door. But the smell of fresh laundry and pancakes from downstairs reminded him he was home.

Ethan sat up, stretched, and took a deep breath. First day of school. His sophomore year. A new season. New goals. New pressures.

He got dressed slowly, pulling on a crisp polo and dark jeans his mom picked out during their back-to-school shopping trip. He slipped on his favorite sneakers, well-worn but still clean enough to pass inspection. Football bag by the door. Notebooks stacked. Backpack zipped. He took one last glance in the mirror. A little leaner. Stronger than last year.

Downstairs, Elle was already at the stove flipping pancakes while Uncle George, hobbling gently with a cane, sipped coffee at the table. He gave Ethan a nod and a smile.

"You ready?" George asked.

Ethan nodded, grabbing a pancake and folding it in half like a taco.

"Mentally or physically?" he joked with a mouthful.

Elle handed him a lunch bag. "Both. And behave."

The car ride to school was filled with light conversation...Uncle George was teasing Ethan about being "too cool" to wave at his mom in public, and Elle was reminding him to stay focused and avoid drama.

When they pulled up to the school parking lot, students were spilling in from all directions, backpacks swinging, music blasting from a few open car doors, laughter ringing in the morning air.

Ethan stepped out of the car and looked around. Everything looked the same, but something felt different. Maybe it was him. Maybe it was everything he'd seen and learned this summer. Or perhaps it was the weight of everything ahead—football, grades, life decisions.

He took a breath, slung his bag over his shoulder, and stepped forward into the crowd.

Sophomore year had officially begun.

The first bell of sophomore year rang through Gerry High's freshly waxed hallways like a starting whistle. The doors swung open, and the noise of summer reunions filled the building—locker doors slamming, backpacks zipping, sneakers squeaking, and students calling out to each other over the low hum of morning announcements.

Ethan grinned as he walked in alongside Marcus, both of them decked out in school-issued football polos. A few freshmen stepped aside when they passed, whispering and wide-eyed.

"Feels different being back," Marcus said, adjusting his backpack strap. "Like… we're not the rookies anymore."

"Yeah," Ethan nodded. "But we're not seniors either. We're like… middle kings."

They both laughed.

Just ahead, Amanda waved them down by her locker, already in a deep conversation with Scott about who got taller over the summer.

"Ethan, did you grow again?" Amanda asked, squinting like a measuring tape was in her eyes.

He shrugged with a crooked smile. "Must've been the protein shakes."

The morning flew by in a blur of schedules, meet-and-greets, and teachers awkwardly trying to pronounce last names. Ethan's locker was still jammed from the previous year, and Keith, now the starting quarterback, was assigned a seat next to him in second-period geometry.

"Good summer?" Keith asked casually.

"Busy," Ethan said.

Keith nodded. "Ready to run it back?"

That was the question everyone seemed to be asking. And Ethan was still wondering what the answer should be.

By lunchtime, the cafeteria was buzzing with conversations about summer jobs, driver's permits, and who dated whom at camp. Ethan found the crew, Marcus, Amanda, Scott, and a few others already seated at their usual table near the windows.

Marcus was mid-rant about the team's new playbook. "Coach better not switch up too much. I just got the old one memorized."

Amanda laughed, poking her fork at a pile of mystery meat. "As long as y'all win games, nobody cares what play you run."

The whole group cheered at that, raising their milk cartons in mock victory.

Later that afternoon, the team gathered on the field after school for the first practice of the season. The sun baked the grass in waves. Helmets gleamed. Whistles pierced the air.

Coach Lanning was already barking instructions, clipboard in hand.

"Gentlemen! Welcome back. This year's not about coasting. This is where we find out who wants it and who talks about it. Understand?"

"Yes, sir!"

Ethan took his place on the line, heart pounding not from nerves, but from something deeper. A hunger. A mission. The camps were over. The summer was done. This was where it mattered.

And so began the long march toward fall.

The weeks that followed fell into a rhythm of day classes, afternoon practices, and game nights under the lights every Friday. Gerry High's sophomore squad showed promise early in the season, racking up a few strong wins that had the student section buzzing with chants and school spirit.

Ethan played with fire. Every camp, every drill, every sleepless night reviewing film seemed to fuel his determination. But even with all the progress he and Marcus had made over the summer, things didn't always click on the field.

Keith, the new junior quarterback, had raw talent, but he wasn't Chris. His timing was off, and the chemistry was still forming. Missed passes, fumbled snaps, and shaky calls began to wear on the team. Tensions flared in the huddle. Ethan found himself clenching his jaw after every miscommunication, trying to lead without stepping on toes.

Coach Lanning pulled him aside after one game. "You can be a leader, Phillips, but yelling won't win you loyalty. Lead with your heart, not just your voice."

Uncle George echoed the same sentiment after watching from the bleachers. "You're not a one-man army," he said with a half-smile. "Trust the team, even when it's hard."

Mid-season brought wins, losses, and late-night talks at home. Ethan journaled more. Slept less. He wasn't just chasing touchdowns; he was chasing something deeper. A reason. A legacy.

Then came the playoffs.

Next week, Gerry High barely secured their spot in the playoffs, squeezing in with just enough wins to qualify. But it didn't matter; the energy around school was electric. After last year's deep run, just making it back sparked hope. Students filled the hallways with chatter about the upcoming games, teachers wore team colors, and local businesses displayed "Go Gerry!" signs in their windows. The entire town rallied behind the team, proud to see the Hawks make another shot at the title. Crowds from neighboring communities packed the bleachers, eager to witness another playoff journey. When Gerry High clinched the first-round victory, cheers echoed late into the night, and for a moment, it felt like nothing could stop them.

The semi-finals started the following week. The roar of the stadium felt different this year. It wasn't as deafening, not as wild or hopeful. Gerry High's football team had clawed its way into the playoffs, but something was missing, something Ethan couldn't quite put into words.

It was the first season without Chris under center. He had graduated the year before, leaving behind big cleats to fill and a legacy built on grit, calm leadership, and unshakable chemistry with the team. Now, Keith, a junior with a powerful arm and a lot to prove, was in charge of the offense. He was talented, no doubt, but not yet trusted.

Marcus, now at the wide receiver position with muscle from his summer training and crisp routes sharpened by sweat and repetition, had stepped up in every way he could. So had Ethan. The two had sacrificed nearly every week to elite football camps, missing out on pool parties, late-night movies, and even a few lazy mornings to get better.

So, when they stood on the field that cold November evening, with the scoreboard flashing 17–24, the bitter taste of falling short clung to Ethan's tongue like smoke. They had lost in the second round of the playoffs. The stands had gone quiet. Some of the seniors were already crying. The dream had ended, again.

In the locker room, the air was thick with silence. Helmets clanked onto the floor. Cleats dragged. Ethan sat with his back against the concrete wall, staring at the scuffed tips of his cleats. Marcus was beside him, face buried in his jersey.

"I can't believe this," Marcus whispered, low enough only Ethan could hear. "We worked all summer, man. All of that, and for what?"

Ethan didn't answer. His jaw clenched. His fists curled.

Coach Lanning stepped into the center of the room, his hat in one hand and his whistle looped around the other. He didn't yell. He didn't pace. He just stood still.

"I'm proud of you," Coach Lanning began, voice even, steady. "You gave this season everything you had. But I need you to hear this not as your coach, but as a man who's seen a lot of young boys grow into men and forget what matters along the way."

The players slowly lifted their eyes. Even Keith looked up from where he sat, towel draped over his head.

"This game is bigger than stats. Bigger than wins. Bigger than even this school," Coach continued. "Some of you are mad. Hurt.

Confused. I get it. But I want you to remember this moment, because this right here, right now, is where your real training begins."

A few players shifted, listening harder.

"You don't learn much from winning," Coach said, nodding. "But from loss? That's where you find out who you are. You learn how to lead, how to trust, how to hold each other up when things don't go your way. And if you don't, then no camp, no playbook, no scholarship will ever make you a champion."

Silence. A heavy, sobering silence.

"Ethan. Marcus." Coach looked directly at them. "You two trained hard this summer. I saw it. We all saw it. But leadership isn't just about effort, it's about connection. You have to bring others with you."

Ethan lowered his head. Those words hit hard.

"Keith," Coach added, "you've got a good arm. But you've been trying to do it alone. That's not how we win here."

No one argued. No one dared.

Coach stepped back and took a long breath. "Now go home. Hug your families. Eat something good. And come back next season ready, not just better, but wiser."

The season was over. The final scoreboard had long gone dark, but the sting of the semifinal loss still echoed in the hearts of the players. Monday morning at Gerry High felt quieter than usual. There were no roaring chants in the hallways, no high-fives in the cafeteria. Even the trophy case outside the gym seemed to wear a heavier shadow. But beneath the silence, pride still lingered.

Teachers offered encouraging nods. The principal made a morning announcement applauding the team for their dedication and resilience. Around town, the support never wavered. Kayla's Ice Cream Parlor posted a hand-painted sign that read, "We're Still Proud of You!" and gave out free cones to anyone wearing Gerry gear. Even in defeat, the Hawks had brought the town together again.

At home, Uncle George gave Ethan some space that evening, sensing the disappointment written in every step his nephew took.

Later, as the house settled and the TV dimmed to background noise, George walked into Ethan's room and sat at the edge of the bed.

"You okay?" he asked gently.

Ethan stared at the floor. "I thought we were gonna win it all."

"I know. You gave it everything."

"It just doesn't feel like it was enough."

George nodded, taking a breath. "Sometimes, the scoreboard lies. It only tells you the outcome, not the heart you put in. Not the hours. Not the leadership. Not the fight."

Ethan looked up, eyes tired but listening.

"You're more than one game," George said. "And real greatness isn't always proven on the field. It's shown in how you lead, how you grow, how you bounce back."

Ethan nodded slowly. The words didn't erase the hurt, but they anchored something deeper in perspective.

Uncle George stood, gently squeezing his shoulder. "Rest tonight. We'll talk more tomorrow. I'm proud of you, Ethan. And so is this whole town…win or lose."

As Uncle George stood and quietly left the room, the soft click of the door closing behind him left Ethan alone with his thoughts. The room was dim, lit only by the faint glow of the hallway light sneaking through the crack beneath the door. His journal sat on the nightstand, open to a blank page, pen resting on top like it was waiting for him.

He stared at it for a long moment.

Usually, this was when he'd write after a big game, after a lesson, after a moment that carved something into his heart. But tonight, the words weren't ready. He picked up the pen, paused, then slowly set it down again.

"Tomorrow," he whispered to himself, pulling the covers up to his chest. "I'll write it all down tomorrow."

With a heavy sigh, he turned over, closing his eyes, letting the silence of the night cradle him. Outside, a soft wind tapped against the window, a quiet reminder that winter was slowly stepping in.

By the end of the week, the school hallways were buzzing again, not with game talk, but with countdowns. Christmas break was right around the corner. Decorations filled the classrooms, lockers were wrapped in holiday paper, and students exchanged secret Santa gifts and candy canes. Teachers wore reindeer headbands and ugly sweaters, and festive music slipped through classroom speakers during study periods.

Ethan tried to enjoy it; he really did. But the season felt different this year. The loss still lingered, and his heart hadn't fully caught up with the holiday cheer. Still, he smiled when Amanda gave him a peppermint hot chocolate and even laughed when Scott wrapped his entire locker in duct tape and gift bows.

Little by little, the holiday spirit made its way in.

By the time the final bell rang on the last day before break, students poured into the hallways, tossing notebooks into backpacks and making plans for snowball fights, sleepovers, and late mornings. Ethan walked out the front doors of Gerry High, his breath forming small clouds in the cold December air, and zipped up his jacket.

Christmas was coming. And whether he felt ready for it or not, it was here.

Chapter 27
Home for the Holidays

Christmas break had finally arrived, but Ethan wasn't in the mood for snowy road trips or picturesque cabins tucked away in the mountains. When his mother brought it up, complete with brochures and cozy fireplace pictures, he politely declined.

"I just want to stay close this year," he told her.

She didn't push. She could see the weight still lingering on him after the season ended. So, she nodded and shifted plans. Home would be their holiday escape this year.

Ethan wasn't alone in wanting to keep things local. Marcus had already pitched the idea of a Christmas Bash at his place, complete with a game tournament, music, food, and their traditional gift exchange on Christmas Eve. Amanda and Scott were all in. Marcus also invited three of his best cousins to the party.

The house was buzzing with teen energy by late afternoon. Laughter spilled through the rooms as Ethan, Marcus, Scott, and his cousins argued over playlist choices and untangled a string of lights that refused to cooperate. Amanda arrived with a tray of Christmas cookies and an armful of wrapped gifts, her eyes lighting up when she saw the decorations Marcus's mom had put up.

They played card games, watched a holiday comedy that made them all laugh too hard, and shared stories about childhood Christmases. The night was loud, joyful, and precisely what Ethan didn't realize he needed.

Amanda didn't stay overnight; her sister Kiera arrived around 11:30 to pick her up, waving from the driveway. "Merry Christmas, boys," she called out before pulling away.

As the night settled, Scott dozed off on the couch with half a candy cane in his hand, and Ethan sat by the fireplace, staring at the glow. It felt peaceful. Real.

Meanwhile, Elle and Uncle George had accepted an invitation to a Christmas party at Sara's house, George's girlfriend of almost a year now. Elle liked her, even if she playfully teased George about finally settling down. Aunt Helen had driven to her sister Evelyn's for the night, bringing peach cobbler and a game of charades no one ever won.

Everyone had found their way to celebrate.

But the entire family had agreed Christmas dinner would be at Aunt Tricia's house the following evening. That was tradition, and no one missed it.

For now, though, Ethan was content. No lights from a distant cabin. No mountain views.

Just home. Just quiet joy. Just the people who mattered most. The next morning, the house was still. Faint sunlight peeked through the frosted windows, casting soft shadows on the living room floor. Everyone was still asleep. Ethan stirred awake on the couch, rubbing the sleep from his eyes as the scent of cinnamon rolls drifted from the kitchen.

He stood and stretched, yawning before wandering into the kitchen where Marcus's mom stood in a cozy cardigan, icing a fresh tray of pastries. A mug of steaming cocoa sat on the counter beside another she was already sipping.

"Merry Christmas, Ethan," she said, smiling as he entered.

"Merry Christmas," Ethan replied, his voice still gravelly with sleep.

He took the cocoa and sat across from her at the kitchen table. For a few moments, they didn't speak. It wasn't awkward, just peaceful. Ethan watched the snow gently fall outside, tiny flakes dancing against the windowpane.

Within thirty minutes, Elle arrived to pick up Ethan from the sleepover. Once in the car, Ethan said, "Merry Christmas."

"Merry Christmas."

"You doing okay?" she asked softly.

Ethan nodded but then shrugged. "Yeah… just tired, I guess."

She tilted her head, studying him with that motherly gaze that always saw through the surface.

"I know this season didn't end the way you hoped," she said. "But I'm proud of how you handled it. You showed maturity… leadership. Not every win shows up on a scoreboard." Finally home, Ethan went to the kitchen with his mom for another round of hot chocolate.

Ethan stared into his cup, thinking about the playoff loss, the silence on the bus ride home, the look on Keith's face after the final whistle.

"I just wanted it to mean something," he said quietly. "All those camps… all that work."

Elle reached across the table and gently touched his hand. "It did mean something. You're growing not just as a player, but as a person. That's the part that lasts."

He didn't say anything at first, but the words sank in. Slowly, he gave her a slight nod.

"You ready for Aunt Tricia's later?" she asked, lightening the tone.

"Yeah," he smirked. "You think she's making that crazy sweet potato pie again?"

Elle laughed. "You know she is. And she'll send you home with three slices whether you ask or not."

They both chuckled, sipping their cocoa as the house warmed with the quiet joy of Christmas morning. No chaos, no noise, just a mother and son, holding space for all that had been, and all that was still ahead. By mid-afternoon, the snow had settled like a soft white blanket over the streets, and the roads were lined with twinkling lights and inflatable reindeer. Elle drove slowly through the quiet neighborhood, Ethan riding in the passenger seat with a tray of macaroni and cheese on his lap, carefully balanced to avoid any spills.

They pulled into Aunt Tricia's long driveway, where several other cars were already parked, including Uncle George's, Aunt

Helen's, and Amanda's family van. The scent of pine and roasting meat met them before they even reached the front porch.

"Here we go," Elle said, glancing over with a smile. "The annual Christmas noise fest."

Ethan chuckled. "I'm ready."

Inside, the house buzzed with laughter, voices, and the occasional clatter from the kitchen. Children darted through the hallway, their socks sliding on the hardwood floor. Aunt Tricia greeted them at the door with her usual dramatic flair, a bright red sweater dress, holiday earrings that jingled when she hugged, and arms wide open.

"Merry Christmas, baby!" she said, pulling Ethan into a firm embrace. "You look taller since Thanksgiving! Elle, put that dish down and come get some cider."

The living room was filled with relatives: cousins, friends, siblings, and in-laws, each adding to the joyful chaos. Holiday music played in the background as everyone mingled. The Christmas tree was beautifully decorated in red, gold, and green, and underneath it, a growing pile of gifts waited to be unwrapped.

Uncle George sat with his leg propped on a pillow, still taking it easy after the accident. He smiled when Ethan came over.

"Hey champ," he said. "Heard you've been quiet lately."

"Not anymore," Ethan said with a smirk, then sat beside him. "It's good to see everyone."

They talked for a few minutes before Marcus showed up with their parents. Amanda was in the kitchen eating pie when she saw him enter the house. She waved excitedly and ran over with a gift bag.

"Don't open it yet," she warned. "We're doing a gift exchange after dinner."

Marcus nodded in agreement. "You better have something good for me," he teased.

Ethan grinned. "We'll see."

The dinner spread was impressive, with baked ham, turkey, green beans, cornbread, candied yams, cranberry sauce, and Aunt

Tricia's infamous sweet potato pie, which had its own table. Laughter echoed through the dining room as they ate, told stories, and shared memories of past holidays.

After dinner, the gift exchange began. Names were drawn from a bowl earlier in the week, and each person took a turn handing out their gift. Ethan gave Amanda a sketchbook with her name etched on the front and a new set of colored pencils. She looked stunned and hugged him tightly.

"I love it. You actually listened when I said I wanted a new sketchbook," she whispered.

Ethan smiled. "Of course."

Marcus opened his and found a custom phone case with their football number and a goofy photo of them mid-game on the back.

"You're ridiculous," Marcus laughed. "But this is perfect."

When it was Ethan's turn, Amanda handed him a rectangular box wrapped in shiny red paper. He opened it slowly, revealing a leather-bound journal with his initials engraved in the bottom corner.

"You said the old one was almost full," she said, shrugging shyly. "Figured you'd need a new one."

Ethan looked at her, speechless for a moment, then said quietly, "Thanks. This means a lot."

As the night wound down, they played board games, took family photos, and lounged on the floor, surrounded by food and joy. Aunt Helen told her usual exaggerated childhood stories, and even Elle danced a little in the kitchen when her favorite old-school holiday song came on.

Later, Ethan sat near the tree, staring at the twinkling lights. He wasn't thinking about football, finals, or losses. Just this moment surrounded by love, wrapped in laughter, and grounded in the kind of peace that reminded him he didn't need to chase the world to feel whole.

And for now, that was enough. New Year's Eve arrived quietly at the Phillips household. There were no fireworks or countdowns, just soft music on the radio, a glowing fireplace, and the calm of a family choosing peace over noise. Elle and Uncle George watched the ball drop on TV while Ethan stayed in his room, scribbling a few thoughts into the last few pages of his old journal. The words came slowly, but they were honest: "I didn't win everything this year, but I didn't lose myself either. I guess that counts for something."

When the clock struck midnight, he whispered, "Happy New Year," to no one in particular and closed the journal for the last time.

By the time January faded into February, the grind of the second half of the school year had set in. The winter cold was persistent, the hallways at Gerry High were lined with college posters, and the teachers reminded the students daily that the year wasn't over yet. Ethan had already begun weight training again with Marcus and Keith after school, preparing for what they hoped would be a stronger season in the fall.

One Friday afternoon after practice, Coach Lanning pulled Ethan, Marcus, Keith, and Lamar aside. They had just finished their drills and were catching their breath when the coach motioned them over to the bleachers.

"I've been watching you four since the start of last season," he began, his tone measured and serious. "There's potential here, strong potential. So, here's the deal. There are three elite-level football camps this summer: one in Dallas, one in San Diego, and one out in Kansas City. These aren't your average summer camps. College recruiters, pro-level trainers... It's where real decisions start getting made."

The boys looked at each other, wide-eyed.

Coach continued, "But it's not cheap. You're flying, staying in hotels, eating out. I'll call each of your parents to explain. If you're serious about going pro or even getting the kind of scholarships most kids dream about, this is the route."

Ethan swallowed hard. The excitement in his chest clashed with the anxiety that crept in just as quickly.

That evening, he sat across from his mother at the kitchen table, sharing every detail Coach had told them. Elle listened carefully, her face shifting from curiosity to concern.

"Three states? By plane?" she asked, her brow furrowed. "Ethan, that's a lot of traveling and without me?"

"I know," he said softly. "But Coach said this is big. It could open doors."

She didn't respond right away. Her fingers tapped gently on the rim of her coffee mug.

"I don't like the idea of you traveling across the country without family," she finally said. "Especially now with so much changing."

Just as the silence settled, Uncle George walked in, still in his business attire from teaching all day. "What's going on?" he asked.

Ethan filled him in, watching as his uncle's face grew thoughtful.

"Well," George said, nodding slowly. "Sara and I were planning a trip in June, but I could move some things around. If I can swing it, I'll go with him. At least for two of the camps. We'll figure something out."

Elle looked at her brother, still hesitant.

"I'd feel better if you were there," she admitted. "But I still want to talk to the other parents. If Marcus and Keith are going, then I need to know what kind of arrangements they're making, too."

Uncle George smiled. "Good. Then let's have a parent meeting. Talk it all out. See if we can coordinate flights or lodging together."

Ethan looked between them, hope slowly spreading across his face.

Elle still wasn't thrilled about the idea, but something in her shifted. She could see the spark in her son's eyes, his hunger, his belief in himself. That mattered too.

"All right," she said finally. "We'll talk to the other parents. But if anything feels off, you're not going."

Ethan nodded quickly. "Deal."

He didn't want to push it. He just wanted the chance. Later that week, the scent of roasted beans and warm cinnamon muffins filled the air as Elle stepped into Gerry Corner Café, a quiet coffee shop tucked between a used bookstore and a flower boutique in the downtown area. The bell above the door jingled softly as she entered, spotting Mrs. Ramirez, Marcus' mom, already seated at a corner table with two large coffees and a small notepad open in front of her.

"Elle! Over here!" she waved.

Elle smiled politely and made her way over just as Keith's dad and Lamar's mother walked in behind her. Everyone had carved out time from their busy schedules to gather in one place, proof of just how serious this trip had become.

Uncle George came in a few minutes later, limping slightly but refusing to use his old walking stick. "Just in case anyone forgot," he joked, "I'm still healing."

"Don't push it," Elle muttered under her breath, handing him a bottle of water.

The group exchanged greetings, small talk slowly fading into the heart of the matter as coffees were poured and chairs pulled in tighter.

Mrs. Ramirez leaned forward first. "So, Coach Lanning told us about the camps in Texas, California, and Kansas, right?"

"Yes," Elle confirmed. "Ethan came home excited, but it's a lot to process. Three camps, three states, flights, hotels, meals, all during the summer."

"And safety," added Lamar's mom, her tone firm. "We're talking about our boys being hundreds of miles away."

Uncle George nodded. "That's why I wanted to step in. If Elle can't travel this time, I'm willing to adjust my schedule and go with the boys. Sara understands. At least I'll be there for two of the camps, if not all three."

Keith's dad spoke next. "If we can coordinate the schedule, maybe we can tag team it. I can chaperone the California trip. I have family out there, so I could make it work."

"That helps," Elle said, jotting it down. "Maybe we can book group flights, too. If they're all on the same itinerary, that eases my nerves a bit."

They continued planning for nearly an hour—discussing logistics, creating an emergency contact list, exploring hotel options near the campuses, and estimating costs. It wasn't going to be cheap, but they all agreed: the exposure their sons would get at these elite camps could change their futures.

Before they left, Mrs. Ramirez smiled and looked around the table. "You know what I love about this? We're all in it together. These boys, they've got a whole community behind them."

Elle looked down at her coffee cup, then back up. "They're not just chasing football dreams. They're learning responsibility, teamwork, and how to handle life away from home. That matters too."

Uncle George raised his bottle of water slightly. "To the next level."

They all echoed the sentiment in their own way, a toast to hope, growth, and the summer that would shape their sons' futures.

Chapter 28
Miles from Home

Ethan folded his last pair of athletic socks and tucked them neatly into the corner of his duffel bag. His room was quieter than usual, no music, no TV, just the soft hum of the ceiling fan spinning above him. Three states. Three camps. Three chances to make everything count.

He zipped the bag closed and looked around the room, as if memorizing it. The bookshelf in the corner was half-filled with sports biographies, his favorite graphic novels, and the framed photo of his mom and Uncle George at his eighth-grade graduation. The "Dream Big" banner was still pinned above his closet. He was leaving for nearly a month, and something about it felt heavier than it should have.

Downstairs, Elle stood at the doorway with her arms crossed, watching as Ethan and Uncle George loaded the trunk of the car. The sun was rising, casting an orange-pink hue across the quiet neighborhood. Birds chirped faintly in the trees. It was too early for goodbyes, but that didn't stop her from feeling it anyway.

Ethan stepped up to her, bag slung over his shoulder.

"You sure you're gonna be okay while I'm gone?" he asked, gently bumping her shoulder with his.

Elle smiled. "I'll be fine. The house might be quieter, but that's not always a bad thing."

He chuckled softly, but his eyes searched hers, still concerned.

"You call me when you land. And every day in between."

"I will," Ethan nodded. "Promise."

She pulled him in for a tight, warm, and lingering hug. "I'm proud of you, Ethan. No matter what happens out there, keep being you."

Uncle George honked the horn lightly from the car. "We've got a flight to catch!"

Ethan grinned, gave her one more squeeze, and then jogged toward the car. Before getting in, he turned around and waved. Elle stood in the driveway, waving back, her heart full and her eyes just a little misty.

As they drove toward the airport, Ethan stared out the window, the morning light washing over the road ahead. His mind buzzed with anticipation. He wasn't just heading to football camps; he was stepping into something bigger. Something unknown.

Miles from home, but not alone. The airport buzzed with early-morning energy: announcements over the intercom, the screech of suitcase wheels on polished floors, and the low hum of travelers hustling through terminals. Ethan and Uncle George made their way through the sliding doors of Terminal C, spotting Coach Lanning and the others near the check-in counters.

Keith was already there with his dad, holding a giant bottle of a sports energy drink and grinning like this was the start of a vacation. Marcus stood beside his mom, who was triple-checking his documents and peppering him with last-minute reminders. Lamar and his older brother, who'd flown in from college to see him off, laughed about something on their phones.

"Yo!" Marcus called out when he saw Ethan. "You ready for this Texas heat?"

"As ready as I'll ever be," Ethan replied with a smirk, fist-bumping him.

Elle had decided not to come to the airport—it would've made the goodbye too emotional. But she'd texted Ethan five times already that morning. He had responded to each with a thumbs-up and a heart emoji. Uncle George handled checking them in and confirming their boarding passes and luggage, while the group of parents exchanged small talk and contact info.

Coach Lanning pulled the boys into a quick huddle.

"This is a business trip, fellas. But that doesn't mean you can't enjoy it. Represent your families, your school, and yourselves well. I'll check in with each of you throughout the week, but remember you only get one shot to leave a first impression with these recruiters."

The boys nodded solemnly. Lamar stretched his arms behind his head. "Let's get it."

Security moved quickly. Before they knew it, they were walking down the jet bridge, backpacks slung over their shoulders, with overhead lights guiding them into the cabin. Ethan took a window seat beside Marcus. Uncle George sat a few rows behind, already flipping through a magazine someone had left in the seat pocket.

As the plane rolled back from the gate, Ethan stared out the window. His heart beat a little faster. He'd been on a plane before…but this trip felt different. More serious. Bigger. A mix of nerves and adrenaline stirred in his chest.

"You good?" Marcus asked, popping a piece of gum into his mouth and offering Ethan one.

Ethan nodded. "Yeah. Just thinking about everything."

Marcus grinned. "Well, stop. You're thinking too hard. We're about to crush this camp."

The engines roared to life. As the plane lifted off the runway and climbed above the clouds, Ethan leaned back in his seat. Texas was a couple of hours away. The first elite camp was just getting started.

But so was the next chapter of his journey. The Texas sun greeted them like a slap to the face.

As the boys stepped off the plane and onto the tarmac at Longfield Regional Airport, the heat wrapped around them thick and unrelenting. Lamar pulled off his hoodie the moment they hit the jet bridge. "Man, it's like walking into a toaster."

Ethan chuckled, adjusting his duffel bag. "We ain't in Gerry anymore."

After grabbing their luggage and loading into two rental vans, the group made the 40-minute drive to the camp facility Lone Hill Elite Gridiron Academy, a sprawling campus of turf fields, training rooms, dorm-style cabins, and meeting halls tucked between dry hills and oak trees. The entrance sign boasted in big white letters: "Where Legends Are Built."

It wasn't an exaggeration.

As they pulled up to the main check-in center, dozens of other high school athletes from around the country were already arriving… guys tall as college players, with duffels over their shoulders and coaches trailing behind them. Some wore branded gear from powerhouse schools. Others looked just as wide-eyed as Ethan felt.

A camp coordinator, clipboard in hand, met their van and directed them toward registration.

"Ethan Phillips, right?" the woman said with a Texas twang, flipping a page on her list. "You're in Cabin B with Marcus, Keith, and Lamar. Head around the back, drop off your bags, and meet us at the orientation field at 5 o'clock. Dinner follows at six."

Uncle George gave Ethan a quick fist bump before they separated. "Call me tonight. And remember what we talked about…you belong here, no matter where they came from."

Ethan nodded, taking a deep breath as he followed his teammates past the rows of cabins, each one painted a dusty shade of tan with metal roofs and cold concrete steps.

Inside their cabin, the air conditioning hummed weakly, a relief after the drive. The room had four twin beds, four sets of shelves, and one small bathroom. No TV, no distractions. Just cleats, tape, and turf dreams.

That evening, the boys gathered on Field A with nearly a hundred other athletes. Coaches from major colleges, some with recognizable names, others more obscure, stood with clipboards and sunglasses, watching like hawks. The lead camp director gave a welcome speech, then blew the first whistle.

What followed was five straight days of grueling intensity.

Each morning began with warm-ups at 7 a.m., followed by position drills from 8 to noon. They broke for lunch, returning by 2 for team scrimmages and combine-style testing, which included forty-yard dashes, shuttle drills, and bench presses. Dinner came at 6:30, and evenings were filled with film reviews and guest speakers, former EFL players, current D1 coaches, and motivational speakers who reminded them that talent alone wasn't enough.

By midweek, Ethan's calves burned, his knuckles were scraped raw, and he was sure his arms couldn't lift another weight.

But he was also rising.

He beat his personal best in the vertical jump. Ran a 4.52 in the 40-yard dash. Caught a perfect spiral during the final scrimmage of the day that got a nod from one of the visiting coaches.

One night, while lying on his bed with his forearm over his eyes, Ethan whispered, "I think I'm finally catching my rhythm."

Marcus, who was finishing off a protein bar in the bunk across from him, said, "You're not catching it. You're owning it."

They all laughed.

On Friday afternoon, the final day, Ethan stood beside Marcus, sweating and exhausted, as they handed in their performance packets. His name had been circled on three different college scout sheets.

As they loaded up the van for the airport, Uncle George clapped him on the back.

"One down," he said. "Two more to go."

Ethan grinned. "Let's do this."

Back in Gerry, at the local community clinic, Elle had just finished charting notes from her last patient when the front desk nurse's voice buzzed urgently over the intercom.

"Trauma code incoming, EMS is en route with an unconscious male, suspected overdose."

Elle slipped on her gloves and joined two nurses and a physician at the trauma bay, prepping IV fluids and oxygen lines. Within minutes, the doors burst open, and paramedics wheeled in a man, mid-30s, twitching and barely conscious, his pupils dilated.

"Fentanyl," one paramedic barked. "Found unresponsive at a transit stop. Heart rate dropping. We gave Narcan, but he's fighting."

Elle moved quickly, helping secure the airway while another nurse inserted an IV. The man jerked, groaning, his eyes fluttering open just as they began resuscitative measures.

"Let's stabilize his vitals," the doctor said, moving to inject a sedative.

That's when it happened.

In a flash, too fast to register, the man's arm twisted upward. A small blade no longer than a scalpel slid from beneath the cuff of his long sleeve. Before anyone could react, he slashed outward.

Elle felt a burning sting across her forearm, the cut deep and sharp. She gasped, stumbling back as blood began to soak through her sleeve.

"Get security!" someone shouted. The attending doctor lunged forward and drove in the second injection.

The man's body slackened, breath hitching.

But before the medication could fully drag him under, his head turned sharply toward Elle.

His pupils widened, black and endless, locking her in place.

With a breath that scraped the air like broken glass, he whispered....

"*Almost.*"

The word did not fall.

It lingered, a curse that seemed to seep into the walls themselves.

No one moved.

The room became ice.

The monitors beeped steadily again, his heart rate normalizing under sedation, but the room was no longer the same.

Elle clutched a towel to her wound. The other nurse looked at her, pale.

"Did he say...?"

"Yeah," Elle murmured, her voice trembling. "He did."

The doctor shook his head, brows furrowed. "Another case tied to drugs. People need to stay off them."

He waved his hand, signaling everyone to finish up and reset the room. No one said anything else. But as they moved around, the tension in the air lingered like a whisper that hadn't finished its sentence.

Back in Kansas, the evening settled into a hush as the boys returned to the hotel after dinner. As they prepared for camp on Monday, Ethan had just stepped out of the shower, towel slung over his shoulder, when Uncle George's phone buzzed on the nightstand. George answered quickly, his voice shifting into a serious, quiet tone.

Ethan wasn't trying to eavesdrop, but something about the way his uncle stepped toward the window, the way he lowered his voice, made him pause mid-step.

"Wait, slow down… What do you mean you were cut?"

Ethan froze.

Uncle George kept listening, glancing back once to see if Ethan was in earshot. But it was too late.

"No, Elle, no…listen. Are you okay now? Did they bandage it? What hospital? Did they catch him?"

Ethan's heart pounded.

His mother.

Cut?

Hospital?

The room felt smaller by the second.

"I'll talk to you later," George said. "We won't tell Ethan. No need to worry him."

Too late.

The lump in Ethan's throat grew heavy. He grabbed his phone and slipped out of the room without saying a word. The hallway outside felt colder than it should have, and by the time he made it to the hotel lobby, he was already trying to breathe through the panic.

Marcus and Keith were sprawled out on the couches, talking about plays from the last day of camp.

Ethan sat down beside them, quiet.

"You good?" Marcus asked, catching the look on his friend's face.

Ethan nodded too quickly. "Yeah… just needed some air."

He stared ahead at the quiet lobby fountain, the soft bubbling water doing little to settle his nerves. He didn't say a word about what he heard. Not yet.

But he couldn't stop thinking: What if Uncle George hadn't answered? What if they never told me?

He wanted to call her. To hear her voice. But something inside told him to wait.

To pray.

And so, instead, he stared at the water, his thoughts racing, his chest heavy with worry, while his friends carried on unaware that Ethan's world had just tilted, again.

Chapter 29
Unshaken Focus

The sun was barely rising over the Kansas horizon when Ethan zipped up his duffel bag and sat at the edge of the hotel bed, waiting for Uncle George to finish brushing his teeth. The camp shuttle wouldn't be there for another thirty minutes, but Ethan hadn't been able to sleep much, not after what he overheard last night.

As Uncle George walked out of the bathroom, towel slung over his shoulder, Ethan looked up.

"Can I ask you something?"

George paused, giving a knowing glance. "You heard me on the phone last night."

Ethan nodded. "What happened to Mom?"

George sighed, sitting on the bed across from him. "She's okay. Really. She was at work, helping a patient who came in with a suspected overdose. Things got a little out of control, and… she got a small cut on her forearm. Nothing serious. She's bandaged and back home resting."

Ethan clenched his jaw. "She got cut. At work?"

George raised his hand gently. "I know, I know. It sounds worse than it is. She told me herself, she's alright. And she didn't want me to tell you. Not yet."

"So why didn't you just tell me last night?" Ethan's voice cracked with restrained frustration.

"Because she didn't want you distracted. She wanted you to keep your focus. We'll call her together tonight so she can explain in her own words."

Ethan lowered his head, rubbing his hands together. He hated not being there. Hated the thought of his mom getting hurt while he was chasing dreams states away. "I just don't like her being hurt, working so hard. She shouldn't have to do all that."

"I know," George said softly. "But she's strong, Ethan, just like you. Right now, she wants you to stay locked in. This opportunity, these camps…this is your time."

Ethan nodded slowly, inhaling through his nose.

"I want to play professionally one day," he said quietly. "Not just for me, but so she doesn't have to work another day in her life. You either."

George's eyes warmed with pride. "You've got a good heart, son. Just remember, greatness doesn't come without a storm or two."

Just then, the phone buzzed. The camp shuttle had arrived early.

Ethan grabbed his gear and stood up. "Let's go."

The ride to the Dinslow State Elite Football Institute was quiet. The other boys joked and chatted, but Ethan remained still, headphones in, gaze out the window. His mind shifted between the turf and his mom. The pain of not being home lit a fire inside him, a fuel unlike anything he'd ever felt.

That morning, the trainers pushed them through weighted sled drills, route running, and 7-on-7 matchups. Ethan was locked in. Every sprint, every snap, every catch, he gave it everything. Sweat poured down his face, his cleats dug into the grass like he was anchoring dreams beneath him.

His coaches noticed.

"He's laser-focused," one whispered.

"Kid's got something to prove," another nodded.

By afternoon, when they broke for lunch, Marcus slapped him on the back. "Yo, you good? You're a beast today."

Ethan smirked. "I've just got things on my mind."

They continued the day with footwork stations and defensive-timing drills. By the time the sun dipped into the Kansas sky, Ethan felt the soreness deep in his bones, but also a deep sense of purpose.

He wasn't just playing football anymore.

He was building a future for his mom. For his uncle. For everything they had given up, so he could chase this dream.

And he wasn't going to let a single setback on or off the field take that away. That night, after the camp day ended, Ethan sat on the edge of the hotel bed with his phone pressed to his ear. Marcus and Keith were in the hallway, grabbing snacks, giving him a little privacy. Uncle George sat across the room, flipping through channels on mute, watching with quiet eyes.

"Hey, baby," Elle's voice came through with a tired but warm tone.

"Mom," Ethan exhaled, sinking into the bed. "Uncle told me. About what happened at work."

Elle took a soft breath. "I figured he would."

"You okay? Like, really okay?" His voice cracked.

"I'm fine, sweetheart. It was just a medium-sized cut. It's a little deep, but the doctors treated it, bandaged it up, and I'm back home resting."

"But how did it even happen?"

"There was an overdose patient brought in by EMS. He was unstable. Violent. While we were trying to stabilize him, he slipped a blade out somehow. Caught me on the forearm before anyone could react. That's all."

Ethan sat in silence, his jaw tightening.

"I don't like this," he muttered. "You're working in that clinic, dealing with stuff like that. You shouldn't have to."

"I know," she replied gently. "But it's my job, and it's part of helping people. I promise, I'm being careful."

"Still," he mumbled, rubbing his forehead, "if I had already made it big, you wouldn't be working there. You wouldn't be getting hurt."

There was a pause.

"You don't have to carry that weight, Ethan," Elle said softly. "It's not yours to hold right now."

"But I want to."

A brief silence passed before she said, "Then let that be your fire. Not your burden."

Ethan nodded, wiping the corner of his eye. "You didn't even go to the main hospital, did you?"

"It was taken care of on-site. Just a few stitches. Nothing worth worrying about."

She didn't mention the words the man said before sedation.

Didn't describe the look in his eyes.

Didn't bring up how her coworkers exchanged uneasy glances afterward.

Didn't tell him how something felt... off.

It could wait.

"Go rest, Mom," Ethan finally said. "I'll call you again tomorrow."

"I love you, Ethan."

"Love you too."

As the call ended, Uncle George looked over. "Feel better?"

Ethan nodded, then stood and went to grab a bottle of water from the mini fridge. "She's strong," he said. "But I just feel like something's... off."

George didn't press. "Focus on the game. That's what she wants. Everything else, we'll deal with later."

Ethan gave a slight nod.

But in the back of his mind... the unease lingered. By the end of the week, the Kansas sun had hardened the boys' grit even more. The workouts were intense, more mental than physical at times. Coaches drilled them on defensive reads, special team strategies, and mid-game adaptability under pressure.

Ethan found himself lining up against older players, some of them already committed to big-name universities. He got beaten on more than a few routes, but he didn't flinch. Every failure added a new layer to his skill set. Lamar and Marcus were equally locked in. Coach Lott, a tough but respected legend in the region, kept telling them, "Out here, you either grow or go. There's no middle ground."

By Friday morning, the boys were exhausted in the best way…sore, sun-drenched, and more confident than ever.

Uncle George pulled Ethan aside before leaving for his return flight. "You're locked in, and I'm proud of you. Finish strong. I'll be waiting when you get back."

Ethan hugged him, something he hadn't done in a while without thinking. "Thanks for being here, Unc. For everything."

Lamar's dad, Mr. Jordan, had flown in the night before. He was quieter than Uncle George but equally present. He took over chaperone duties seamlessly, giving the boys space while keeping them in check.

"Let's finish strong," Mr. Jordan said after checking them into the airport early Saturday morning. "California's next, and trust me, that's where things go from fast to fierce."

They boarded their flight bound for California, and as soon as they landed, the mood shifted.

Madison's mansion was jaw-dropping.

A winding driveway led to a three-story modern estate perched above the coast in the hills of Crestview Bay. The front doors opened to a marble foyer with glass walls overlooking an infinity pool. Madison, a poised and confident heart surgeon with a welcoming smile, greeted the boys like family.

"You're welcome here. Just don't break anything older than you," she joked, guiding them through the house.

The boys tried not to gawk. Tried, but failed.

The basement alone felt like something out of a movie: a full-size theater room with recliners, a three-lane bowling alley, an LED-lit arcade room, and a snack bar that looked like a private concession stand.

Outside, they had access to:

A professional-sized basketball court,

A private tennis court,

A putting green and mini golf course,

A whole go-kart track that looped around a waterfall feature,

And a built-in fire pit near the pool with surround-sound music.

"I changed my mind," Marcus said, flopping onto one of the oversized pool loungers. "Forget camp. Let's stay here forever."

"Yeah, this is like athlete heaven," Ethan added, mouth open as he walked barefoot across the cool patio tile.

But Mr. Jordan wasn't having it.

"This place is a gift," he said, firm but kind. "You'll appreciate it after camp."

And he meant it.

By Monday morning, they were up before dawn, riding out to Greenhouse Elite Football Camp, tucked in the sun-scorched outskirts of Ridgeview County. The west coast sun was brutal. The drills were brutal. And the competition was on another level.

"Out here," one coach told them, "we don't care about stars. We care about the heart."

The boys were tested in ways they hadn't experienced before, especially on defense. The West Coast style of play was faster, more explosive, and required a higher IQ on both sides of the ball. Ethan learned how to read hips and anticipate breaks, shaving precious milliseconds off his coverage. Marcus finally started wrapping up on open-field tackles instead of swinging wide. Lamar began playing with finesse and speed, rather than relying on brute strength. Keith improved his quarterback reads and play selection.

They also hit the gym after camp hours. With Madison's home gym fully equipped like a pro athlete's training center, each of them gained between 5 and 10 pounds of healthy weight. Their bodies bulked up. Their confidence shot up.

The week flew by.

Nights were spent unwinding by the fire pit or taking dips in the pool under the stars. Madison made them smoothies every morning before training and listened to their camp updates like a proud aunt. Even Mr. Jordan smiled more especially after watching his son go toe-to-toe with a 5-star recruit during a scrimmage and come out on top.

The final night before heading home, the boys sat in the theater room watching old college game footage and eating popcorn.

"I don't want this to end," Ethan admitted.

"Me neither," Lamar said. "But this… this changed us."

"Facts," Marcus added. "Now we're ready. No excuses."

They didn't know it yet, but these three camps had transformed them, not just as players, but as young men with vision, resilience, and an edge. The next morning, the sun rose slowly over the western skies as Flight 812 from San Diego touched down at Gerry Airport. After nearly a month of nonstop drills, competition, sweat, and dreams coming to life, Ethan stepped off the plane feeling like a new version of himself. Stronger. Sharper. Hungrier.

He looked to his right. Marcus was yawning, Lamar was stretching his legs, and Keith was adjusting the duffel strap over his shoulder. Despite their exhaustion, there was a silent acknowledgment between them. They had survived three of the most brutal football camps in the country and came out better for it.

As the boys exited the terminal, a warm rush of familiarity greeted them, along with their families.

Elle stood near the arrival gate, her eyes searching anxiously until they locked on Ethan. A wave of relief swept over her as she opened her arms, and he stepped into them without hesitation. She held him close, the kind of embrace that melted miles and months of worry.

"I missed you, baby," she whispered.

"I missed you, too," Ethan murmured, surprised by how much he needed this exact moment.

Nearby, Marcus's mom was dabbing her eyes. Lamar's dad gave him a one-armed hug and patted Keith on the shoulder. Parents were everywhere, offering congratulations, loading up luggage, and snapping a few photos. Uncle George wasn't there; he had left for Hawaii with Sara the day before, a long-planned vacation that overlapped the last leg of camp.

"I'm so proud of you," Elle said, stepping back to get a better look at him. "You look... different."

"I feel different," Ethan replied. "In a good way."

Once the luggage was claimed and the greetings had settled into conversations, the boys regrouped one last time near the exit doors.

Marcus nudged Ethan. "Let's take a few days to chill. I need to sit still and not think about football for like... twenty-four hours."

Keith chuckled. "I'm sleeping in for a week."

Lamar grinned. "Same here. But after that? We gotta talk about everything. What we learned, what we're doing next. I got plays I wanna break down."

Ethan nodded. "Yeah. Let's meet up by the weekend."

Before heading to their separate cars, they did their usual quick handshake-hug, a signal of loyalty and brotherhood that had deepened over the summer.

"Oh," Marcus added, walking backward toward his mom's car, "Coach Lanning said he wants to do a video call with all our parents. Said he wants feedback and to hear how we all handled the camps."

Ethan raised a brow. "You think he's trying to see who's ready for the fall?"

"Probably," Lamar said. "Or maybe he just missed us."

They all laughed, then parted ways.

As Ethan slid into the passenger seat of his mom's car, his duffel bag tossed in the trunk, he leaned back and exhaled.

"Home," he whispered.

Elle smiled over at him as she started the car. "And just in time for the weekend. I made your favorite."

"Mac and cheese?"

"With smoked turkey legs and honey-glazed carrots."

Ethan grinned. "You really missed me, huh?"

She glanced at him. "More than you know."

They drove in comfortable silence for a few miles. The city hadn't changed, but Ethan had. And though the season ahead still held

pressure, expectations, and possibly even dangers he couldn't yet see,
he was home, loved, and full of purpose.

Chapter 30
Quiet Before the Whistle

Monday morning came like a soft exhale. For the first time in weeks, Ethan didn't have to set an alarm. He lay sprawled across his bed, the sheets tangled around his legs, the faint scent of chlorine and sunscreen still clinging to his skin. His duffel bag sat half-zipped in the corner, untouched since arriving home from California. He didn't care. Not today.

Sunlight spilled through the window, warming the hardwood floor where Samson lay curled up, tail flicking slowly as if he, too, understood that today was a day for stillness.

Ethan stretched, yawned, and sank back into his pillow. No whistles. No drills. No boarding calls, name tags, or cafeteria lines. Just the peaceful hum of the ceiling fan and the distant chirp of birds outside the house.

Downstairs, he heard the soft clatter of dishes as his mom made breakfast. She hadn't rushed him to unpack or asked about the camp yet. She just hugged him long and hard when he landed, whispered, "I missed you," and let him be. That grace meant more than any lecture or praise.

He picked up his phone. A group text from Lamar and Marcus had come in around 10 p.m. the night before:

Lamar: "Still recovering from Cali. Aunt Madison tried to feed me steak three times a day."

Marcus: "Back in my bed, thank you, Lord. But yeah… we NEED to talk about these camps soon."

Ethan: "Let's rest tomorrow. Wednesday afternoon meet-up?"

Lamar: "Bet."

Marcus: "Cool. And Coach Lanning said he wants to video-call the parents later this week. You know he's about to give us a post-camp breakdown."

Ethan smiled at the screen, thumbs poised over the keyboard, then thought better of it and tossed the phone aside. He wasn't ready to talk about football again, at least not yet.

Later that week, on Wednesday afternoon, the living room was hushed for a weekday. Elle sat on the couch with her laptop open, her hair pulled into a soft bun, glasses perched on the bridge of her nose. Ethan sat at the kitchen counter, a bowl of cereal in front of him and the laptop charger coiled like a snake beside his elbow.

"Coach Lanning just sent the video link," she said. "He wants to start in ten."

Ethan nodded, finishing the last of his cereal. "Did he say what it's about?"

"Somewhat. Just a reflection call with parents and players. He said something about 'building momentum before the school year.'"

Elle turned the laptop so the camera could capture them both. Ethan leaned in, wiping his mouth with a paper towel.

One by one, familiar faces began appearing on the screen: Coach Lanning in his usual ball cap, Marcus's mom in a bright yellow blouse, Lamar's dad sitting in a home office lined with football trophies. A few other parents and players joined in, yawning or sipping coffee.

Coach Lanning smiled and raised a hand.

"Alright, everyone, good to see you all. I won't keep you long. I just wanted to thank each of you for supporting your sons this summer. Those camps weren't easy, but they were necessary. I've watched these boys grow in ways that stats don't measure. Leadership. Accountability. Humility."

He looked directly into the camera, as if speaking to each family individually.

"You can't coach character, not really, not unless kids have people at home who are rooting for more than just touchdowns. And I see that in all of you. So, thank you."

Several parents smiled or nodded. Ethan glanced at his mom. She gave a quiet, proud smile but said nothing.

Coach continued, "Now, we've got preseason starting in a couple of weeks, and I want you all to talk to your sons. Not just about goals, but about their identity. Who they are outside of football. Because life will test that, I promise you, it will."

The screen fell into a thoughtful silence.

Coach Lanning leaned back in his chair. "That's it for me. Boys, enjoy your downtime. Parents, thank you again. I'll be sending fall schedules out soon."

After the video call ended, Elle slowly closed the laptop.

"You've got a good coach," she said.

Ethan nodded. "Yeah. He sees more than what's on the scoreboard."

He stood, grabbed his bowl, and paused. "Mom?"

"Yeah, baby?"

"I want to talk about Dad soon. Just not today."

Elle's lips parted, then closed. She nodded once. "Okay. When you're ready."

Ethan walked to the sink, rinsing out his bowl, and looked out the window. For the first time in a while, the future didn't feel like a race. It felt like a slow, steady walk toward something that might finally make sense. Friday afternoon rolled in with a lazy heatwave. The kind of heat that made sidewalks shimmer and cicadas scream from the treetops.

Ethan biked over to Lamar's house, where Marcus was already waiting on the porch, sipping flavored water and scrolling through his phone. The air smelled like charcoal and cut grass, typical summer staples in the neighborhood.

"Yo," Ethan greeted, hopping off the bike and wiping sweat from his brow.

Lamar opened the door and waved them inside. His family's den was cool and comfortable, with a stack of leftover takeout containers on the kitchen counter and the sports channel playing softly in the background.

The three collapsed onto beanbags and worn couch cushions, letting out a collective sigh.

Marcus was the first to speak. "So… those camps were no joke."

"For real," Lamar agreed. "I'm still sore from that Thursday scrimmage. Aunt Madison had me soaking in Epsom salt like I was a retired linebacker."

Ethan chuckled. "Same. And I haven't even opened my cleats bag yet. Just the thought of smelling it…"

They all groaned in unison.

Then the conversation turned serious.

"What y'all think Coach meant during the video call?" Marcus asked. "That part about identity."

Lamar leaned forward. "I think he's warning us. Like, don't let football be the only thing that tells us who we are. 'Cause one injury or one bad season, and you don't even know your name anymore."

Ethan nodded slowly. "Yeah. I've been thinking about that too. Camps made me realize I love the game, but… it ain't everything."

The boys sat in silence for a moment, absorbing their own words.

Then Lamar broke it: "Okay, enough of the deep talk. Let's agree next year, no more three back-to-back camps."

"Agreed," Marcus said.

"Signed in blood," Ethan laughed.

On Sunday, July 4, it was Sara's Family Cookout, the sun was high, and the grill was hot. Sara's backyard was buzzing with energy.

Ethan had never seen so many people he didn't know all in one place and all somehow related. The yard was huge, complete with a pool, two picnic tables, a shaded patio, and a bouncy house in the corner for the younger kids.

Sara, radiant in a red sundress, welcomed them warmly. "Ethan! You made it. Come on, let me introduce you to the crew."

She walked him and Uncle George around, smiling like a proud aunt showing off her favorite student. Ethan met her parents, her two brothers, one sister, a dozen cousins, and even a few aunts and uncles who immediately complimented his height and handshake.

After an hour of fun playing ring toss and eating three hot dogs with bags of potato chips, came the moment.

A tall, lean kid with a sharp jawline and a smug expression walked over from the basketball court.

"You're Ethan Phillips, right?" the boy asked.

Ethan blinked. "Yeah… and you are?"

"Jaylen. Deskfloor Academy Eagles." The boy smirked. "We played y'all in the semis. I had two sacks in that game."

Ethan kept a neutral face. "Okay."

"Your quarterback was trash, man. Kept running scared. Y'all folded once we started applying pressure. I watched your highlight reel. Y'all overrated."

A few nearby kids laughed nervously. Ethan's jaw tightened. He didn't take the bait.

"I'm gonna go grab some lemonade," he said coolly.

He turned toward the picnic table when suddenly—shove.

Jaylen pushed him hard in the back, causing Ethan to stumble and knock over a whole pitcher of lemonade onto the tablecloth. Cups scattered, and a watermelon slice went tumbling off the edge.

The crowd went silent.

Sara's dad stood up immediately. "Hey! That's enough!"

"Jaylen!" shouted one of the aunts. "What is wrong with you?"

Uncle George was already moving. His expression was tight lips pressed together, jaw flexed, eyes blazing.

Ethan froze, fists clenched, but still said nothing.

George put a firm hand on Ethan's shoulder and turned to Sara, who rushed over apologizing.

"I am so sorry," she said, flustered. "That's my nephew, and he…he's always had a mouth on him. I'll handle it, George. Please don't go."

But George shook his head. "I'm not keeping him in this. I won't expose him to stuff like this, not even for a cookout. We're leaving."

"Please, just…"

George didn't raise his voice, but his tone was final. "I respect you, Sara. But this is not right. This ain't it."

He ushered Ethan toward the gate, his grip protective, fatherly.

The car ride was quiet at first. George's knuckles tightened on the wheel, eyes locked on the road. Ethan stared out the window, the scene at the picnic playing over and over in his mind.

After a few miles, Ethan spoke.

"I didn't even say anything back to him. I let him talk. I got tired of hearing it and got up to walk away, and he still, he still tried to make a scene."

George nodded slowly. "I know. I saw it."

"I wanted to swing on him," Ethan admitted, voice low. "But I didn't."

"I know that too."

Silence stretched again.

George finally sighed and looked at Ethan during a red light. "You showed restraint. That takes strength. More than people give credit for."

Ethan glanced at him. "You're not mad?"

"I'm proud." George's voice was calm. "You could've reacted like most would've expected you to. You didn't. You showed character. That means more than sacking some loudmouth on the field or winning an argument."

The light turned green, and they rolled forward.

"You were bigger than the moment," George added. "And that matters. Even when it hurts."

Ethan swallowed hard, the fire in his chest cooling. "Thanks, Unc."

George gave a small smile. "Anytime, kid. You keep proving who you are one decision at a time." The front door closed with a soft click, but the weight of the evening slammed against the walls like a storm that hadn't passed.

Ethan didn't say a word. He kicked off his shoes at the bottom of the stairs and climbed each step slowly, his jaw clenched, eyes dark and unfocused. His ears were still ringing with Jaylen's voice, his body still tense from restraint.

He pushed open the door to his room and shut it behind him with more force than he meant to.

Then he just stood there.

The room was familiar, safe, but his chest was tight, like he couldn't breathe in the air he knew best. He sat on the edge of his bed, palms resting on his knees, eyes fixed on the floor.

Anger pulsed through him…hot, raw, unresolved.

Downstairs, he heard Uncle George's voice drift into the living room where Elle was sitting with a book. George didn't bother sitting. He stood with his hands on his hips, pacing in front of Elle as he recounted what happened.

"That boy, Sara's nephew, targeted Ethan. Called out his school, mocked his team, and then shoved him from behind. Spilled lemonade all over the picnic table. It wasn't teasing, Elle. It wasn't very nice. Meant to provoke him."

Elle's eyes widened. "What did Ethan do?"

"He walked away," George said firmly. "He got up. Said nothing. Tried to remove himself from the situation."

A pause.

Elle put her hand over her mouth, eyes welling slightly. "Oh… my baby."

George softened his tone. "He didn't swing. He didn't curse. He didn't even raise his voice. But I saw the look in his eyes. That boy got under his skin, and Ethan walked away anyway. That's character.

That's maturity. And I wasn't about to let him sit there and stew in that kind of mess while people excused it as 'just kids being kids.' So, I brought him home."

Elle exhaled and nodded slowly. "Thank you."

George rubbed the back of his neck. "Sara was embarrassed. She asked us to stay, but... I'm not gonna put Ethan in places where he's disrespected to keep peace."

Elle stood and wrapped her arms around George. "You did the right thing."

Back upstairs, Ethan stared at the blank page in his journal.

The leather-bound notebook sat in his lap, the pen in his hand unmoving. The pages before it were full of camp reflections, play breakdowns, weight goals, and quotes from Coach Lanning.

But this page… this page wasn't about football.

It was about fire.

He clicked the pen and began to write, his handwriting sharper than usual, pressed deep into the paper:

July 4

I hate that people can get away with running their mouths and still feel like they're on top. I hate how much it bothered me. I tried to walk away. I tried to be the bigger person. But it still doesn't feel good.

That kid pushed me, and I wanted to shove him through the picnic table.

But I didn't.

I hate that I still feel like I lost something.

Everyone always says, "be the bigger person," but no one talks about how being bigger sometimes feels like being silent, like swallowing your pride, your heat, your scream.

I walked away, and it still hurts.

I don't know what I was supposed to do to feel peace about it.

I'm tired of having to prove I'm not like "them."

I'm just tired.

He stopped writing, the pen hovering over the page.

Then, as if trying to end it on a note of control, he scribbled one last line:

But I know who I am. And that has to be enough.

Ethan closed the journal gently and placed it on his nightstand. His chest was still heavy, but something about seeing the words on paper made the storm feel less overwhelming.

He lay back on the bed and stared at the ceiling.

Quiet.

But not silence.

Chapter 31
When Summer Fades

The days after the Fourth of July passed quietly, like sunlight slowly dimming behind the trees.

Ethan didn't talk much about what happened at Sara's house. He didn't need to. Uncle George never brought it up again, and Elle gave him space, checking in with warm eyes, gentle questions, and plenty of his favorite meals.

For the first time in a long while, Ethan had no schedule. No weight room alarms. No cleats waiting by the door. Just empty days filled with soft mornings and slow afternoons.

Somewhere between July 10 and the first week of August, the rhythm of summer returned. He mowed lawns with Marcus twice a week, made a few extra bucks, and sometimes helped Lamar organize his grandfather's garage. Most nights, he fell asleep listening to the hum of cicadas and the distant crack of neighborhood fireworks, even after the holiday had long passed.

He found himself journaling more about things that had nothing to do with football.

One entry read:

"Peace doesn't always shout. Sometimes it whispers after you walk away."

He didn't know if it made sense to anyone else, but it felt right. Later in the week, he received an email from Coach Lanning about the preseason schedule. It stated that practice resumed on August 7. Ethan read it three times and then left his phone face down on his dresser. He wasn't dreading it, but something had shifted. Football was still his passion, but it wasn't his identity. At least, not anymore.

Uncle George noticed.

"You okay?" he asked one night after dinner, both of them on the porch watching the sky shift colors.

"Yeah," Ethan said. "Just thinking more than usual, I guess."

George nodded. "That's not a bad thing. Some boys only think with their cleats."

Ethan smirked. "I used to."

George leaned back in his chair. "You're growing, E. And not just in height. I see it. And I'm proud of it."

The first day of practice, the turf was hot. The air was thicker than it had any right to be. Coach Lanning's whistle sliced through the morning fog as the team gathered for warm-ups.

Ethan spotted Marcus already stretching, his hair damp with sweat. Lamar jogged in moments later, grinning like he never left.

"Y'all ready?" Lamar asked.

"No," Ethan said, pulling on his gloves. "But we're here."

The team started running drills, and just like that, summer began to fade.

The weight of the pads. The sound of cleats scraping turf. The rhythm of quarterbacks calling cadence.

It all came rushing back.

Coach Lanning walked up behind Ethan during drills and gave him a firm pat on the back.

"Still got it," he said. "But don't think I didn't notice…something's different about you."

Ethan looked over. "In a good way?"

Coach smiled. "The best way."

A few days before school started, Ethan sat in the old swivel chair at the local barbershop. The bell jingled each time a new customer came in, but no one was in a rush.

Carter lined him up while talking to another man about high school ball.

"Gerry got some dogs this year," the man said. "But they'd better protect that QB better than they did last season."

Ethan listened without saying a word, a smile tugging at the corner of his mouth.

"Ethan," Carter said, "you ready for junior year?"

Ethan nodded. "I think so. Trying not to overhype it."

Carter leaned in with the clippers. "Don't hype it, own it. Quiet confidence. That's how you lead."

Ethan let the words settle. He liked that.

***

The first day of junior year, the morning air felt different…cooler, sharper, laced with the scent of dew and pencil shavings. Ethan stood in front of the mirror, buttoning a crisp black polo shirt and dark jeans. His backpack leaned against the doorframe like an old friend.

Elle peeked into the room. "You look sharp, baby."

"Thanks, Ma."

She walked in, brushed a bit of lint from his collar, and looked him over the way only a mother could. "Junior year. You ready?"

Ethan thought about the cookouts, the camps, the shoves he didn't return, the words he swallowed, the miles he ran, and the journal entries he hadn't let anyone read.

He nodded slowly. "Yeah. I'm ready."

Downstairs, Uncle George was waiting at the table with two sausage-egg sandwiches and a bottle of orange juice.

"Eat up," he said. "You've got a long year ahead."

Ethan sat, took a bite, and smiled.

For the first time, school didn't feel like just another season to get through. It felt like a new chapter.

Not because everything was perfect.

But because he wasn't the same.

Moments later, Ethan arrived in the school parking lot, which was buzzing with life.

Doors slammed shut. Music blasted from cracked windows. Girls hugged each other like they hadn't seen each other in ten years instead of ten weeks. Guys threw their backpacks over one shoulder and leaned against cars like nothing had changed.

Ethan stepped out of Uncle George's truck and adjusted his bag. The sun glinted off the hood as George gave him a nod.

"You got this," he said.

Ethan nodded and closed the door.

Inside the school, it smelled the same disinfectant, floor wax, and a hint of teenage cologne. But it felt different this year. He felt different.

He passed a group of juniors at their lockers, some tossing jokes, some scrolling through their phones.

"Yo Ethan!" someone called from behind. Marcus jogged up beside him, Lamar a step behind.

"Man, this hallway's packed," Marcus said. "You'd think they were giving away free tennis shoes."

"First day energy," Lamar added, bumping fists with Ethan.

They walked toward the main hallway, nodding at familiar faces. A few underclassmen glanced their way, whispering. Ethan caught the words "varsity guys" and "Phillips," but he tuned them out.

He wasn't walking into this year for anyone else.

They paused near the large bulletin board where class rosters were posted.

"I'm in Pre-Calc with Ms. Lain," Marcus said, scanning his schedule. "Period 2."

"Got Chemistry with Coach Brenner," Lamar added. "Not bad."

Ethan looked at his own. First period hit him like a cold splash of water.

"Valentine. Room 204. AP Pre-Calc."

Marcus raised his brows. "Dang. You're in with the calculators-for-fun crowd."

Lamar elbowed him. "Man, Ethan's smart. He belonged there before half of them even knew what Pi was."

Ethan smirked but said nothing. He looked down at his schedule once more.

Ethan adjusted the strap on his backpack and glanced down at the schedule again:

"1st Period – AP Pre-Calc Ms. Valentine"

Most of his teammates were in regular math or study hall, but Mrs. Duncan, his guidance counselor, had told him months ago, "Ethan, I'm placing you in advanced math and science next year. You've got the mind for it. Don't let football hide that."

So here he was. Climbing the stairs. No shoulder pads. Just a mechanical pencil and a quiet determination.

He walked into the classroom five minutes early. Posters of famous mathematicians lined the walls. A countdown clock read "SAT: 228 Days."

Ms. Valentine stood at the whiteboard, scribbling in red marker. She looked up over her glasses.

"Name?"

"Ethan Phillips."

She paused. "Ah. Football, right?"

He nodded. "Yes, ma'am."

"You sure you're in the right room? This is AP Pre-Calc, not Phys Ed."

Ethan kept his tone even. "Mrs. Duncan placed me here."

"Alright then," she said with a shrug. "Have a seat."

It has been three days of being in Ms. Valentine's class, and she hasn't hidden her skepticism. She handed out pop quizzes like snacks, rarely offered praise, and left curt, vague comments in red ink like "Think deeper" or "Are you trying?"

Ethan noticed a pattern: other students got second chances.

He didn't.

Kyle Matherson bombed a quiz and got to retake it.

Ethan missed one formula on a five-question warm-up and heard:

"Mr. Phillips, I hope you're not relying on your playbook to get through this class."

The class chuckled. Ethan didn't.

After class, Ethan stayed behind. "Ms. Valentine, on the quadratic review, you marked number four wrong, but I checked it. I think it's actually correct."

She raised an eyebrow. "Interesting. Most athletes don't double-check their work."

Ethan stayed steady. "I just want to understand."

She glanced at the paper, sighed, then nodded. "You're right. I'll update it."

No apology. No respect.

Just another subtle jab.

At lunch, "You good, bro?" Lamar asked, eyeing Ethan's barely touched lunch.

Ethan sighed. "Valentine. Still treating me like I snuck into class through the locker room."

Marcus frowned. "Ain't she the one who said you don't belong?"

"Didn't say it like that," Ethan said. "But she doesn't have to."

"You gonna drop it?" Lamar asked.

"Nope."

"Good," Marcus said. "You're more than shoulder pads and cleats. Let her choke on them A's."

That night, Ethan sat at the dining table, math notes spread wide, calculator buzzing quietly. Elle passed by and paused.

"You okay?"

"I just want to ace this quiz."

"You don't have to prove anything, baby."

"I know." He looked up for a moment. "But I kind of want to."

Elle touched his shoulder. "Then do it with grace. Quiet storms leave the deepest marks."

Ethan nodded, turning back to the page.

This wasn't just about math anymore. It was about value. And showing up fully, even when someone doesn't expect you to.

On Thursday morning, the hallway buzzed as students spilled out of homeroom and shuffled toward first period. Locker doors slammed. Sneakers squeaked. The PA system crackled out a barely audible announcement about parking permits.

Ethan moved with purpose.

He adjusted his backpack strap and climbed the steps to the second floor. Room 204 loomed ahead, its door slightly ajar. His palms weren't sweaty, but his heartbeat was quiet with focus. He had taken Ms. Valentine's quiz two days ago, five problems, all heavy with layered equations and hidden tricks.

He had double-checked every answer.

As he entered the room, Ms. Valentine was already at her desk, a stack of graded quizzes in her hand. Her eyes flicked up to acknowledge him, then back to her stack. The rest of the class trickled in, chattering lightly.

When the bell rang, she stood.

"Let's keep things efficient today. You'll get your quizzes back first."

She began moving through the rows, handing them out. No words. Just papers sliding across desks. Some students flipped theirs quickly. A few groaned. One girl muttered, "Ugh, seriously?"

Ethan kept his eyes forward. Then she stopped at his desk.

She didn't speak right away. Just placed the quiz face down and paused for a second, barely perceptible before moving on.

Ethan waited until she returned to the front of the room before turning it over.

100%.

Written in red ink, but this time it wasn't harsh. Just… clear.

No comments. No sarcasm.

Just a quiet number circled at the top.

He stared at it for a moment, not smiling, not reacting outwardly, but something unlocked in his chest. The pressure. The questioning. The need to prove something.

He didn't need the class to clap.

He didn't need Ms. Valentine to make a speech.

He just needed that one moment of knowing he was more than they thought and had always been.

From the front of the room, Ms. Valentine cleared her throat.

"Most of you will need to review exponential functions this weekend. But one or two of you… handled it well."

She didn't look at him.

But she didn't have to.

As class went on, Ethan's pencil moved easily through the warm-up problems. His mind was sharper. Lighter.

At the bell, he gathered his things and started toward the door.

As he passed Ms. Valentine's desk, she glanced up, not cold this time. Measured.

"Good work, Mr. Phillips," she said. Quiet. Controlled. But real.

Ethan paused.

"Thank you, ma'am."

Then he walked into the hallway, the quiz folded neatly into his notebook like a quiet trophy.

Chapter 32
Quiet Influence

The Monday after the quiz results, Ethan walked into Room 204 with the same quiet resolve he'd carried all week. He had earned his grade, and even if Ms. Valentine hadn't thrown him a parade, something shifted that day, a weight lifted, even if just slightly.

As he slid into his seat near the window, he noticed Kyle Matherson, the quiet kid from the robotics team, glancing his way.

When class ended, and students began packing their things, Kyle hesitated near Ethan's desk.

"Hey," he said, voice low. "You, uh… You got a hundred on that quiz, right?"

Ethan nodded. "Yeah."

Kyle shifted his weight awkwardly. "Think you could help me understand question three? I've been stuck since Monday."

Ethan blinked. He hadn't expected that. But he nodded. "Sure. You want to meet in the library after school?"

Kyle smiled and was relieved. "Yeah. Thanks, man."

Ms. Valentine, still erasing the whiteboard, glanced their way. If she heard the exchange, she didn't comment. But her gaze lingered a second longer than usual.

The library was nearly empty after school. Ethan and Kyle sat at one of the back tables near the windows. They spent twenty minutes going over exponential decay and growth rates. Kyle listened closely, nodded a lot, and by the end of it, actually solved a sample problem on his own.

"I think I got it now," he said, pushing his notebook forward. "You explain it better than she does, honestly."

Ethan chuckled. "Don't let her hear you say that."

Kyle grinned. "You ever think about tutoring?"

Ethan shrugged. "Not really. I just… like helping when I can."

By Friday, word had gotten around. Two more students asked Ethan if he could help them review before the next quiz. He agreed, even though football practice had picked up with playoff season approaching. He just had to balance his time right.

Coach Lanning noticed the shift in him, too.

"Phillips," he said after practice one day, "I heard you're helping some of your classmates study."

Ethan wiped sweat from his brow. "Yes, sir."

Coach nodded. "Proud of that. Keep it up. Character shows up off the field, too."

As the days rolled on, the fall air grew sharper, and football talk consumed the halls of Gerry High. Posters were everywhere. The Gerry Hawks were headed into the playoffs with one of their strongest seasons yet.

The first game came fast, and Ethan was ready. He lined up under the stadium lights, cleats biting into turf, breath visible in the night air. When the ball snapped, everything else disappeared.

The Hawks dominated.

The following week, the stands were even fuller. The pressure was heavier. Ethan didn't flinch.

And then came the state semifinal against none other than Deskfloor Academy.

It was personal now.

Jaylen, the same boy from the Fourth of July cookout, was on the opposing sideline, smirking like old memories never faded.

Ethan met his gaze once. Just once. Then he walked away.

On the field, he let his performance speak louder than his voice.

Two touchdowns. One game-saving tackle. Zero trash talk.

Gerry High advanced.

The state championship game was held two weeks later in a packed stadium under a sky thick with clouds.

Ethan stood at midfield, helmet tucked under his arm, teammates shouting, coaches pacing.

As the national anthem ended, he closed his eyes briefly and whispered, "God, help me play with strength and humility."

The whistle blew. The game began.

It wasn't easy. The opposing team was disciplined and strict. But Gerry's line held firm, and Ethan's focus never wavered.

When the final seconds ticked down and the scoreboard flashed 28–21, the stands erupted.

State champions.

His teammates mobbed Ethan, lifted him on their shoulders, doused him in sports drinks, and pulled him into photo after photo.

But later that night, when it was quiet, he found himself alone in the locker room.

He pulled out his journal and stared at the blank page.

Then he wrote:

"I didn't win this. We did. And God gave me the strength to finish."

He set the pen down and let the stillness wash over him.

For the first time in a while, he felt at peace. The locker room lights buzzed overhead as Ethan closed his journal, slid it back into his bag, and stood to leave.

Outside, the stadium lot was mainly empty, the night sky stretching wide and starless. But parked near the player's exit was Uncle George's truck and beside it, Elle, bundled in her fleece coat, waving with both hands as if he'd just returned from war.

"STATE CHAMPS!" she shouted, her voice thick with pride and joy.

George leaned against the passenger side with a grin that hadn't faded since the final whistle. "Come on, MVP. We're taking you out."

Ethan laughed, tossing his bag into the back. "Where?"

Elle opened the back door and slid in. "You'll see."

Within 20 minutes, they arrived at the All-Night Diner at 1:12 a.m.

Neon lights flickered above the worn-out sign that read Local 24-Hour Grill. The windows were fogged from the warmth inside, and a red vinyl booth in the corner had just been wiped down when the trio walked in.

A waitress with tired eyes but a kind smile handed them laminated menus. "You folks celebrating something?"

Elle beamed. "Our boy just won the state championship again."

The woman lit up. "Well, then dessert's on the house."

Ethan didn't care much for dessert right now; he just wanted food. Real food. He ordered a bacon cheeseburger with seasoned fries and a chocolate shake. George got a skillet meal with everything. Elle settled on pancakes, eggs, and sausage.

They ate slowly and laughed loudly. They replayed the game's best moments, teased George for yelling at the refs, and watched Elle tear up as she shared her pride.

Then, somewhere between the last bite of fries and a shared slice of pie, George leaned back and looked at Ethan seriously.

"You handled yourself like a grown-up out there," he said. "Not just on the field, but after. You kept your head. Led your team. Walked in humility. That's bigger than any trophy."

Elle reached across the table and took Ethan's hand. "We love you, baby. We're so proud of the man you're becoming."

Ethan swallowed hard, his heart full. "Thank you… Both of you. For everything."

They didn't need to say more. The silence was golden. Filled with the kind of love that didn't shout. It just sat with you, stayed warm beside you, and reminded you that you weren't alone.

The first snow fell just two days after the state championship game. Light and feathery at first, it dusted the streets of Gerry with soft white, coating rooftops and blanketing driveways like a reminder to slow down.

Ethan had barely gotten used to the quiet again. The buzzing of school had dimmed, and the news interviews had stopped calling. Christmas break had officially started, and for the first time in months, he had no obligations but to sleep, spend time with his family, and the promise of peace.

What he didn't expect was the surprise George had been planning behind the scenes. "Hey, kid, pack some clothes," shouted Uncle George from downstairs.

"Wait…what do you mean, pack a carry-on?" Ethan asked, suitcase already in hand, standing in the living room with his mom and uncle.

George smirked and zipped up his duffel bag. "I mean what I said. Shorts, T-shirts, flip-flops. No coats. No snow boots. Trust me."

Elle laughed from the hallway, pulling down a beach hat and sunglasses. "Your uncle has been dying to tell you for two weeks."

"Tell me what?"

"We're flying to St. Thomas," George said. "Merry Christmas, kid."

Ethan blinked. "Wait for real?"

"Real palm trees, real sunshine, and real relaxation," Elle said, already grabbing her passport. "You earned it. We all did."

Ethan couldn't help but smile. The championship win had been big, but this? This felt personal. Like love wrapped in sunshine.

On December 23, the ocean air & peaceful skies met the family as they landed on the island.

St. Thomas greeted them with warm breezes and blue skies that didn't seem to end. Their hotel overlooked the coast, balconies wrapped in ivy and hammocks swaying beneath palm trees.

Ethan stood barefoot in the sand that first evening, toes digging into the grains while the waves brushed the shore like whispers. Elle was sipping fruit juice in a beach chair. George had already made friends with the locals and found a dominoes game near the outdoor bar.

It was quiet. No camera flashes, no coach's whistles. No, Ms. Valentine.

Just family. Just peace.

That night, they had dinner under the stars. Lobster, jerk chicken, and mango-glazed ribs filled the table. Music played softly from a steel drum band, and laughter filled the space between courses.

"George," Elle said, "this was the best idea you've ever had."

George leaned back and put his hands behind his head. "Told y'all. Can't spell Christmas without a little island breeze."

Ethan looked around the table and realized he hadn't felt this light in months.

On Christmas morning, they exchanged small gifts on the hotel balcony. Elle gave Ethan a leather-bound travel Holy scriptures with his name etched into the front. George gifted him a waterproof sports watch.

"I know you got game on the field," George said, "but never lose track of time where it counts."

Ethan opened his mouth to respond, but the lump in his throat was too tight.

Instead, he nodded.

"Thanks, Unc. Thanks, Ma. For everything."

Elle wrapped her arms around him, and they just stayed there for a mother-son moment, both a little sunburned, both a little emotional.

Later that day, they took a boat ride around the island. They snorkeled in crystal-clear waters and ate fried plantains from a beach stand run by an older woman who called Ethan "Island Champion" after George bragged about the state title.

That night, lying in bed with the windows open and the waves singing him to sleep, Ethan pulled out his journal.

He didn't write. He just held it. And for some reason, that was enough. Their last full day on the island was one for the scrapbook.

They started early with a cave tour on the northern edge of the island, ducking through narrow passageways, marveling at ancient rock formations and clear underground pools that shimmered with light. Ethan led the way, flashlight in hand, laughing every time Elle screamed at the sound of a bat or a sudden drop of water.

"That better be water," she said, swatting at her hair. "If something crawls on me, I'm never coming back to the island."

George chuckled behind her. "You'll be back to paradise, Elle."

After the caves, they changed clothes and took a short hike through a tropical forest, where the scent of wild guava and sun-ripened leaves filled the air. They stopped to take pictures under an old banyan tree, its thick roots curling up from the ground like something out of a fairytale.

Ethan stood in the middle of it all, sweat on his brow, sunlight dancing between the leaves. For a moment, he closed his eyes and breathed it in.

Freedom.

Later that afternoon, they boarded a boat for a casual tour along the western edge of the island. Their guide, a barefoot man named Ray who claimed to have once been a reggae drummer, pointed out hidden beaches, coral reefs, and local homes built into the cliffs.

As the sun began its slow descent, they docked near a street market alive with color and music.

Ethan wandered from booth to booth, picking up hand-carved coasters with palm-tree engravings, T-shirts with phrases like "Salt in My Soul" and "Built for Island Life," and a bracelet for Marcus with a coconut-shell bead.

At one table, a woman with silver hair and sun-worn hands held up a shirt and said, "You look like a strong one. This one's for warriors."

Ethan smiled and bought it on the spot.

That evening, they returned to their hotel just before sunset and dressed for one last dinner by the sea.

The restaurant patio overlooked the water, with lanterns strung across the railing and live guitar music playing softly in the background. The air was warm and fragrant with spices.

Ethan ordered grilled shrimp with rice and plantains. George went all-in on a plate of jerk ribs, and Elle ordered red snapper with coconut cream sauce.

Their conversation was light, full of teasing and story-swapping.

Elle raised her glass of fruit punch halfway through the meal. "To peace, to family, and to rest. Because Lord knows, we don't get enough of it."

George raised his own. "To fresh air and no referees."

Ethan laughed. "And to the woman who thought I was a warrior."

They clinked glasses, no champagne, no spectacle, just gratitude.

After dessert, they walked barefoot along the beach, letting the waves chase their toes. George told a story about how he almost got left behind on a cruise ship once, and Elle howled with laughter the whole time.

It was simple. It was sacred.

It was enough.

The Next Morning at the airport, Ethan stood on the tarmac, one last breeze brushing his face as they climbed the steps to the plane. He turned around, took a deep breath of ocean air, and held it.

"Ready?" George asked, stepping past him. Ethan nodded. "Yeah. I'm ready."

But deep inside, a small part of him wished they could stay just one more day. "I'm gonna miss this place," he said.

"You and me both," Elle replied, adjusting her carry-on. "But reality's waiting."

George chuckled. "Cold, snow-covered, homework-filled reality."

Ethan smirked. "Sounds awful."

They handed over their boarding passes and headed toward the jet bridge. Vacation was over. But something about the trip stuck to Ethan's heart like a breeze he didn't want to forget.

Back in Gerry, it was New Year's Eve.

They kept it simple.

A few snacks. Sparkling cider in paper cups. A blanket was thrown over the couch while a countdown played on TV. Just Ethan, Elle, and George, wrapped in warmth while the year ticked down.

At midnight, they clinked cups and yelled over the firework pops from the neighborhood.

"To peace," Elle said.

"To vision," George added.

Ethan nodded quietly. "To finish what we started."

Back at school, by the time the New Year had come and gone, the energy had shifted. The buzz of football faded into yearbook photos, senior prep talks, and college chatter. Though he was still a junior, Ethan could feel it coming, his time.

His inbox started filling up with emails from recruiters and college coordinators. Coaches left messages for his mom. Brochures piled on the kitchen counter: Briarstone University, Winslow State, Greywood College, Northwood Gridiron Institute, and Rockdale University. The stack was taller than the cereal boxes.

Ethan would stare at them in the mornings over toast, flipping through glossy pages filled with stadium shots, scholarship promises, and words like legacy and future.

As March drifted into spring break fever, Elle walked into the living room with a clipboard on one Saturday morning, reading glasses halfway down her nose.

"Alright, young man," she said. "It's time."

Ethan looked up from his phone. "Time for what?"

She waved the clipboard. "College tour planning. Spring break is next month, and these schools aren't gonna visit themselves. I've already spoken to a few coaches."

Ethan raised a brow. "All of them?"

"There are over ten," she said, sitting beside him. "Too many. I told them you'd narrow it down to five. Late April into early June, we'll start visits."

He leaned back on the couch. "Only five?"

"Yes. Because I am not spending my whole summer living out of a rental car and hotel breakfasts." She gave him a look. "And besides, Aunt Helen and Aunt Tricia are dragging me to the Cayman Islands for the Fourth of July. I already said yes."

George looked up from the kitchen. "Wait, y'all going to the Caymans without me?"

Elle rolled her eyes. "You can come. But you better not expect me to answer college emails from a beach chair."

Ethan grinned. "Fair enough."

Later that night, in his room, Ethan pulled out the brochures and spread them across his bed like trading cards.

Everyone had something flashy to offer: bigger facilities, legendary coaches, promises of national coverage. But underneath the sparkle, he could feel the weight of the decision growing.

He picked up a brochure from Iron Water State University, a top D1 school just two states over. One of the coaches had already called twice. It had everything: strong academics, professional connections, and the potential for a full-ride scholarship.

He put it in the "maybe" pile.

Then he stared at the others.

For the first time, he wondered… What happens to who I am when all this becomes real? He went downstairs to be with his uncle and mom.

The living room coffee table was covered with brochures, scribbled notes, and a half-eaten bowl of trail mix. Ethan sat cross-legged on the floor, sorting flyers into little piles while Elle flipped through her handwritten list of school contacts. Uncle George was stretched out on the couch with a toothpick in his mouth, watching the whole thing like it was draft night.

"I still think five is too many," George said. "Back in my day, you picked one and hoped for a letter in the mail."

Ethan smirked. "Well, times have changed, Unc. And these schools actually want me."

Elle looked up from her clipboard, glasses perched on her nose. "And we're going to be selective. No hopping all over the country in July. I'm not missing my Cayman Islands trip for anybody's admissions tour."

Ethan laughed. "I hear you."

He reached for the last brochure on the table and held it up.

"Alright. Here's my five."

He spread them out like cards on the table.

Briarstone University: "They've got history, strong football culture, and a solid academic support system."

Rockdale University: "Coach Jacobs said I could come in and compete for the defensive end spot right away."

Greywood College: "Smaller, but the program is disciplined. I like their staff."

Stonebrook State University: "Full ride. Big program. Professional attention. It's tempting."

Winslow State: "It just feels right. They've been the most consistent since last season."

George gave a slow nod. "That's a solid list."

Elle leaned forward, her fingers tapping thoughtfully on the Stonebrook brochure. "I like Greywood for the balance. And Rockdale's coach sounded very organized when I spoke with him briefly last month."

Ethan raised an eyebrow. "You already called them?"

Elle smiled. "Just to get a feel. But now that you've picked your five, I'm sending official emails out in a couple of days."

On Tuesday night, the house was quiet, except for the clicking of Elle's keyboard and the hum of the dishwasher in the background. Ethan came down the stairs in a hoodie and socks, rubbing his eyes.

"You still working on that?" he asked.

Elle didn't look up. "I've emailed all five schools. Gave them your academic and athletic profile, linked some film, and requested spring visit windows."

He sat down across from her at the table. "All of them?"

She finally looked up, proud and tired. "Yep. And I already heard back from three."

"Seriously?"

She nodded. "Stonebrook booked you for mid-April. Greywood and Rockdale are sending paperwork. I'm pushing for one in April, two in May, two in June. That way, I can sip coconut water in peace by July 1st."

Uncle George walked into the kitchen and opened the fridge. "You get her flights booked, too, Ethan?"

Ethan chuckled. "Sounds like I need to."

Elle closed her laptop with a satisfied snap.

"You made your picks," she said softly. "Now it's time to walk into them."

Ethan nodded slowly.

"I'm ready."

But even as he said it, he couldn't shake the quiet voice in the back of his mind, the one that whispered, "Ready for what?"

Chapter 33
First Look at the Future

On April 17, the family arrived at Stonebrook State University. The moment Ethan stepped out of the rental car, he felt that mix of nerves and wonder that came with stepping into unfamiliar territory.

The campus stretched wide before him, neatly trimmed lawns, red brick buildings with white columns, students biking between class halls, and the soft hum of life unfolding in every direction. The air smelled like coffee and spring rain.

"Whew," George said, climbing out from the driver's seat. "This place is... something."

Elle adjusted her sunglasses and gave Ethan a proud nod. "You could belong here."

Ethan slung his backpack over one shoulder. "We'll see."

They walked toward the welcome center, where a banner hung above the door:

"Stonebrook State Spring Prospect Weekend Welcome, Class of Tomorrow."

Inside, everything was polished. Bright. Energetic. Coaches stood near the entrance, greeting families and handing out itineraries. A junior athlete named Terrence was assigned as Ethan's student guide, a linebacker with a quick smile and way too much energy for 9 a.m.

"You're from Gerry, right?" Terrence asked, handing Ethan a folder. "Let me guess, snow boots and Friday night lights?"

Ethan grinned. "Something like that."

On the campus tour, they walked across campus as Terrence pointed out key spots, the weight room, the student-athlete center, the practice fields, and the academic advising wing.

"Here's where they feed us," Terrence said, gesturing to a modern cafeteria with glass walls. "Food's solid. Not your grandma's pot roast, but it won't kill you."

Ethan chuckled.

Elle took pictures on her phone. George asked questions about dorm security and meal plans. Ethan just tried to absorb it all. The buildings. The pace. The faces. The way everything seemed like it was waiting for him, and not at the same time.

Later that afternoon, they met with Coach Drayton, the offensive coordinator, and a couple of other staff members. The office smelled like leather and sports drinks, and the walls were lined with photos of players who had gone on to play professionally.

"We've been watching your film, Ethan," Coach Drayton said, shaking his hand firmly. "You've got field vision, quick feet, and patience in the line. Those are rare for a high school defensive end. We think Stonebrook could shape you into something special."

Ethan sat up straighter. "Thank you, sir."

"We're offering a full ride," the coach continued. "Academic and athletic. It's early, but we're confident you'd be a good fit."

Elle gave a tight smile. George nodded slowly.

Ethan's heartbeat was faster. Full ride. Special. Fit.

It was everything he wanted to hear.

But somewhere in the middle of all that praise, something small tugged at him. He hadn't prayed about this visit. He hadn't journaled about it. He hadn't even opened his holy scriptures since the Christmas trip.

He pushed the thought away and smiled again.

That evening, back at the hotel, Ethan sat on the edge of the bed, flipping through the Stonebrook folder.

Practice schedules. Tutoring support. Alum success stories.

It all felt so real now.

Elle stepped out of the bathroom, drying her hands. "So… what do you think?"

"It's… impressive," Ethan admitted.

George looked up from the chair in the corner. "You looked like you belonged today."

Ethan nodded, then hesitated. "You think I'm ready for something like this?"

Elle smiled. "We wouldn't have driven twelve hours if we didn't."

He looked back at the folder. Then, in his backpack, where his journal was buried beneath his hoodie.

He didn't reach for it.

A few weeks later, on May 12, the family was heading to Winslow State.

The trip to Stonebrook State had left an impression, but it also left Ethan thinking more deeply than he expected.

He hadn't said much about it afterward. Not in the car, not back at school, and not even to Marcus or Lamar when they asked how it went. On the outside, he nodded and gave the safe answers: "It was cool," or "They treated me good."

But something lingered. No doubt.

Not exactly excitement either.

Just… weight.

A feeling that all of these campuses, handshakes, folders full of bold-lettered promises were starting to shape a version of himself he wasn't sure he fully recognized yet.

Still, the next visit was already locked in.

The drive to Winslow State was longer, quieter. George had let Ethan handle most of the directions, and Elle had packed sandwiches and fruit in a cooler bag.

The campus wasn't as polished as Stonebrook's. It was older, with ivy-covered buildings and a wide-open quad that buzzed with spring energy. A live band played near a student union where tour groups gathered under a banner that read:

"Welcome Prospects, Your Future Starts Here."

Their host was a tall, friendly senior named Khalid, built like a linebacker.

"You play?" Khalid asked as they shook hands.

"Tight end and defensive end," Ethan replied.

Khalid grinned. "Double duty. That's what I like to hear. Let's get you the full tour."

The campus life was giving up close and personal. The tour was more individual than the one at Stonebrook. Less flash, more conversation. Khalid introduced Ethan to players who had been there three or four years, guys who looked tired, grounded, but confident. Some were majoring in sports medicine, others in business, and a few in engineering.

"It's not just about ball here," one of them said. "You grind, yeah, but they expect you to show up in the classroom too."

George liked that. Elle did too.

Ethan listened. Watched. Took mental notes.

Winslow didn't try to impress.

It just… was.

Later in the afternoon, they stood along the sideline watching the team run through spring drills.

A coach with a clipboard leaned over to Ethan. "We've seen your film. You don't just move, you read. That's rare. Especially in a two-position athlete."

Ethan nodded, saying little. His eyes stayed fixed on the tight ends going through blocking drills and red zone sets. He noticed how they worked, not just the physical part, but how they communicated, reset, and adjusted on the fly.

He could see himself there. Not for the name. Not for the lights.

But maybe… for the process.

After the family left the university that evening, they headed to a local diner to eat.

That night, they didn't stay at a fancy hotel. They stopped at a modest roadside diner just outside town. Booths lined the windows. The floors were worn, but the place smelled like home fries and hot syrup.

Over pancakes and grilled chicken, Elle pulled out her phone and started a pros-and-cons list for Winslow.

George was quiet, sipping coffee and watching Ethan think.

"So?" Elle finally asked. "Is this one a maybe or a 'no way'?"

Ethan leaned back and exhaled.

"It's different," he said. "But I liked how real it felt."

"That's something," George said.

Elle nodded. "Okay then. One more visit next week, and then we can start narrowing down. I still plan to be on a beach by July."

Ethan laughed.

But as he looked out the diner window, watching a few college students walk by in worn-out hoodies and backpacks slung low, he couldn't help but wonder:

What happens if all of this becomes my whole life? He thought to himself.

After the trip to Winslow, the conversations at home got quieter.

Ethan spent more time alone, reviewing brochures and campus maps in his room, flipping through highlight videos and social media tours, but not really saying much. He wasn't avoiding the process; he just needed space to feel it, to sort through what each visit stirred in him.

Elle noticed. George did too. They didn't push. They just kept the plan moving.

Two weeks later, the family headed to Briarstone University, the third stop on the list and the one Ethan had been the most unsure about. On paper, Briarstone had it all: state-of-the-art athletic facilities, elite academic programs, and a long reputation of producing professional-level athletes.

Still… something about it made him uneasy. He couldn't explain why.

After arriving at Briarstone's campus, it was immaculate. Perfectly landscaped. The buildings stood tall and symmetrical, lined with sharp glass and stone architecture. Everything looked like it belonged in a magazine spread.

Their tour host, a junior named Chase, met them near the athletic complex. He was charming, well-spoken, and dressed like a sportswear brand already sponsored him.

"You're Ethan Phillips?" Chase asked, giving him a confident nod. "Man, we've been hearing about you. Dual position? That's gold here."

Ethan gave a polite smile. "Thanks."

Chase launched into the tour, pointing out luxury dorms, athlete lounges with built-in gaming stations, and the player-only dining hall that looked more like a resort buffet than a cafeteria.

Elle raised an eyebrow. "Wow."

George crossed his arms, taking everything in.

Later, they were escorted into the indoor training facility, a massive structure filled with turf fields, high-end lifting stations, and wall-sized digital monitors that tracked performance metrics in real time.

A coach introduced himself, Coach Ryland, smooth, persuasive, and a little too polished.

"We believe in winners here," he said, looking directly at Ethan. "You want to dominate at the next level? Briarstone is the launchpad."

Ethan nodded slowly, glancing around the room at posters of former players holding trophies, striking power poses, and standing next to luxury cars.

There was no mention of academics. No questions about who he was outside of football. No interest in the character-building Winslow emphasized.

Just results.

Just reputation.

Just winning.

Back at the hotel, Ethan barely touched his dinner. Elle scrolled through the day's photos but didn't say much. George clicked the remote, flipping through channels before finally turning it off altogether.

"So," George said, breaking the silence. "What's the verdict on Briarstone?"

Ethan leaned back in the stiff hotel chair. "It's… nice."

"But?" Elle asked.

He shrugged. "I don't know. It just felt… off."

Elle sat up. "Off how?"

"Like it was more about what I could do for them than what they could do for me."

George gave a quiet nod. "That's the kind of thing you have to listen to, son. Not everything that shines is meant to be picked up."

Ethan sat there in silence, the weight of it pressing heavier now. He hadn't written anything down. He hadn't prayed. He hadn't opened his journal in months.

The folder from Briarstone sat untouched at the foot of the bed.

The final days of school felt like a blur.

Final exams came and went, and hallways buzzed with the familiar tension of report cards, locker cleanouts, and yearbook signatures. Ethan turned in his last paper for Advanced Biology, and Mr. Grissom, still skeptical of football players, handed it back with a raised eyebrow.

"Solid work," he muttered. "Didn't expect it."

Ethan didn't respond. He didn't have to. The A-minus at the top of the page said enough.

The classroom was emptied behind him as he lingered near the window, watching teammates toss water bottles at each other in the courtyard. His muscles ached from spring practices, and his mind still hadn't fully settled from Briarstone.

One more visit this week. Then maybe… he could exhale.

The early summer heat crept in slowly as they drove across state lines toward Rockdale University, the fourth school on Ethan's list.

Unlike Briarstone's polished image or Winslow's raw grit, Rockdale struck a different tone entirely. The town surrounding the campus was quiet, filled with mom-and-pop diners and antique bookstores. It wasn't flashy, but it had a sense of history like something that had been built here and earned, not just designed.

Their tour began at the admissions building with a soft-spoken junior named Victoria, a former track athlete who now studied education.

"Rockdale's big on mentorship," she explained. "Coaches here are more like father figures. It's competitive, don't get me wrong,

But it's the kind of place that keeps you grounded."

That word stayed with Ethan all day. Grounded. The head coach, Coach Dillard, was a former lineman with deep laugh lines and a firm handshake. He looked Ethan in the eye when he spoke, not at his stats sheet.

"You play tight end and defensive end? That takes grit," Coach Dillard said. "We like grit here. And we like thinkers."

Ethan blinked. "Thinkers?"

"Players who think through plays. Who reads defenses? Whoever studies, asks questions, and wants to grow. That's what makes someone coachable. And we've watched your film. You've got it."

Ethan couldn't help but smile. It was the first time he'd heard it said like that.

Later in the tour, they passed an old brick chapel tucked behind the main quad. A small sign read: "Open to All: Sit, Pray, Reflect."

Ethan slowed down, glancing at it as they walked by. George noticed.

"Want to go in?" he asked.

Ethan hesitated. Then nodded.

Inside, the space was simple wooden pews, stained glass, and a faint smell of wax and dust. It reminded him of home. Of Sunday mornings with his mom. At times, he would write in his journal after church, praying for guidance, but he wasn't sure he heard anything anymore.

He sat down quietly for a moment, not saying anything out loud.

But in his heart, he whispered:

God, I'm still listening. Even if I don't talk like I used to… I'm still here.

As they drove home under a pink-orange sky, Ethan rested his head against the window, the chapel still fresh in his mind.

"Rockdale's different," he said quietly.

Elle smiled from the front seat. "That a good different or a no-thanks different?"

Ethan shrugged. "It felt… peaceful."

George chuckled. "Peaceful is rare these days." "Yeah," Ethan murmured. "I liked that."

Another week has gone by of visiting college campuses. By the time they reached Greywood University, summer had already settled in. Warm wind slid through the car windows, and the air smelled like fresh-cut grass and hot pavement.

It had only been three weeks since Rockdale, but something in Ethan felt different now, calmer, less frantic. He had been to four schools, each with its own tone, pace, and message. His mind wasn't made up yet, but the fog was lifting.

Elle pulled into the campus parking lot, glancing at her phone. "Our tour starts at 10. Let's grab some water first. It's supposed to be almost 90 degrees today."

George looked over at Ethan, who hadn't said much during the drive. "This is the one you're most excited about?"

Ethan thought for a second, then nodded. "I just want to see if it feels real."

Greywood University was set on a sprawling hilltop, with ivy-covered buildings and wide, shaded sidewalks. The campus felt lived in. There were chalk drawings near the library, hammocks hanging between trees, and students walking in flip-flops with earbuds in.

It was alive, but not trying too hard.

The football facility was modest compared to Briarstone's, but still impressive. The head coach, Coach Harvell, was a soft-spoken former player with a quiet command. He greeted Ethan with a simple handshake and a question:

"What kind of man do you want to be when football ends?"

Ethan blinked. "What?"

Coach Harvell smiled. "I didn't ask what kind of player you want to be. I asked what kind of man."

Ethan hesitated. "I'm… still figuring that out."

"That's a fine answer," the coach said. "And the right time to start asking."

They sat together in the film room and broke down clips of Ethan's games. The assistant coach pointed out moments where his football IQ showed his ability to block blindside, track down runners from the edge, and anticipate coverage.

"You're more than just size and speed," the coach said. "You're a student of the game. We can build on that."

Ethan couldn't help but grin. He hadn't heard that phrase since Coach Lanning said it in his first year of high school: "student of the game." Back then, it felt like a title. Now it felt like an invitation.

After the tour ended, Ethan asked to walk alone for a bit. Elle and George found a shaded bench while he headed up the trail behind the athletic building.

The hill overlooked most of the campus. He could see students tossing frisbees, couples reading under trees, and a professor holding an impromptu lecture on the grass. It was peaceful, but alive.

He reached into his backpack and pulled out his journal, the one he hadn't opened since earlier this year.

He didn't write. Not yet.

But he flipped through the pages, reading past entries, prayers, goals, struggles.

A lump formed in his throat.

He didn't realize how much he missed this version of himself, the one who slowed down, reflected, and actually talked to God instead of just hoping he was on the right path.

He closed the journal softly, then whispered under his breath:

I haven't forgotten. I'm just... figuring it out.

On the way home, they stopped at a diner off the interstate.

Elle ordered pancakes and sausage. George got a BLT with extra mayo. Ethan just sipped water, his appetite lost in thought.

"So?" Elle asked, watching him.

"I think I've got it," he said.

"Top pick?"

"No," Ethan replied. "Top two. I need to pray on it."

George raised his glass. "That's all we ask. Pray first, commit second."

They clinked glasses. Root beer. Orange juice. Water.

The sun dipped low behind the highway signs as they pulled back onto the road. He was quiet, content, and one step closer to whatever came next.

Chapter 34
The Decision

The house was quiet when they pulled into the driveway.

No porch light. No TV humming in the background. Just the crunch of tires on gravel and the soft creak of the front door opening as Ethan stepped inside. His legs ached from the long car ride, and his eyes were heavy, but his mind was wide awake.

He took the stairs two at a time and dropped his bag by the door of his room. The familiar scent of laundry detergent and his worn-out sneakers greeted him like an old friend. He sat on the edge of his bed, staring at the floor for a long moment before reaching over to his bookbag.

The journal.

He hadn't written in it in months, not since early spring. But now, as his fingers traced the worn edges of the leather cover, something inside nudged him. It wasn't just a habit. It was home.

He opened to a blank page, took a deep breath, and began to write.

He began:

God, thank You for this moment.

Thank you for allowing me to live out a dream that started in my backyard with a beat-up football and no clue where it would take me.

Thank you to my mom for her strength, her sacrifices, and her love that never ran out. For my Uncle George, who didn't just step in, he showed up every time. He raised me into a young man with grit and vision.

Thank you to Coach Lanning, who believed in me back when I barely believed in myself, and to Lamar, Marcus, Amanda, and Scott, who are my real friends who stood with me even when the world was loud.

Most of all, thank You for giving me peace about this decision. I'm choosing Greywood.

Coach Harvell saw me. Not just the athlete, but the man I'm trying to become. I feel like that's where I belong.

So here I go, next chapter, same Author.

Ethan closed the journal gently, resting his hand on top of it for a moment as if sealing the words in his heart.

He stood, stretched, and made his way downstairs.

The living room was dim, lit only by the soft glow of a side lamp. Elle was curled up on the couch with her legs tucked beneath her, a bowl of popcorn resting on her lap. Uncle George sat beside her, phone pressed to his ear, chuckling with Sara on speaker.

"Yeah, yeah, the tour went great," George said. "He's upstairs now, probably passed out."

Ethan cleared his throat.

Elle looked up. "Hey, baby. You okay?"

George turned, then smiled and held up a finger to Sara. "Hang on, he's got something."

Ethan stepped forward, standing tall but nervous. "I made my decision."

Elle sat up straighter. George ended the call.

"Greywood," Ethan said. "That's the one."

Elle's eyes filled instantly with tears. She didn't say anything, just nodded, pressing a hand to her mouth.

Uncle George grinned widely. "You sure?"

"Yeah," Ethan said, a quiet conviction in his voice. "I felt something there. Peace. Like it was where I'm supposed to be."

George stood and clapped a hand on Ethan's shoulder. "Then that's all that matters."

Elle pulled him in for a hug, whispering, "I'm proud of you. Always."

They stood like that for a while for a big celebration, no fireworks. Just family. Just love. Just the calm after a long journey.

Later that week, Ethan stood in the backyard under the early morning sun, cell phone pressed to his ear. Birds chirped in the trees, and the faint hum of a neighbor's lawnmower buzzed in the distance. He shifted his weight from one foot to the other, pacing the grass as the phone rang.

"Coach Lanning speaking."

Ethan smiled. "Hey, Coach, it's Ethan Phillips."

There was a pause, then a warm, familiar tone. "Ethan! I've been wondering when you were going to call me. What's the verdict?"

Ethan took a breath. "Greywood. I'm committing."

"Greywood?" Coach Lanning said, "Then let out a whistle. "That's a solid program. I know Coach Harvell personally. He's the real deal."

"Yeah. I felt it," Ethan replied. "It wasn't just football. It was… something more."

"That's what I like to hear. Son, I'm proud of you. Not just for making a choice, but for thinking it through the way you did."

"Thanks, Coach."

"Keep working. This summer's not a vacation, it's preparation. Let them see who you are before you even set foot on campus."

"You got it."

"And Ethan?"

"Yeah?"

"Don't stop writing."

Ethan chuckled, glancing back toward his bedroom window. "I won't." The call ended.

The next morning, Ethan headed to Walker's Market, which sat on the corner of Maple and 7th, with faded green awnings and a neon sign that buzzed faintly every time someone walked in. The summer job wasn't glamorous, but it paid, and that was all Ethan cared about.

He pulled on the black polo with the red "W" stitched over the chest and headed toward the employee entrance. Marcus was already there, leaning against a stack of watermelons, sipping from a slushy.

"Took you long enough," Marcus grinned. "You miss orientation?"

Ethan punched his shoulder. "Nah, I'm early. You just camp here."

Scott popped his head out from behind the automatic doors, holding a pricing gun in one hand. "Let's make a bet first one to drop a box of canned beans owes us all fries."

"Deal," Ethan said, adjusting his name tag.

The three fell into a rhythm quickly, stocking shelves, pushing carts, and helping customers find whatever they couldn't pronounce. It wasn't hard work, but it kept them busy. Kept them grounded.

Across the street, Amanda stood behind the counter at Benny's Burgers, flipping patties and calling out order numbers with the headset slightly crooked on her head. Now and then, she'd glance through the large front window, her eyes landing on Ethan restocking bananas or joking with Marcus.

At lunch, they all met up on the shaded benches between the two buildings.

Amanda tossed a burger wrapped in foil toward Ethan. "Don't say I never looked out."

Ethan caught it with one hand and laughed. "Only if you got extra pickles."

"You're welcome," she smirked, sitting down with her tray of fries.

Marcus leaned back, arms behind his head. "So, one last summer before life really changes, huh?"

"Yeah," Ethan said quietly, unwrapping the burger. "It's all moving fast now."

Scott raised a fry like a toast. "Then let's enjoy the ride."

They clinked fries together, laughing like they had done every summer before, but all of them knew this one was different. This was the last normal before everything changed.

It has been almost two weeks since Ethan started his summer job. He enjoyed working and hanging out with his friends. One evening, Ethan pulled into the driveway just as the sun dipped below the trees, casting a warm amber glow over the neighborhood. He tossed his Walker's Market name tag onto the passenger seat, yawned, and made his way up the front steps.

As soon as he opened the door, the sound of suitcase wheels clattering and drawers opening filled the house.

"Mom?" he called.

"In here!" Elle's voice floated from the main bedroom.

Ethan stepped inside and blinked at the chaos. Elle had half her closet emptied onto the bed, a beach hat balanced on her head, and sunscreen bottles spread across the dresser.

"What's going on?" he asked, eyebrows raised.

"Packing for the Cayman Islands," she said with a grin. "Aunt Helen and Tricia already texted they're bringing way too much, so I figured I might as well join them."

Uncle George appeared in the hallway holding a small duffel bag. "Sara and I are heading to Texas. Her grandfather is turning 90. Big family gathering."

Ethan looked between them. "Wait… why are y'all leaving me here alone?"

Elle paused mid-fold. "You're a big boy. You're 17, you have a job, a driver's license, and your key."

Uncle George chimed in, "Just don't burn the house down or throw a wild house party for the cops to show up. I don't need the neighbors calling me again like last year when you and Marcus 'accidentally' set off fireworks on a Tuesday."

Elle laughed, wagging a finger. "And I better not see us trending on Gerry County's Facebook page under 'Local Teen Chaos.'"

Ethan held up both hands, grinning. "I won't! I promise."

"Well then, that settles it," Elle said, zipping her suitcase. "We'll see you in a week."

Uncle George ruffled Ethan's hair. "Go to work and try not to miss any days. Got it?"

"Got it."

"Love you, kid."

"Love you too, Uncle G."

Elle leaned in for a quick hug. "Love you, sweetie. Call if you need anything, and there's money on the counter for groceries."

Ethan nodded, watching them walk out the door, luggage in tow. As the door clicked shut, the silence fell heavy over the house.

He looked around, dropped his keys on the counter, and whispered, "I've never been home alone before."

He stood there for a moment, unsure what to do. The fridge hummed. The clock ticked. The silence grew louder.

Then he smiled.

Later that night, by 8:00 p.m., the house was alive with music, laughter, and the smell of pepperoni pizza.

Ethan had called the crew.

Marcus showed up first, arms loaded with two 2-liter bottles of soda and a bag of sour gummy worms.

Amanda drove over to his house, carrying two bags of candy and a deck of cards. "Let's make this a snack-filled night."

Ethan held the door open for Scott, who came dragging a crate of video games, a small speaker, and a Bluetooth projector.

"I brought all the latest games and music," Scott announced, kicking off his sneakers. "Let's go."

Ethan had a stack of potato chip bags ready on the kitchen island. "Grab what you want."

They turned the living room into a full-blown hangout spot… cushions on the floor, lights dimmed, the projector screen glowing on the wall. Laughter bounced off the walls as they played games, talked about summer jobs, and joked about school.

At one point, Amanda tossed a pillow at Marcus. "If you lose again, you're banned from using the controller for life."

Ethan sat back, grinning. "This… this is better than any party."

No drama. No pressure. Just friends, food, and a moment of peace in a house that, for the first time, was truly his, at least for a week.

Meanwhile, in Texas, Uncle George hadn't been there since Ethan's elite football camp, but the moment he stepped onto Sara's grandfather's land, he felt like he'd known the family forever.

The old farmhouse sat at the end of a long gravel driveway, surrounded by rolling hills and tall oaks. Strings of lights crisscrossed the yard, tables were loaded with smoked brisket, ribs, and peach cobbler, and the smell of hickory wood filled the air.

Sara's grandfather, Mr. Henley, sat in a wooden rocking chair near the porch, smiling as guests took turns hugging him, snapping photos, and sharing stories. He wore a custom-made "90 & Still Kickin'" T-shirt and waved a cane like a king holding court.

Uncle George helped flip meat on the grill with Sara's brothers, tossed a football with a few of the younger cousins, and even danced a slow two-step with Sara when the country band started playing under the stars.

Later that evening, Sara leaned over with a grin. "So, still think my family's too loud?"

George laughed. "Absolutely. But it's a good loud."

They toasted with sweet tea and carved out a corner on the porch just for themselves. He hadn't felt this relaxed in a long time.

Over in the Cayman Islands, Elle's toes sank into the white sand as the turquoise waves rolled gently onto the shore. She hadn't been on an all-girls trip in over a decade, and this trip, with Helen and Tricia, was long overdue.

Their beachfront resort offered everything: fresh fruit delivered to the room every morning, hammocks between palm trees, and a long list of excursions. They soaked in every second.

The sisters snorkeled near coral reefs, went horseback riding through shallow waters, and laughed until their stomachs hurt during a rum distillery tour. On the last night, they ate jerk chicken and fresh conch under a canopy of stars, music drifting from a nearby steel drum band.

"Let's make this a tradition," Helen said, holding up her tropical drink.

"Yes, but next time," Tricia added, "we're bringing the boys."

Elle chuckled. "Not Ethan. That boy would be trying to play football with the local teens on the beach instead of relaxing."

Still, she missed him.

At the street market, Elle picked up a handcrafted bracelet made of green sea glass and a T-shirt reading "Cayman Strong" in bold letters. "Something for my baby," she whispered, smiling.

By the end of the week, Ethan had cleaned the house, taken out the trash, and even mowed the lawn twice.

He heard the door open just before dinner on Sunday.

"Anybody home?" Uncle George's voice echoed through the hallway.

"Living room!" Ethan called out.

Elle walked in behind him, her skin sun-kissed and her arms full of bags.

"Well, look who didn't burn the house down," she teased, setting her purse on the counter.

Uncle George gave him a firm pat on the back. "You look taller. Must've been all that pizza."

They all laughed as Ethan leaned against the counter, grinning.

"I got you something," Elle said, reaching into one of the bags and handing him the green sea glass bracelet. "It's supposed to bring good energy."

Uncle George tossed him a Texas hat. "Don't get ideas, it's just a souvenir."

Ethan held both gifts in his hands, genuinely touched. "Thanks. I missed y'all."

"Missed you too, sweetie," Elle said.

Uncle George added, "We're proud of you. This house was still standing. That's saying something."

They shared a family dinner that night, nothing fancy, just spaghetti and garlic bread, but it was one of those moments that made Ethan realize how much he still needed them, even as everything around him started to change.

Chapter 35

The Final First Day

The last week of summer slipped away like sand through fingers, slow at first, then suddenly gone.

Ethan stood at the bathroom mirror on a crisp Monday morning, brushing down his waves with steady strokes. His new senior hoodie hung freshly washed on his bedroom chair, and his sneakers were spotless, lined up by the door just like always. But this year... it felt different.

He glanced at the calendar on his desk. August 21.

Senior Year.

Downstairs, the smell of cinnamon toast and scrambled eggs wafted through the house. Elle was in the kitchen, humming softly to the gospel playlist coming from the speaker. Uncle George sipped coffee at the counter, dressed in his usual cargo pants and polo shirt.

"Big day," he said, nodding as Ethan came down the stairs.

"Yeah," Ethan replied, slinging his backpack over one shoulder.

Elle turned from the stove and beamed. "Look at my baby. Last first day."

"Don't start, Mom," Ethan laughed.

She reached up to fix the collar on his hoodie. "Promise me one thing?"

"What's that?"

"Don't rush through it. I know you've got plans and dreams and recruiters calling. But take it all in, alright? This year only comes once."

"I will," he said softly.

They all ate breakfast together, sharing quiet glances and half-smiles. No one had to say it out loud; senior year had arrived, and nothing would be the same again. Ethan exited the house and entered his vehicle. He placed his bookbag on the passenger seat, started the engine, and left the driveway, en route to Gerry High.

The parking lot at Gerry High buzzed with excitement and nerves. Seniors stood in small clusters, showing off summer tans, retelling travel stories, and debating the best electives to avoid doing any real work.

Ethan parked his car, his own car, and stepped out, feeling every bit like a senior. Marcus and Scott pulled up a minute later, blasting music through the open windows.

"Look who finally gets to walk in like a king," Marcus shouted, tossing Ethan a football.

"Man, I've been waiting for this day since ninth grade," Scott grinned.

They dapped each other up, falling in line like they had every year, but this time at the front of the school, not the back.

Inside, the walls were lined with "Welcome Back Seniors!" posters, and the staff had created a balloon tunnel leading into the commons.

Amanda met them at their lockers. "Already tired and it's only first period," she joked.

"Just wait till finals week," Ethan smirked. "You'll be crying in the stairwell again."

Amanda rolled her eyes, but the teasing felt easy, familiar.

Ethan accessed his locker and placed his bookbag inside. He then retrieved his binder to review his class schedule.

Ethan's schedule was packed with AP Science, Advanced Math, Senior English, Weight Training, and two electives that Coach Lanning had nudged him into for "mental balance."

But what caught Ethan off guard was how the halls felt smaller now. Teachers called him by name. Underclassmen stared in awe. He wasn't just on the football team anymore; he was the team captain, the big man on campus.

In the weight room, Coach Lanning pulled him aside.

"This is your year, Phillips. You already know what's coming. Scouts. Pressure. Expectations. But I want you to remember lead by example. And don't let the hype make you forget who you are."

"I got you, Coach," Ethan nodded.

Lanning clapped him on the back. "I know you do."

As Ethan walked out of the gym, a calm settled over him. The buzz of senior year had officially begun, and with it, the weight of every decision, every practice, every class. But he was ready, or at least he hoped he was.

The summer sun lingered a little longer that evening as Ethan walked toward the Gerry High football field. His senior year had finally arrived. The grass felt familiar beneath his cleats, but everything else felt elevated. The drills were more complex. The expectations are higher. The stakes are heavier.

Coach Lanning blew his whistle. "Let's tighten it up, Hawks! Season openers are in three weeks, no time for senioritis. Ethan gets the tight ends lined up. Marcus, rotate out."

The team sprang into motion. Ethan took control like a second coach on the field. He barked out the play, adjusted a teammate's stance, and snapped back into position. The sweat running down his face didn't bother him. This was his home, his sanctuary.

Lamar jogged up beside him. "Yo, you look like you slept in that uniform, bro."

Ethan smirked. "Better than looking like I never played."

"Man, shut up," Lamar grinned, jogging off to his spot.

Practice ran long. The team broke down just before dusk.

"Hawks on three!" someone shouted.

"One, two, three HAWKS!"

The echo of the chant lingered in the air as the players walked off the field, talking about the upcoming game, college offers, and weekend plans. Ethan stayed behind a little longer, stretching at the

50-yard line, silently grateful. His final season had begun, and he was ready.

Later that night, Coach Lanning sat in his office reviewing last season's game film. The hum of the old ceiling fan blended with the low volume of the video highlights. The Gerry Hawks looked sharp…even sharper this year.

The office phone rang.

"Coach Lanning."

A calm, level voice responded. "Good evening, Coach. I represent Premier Star Athletics. My name is Dawson. We've been following a few of your athletes, particularly Ethan Phillips."

Coach raised an eyebrow. "Premier Star? That name's new to me."

"We're a selective agency. Very… exclusive. We specialize in lifestyle development, branding guidance, and long-term positioning. We identify early."

Lanning leaned forward slightly. Something about the voice…it wasn't shaky, but it was hollow. Calculated. Lacking any warmth or energy.

"Where are you based?"

"Oh… all over," Dawson replied smoothly. "We're mobile. We come to those who are…. open."

Coach Lanning sat back. The voice was unnerving, too polished, too impersonal.

"You want to talk about a kid, you come in person. Meet the coaches. Shake hands. Watch the film with me. I don't entertain shadows over the phone."

A soft chuckle crept through the line.

"Understood, Coach. We'll be watching. Very closely."

Click.

Coach stared at the phone for a long second.

He reached for Ethan's player folder and wrote on the back:

Premier Star Athletics felt off. Not right. Be alert.

He closed the file slowly, a strange chill settling into the room.

Something about that call didn't feel like scouting.

It felt like surveillance.

The next day at the senior picnic, the morning sun peeked over the school building as Gerry High's senior class poured into the back courtyard, laughing, shouting, and catching up. The annual senior picnic was in full swing, grills fired up, music pulsing from large speakers, folding tables packed with snacks, and inflatable games set up across the lawn.

Ethan strolled in wearing his team-issued Hawks shirt and gym shorts. He gave a few high fives and nodded to classmates he hadn't seen all summer. Marcus and Scott were already near the food table, stacking plates high with burgers and pasta salad.

"Bout time you showed up!" Marcus called.

"I had to make sure I didn't wear the same thing as you," Ethan joked.

They grabbed seats under one of the large white tents. Amanda wandered over with a Capri Sun and two bags of chips, tossing one onto Ethan's plate. "You're welcome."

Ethan smiled. "Appreciate it. How's the burger line?"

"Longer than the financial aid office," she smirked.

The day felt lighter, even carefree. For a few hours, there were no recruiters, no practices, no expectations: just classmates, summer memories, and the bittersweet thrill of a senior year officially underway.

Still, Ethan couldn't shake a faint feeling in his chest, like something was watching, or waiting.

As the group lounged under the tent, someone brought up the upcoming senior trip.

"Where are we going for Christmas? I heard they're thinking ski resort!" a girl shouted.

"I vote somewhere warm," another student chimed in. "Spring Break should be beaches, not snow boots."

Then came the mention of Prom suits, dresses, limos, and after-parties.

The football players, however, had one goal that rose above all the rest.

"We need that third championship," Marcus said seriously.

"For real," Lamar added. "Ninth grade. Eleventh. Let's finish it right with our senior year."

Ethan nodded slowly. "Let's leave our mark. Win it all one last time."

Lamar raised his bottle of soda like a toast. "To the three-peat."

"Three-peat!" the table echoed.

Still, Ethan couldn't shake a faint feeling in his chest, like something was watching, or waiting.

Later that week, Gerry hosted a prep rally for the seniors to kick off the football season. The gym pulsed with noise. Students waved signs, cheerleaders flipped, and the marching band blared the school anthem. The senior pep rally roared with energy as the football team was introduced one by one.

When Ethan's name was called, the crowd erupted. He smiled, jogging out with Marcus and Lamar beside him. Conner raised his hands, hyping the crowd.

The principal spoke last, giving a short speech before announcing early dismissal.

"You've earned it, seniors. Now go enjoy your afternoon… responsibly!"

While most of the student body flooded out into the parking lot, the football players turned toward the locker room.

"No days off," Marcus said.

"Let's get it," Ethan added.

They changed quickly and hit the field early, footballs flying across the turf before most students had even cleared the school driveway. Laughter, motivation, and anticipation buzzed through the air.

They were ready. And this year, it was personal.

Three weeks later, the first Friday night under the lights had finally arrived.

Gerry High's stadium buzzed with energy. Students in gold and blue shirts packed the bleachers, the marching band was tuned and lined up, and cheerleaders waved pom-poms in the thick August air. The Hawks were back.

And so was Ethan.

Still standing at 6'6" and 265 pounds of pure muscle, Ethan had become a force on both sides of the ball, tight end and defensive end. His combination of speed, strength, and high football IQ made him nearly unstoppable. Coaches, teammates, and even rivals noticed.

Beside him, Lamar held down the offensive line at left tackle, broad, silent, and deadly in protection. Marcus had grown leaner and faster, running routes with crisp precision as a wide receiver. Conner, their starting quarterback, had matured into a confident leader with a sharp arm and quicker reads.

The locker room was loud with excitement before the game. Shoulder pads clanged, cleats tapped against tile floors, and energy crackled in every direction.

"Let's set the tone tonight!" Coach Lanning shouted above the noise. "This is our house. Protect it. No slow starts hit hard from the whistle!"

Ethan pulled his helmet over his head and looked to Lamar, Marcus, and Conner. No words were needed. This was the moment they'd trained for all summer.

The team poured onto the field to a roaring crowd.

Kickoff.

The first few plays were fast, aggressive, and gritty. Ethan caught a first-down pass, broke a tackle, and dragged two defenders before being brought down. On defense, he shed a block and dropped the running back for a loss. Marcus sprinted down the sideline for a 40-yard touchdown. Conner threaded a needle between two safeties to keep the drive alive. Lamar flattened anyone who got too close to the pocket.

By halftime, Gerry led 21–3. The crowd was electric. The team was clicking.

But Ethan wasn't done. In the third quarter, he delivered a blindside sack that echoed through the stadium. Then, a leaping touchdown grab over two defenders had the crowd on its feet.

Final score: 35–10.

The first game was a statement.

In the locker room after, Coach Lanning stood on a bench. "That's how champions start a season! But we're not done. This is one step in a long journey. Stay hungry!"

The boys pounded lockers, shouted, and high-fived.

Ethan sat down to unlatch his cleats, sweat soaking through his jersey.

One win down.

Eleven more to go.

And if he had anything to do with it, this would be the year they left their mark on Gerry High forever.

The lights of Gerry High still glowed faintly in the distance as Ethan pulled into the driveway. The roar of the crowd was gone, now replaced by crickets, porchlight hum, and the low flicker of the living room TV.

Inside, the scent of lemon tea and baked chicken welcomed him like a hug.

Uncle George and his mother were already home, still dressed in their Hawks gear. Elle was curled up on the couch, a warm blanket across her lap, while George sat in the recliner with his arms folded like a coach still analyzing plays.

"There he is!" George called out as Ethan stepped inside, his duffel bag slung over one shoulder. "The man of the hour."

"Good game, baby," Elle added, her eyes gleaming with pride. "You were all over that field tonight."

Ethan smiled, tired but satisfied. "Thanks, y'all. I'm gonna shower quick."

Upstairs, the hot water helped wash away the weight of the night sweat, adrenaline, and the lingering ache in his shoulders. But beneath it all, a fire still burned.

This was just the beginning.

When he came back down, hair damp and hoodie zipped up, he found his mom in the kitchen pouring tea into two mugs.

"Want some?" she asked.

"Nah, I'm good. But I do wanna talk to you about something."

Elle raised an eyebrow.

He leaned against the counter, hands in his pockets. "The senior trip. It's in December, right after finals. A couple of the guys want to go to Florida. Beach house, jet skis, all that. Some are talking about the mountains, maybe a cabin. Can I go?"

Elle set the mugs down slowly. "Where are the chaperones in all this?"

Ethan grinned. "Still being figured out."

"Mmhm," she said, giving him the look. "Well, I'll need full details, names, and a contact list before I give a real answer. But… you've earned the conversation."

"That's all I needed," Ethan said, his grin widening.

Uncle George walked in just then, rubbing his beard. "You boys gonna celebrate all year or get serious about that ring?"

Ethan turned to him, face straightening with purpose.

"I want that third championship, Uncle G. We all do, me, Marcus, Conner, Lamar. We're not playing around this year. Every practice counts. We're leaving with a mark."

George nodded, the corner of his mouth twitching into a proud smirk. "Now that's what I like to hear."

"Did you see us tonight?" Ethan added. "We played like one heartbeat. Like we already knew how the story ends."

Elle smiled softly from the kitchen. "You boys are writing your ending. Just make it count."

Ethan looked between them, feeling the gravity of it all settle in.

He wasn't just playing for trophies.

He was playing for legacy.

Chapter 36
The Sound of Tomorrow

The house had gone still.

The TV was off. The kitchen lights dimmed. The clink of mugs and game talk had faded into the soft murmur of the night.

Ethan lay in bed, the sheets twisted around his legs, one arm tucked under his head. His body ached in all the usual places…shoulders, knees, hamstrings, but it was a good kind of ache. A winning ache.

He stared up at the ceiling, listening to the slow tick of the clock on his dresser and the faint rustling of trees outside his window.

So much had happened.

But all he could think about was one thing.

"God… if this is the beginning, let me finish well."

It wasn't fancy. It wasn't a long prayer.

Just a whisper between him and God who'd carried him this far.

He closed his eyes, muscles finally giving way to rest. The world faded into silence, but one word remained tucked like a promise in his chest…..Legacy! He said to himself before falling to sleep. October melted into November like the last slow pour of maple syrup.

School days blurred together with chalk dust, cafeteria noise, and sleepless nights spent studying for midterms. Ethan found himself moving between morning workouts, back-to-back quizzes, film sessions, and late-night cramming sessions where even Marcus fell asleep with a textbook open on his chest.

But somehow, they made it.

Midterms came and went. Grades weren't perfect, but they were solid, good enough to keep everyone eligible, and good enough to keep the seniors on track for graduation.

Coach Lanning didn't let up.

"If you can memorize a playbook, you can pass algebra!" he'd shouted after a particularly sluggish Tuesday practice. "Push through. Finals are coming. Playoffs too. You're not average — act like it."

Thanksgiving came with just enough time for rest. Ethan woke up that Thursday to the smell of sweet potato pie, roasted turkey, and cinnamon-heavy cider brewing in the kitchen. Uncle George carved the turkey while Elle hummed along to a gospel song playing from her phone.

"Thankful for this family," George said before they prayed over the food. "And for this young man right here."

He clapped a hand over Ethan's shoulder.

Ethan smiled sheepishly but nodded. "Thankful for both of you. And for another shot at something bigger."

By that night, after the dishes were done and leftovers packed away, Ethan sat on the couch scrolling through highlight videos and rankings. Gerry High was now 9–1.

One more regular-season game.

Then the playoffs.

The team was clicking like never before, offense humming, defense swarming, and special teams turning heads.

The Gerry Hawks weren't just good.

They were feared.

The final game of the season was a bloodbath. Ethan forced two fumbles. Marcus returned an interception for a touchdown. Conner threw a perfect 40-yard spiral into the end zone where Lamar, for the first time all year, lined up as a fullback and caught it one-handed.

Coach Lanning nearly lost his mind on the sideline.

When the final whistle blew, the Hawks were 10–1 and officially playoff-bound.

As the crowd erupted, players tackled each other in celebration. Ethan stood in the middle of the field, helmet in hand, heart pounding.

They'd done it.

But this wasn't the end.

This was just the next level. The Friday night air bit sharply against their skin as the team jogged onto the field for warmups. Breath came in white puffs. Their cleats crunched the frosted turf like fire igniting flint.

First round. Playoffs. Everything counted now.

The bleachers were packed with bundled-up parents, alums, and reporters. School flags waved like battle colors. Drums pounded from the marching band, and chants echoed from the crowd like a war cry.

In the locker room, the heat blasted, but the tension was colder than anything outside.

No one was talking.

Shoulder pads creaked as players adjusted their gear. Gloves were tightened. Tapes rewrapped. Even the music was off.

Then Coach Lanning stepped in.

Clipboard in hand. Whistle tucked under his chin. Voice steady, but sharp.

"Look at me," he said.

Every player turned. Every eye locked in.

"You've come too far to forget who you are."

He strolled across the locker room, looking at each player one by one.

"Some of you came into this program as skinny freshmen who didn't even know how to hit right. Some of you didn't think you'd start. Some of you were told you'd never make it past week two. But here you are. You bled for this. You lifted for this. You stayed after practice for this."

He paused. The room was still.

"This game? It's not just about skill. It's about grit. It's about the heart. When they line up against you tonight, they're not just playing the Hawks. They're playing a legacy." He turned to the seniors.

"Ethan. Marcus. Conner. Lamar. All of you. This is your moment. You set the tone, you lead the way. Every guy on this team is looking at you right now.

You want that third ring?

Then show it.

Take the first step… right here, right now."

Ethan nodded slowly. His jaw clenched. Every muscle in his body felt like it had been waiting for this night.

Coach Lanning raised a single finger. "One game at a time. One play at a time. Leave it all out there, and don't walk off that field with any 'what ifs.' You hear me?"

"Yes, Coach," they answered in unison.

"Say it as you believe it!"

"YES, COACH!"

He slammed the clipboard down on the bench.

"Then let's go shock the state."

The locker room exploded. Helmets clanged. Fists pounded lockers. Voices roared like thunder.

Ethan grabbed his helmet, looked over at Marcus, and said, "Let's start writing history." The playoffs weren't just games.

There were battles.

Four rounds. Four different teams. Four different towns that tried to end their story.

And still, Gerry High refused to fall.

Game by game, the Hawks clawed and climbed. A last-second field goal in round two. A blocked punt by Marcus in round three. Ethan recovered a fumble and ran it back 30 yards in the semifinals. The scoreboard barely mattered anymore.

What mattered was the will.

And this team had it in every bone.

By the time they arrived at the state championship, nerves had turned into steel. The whole town had followed them: parents, teachers, little league kids, even the local sheriff. Gerry was practically shut down. Banners hung from storefronts. A parade was already being whispered about.

The game was held at a massive university stadium with bright lights, televised, and scouts in the press box.

But Gerry wasn't here to be watched.

They were here to win.

From the opening kickoff, it was war.

Ethan broke through the line like a hammer on every snap. Marcus laid two brutal tackles that had the crowd gasping. Conner's passes were clean. Lamar was unstoppable. Still, the other team, Pillow Didge, wasn't backing down.

Halftime: tied 14–14.

By the fourth quarter, it was 28–28. Everyone was breathless. Coaches screamed. Cheerleaders chanted. Fans were on their feet.

One minute left.

Final drive.

Coach Lanning called a timeout.

In the huddle, sweat dripped from every brow. Ethan looked at his brothers, some of them banged up, limping, taped, tired, but no one was quitting.

"Last play," Conner said. "One shot."

They lined up at the 35-yard line.

"Blue 42… set… hike!"

Conner dropped back. Lamar blocked like a brick wall. Ethan slipped out and curled across the middle of the open space.

The ball flew.

Time slowed.

Ethan reached…

Caught.

He planted his foot and spun past one defender.

Then another.

The safety came in too late.

Touchdown.

The crowd erupted like a volcano.

Ethan dropped to his knees in the end zone, tears pouring down his face as his teammates swarmed him.

Champions.

The horn blasted. Fireworks exploded over the field. Reporters rushed in. Coach Lanning hugged every player like a father seeing his sons grow up in one night.

But the best moment came seconds later.

The entire student body stormed the field.

Hundreds of them.

Waving flags and screaming and crying, lifting the players onto their shoulders. Confetti flew from the stands. Band horns blared the fight song louder than ever before.

Even the mayor was there, shaking Coach Lanning's hand and clapping Ethan on the back.

Elle found her way through the chaos, arms wide open. Ethan dropped everything and hugged her tight, letting her cry into his jersey.

"You did it, baby," she whispered. "You really did it." As the sea of gold and blue swelled across the field, cheers turned to chants, chants into hugs, and hugs into the unforgettable blur of victory.

Ethan, still catching his breath, was surrounded by cameras flashing, microphones shoved into his face, and students lifting their phones to capture every second. Seniors stood side-by-side for interviews, grinning like kids who just won the world.

But not far from the crowd…

Three men stood still.

They weren't in team colors. No school badge. No media lanyards.

Just colorful coats, leather gloves, and curious, unblinking eyes.

One leaned against the back rail of the end zone, scribbling on a notepad—though no one saw where the paper came from. The second stood near a news crew, arms crossed, lips moving but no sound coming out. The third, taller, and thinner figure seemed to weave in and out of the crowd without brushing against a single person.

They were unnoticed.

Until one reporter, setting up a new camera angle, turned suddenly and muttered, "Why are you standing so close to me?"

The thin one answered, with a voice as flat as winter wind,

"I'm taking notes."

The reporter blinked. "Okay… weird," he said, stepping away quickly to interview Coach Lanning.

He looked back, just once.

Now the man was standing beside another reporter.

Still.

Too still.

No blinking. No breathing. Just… watching.

The reporter shivered.

"What is wrong with that guy?" he whispered to himself.

And still, the crowd celebrated.

The cameras kept rolling.

But somewhere in the shadows, evil was listening.

Uncle George, standing nearby with pride in his eyes, just nodded. "Told you this was your year."

As the night wore on, the stadium lights glowed against the winter sky. But for Ethan, the real light was something deep, unshakable.

They had finished the mission.

"Legacy: complete," he whispered. The field was clearing now.

Confetti still floated through the air as snowflakes, and echoes of victory hung over the stadium, but the crowd had begun to disperse. Students headed to their cars, parents waved from the gates, and volunteers collected water bottles and dropped gloves.

Ethan walked off the field beside Marcus, both of them sweaty, bruised, and smiling like kids on Christmas.

"That was crazy," Marcus said, slinging his arm around Ethan's shoulder. "Third ring. We really did it."

"Yeah," Ethan said, grinning. "The whole town showed up, too. Coach said it'd feel like this, but I didn't believe him until now."

As they headed toward the locker room tunnel, Ethan reached down to adjust his shoulder pads…

Then it happened.

A man brushed past him too fast, hard enough to knock him slightly off balance.

Ethan turned. "Oh, sorry about that, sir."

The man stopped briefly. Dressed in a colorful wool coat, no team gear, no emotion on his face. His eyes were sharp and oddly glassy, like mirrors without reflection.

He gave a faint smile.

"It's okay. See you around."

Then he turned and walked away, in calm, deliberate steps toward the parking lot, disappearing into the shadows between the stadium lights.

Marcus furrowed his brow. "What was up with that guy?"

Ethan shrugged, still watching him walk. "I dunno. Maybe he's just rude. Didn't even say excuse me."

Chapter 37
Just a Weekend

The final bell of the semester rang through the halls of Gerry High like a choir set free.

Backpacks slammed shut. Lockers banged closed. Seniors burst from classrooms with loud cheers and winter coats slung over their shoulders. The first flakes of snow had started falling just that morning, dusting the sidewalk and hinting at a real white Christmas.

School was out. Christmas break had officially begun.

Ethan walked out the front doors with Marcus, Lamar, and Conner. Their championship rings hadn't even been sized yet, but the glow of victory still clung to them like cologne.

"No homework. No alarms. No film study. No Coach Lanning yelling about pad level," Conner said, spinning in a slow circle on the sidewalk. "This is freedom, boys."

Marcus nodded. "Yeah, and just in time for the cabin trip."

The seniors had planned it weeks in advance, a weekend getaway, Friday to Sunday night, back by Monday morning. Just 30 students had signed up, mostly tight-knit classmates and a few football players. Everyone else had made other plans.

According to Amanda, at least six other senior groups were doing their own thing for Christmas break: a trip to Chicago, a ski lodge in Pennsylvania, a cruise out of Miami, and even two students tagging along on college tours. But the cabin trip?

That was for the ones who wanted something a little quieter. A little closer.

Amanda's dad, Mr. Blackwell, had agreed to chaperone the cabin weekend, along with three other parents: Marcus's mom, a math teacher named Mr. Holland, and Mrs. Ruiz, who ran the PTA and made hot cocoa like a religion.

"It's just a weekend," Amanda had said in the group text.

"Cabins, food, snow, laughs. Then back to reality."

Ethan was okay with that.

He needed the break. His body still ached from the championship game, and his mind had been on overdrive for months. A cabin sounded like peace. A weekend of quiet before everything ramped up again: college letters, senior projects, and signing day.

Besides, he hadn't had real downtime with his friends since the summer.

He just wanted to be normal for a few days.

No crowds.

No cameras.

No pressure.

Just snow, jokes, and sleep.

That was the plan. He entered his vehicle and drove to his residence.

When Ethan arrived home, he tossed a hoodie into his duffel bag, then another pair of sweats. He checked his phone group chat, blowing up with last-minute snack lists, speaker requests, and questions about the hot tub situation.

He shook his head, amused.

"Amanda's trying to organize a movie night, but Lamar's trying to bring a karaoke machine," he muttered to himself, zipping up his bag halfway. "This trip's gonna be chaos."

From downstairs, he heard the soft clinking of dishes and the hum of gospel music coming from the kitchen speaker. He grabbed his charger and headphones, stuffing them in the front pocket of his bag, then made his way down the steps.

Elle was at the stove, stirring something warm and sweet-smelling, blueberry cobbler or maybe apple crisp… a soft, buttery aroma wrapped around the house like a blanket.

"You finished packing?" she asked without looking up.

"Just about," Ethan said. "Leaving in twenty. Marcus's mom is doing the first round of pickups."

Elle turned, wiping her hands on a towel. She looked him over like a mother does not to admire, but to inspect. Was he eating enough? Did he look tired? Was he hiding something?

"You sure you got enough warm clothes? You boys act like you're heat-resistant."

"I packed layers, Ma. I'm good."

She came closer, gently tugging at the zipper of his jacket. "And what about your boots? Those cabin trails get icy. I don't want you out there slipping around thinking you're invincible."

Ethan gave a small smile. "I got my winter boots. I'll be fine."

Elle didn't let go right away. She held the collar of his coat in her hands, then looked him in the eyes.

"You know I trust you, right?"

He nodded.

"But the woods can be tricky," she continued. "There's no city noise out there. No streetlights. No quick help. I want you to stay sharp. Don't go wandering off, especially at night. Stick with your group. Use wisdom."

Ethan softened. "I will."

"And if anything feels… off, you come home. You understand?"

"Yeah," he said. "I understand."

Elle reached up and smoothed the side of his face like she did when he was ten. "You've got a good head, Ethan. Keep it. Don't let the fun make you forget the foundation."

"I won't."

She finally smiled. "Alright. Have a good time. But if I get a call from a ranger saying y'all went skinny dipping in a frozen lake, I'm sending Uncle George with the belt."

Ethan laughed. "Now that's terrifying."

She handed him a wrapped container. "Take this with you. Apple cinnamon bread. Might keep you warm when the snacks run out."

He leaned in and hugged her. "Love you, Ma."

"Love you more."

Outside, a horn honked.

Ethan slung the duffel bag over his shoulder and headed to the door.

The woods were waiting. The van smelled like fruit snacks, cocoa butter, and teenage excitement.

Ethan sat in the back row, legs stretched out over his duffel bag, earbuds dangling but not playing anything. The ride was already full of laughter and noise, the kind only seniors, finally free from school, could create.

Marcus was up front next to his mom, who was focused on the icy road ahead, humming gospel music under her breath as if that could balance the chaos behind her.

Lamar and Conner were dead center in the middle row, arguing over playlists like it was life or death.

"I'm telling you, we need to start with R&B," Conner said, holding his phone like a sacred scroll.

Lamar groaned. "Bruh, it's a cabin trip, not prom. Play something that gets the vibe right."

"Exactly. R&B is the vibe."

From the back, Amanda leaned forward over the seat. "Can we not spend the whole trip arguing about music? Pick a winter playlist and rotate the DJ every hour."

Ethan smirked. "You do know you just guaranteed four hours of Christmas trap remixes, right?"

"Good," Amanda said, tossing him a candy cane. "Consider it a festive punishment."

The rest of the students in the van laughed. Someone pulled out a portable speaker. A few started recording for their social media stories, "#Cabin Weekend," which is already trending among their private pages.

Outside the windows, the trees became taller and denser. Houses disappeared. Signal bars dropped. Snow thickened along the shoulder of the two-lane road.

"Y'all notice it's getting real country out here?" Marcus said, glancing nervously out the window. "Like… don't-get-a-flat-tire kind of country."

Marcus's mom chuckled from the driver's seat. "That's why we brought chains and emergency blankets. And don't act brand new. Y'all wanted the woods."

"I wanted 'rustic and cozy,' not 'Deliverance,'" Lamar muttered.

Laughter filled the van again.

Ethan leaned back in his seat, letting the noise wash over him. These were his people. His crew. His teammates. His classmates. His friends. It felt good to be here, to be normal, to ride.

The vans crunched slowly down a long gravel road lined with towering pine trees, their branches heavy with snow. The headlights cut through the fading daylight as they passed a wooden sign painted in forest green:

"Gerry Pines Retreat: Rest, Reflect, Reconnect."

Lamar leaned forward, peering through the windshield. "Okay, that's corny. But those cabins are kinda tough."

Three rustic log cabins stood at the end of the clearing, each one spaced a few yards apart, their roofs blanketed in snow, chimneys already smoking, and soft golden lights glowing from the windows.

"Looks like something off a postcard," Amanda said from the front passenger seat.

Each cabin had a wide porch, wooden rocking chairs, and a split-rail fence wrapping around the perimeter. A small lake sat just beyond the trees behind the last cabin, frozen over with a sheen of silver under the early evening sky.

As the vans parked, the students piled out, wide-eyed and shivering.

"Okay!" Amanda's dad, Mr. Blackwell, shouted as he climbed out of the second van, his clipboard in hand. "Everyone, grab your stuff and gather around. We've got cabin assignments and weekend rules."

"Rules?" Marcus groaned, dragging his duffel.

"Don't worry," Mr. Blackwell said with a smirk. "They're simple: don't die, don't set anything on fire, and don't test my patience."

Laughter broke out as students circled up.

Each cabin would host ten students and at least one chaperone.

Cabin 1: Mr. Blackwell with Ethan, Marcus, Conner, Lamar, Amanda, and five others.

Cabin 2: Mrs. Ruiz and her group, mainly the quieter students, yearbook staff, and two drama club kids who brought board games and hot cocoa mix.

Cabin 3: Mr. Holland, the math teacher, had already started unpacking board games and a first-aid kit before anyone got out of the van.

"Cabins have wood-burning stoves and working bathrooms," Mr. Blackwell continued. "Phones work, barely, so don't count on social media saving you. You want warmth? Chop wood. You want Wi-Fi? Pray."

The group laughed again and began hauling bags inside.

Inside Cabin 1, the smell of cedar, pine, and faint smoke filled the air. Bunk beds lined the walls, and a fireplace crackled in the main room. Thick blankets were folded at the edge of each bed, and a basket of snacks sat in the middle of the shared living space with a handwritten welcome note.

Conner tossed his bag on the top bunk. "This is nicer than my grandma's house."

Marcus opened a window slightly, letting in crisp air. "I might not leave."

Ethan stood in the middle of the room, letting the warmth settle over him while he lay across the bed.

Outside, snowflakes started falling again, slowly, gently, and softly. The laughter of students echoed between the trees. A fire pit was already being prepped in the clearing between the cabins.

The fire cracked and popped as long as logs were stacked high and glowing orange, sending little sparks into the snowy air like fireflies with nowhere to go.

All thirty students were gathered in the open clearing between the cabins, bundled up in hoodies, coats, scarves, and blankets. Foldout chairs, tree stumps, and picnic benches circled the fire in a loose, messy ring. Mr. Blackwell stood off to the side with a thermos of coffee, chatting with Mrs. Ruiz and Mr. Holland as they kept a watchful but relaxed eye on the teens.

Someone passed around a Bluetooth speaker. Another passed a bag of marshmallows and chocolate bars to make s'mores.

"This is the part where a bear shows up," Marcus said, roasting two at once. "And I gotta fight it shirtless with a stick."

"You wouldn't fight a bunny rabbit if it looked at you sideways," Amanda teased.

"I'd fight a raccoon."

"Marcus," Ethan said, laughing, "you ran from a squirrel in 10th grade. I remember."

"Okay, but that squirrel was aggressive," he replied defensively. "And I had on slides."

The group burst into laughter. The cold didn't seem to matter anymore; the fire and the friendships were enough to keep the night warm.

Stories started rolling.

Conner told a dramatic tale about getting lost in a Walmart parking lot as a kid. Amanda confessed she entered the wrong house on Halloween, thinking it was her friend's party. Ethan shared how he once practiced speeches in the mirror with a hairbrush and didn't realize his uncle was recording him the whole time.

"Y'all better not let this video resurface when I'm up for a player of the year," he said, shaking his head as they howled in laughter.

The night continued.

Snowflakes kept falling, and someone pulled out a bag of kettle corn. The flames danced higher, casting golden shadows on everyone's faces.

But then, in a brief lull between stories, Ethan caught something out of the corner of his eye.

"You good?" Lamar asked, handing him a s'more.

"Yeah," Ethan said slowly. "Just thought I saw something in the trees."

Lamar turned to look, but the woods were still. Quiet. Undisturbed.

"Probably just your imagination," Lamar said. "Or a deer. Or that squirrel that haunts Marcus."

Marcus pointed his marshmallow stick at them both. "I rebuke that squirrel."

Ethan chuckled but glanced back one more time. The trees swayed gently under the weight of snow. Nothing moved.

But deep inside, a slight chill settled in his chest, one that didn't come from the wind.

Chapter 38
Cabin Weekend

Morning broke quietly and beautifully.

A soft blanket of fresh snow had fallen overnight, covering everything in a smooth white shimmer. The pine trees looked like frosted towers, and the frozen lake gleamed in the morning light like glass.

Inside the cabins, the smell of bacon and cinnamon drifted through the halls. Mr. Blackwell had whipped up a huge breakfast, and Mrs. Ruiz brought over muffins and fresh fruit from her cabin.

Ethan sat at the long table, sipping orange juice while pulling on his hoodie.

"This view is wild," Marcus said, looking out the window. "Like a snow globe but real."

"And cold," Amanda added, wrapping her scarf tighter.

Once breakfast was cleared and bags were packed, the group gathered out front near the cabins.

"Alright, team!" Mr. Blackwell called out, holding a clipboard. "We've got options. Half of you want to hike, half want to sled. So, we're splitting up."

The cheer that erupted was a mix of excitement and groaning.

"Group One will hike with Mrs. Ruiz and me, up through the eastern trail, and it should take about two hours with stops. Group Two stays here and sledding with Mr. Holland behind Cabin Three. No one goes off on their own, got it?"

"Yes, sir!" they all chimed.

The students sorted themselves quickly. Ethan, Marcus, Amanda, and a few others chose hiking. Conner, Lamar, and the louder half of the group headed for sledding, already dragging their gear toward the slope behind the cabins.

"You sure you're not trying to avoid breaking your tailbone on that sled hill?" Conner teased Ethan as they separated.

"Absolutely," Ethan grinned. "I'd rather hike than fly into a tree."

As the groups split, Mr. Blackwell gave one final reminder. "Stay on the marked paths. Don't go wandering off-trail. These woods get thick fast."

They nodded, and soon the groups parted ways, laughter ringing in both directions as footprints crunched into the snow.

The sledding group erupted into chaos as they slid down the hill, crashing into snowbanks and shouting over whose turn was next.

The hiking group, however, crept under the tall canopy of trees, their breath fogging in the cold, boots sinking slightly in the new snow.

Ethan trailed behind a bit, taking in the silence.

"Everything okay?" Amanda called from up ahead.

He looked up. "Yeah… just thought I saw something."

"Probably a rabbit," she said. "Or one of Marcus's ghosts."

Ethan chuckled and started walking again. As they continued hiking, they made their way deeper into the pines, the snow crunching beneath their boots with every step.

The eastern trail snaked through tall evergreens and around gentle slopes that no other footprints had touched. Mr. Blackwell led the group, a trail map in one hand, a hot coffee thermos in the other, while Mrs. Ruiz took up the rear like a proud shepherd.

"This view is wild," Amanda said, snapping a picture of the frozen lake they passed. "Looks like a fairytale."

"Except with less betrayal and more thermals," Ethan replied, grinning.

Marcus stopped suddenly, half-sinking in a drift. "Okay, but why does it feel like we're ten minutes from a bear or a documentary?"

Ethan laughed. "You said the same thing when we went to the zoo."

Amanda pointed to a small wooden marker. "Trail loops back this way. We're halfway through."

They took a break at a scenic overlook where the trees opened wide enough to see the snowy hills stretch into the horizon. Some took selfies, others threw snowballs, and someone slipped trying to sit on a frozen log, which led to ten minutes of unstoppable laughter.

"Not even mad," the girl said, brushing snow off her jeans. "Worth it."

Meanwhile, back behind Cabin Three, the sledding group was in full mayhem mode.

Lamar had built a mini ramp using a pile of snow and was daring anyone brave enough to fly off it. Conner had wiped out twice already, once landing halfway in a bush and once losing a boot mid-air.

"That was the most graceful fall I've ever seen," someone shouted.

"I didn't fall," Conner insisted, crawling out of the snow. "I was just... redistributing gravity."

A pair of girls were filming a slow-motion video of their tandem sled ride while two other students tried to build a snowman and failed miserably, resulting in a snow blob with sunglasses and gummy worms for a mouth.

"I present to you... Snowvin Diesel," one of them declared, bowing.

Mr. Holland stood at the top of the hill, a whistle in hand, watching with equal parts amusement and anxiety. "If someone breaks a leg, I'm calling your gym teacher to explain the physics of poor decision-making."

No one slowed down.

By the time the afternoon sun began to dip behind the trees, both groups were breathless, red-cheeked, and ready to eat like they hadn't seen food in days.

Back at the cabins, the smell of chili, cornbread, and roasted vegetables filled the air. The parents had worked together while the students were out, prepping a hearty dinner and setting out long tables inside Cabin Two.

Snow-dusted boots lined the cabin porches. Scarves were draped over chairs. Someone started a playlist of mellow R&B and holiday classics.

"Best day of break so far," Amanda said, sinking into her seat with a plate full of food.

Ethan nodded, mouth full of cornbread. "And the weekend's not even over."

They all agreed laughing, teasing, passing napkins and hot sauce, trading stories about who wiped out the worst or who saw the prettiest view.

And for a few perfect hours, they weren't students or athletes or seniors worried about the future.

They were just kids, in the woods, making memories as the snow was still falling gently when the smell of bacon, scrambled eggs, and cinnamon waffles floated through the cabin halls.

It was Sunday morning, their final full day together before heading back to the city. The weekend had flown by like a blur of snowflakes and laughter.

Inside Cabin Two, long tables had been set again, this time for breakfast. The parents worked like a well-oiled team—Mr. Blackwell manning the griddle, Mrs. Ruiz and Marcus's mom mixing batter, and Mr. Holland attempting to flip pancakes while being roasted by students every time one hit the floor.

"I'm just seasoning the floor," he joked, holding up a burnt flapjack with tongs. "It builds character."

Ethan and Marcus loaded their plates with eggs, hash browns, and toast.

"Man, this trip's been good," Marcus said. "I don't wanna leave."

"Same," Ethan nodded. "Feels like we hit pause on life for a minute."

Amanda sat across from them, sipping hot cocoa. "We needed it. Senior year's been... a lot."

No one argued.

Between school pressure, sports, college decisions, and figuring out what came next, this weekend had been a rare chance just to be.

After breakfast, Mr. Blackwell stood up and tapped a mug with his spoon.

"Alright, Hawks," he said. "Before we pack up and hit the road, we've got one last activity. Team challenge out in the snow. You've got thirty minutes to build the best snow creation you can. Sculpt it, stack it, name it. Then we vote. Winner gets bragging rights forever and the last chocolate muffin tray."

A cheer went up so loud it rattled the windows.

"Let's go!" someone yelled, already rushing outside with gloves in hand.

Outside, the snow was perfectly light, soft, and fresh from overnight. Students split into teams and got to work.

Amanda's group tried to sculpt a snow unicorn. Marcus and Conner attempted a full snow football stadium, complete with tiny players made from twigs and marshmallows. Ethan joined a group that built a massive snow throne and dared everyone to take photos in it like royalty.

Even the parents got in on it Mr. Holland molded a wonky-looking snow duck, claiming it was "abstract modern art." Mrs. Ruiz added a scarf and called it "Billy the Wise."

By the time the judging came around, everyone was breathless and laughing.

The winner?

The snow throne.

Ethan didn't take his muffin, though he gave it to Amanda, who had somehow managed to keep her gloves clean all weekend.

"You earned it," he said, smiling.

By noon, they were packed and ready.

Bags were loaded. Cabins were checked. Fires were put out. The group circled up for one last photo thirty students, four chaperones, and a weekend full of memories caught in one perfect frame.

As the vans rolled back down the gravel path, the cabins behind them slowly disappeared behind a curtain of snow and trees.

But something stayed with them.

A stillness. A closeness. A memory they'd carry far beyond senior year. The sky was a soft, winter gray when Ethan stepped through the front door; duffel bag slung over his shoulder, boots trailing bits of snow across the welcome mat.

"Home," he mumbled, barely loud enough for anyone to hear.

He dropped the bag, kicked off his boots, and headed straight upstairs.

No fanfare. No unpacking. No distractions.

He walked into his room, shut the door, and flopped face-first onto his bed like gravity had finally caught up with him.

"Best weekend ever," he whispered into his pillow, still wearing half his hoodie and a smirk of satisfaction. His body was sore, but in the best way like he'd lived life fully for the first time in months.

Downstairs, the soft sound of Christmas music floated through the house.

Elle was already in the living room, standing on a step stool and hanging garland around the fireplace. The scent of pine candles and cinnamon clove drifted through the air, mixing with something sweet baking in the oven apple crisp, Ethan guessed.

The tree was already up, full of gold and deep red ornaments. A few wrapped gifts sat beneath it, and a handwritten sign rested on the coffee table that read:

"Jesus is the reason for the season."

Uncle George was on the couch, snoring lightly with the TV on low volume. A football rerun played, but no one was really watching.

Elle smiled as she stepped down and peeled off her gloves. She walked into the kitchen, humming softly and peeking into the oven.

Then she called up the stairs.

"You hungry?"

Ethan rolled onto his back and yelled, "I could eat the whole fridge!"

She laughed. "Well, come down and settle for a plate. You can eat the fridge after Christmas."

A few minutes later, he appeared in the kitchen with hair wild and a face still glowing from the weekend.

Elle studied him closely as he sat down at the table, spooning hot apple crisp into a bowl.

"You look different," she said, pouring him a glass of milk.

Ethan looked up. "Different how?"

"I don't know. Lighter," she said. "Like something finally settled in your spirit."

He thought for a moment. "It did. We laughed. We hiked. Sledded and cooked over fires. I talked for hours. I didn't think about football, school, or pressure. Just… life."

Elle smiled and touched his shoulder gently. "You needed that."

He nodded. "Yeah, I really did."

They sat in a quiet pause, the kind only a mother and son could share a space where no words were needed.

Outside, snow continued to fall softly against the windows.

Inside, there was warmth, rest, and the soft glow of peace.

Christmas was only two days away. Christmas morning arrived in a hush.

The snow had stopped overnight, leaving the neighborhood blanketed in a soft, untouched white. The sun glowed faintly behind gray clouds, casting everything in a gentle light.

Ethan woke to the smell of cinnamon rolls and turkey sausage. Downstairs, holiday jazz played softly from the speaker, and the sound of wrapping paper rustling and mugs clinking filled the house.

He rubbed his eyes, yawned, and reached for his hoodie before heading down.

Elle was already in the kitchen, dancing slightly as she stirred a pot on the stove. Uncle George sat in his recliner, wearing reindeer slippers and sipping coffee like a king.

"Merry Christmas," Ethan said, his voice still scratchy.

"Merry Christmas, baby," Elle said, turning to kiss him on the cheek. "Hope you're hungry."

He laughed. "Always."

After breakfast, they gathered in the living room. The fireplace glowed warm, and the Christmas tree shimmered with tiny lights and golden bows. Ethan handed out gifts while Elle played DJ with the speaker.

Laughter filled the room Uncle George cracking jokes about every present, Elle getting emotional over a framed photo Ethan had printed of them from his last football game, Ethan lighting up when he opened a pair of custom cleats with "LEGACY" stitched on the sides.

But the best gift came in a small envelope at the bottom of his stocking.

It wasn't flashy. No glitter, no bow.

Just a folded letter marked:

"University of Greywood Athletics Department."

Ethan held it for a moment, heart thudding.

Elle watched him carefully. "Well? Don't keep us in suspense."

He opened it slowly.

Inside was a congratulatory letter from the University of Greywood, offering a full athletic scholarship to play football and study physical therapy. Handwritten at the bottom was a note from the head coach:

"We don't just want your talent. We want your leadership. Welcome to Greywood, Ethan."

He stared at the paper for a long second, then looked up, eyes wide.

Elle covered her mouth. "You got it?"

He nodded. "I got it."

Uncle George slapped his knee. "That's what I'm talking about! Let's go!"

Elle stood and wrapped him in a hug, whispering, "I'm so proud of you. But more than football I'm proud of who you're becoming."

A week later, it was New Year's, and the house was quiet again.

Ethan sat on the porch, wrapped in a thick blanket, watching the sky shift from dusk to dark. A few fireworks had already started in the distance, bright colors blooming like flowers against the sky.

He held his phone but wasn't scrolling through it.

Just thinking.

The year had been full. Wins. Losses. Breakthroughs. Growth.

And now a whole new chapter waited on the other side of midnight.

Elle came out with two mugs of cocoa and handed him one, then sat beside him.

"You ready for next year?" she asked.

Ethan took a sip and nodded. "Yeah… I think I am."

She looked up at the sky. "Then say it."

"What?"

She smiled. "Speak what you want this next year to be."

Ethan thought for a moment, then said quietly:

"Purposeful. Focused. And at peace."

Elle bumped his shoulder gently. "Sounds like a good year to me."

As the final seconds of the year ticked away and fireworks lit up the sky, Ethan leaned back in his chair, eyes steady.

He wasn't just hoping for something good.

He was walking toward it.

Chapter 39
Turning Points

The hallways of Gerry High buzzed with new energy as students returned from Christmas break, jackets zipped up to their chins and sneakers squeaking against freshly mopped floors.

The bulletin boards were already updated with college deadlines, senior trip reminders, and the first set of prom announcements.

"Feels weird being back," Marcus said as he and Ethan walked toward their lockers. "Like, break was a dream, and now we're stuck in reality again."

Ethan nodded. "Yeah, but... this is it. Last semester. The countdown's real now."

By mid-February, everything kicked into high gear. It was Signing Day.

The gym was packed. Banners hung from the walls. A stage had been set with a long table, a crisp tablecloth, and a row of college hats.

Conner had already committed to Briarstone University. Marcus was still deciding between two regional schools. Lamar had quietly signed early to a Division II powerhouse and didn't want a big fuss.

But today was Ethan's moment.

With family, friends, coaches, and the entire senior class watching, he sat at the center of the table, a Greywood University hat in front of him.

The announcer read his name, and Ethan picked up the pen.

Full ride. D1 ball. His next chapter.

He signed.

Applause filled the gym.

Coach Lanning clapped him on the back with a proud, wordless nod. Elle stood in the crowd with her phone recording, tears running down her cheeks. Uncle George shouted, "That's my boy!" so loud it echoed.

Ethan stood, placed the Greywood cap on his head, and smiled widely for the cameras.

He'd done it.

By early March, prom talk had taken over the school like wildfire.

Group chats were filled with dress ideas, tux rentals, limo plans, and color themes. The teachers had even added a countdown calendar outside the main office.

"Okay, so we all got dates, right?" Amanda asked one afternoon at lunch.

"I'm taking Mya," said Marcus.

"Lamar's going with Joy from the choir," Conner added. "Don't ask how that happened."

"What about you?" Amanda turned to Ethan.

Ethan looked at her, then smiled. "I was just waiting to ask the right person."

Amanda raised an eyebrow.

He pulled out a folded paper from his hoodie pocket and handed it to her. It read:

"Since I already got the best teammate… want to be my date to prom?"

Amanda stared at it, then smiled.

"About time."

They high-fived like always… but this one lingered just a little longer. By the end of March, the weather hadn't quite made up its mind frost in the mornings, muddy grass by afternoon but spring was coming.

Senior projects were underway, college plans were solidifying, and prom tickets had officially gone on sale. Ethan was balancing workouts, classes, and calls from his soon-to-be Greywood position coach.

The pressure had shifted but it hadn't disappeared.

Only now was there a new kind of clarity.

He wasn't running toward football.

He was growing into a man.

And even in the middle of prom plans, graduation fittings, and school countdowns, Ethan knew…

The real work was beginning. Spring break came and went in a quiet breeze.

While some seniors jetted off to warm beaches and crowded resorts, Ethan stayed home by choice. He used the week to rest, recharge, and refocus. His days were filled with workouts, film study, long walks, and the occasional nap that stretched into the afternoon.

"I'm not wasting my energy on sand and sunburns," he joked to Marcus when asked why he wasn't going on the senior trip to Clearwater Beach. "I'm trying to be college-ready, not camera-ready."

Marcus laughed. "You're weird, man. Focused, but weird."

A few seniors did go on the trip, Amanda included, but others stayed close to Gerry. The ones who remained met up for bowling nights, bonfires, and low-key hangouts that felt more like family than vacation.

By the second week of April, all anyone could talk about was Prom Night.

The school had rented out The Gerry Grand Ballroom, the biggest venue in the county. Rumor had it someone's cousin was flying into DJ, and a local restaurant had offered to cater.

Fittings, shoe orders, and nail appointments flooded every group chat.

Amanda had picked a stunning navy-blue gown with silver detailing. Ethan went with a crisp black tux with a matching navy tie and custom cufflinks that said, "Senior Year."

The day of prom, the school parking lot was replaced by limos, town cars, and luxury rentals, even a classic old school convertible that Lamar borrowed from his uncle.

The energy was electric.

Parents gathered around to snap pictures. Teachers smiled with that "finally, they made it" kind of pride. Everyone looked like royalty.

Before Ethan left, he came downstairs looking sharp, hair lined up, tie perfect, cologne just right.

Elle was waiting with a camera. "Let me get one from the stairs yes, like that. Turn slightly. That's it."

Uncle George stood in the doorway with his arms folded. "Alright, pretty boy. Come here."

Ethan walked over. George clapped a hand on his shoulder and lowered his voice.

"Listen to me. I know tonight's big. You earned it. But don't mess it up trying to prove anything. You drink? You don't drive. You don't get in a car with someone drunk. You call me. You hear me?"

Ethan nodded. "I got it."

Elle stepped in. "And don't stay out too late. Just because you're grown doesn't mean you don't have a mother who will drive through a party and pull you out barefoot in a robe."

He laughed. "Understood."

"Mitchell's house is about thirty minutes out, right?" George asked.

"Yeah," Ethan said. "His parents built this huge place on ten acres. They're cool with the party, and his older cousin is DJ'ing in the backyard."

Elle raised an eyebrow. "Backyard?"

"Yeah, the setup's legit. Lights, games, food, his parents are watching everything. Said they'd shut it down by 2 a.m."

George nodded slowly. "Alright. Just remember fun doesn't mean foolish." "Yes, you can go to the after-party," his mother said with a smile. Ethan was happy. The sky was painted in gold and soft lavender as the sun dipped behind the trees, casting the perfect light across the Blackwell family's front yard.

Amanda stepped outside in a shimmering navy gown, her curls pinned back in an elegant twist, silver earrings sparkling as she moved.

Ethan stood by the steps, adjusting his cufflinks, trying not to stare too obviously.

Mrs. Blackwell clapped her hands softly. "You two look absolutely stunning."

Mr. Blackwell, standing tall in a navy suit of his own, grinned and added, "Y'all might as well walk the red carpet. Forget prom."

Elle stood off to the side with her phone, capturing every angle. "Okay, Ethan, hold her hand… no, not like that, hold it like you're serious about her."

Amanda laughed. "He is serious, Miss Elle."

Uncle George, sunglasses on despite the setting sun, held up his phone. "Smile, champ. This is the one they'll frame on the mantle when y'all get married."

"Uncle George," Ethan said, shaking his head.

"Don't mind him," Elle said. "He's been watching too many romantic movies."

More pictures. One with Ethan and Amanda under the cherry blossom tree. They took pictures of Amanda with her mom, including one of Ethan, Amanda, Elle, and Uncle George all together.

Then the real surprise rolled up.

A party bus—long, sleek, black with neon under-glow and tinted windows pulled into the driveway.

The side door slid open to reveal Marcus, Conner, Mya, and a handful of other seniors already inside, music playing softly as they waved.

Uncle George grinned. "Don't say I never did nothing for you."

Ethan's eyes widened. "You serious?"

"Party bus is yours for the night," George said. "Just don't tear it up."

"Thank you, Unc," Ethan said, fist-bumping him.

"Make some memories," Elle added. "Good, clean ones."

They climbed aboard, the lights inside flashing gently as Amanda sat beside Ethan, both of them still glowing in the camera flashes and fading sunset.

At the Gerry Grand Ballroom, it was dressed in magic. Crystal chandeliers glistened over gold-and-blue themed tables. Tall floral centerpieces shimmered with lights. The DJ booth was set up near a marble dance floor, and the entire room buzzed with elegance and excitement.

Everyone looked grown.

Heels clicked, and laughter echoed, as high school seemed a distant memory for one night. Ethan and Amanda walked in arm-in-arm, turning heads as they made their entrance. They took more photos near the ice sculpture, grabbed plates from the buffet, and danced to everything from slow jams to throwback hits.

Marcus and Mya dominated the dance floor. Conner made everyone laugh with his ridiculous robot dance. Even the teachers chaperoning at the edges couldn't help but smile.

Halfway through the night, a slow song played.

Ethan and Amanda stepped out onto the floor.

He took her hand.

They swayed slowly, not speaking, just moving, present in the moment.

"You know," Amanda whispered, "this night feels like a movie."

Ethan smiled. "Then I'm glad I get to be in it with you."

By midnight, the ballroom lights dimmed, and the party bus headed thirty minutes outside of town to Mitchell's place.

They pulled into a long, paved driveway surrounded by fields and tall trees.

Mitchell's parents had gone all out.

String lights hung between posts in the massive backyard. A whole tent was set up with heaters, music, a dance area, and tables stacked with snacks, drinks, and catered finger foods. Portable heaters glowed warmly in the corners. A fire pit crackled in the back, surrounded by chairs and cozy blankets.

"No alcohol. No smoking. No foolishness," Mitchell's dad had said earlier, and everyone respected that.

Inside, there were games, pool, ping-pong, and music playing just low enough for conversation. Outside, the vibe was pure celebration.

Ethan grabbed a grape soda and leaned against the fence with Amanda, watching friends dance under the stars.

"This is crazy," he said. "I didn't expect it to be this nice."

Amanda looked up at him. "We've made it this far. We deserve a night like this."

He nodded. "You're right."

Across the yard, students laughed, posed for selfies, told stories around the fire, and soaked up every second of a night that felt like the closing of a chapter.

Ethan looked around and smiled.

Safe. Fun. Unforgettable.

Prom faded into memory like the last note of a song.

By the first week of May, reality had returned gently, then all at once.

The seniors of Gerry High walked the halls differently now. Slower. More aware. As if every moment might be their last in these familiar spaces.

Final projects were turned in. Yearbooks were distributed. Lockers started to empty.

Teachers who once chased them for homework now offered hugs and advice. Posters lined the hallways with senior quotes and college commitments:

Conner, Briarstone University-Athletic Scholarship

Lamar, Rinse State, D2

Marcus, Cozy State, Athletic Scholarship

Ethan, Greywood University, Athletic Scholarship

In the cafeteria, the energy had shifted.

There was less noise more reflection.

People signed yearbooks like their words might be permanent:

"Stay real."

"Don't forget me."

"See you at the reunion."

In English class, Ms. Freeman had them write letters to their future selves. Ethan's letter was short, but honest:

"I hope you're still grounded. Still hungry. Still remembering where you came from."

The final bell was only days away.

Caps and gowns were handed out in neat plastic bags. Seniors took turns decorating theirs some with rhinestones, others with glitter and college logos.

Ethan's was simple.

He added the words: "Legacy Begins."

Amanda's cap said: "Still Becoming."

They stood side by side in the senior hallway, looking at the wall of class pictures that stretched back decades.

"It feels weird," Amanda said. "Like... we're about to leave and none of this is coming with us."

Ethan nodded. "Yeah. It's like the last four years were a chapter, and now it's closing."

They paused.

Not because they didn't know what came next.

But because they finally believed it was real.

On the last day of school, the seniors lined up in the gym for the traditional walkout one final lap through the hallways, dressed in caps and gowns, music playing on the intercom, first-year students clapping from the sidelines.

Ethan walked in the front row with Marcus, Amanda, Conner, and Lamar.

His heartbeat was slow and steady.

He passed the library. The locker he used in his first year. The classroom where Coach Lanning first told him he had "something special."

Everything felt louder, even in silence.

Students high-fived them. Teachers teared up. Some clapped. Some just smiled.

As Ethan reached the front doors and the sunlight poured through the glass, he paused.

Amanda squeezed his hand.

"You ready?" she asked.

He looked back once more at all the laughter, the memories, the noise and pressure and growth that had shaped him.

And then he stepped outside the school's double doors for the last time.

Chapter 40
The Final Walk

The following week, the hum of chatter filled the auditorium like a rising tide families taking their seats, proud parents adjusting camera lenses, the occasional burst of laughter echoing off the polished gym walls. Gold and blue balloons danced from the railings, and a banner stretched across the bleachers: "Congratulations, Class of 2012 The Future Is Yours."

Ethan stood in line with his classmates, adjusting the tassel on his cap. The black gown felt heavier than it should've part polyester, part emotion. This was it the end of high school.

He inhaled deeply, scanning the crowd from behind the curtain. There they were his people. His mom was wearing a soft blue dress and clutching a tissue already damp at the corners. Uncle George, in his usual sharp button-up and sunglasses, gave him a nod that said You did it, son. Aunt Helen waved wildly when she caught his eye. Aunt Tricia, dressed like she was headed to Sunday brunch, had a phone ready to record. Around them were cousins, uncles, old church members, and even his little league coach.

They came for him.

The processional music began, and the graduates started walking out two by two. When Ethan stepped onto the gym floor, the roar of his cheering section was unmistakable. He couldn't help but grin.

He found his seat. Principal James gave a short, formal welcome, followed by the valedictorian's speech. Ethan barely heard it his thoughts drifted through time. Coach Lanning's locker room speeches. Early morning practices. Prayers before games. His father's absence. His mother's unwavering faith.

Names were called. Students stood and crossed the stage.

"Ethan Phillipssssss!"

The room erupted. He took the stage, shaking hands with the principal, locking eyes with his family just long enough to see his mother cover her mouth as tears streamed down her face. Uncle George stood to clap, and even Aunt Tricia stood up, filming while shouting, "That's my nephew!"

The diploma felt cool in his hand, but the warmth came from the smiles in the crowd.

After the ceremony, the graduates spilled outside into the early summer air. Families mingled and snapped pictures against a backdrop of blue skies and bright futures.

Ethan posed for photos, one arm around his mom, the other around Uncle George.

"You proud of me?" he asked softly.

"Proud?" Elle sniffled, wiping her cheek. "I'm bursting with joy, baby."

George leaned in. "I told you. I saw it from day one. You're something special. Just don't forget who you are when the noise gets loud."

Ethan nodded, but his eyes drifted toward a group of students already making plans for the after-party. The noise was already loud.

They took more photos some with a cluster of cousins, some with Coach Lanning, who dropped by in slacks and a tie, giving Ethan a firm handshake and a quiet, "You're going far, kid. Stay grounded."

Later, as the crowd thinned, Ethan stood alone near the edge of the school lawn. He looked back at the building's brick walls, tall windows, and all the echoes within them.

For a moment, he thought he heard the faint sound of the freshman hallway laughter, the Coach's whistle, the squeak of gym shoes, and the clink of his locker door.

He smiled and whispered, "Goodbye."

Then, without turning back again, he walked toward the car where his family waited. Later that day, the scent of grilled ribs, honey-glazed chicken, and Aunt Tricia's famous mac and cheese filled the air as laughter floated from the backyard. Paper lanterns swayed gently on strings, and gold and blue streamers twisted around the deck posts, matching Ethan's Gerry High graduation colors.

The long folding tables were covered in plastic tablecloths, already dotted with blue punch stains and half-eaten plates. The sound of jazz played softly through Uncle George's Bluetooth speaker while kids ran barefoot through the grass, tossing a football and begging for cupcakes.

Ethan sat under a canopy with his legs stretched out, a crown of sweat forming along his hairline. His cap and gown had long been discarded for a Bahamas T-shirt and new sneakers; his mom surprised him with them that morning.

"Ethan!" his cousin Darnell called out, lifting a plate piled so high it looked like it might cave in. "Man, you ready for college life? Ain't no mac and cheese like Aunt Tricia's down there!"

Ethan laughed. "That's what care packages are for."

A group of older relatives sat fanning themselves under umbrellas, sipping sweet tea, and sharing stories of their own high school days. Someone mentioned how Ethan used to trip over his own cleats in Little League. Someone else reminded him of the spelling bee he lost in 5th grade by misspelling "gravity."

Elle stood near the grill, smiling as it hurt. She had dreamed of this day, this very moment, for years. Her baby boy was on his way. Not just away from home, but into something greater. Something she couldn't quite protect him from.

"Y'all better get pictures!" Aunt Helen called out, pulling Ethan from his chair. "Come on now, one with your mama! You're gonna look back and wish you took more."

He smiled and leaned beside his mom as flash after flash went off. She held him tightly around the waist, her head leaning against his shoulder for just a second longer than needed.

"You okay, Ma?" he whispered.

She looked up at him, blinking back water in her eyes. "Of course I am, baby. ... don't forget to call me."

"I won't," he promised.

Uncle George stepped in for a photo, followed by a group hug with all the aunts. Even Aunt Tricia, who continually teased him, pulled him tightly and kissed his cheek.

Later, as the sun set, lanterns glowed and the music slowed. The crowd thinned, kids sat wrapped in blankets, and fireflies began to flicker in the grass. Ethan found himself sitting alone at the edge of the yard in a lawn chair, staring up at the twilight sky. His plate was empty, but his heart was whole.

Uncle George came over and handed him a root beer.

"This is your send-off," George said, raising his bottle. "Don't ever say we didn't celebrate you right."

Ethan clinked bottles with him and nodded. "I won't."

They sat in silence for a moment.

"You think I'm ready?" Ethan asked.

George took a long breath. "You're ready. Just remember... everything shiny ain't gold. Stay focused. You got everything in you to do right."

Ethan nodded again but didn't speak.

Because somewhere deep inside, as he looked around the yard one last time at the folding chairs, the laughter, the flickering bug lights, his mom was humming in the kitchen. Ethan was ready for college.

The summer days blurred into a rhythm of sleeping in, late-night runs to the corner store, lifting weights in the basement, and short visits from cousins who were already asking, "When are you leaving?"

Ethan spent most afternoons lounging on the back porch, earbuds in, journaling some days, zoning out others. His duffel bags sat half-packed inside his room: new sheets, shower caddy, extra-long twin bedding. His mom had gone all out.

By mid-August, the breeze had already started to change. A reminder that time was moving whether Ethan was ready or not.

One quiet Thursday afternoon, a familiar car pulled into the driveway. Ethan looked up from his phone as Marcus stepped out in a fitted Cozy University tee shirt, basketball shorts, and sneakers that still looked brand new.

"Yo," Marcus grinned, walking up with that usual confidence and half-sarcastic smirk. "I heard you still got half your socks unfolded."

Ethan smirked. "Nah, I finished those yesterday. Just waiting on you to say goodbye properly."

They bumped shoulders and sat on the porch steps, sipping fruit punch in silence for a moment.

"You leave next week, right?" Ethan asked.

"Yeah. Coach wants us checked in by Sunday night. Full D1 ride, man." Marcus smiled and shook his head like he still couldn't believe it. "Cozy. Can you believe that?"

Ethan bumped fists with him. "I told you that you were gonna be the one."

"Nah, man. We both knew it was you first." Marcus looked out over the yard. "But it's wild. One minute we're in Coach Lanning's office arguing over who missed the block, now... we're packing up our lives."

Ethan nodded. "Feels fast. Too fast."

Marcus leaned back on his elbows. "You nervous?"

Ethan shrugged. "Nah. I'm ready. I think."

"You're gonna kill it at Greywood. That school's lucky to have you." Marcus hesitated, then added, "Just... don't change up, E. I mean that. Stay grounded. Keep praying. Don't let the noise get in your head."

Ethan gave a soft chuckle. "You sound like my uncle."

"Well, your uncle got wisdom. I'm just saying keep your faith close, bro. That stuff matters even more when you're surrounded by everything else."

Ethan looked down at the porch wood grain, silent for a moment. "Yeah. I hear you."

They stood up after a while and hugged one of those strong, brotherly hugs that said more than either could put into words.

As Marcus walked back to his car, he turned around and grinned. "Don't forget the little people when you're on national news!"

Ethan laughed. "Don't forget me when Cozy starts selling your jersey!"

Marcus waved. "We're both going places, man. But don't let the place change you."

Then he was gone.

The car turned out of the driveway, and just like that, one more piece of home drove off with it.

Ethan stood on the porch, watching the street for a while. Then he went inside, looked at the duffel bags by the door, and finally started folding the last of his clothes. Two days later, the drive to Greywood University took just over three hours, but to Ethan it felt like a lifetime. His mother chatted most of the way, pointing out landmarks, reading highway signs aloud, and occasionally asking if he was nervous. He kept his headphones in, nodding or offering one-word answers, not out of disrespect, just... emotion overload.

Uncle George handled the drive, calm and focused as usual. He didn't say much, but now and then Ethan caught him glancing at him in the rearview mirror.

As they pulled into campus, the place buzzed with excitement. Cars were backed up along the curved drop-off loop, upperclassmen in Greywood Orientation shirts shouted directions, and music played from a portable speaker near the freshman welcome tent.

"Welcome to Greywood!" a girl called out, handing them a laminated map and lanyards. "Go Eagles!"

Ethan stepped out of the car and looked around buildings that stretched skyward, manicured lawns, stone pathways, and students everywhere pulling carts or hugging goodbye. It was real now.

Dorm check-in was a blur. The RA handed over a key card and room number, and just like that, they were walking down the third-floor hallway of Reach Hall, past doors already decorated with dry-erase boards and motivational quotes.

Room 312.

Ethan tapped the key card. The door clicked open.

Inside, a lean, dark-skinned guy with short locs and a southern drawl was halfway through unpacking a suitcase.

"Yo!" the guy said, turning toward them with a friendly grin. "You gotta be Ethan. I'm Jamir from Memphis. Special teams."

They dapped each other up, and Jamir nodded toward the empty side of the room. "I saved you the better bed. No roaches. Yet."

Ethan chuckled, easing into the space. "Appreciate that."

The room smelled like new paint and fresh linens. Twin beds lined opposite walls, desks near the window, a single dresser they'd have to share, and a small fridge in the corner, humming quietly.

Elle started unpacking immediately, folding shirts, arranging toiletries in the drawer, even spraying lavender air freshener as if it were home. Uncle George hung up Ethan's team schedule on the corkboard near the desk.

"Looks like you got a good setup," George said, taking a step back. "Small, but it works."

Ethan nodded. "Yeah... It's not bad."

Jamir laughed. "Wait till y'all see the dining hall. They got fried catfish Fridays. It's like my granny's kitchen showed up to college."

The room settled into quiet again as the last bag was unpacked. Ethan's heart felt heavy, like the air had thickened.

Elle looked around the room one last time, smoothing the bedspread, then turned to her son. "You got everything you need?"

He nodded.

"You got Jesus?"

He smiled faintly. "Yeah, Ma. I got Him, too."

She wrapped him in the kind of hug that said, "Don't forget where you came from," and her voice cracked as she whispered, "I'm so proud of you. And I love you so much, Ethan."

"I love you too, Ma."

Uncle George stepped up and hugged him next with a firm, strong, steady embrace.

"Make us proud," he said, clapping Ethan on the back. "And don't lose your head out here. Football's just a game. Character is everything."

"Yes, sir."

They stood in the doorway for a second longer before Elle finally wiped her eyes and said, "Okay... we'd better go."

Ethan walked them to the elevator. As the doors closed, his mom held up her hand in a wave, eyes glistening.

He stood there in the hallway long after the elevator had gone down.

Back in the room, Jamir was already stretched across his bed, watching highlights on his iPad.

"Everything cool?" he asked.

"Yeah," Ethan said, exhaling as he sat on the edge of his bed. "Just... first time away from home, you know?"

Jamir nodded. "Yeah, man. It hits different. But welcome to the rest of your life."

Ethan looked around the room one more time, then out the window toward the vast, unfamiliar campus.

Somewhere in the back of his mind, he thought he heard Coach Lanning's voice, or maybe Uncle George's:

Stay grounded. Keep your faith.

But as the noise of campus life buzzed around him, that voice began to fade.

Chapter 41
Day One Drift

The sun hadn't even cracked the horizon when Ethan's alarm buzzed.

He groaned and slapped at the screen, peeling himself out of bed. Jamir was already up, brushing his teeth and mumbling along to a rap song playing low on his phone.

"Better hurry up," Jamir said, spitting into the sink. "Coach, don't play about time. He said 6:00 a.m. means on the field at 6, not walking in."

Ethan nodded, threw on his Greywood athletic gear, and laced his cleats tight. His body still ached from moving in, but adrenaline was already stirring. This was his dream. This was where the grind began.

The first workout was brutal.

The weight room pulsed with music and sweat. Coaches barked orders. Trainers circled with clipboards. Players grunted through sets of squats, sled pushes, and pull-ups.

Ethan pushed through, matching reps with linemen bigger than he'd ever seen in high school. At one point, the strength coach stopped him and said, "I like that motor, Phillips. Don't lose it."

By the end of the session, Ethan's shirt was soaked, his arms trembling from fatigue. But he felt alive.

Jamir gave him a fist bump as they headed toward the locker room. "Welcome to Greywood."

After showers and a quick breakfast, they had a first-year orientation block: ID cards, campus tours, and mandatory safety briefings. By noon, Ethan was already exhausted, slumped back in his chair during a financial aid info session, half-listening as a counselor explained meal plans.

Later that afternoon, Ethan and Jamir grabbed food from the dining hall. They had catfish, just like Jamir said. The two sat by the window near a group of other athletes: a few from track, one from women's basketball, and a cornerback named Malik who introduced himself like a comedian.

Ethan laughed for the first time all day. Everyone talked fast, debating music, hyping up an off-campus lounge called "Vibe Fridays," and bragging about their first imaging deals.

Ethan listened, intrigued, but quiet. Still figuring out who he was supposed to be in this new space.

That evening, the hallway buzzed with noise. Students played music, propped their doors open, or lounged in the common room watching basketball highlights. Jamir pulled out his gaming system and said he'd be up late gaming with his boys back home.

Ethan stepped into the hallway to breathe.

Across the hall, someone had their door cracked. A soft gospel tune floated out, and it reminded him of his Aunt Helen's house.

He paused.

It was a song his aunt used to hum while cooking. A song he hadn't thought about in years.

He stood there for a second, considering. He could knock. Say hello. Ask who was playing it. Maybe it was another church kid. Perhaps a group of believers met here on campus.

But then someone called out from down the hall.

"Yo, E! We're heading to the gym for a late run! You in?"

Ethan turned. "Yeah…yeah, give me a sec."

He looked back at the cracked door. The music was still playing.

He took one more step toward it...

Then he turned the other way.

The door closed behind him.

Later that night, he dropped onto his bed, too tired to pray. He stared at the ceiling until sleep pulled him under.

No prayer. No journal. No reflection.

Just the hum of campus nightlife

and the distant echo of a gospel song he ignored.

The first whole week at Greywood moved like clockwork…early lifts, back-to-back classes, study hall, evening walkthroughs, and sleep when his body finally gave out.

Ethan's weekdays were mapped down to the minute. His mornings started before dawn in the athletic facility, running drills in the fog with the offensive line, while the strength coach, Coach Tarlow, hollered from the sideline like a drill sergeant.

"You want that professional pipeline? Earn it!"

Classes were manageable but demanding. Ethan took Intro to American Government with Professor Hensley, a soft-spoken woman with a sharp tongue when students weren't prepared. Then came Public Speaking with Mr. Dwyer, who paced around the room barefoot, as if he were being videotaped.

His favorite class, if he had one, was Foundations of Leadership taught by Dr. Quinn, a retired Navy officer who called everyone "cadet" whether they played football or not.

Between classes and workouts, there wasn't much time for anything else. Ethan ate fast, dressed fast, and moved fast.

But the drift came slowly. It started on Sunday.

That first weekend, he intended to go to the campus chapel service. He even set an alarm.

But Saturday night, Jamir had invited a few guys over to play video games. They ordered wings, watched film clips from last season, and talked trash deep into the night.

When Sunday morning came, the alarm buzzed.

Ethan rolled over, hit snooze, and never got back up.

He told himself he'd watch a sermon online later. He didn't.

His journal stayed zipped in the suitcase.

The one his mom had placed on top of his clothes, slid in a note on the first page:

"Don't forget who you are. Let your light shine. – Mom"

He saw the note once when he unpacked, smiled, and never opened the journal again.

Calls from home came less frequently.

The first time his mom called, he answered.

The second time, he texted: In meetings, love you.

The third time, he forgot to respond until two days later.

Uncle George sent him a motivational quote on Wednesday. Ethan replied with a thumbs-up.

During study hall one night, Malik leaned over and said, "Yo, we're hitting Vibe Lounge this weekend. Freshman night. You in?"

Ethan smirked. "What is it?"

"Just music, girls, food, you know. Break the routine. You need it. Greywood doesn't own your soul, bro."

Ethan didn't answer, but the idea settled in.

Thursday night, he sat in his dorm bed, scrolling through photos on social media.

One from back home: his church choir was doing a youth takeover service.

His mom was tagged, standing next to the podium.

The comment read: So proud of Ethan. You raised him right.

He stared at the picture for a long time. Thought about liking it. Didn't.

On Friday morning, Jamir stood in front of the mirror fixing his collar. "We're hitting Vibe tonight, right?"

Ethan hesitated. "I'll think about it."

Jamir tossed him a clean black polo shirt. "Think about it in this. You need a break from all this good-boy tightness."

Ethan caught the shirt and stared at it in his hands.

He didn't say yes.

But he didn't say no.

The noise of Greywood life grew louder.

The spiritual stillness faded quieter.

And somewhere between classes and training tables,

Between ignoring calls and skipping chapel...

Friday night came like a storm cloud ready to burst.

The dorm hallway was electric. The music was thumping behind closed doors, cologne hanging thick in the air, and laughter bouncing off the walls. Ethan sat on the edge of his bed, staring down at the black polo shirt Jamir had tossed him earlier that morning.

It was folded neatly across his lap, untouched. The tag still clung to the collar like a warning.

"You coming, right?" Jamir asked, buttoning his shirt and dabbing cologne behind each ear. "Man, Vibe's gonna be crazy tonight. They say the seniors usually show out for this one. DJ is spinning."

Ethan didn't answer. He slipped on his sneakers but didn't move.

"You alright?" Jamir asked.

"Yeah," Ethan lied.

Jamir nodded and grabbed his wallet. "You'll feel better once we get there. Get outta your own head."

As Jamir left the room, he smacked the door frame twice. "Ten minutes, E. I'll be downstairs."

Ethan sat in silence.

He looked at himself in the mirror. Shirtless, athletic build, clean cut, he looked like someone who had it all together. But something inside felt off. Heavy.

He grabbed the black polo and started to pull it over his head.

Then there was a knock at the door.

Tap. Tap.

He expected Jamir, but when he opened it, he saw a girl he didn't recognize standing in the hallway. She wore an oversized sweatshirt and carried a small paper bag.

"Hey," she said softly, "are you Ethan?"

"Yeah...?"

She smiled nervously. "Sorry. My name's Kiana. I'm in 320. I ran into your mom during move-in week. She gave me a bag of muffins to give to you and said, 'Don't forget to check on him now and then.' I've had them all week, but I kept forgetting."

Ethan blinked, caught off guard. "Wait, she talked to you?"

Kiana nodded. "She said you might act tough, but you had a soft heart. I was like, 'Cool, stranger-mom info,' but… I dunno. I felt bad about forgetting. I figured tonight was as good a time as any."

She held out the small bag. It smelled faintly of cinnamon and brown sugar.

He took it, still in disbelief. "Thanks."

She shrugged. "Anyway, have a good night. If you ever wanna come to Holy Scriptures Study, we meet Tuesday nights in the common room. Just a few of us. Nothing crazy. No pressure."

He opened his mouth to respond, but all that came out was, "Okay."

She smiled and walked away.

Ethan closed the door slowly and sat on his bed.

He opened the bag.

There were four small muffins wrapped in a napkin. On top was a sticky note in familiar handwriting:

"Just a taste of home. Love you. – Mom"

He stared at it for a long time. His hand trembled just slightly.

His phone buzzed.

Jamir: We are downstairs. You coming or nah?

Ethan looked from the phone to the shirt, to the muffins, then to the sticky note.

His chest tightened. For the first time in a while, he felt something.

Conviction. Memory. Stillness.

He leaned back in bed, shirt still in hand, and stared at the ceiling.

The music in the hallway grew louder. Voices echoed, footsteps hurried past his door. The party was waiting. But he didn't move.

Not for a while. Not until the noise finally faded.

He didn't go that night, but he would another time.

Soon. Sunday morning came quietly.

Outside, the church bells at nearby Greywood Chapel chimed nine times, soft and hollow, carried by the breeze across Greywood's still-sleeping campus.

Ethan heard them.

He lay in bed with the covers pulled to his chest, eyes open, staring at the ceiling. His phone buzzed with a calendar reminder:

"Chapel Service at 10:00 am, Greywood Student Union, Room 102."

He reached for the phone, silenced it, and tossed it face down on the dresser.

Across the room, Jamir was snoring, clearly recovering from whatever Saturday night had cost him.

Ethan sat up for a second. He swung his legs off the bed.

Part of him wanted to go.

He thought about Kiana's offer. Thought about his mom's voice. Thought about how good it would feel to be in the presence of peace again.

But instead, he grabbed his earbuds, opened his Spotify playlist, and drowned the thought in music.

He didn't move until noon.

And when he finally got up, he went straight to the dining hall. The chapel service had already ended.

He never looked back.

It started like any other night.

Music in the hallway. Guys shouting jokes down the stairwell. Girls knocking on doors, giggling as they moved in packs. Flyers had gone out on campus all week:

VIBE FRIDAYS AT 10 PM: OFF-CAMPUS HOUSE PARTY

Free entry, food, music, vibes only. No drama.

Jamir was already dressed, wearing ripped jeans, a gold chain, and white tennis shoes so clean they could blind headlights.

"You ready this time?" he asked, stuffing gum in his mouth.

Ethan nodded. No hesitation.

"Yeah. Let's go."

The house was just off campus, a three-story rental packed with bodies and bass. Strobe lights flickered behind tinted windows, and music thudded through the walls like a heartbeat.

The living room was packed. People danced, cups in hand, laughter bouncing off every corner.

The kitchen smelled like liquor and hot wings. A punch bowl glowed unnaturally red. Smoke hung low in the back hallway.

Ethan followed Jamir in, trying to act casual and trying to blend in. But his senses were overloaded: too many faces, too many sounds, too much energy.

It was everything he'd once promised himself he wouldn't get pulled into.

But here he was.

In the corner, a girl waved him over. Jamir grinned and said, "I told you Greywood parties differently."

They dapped up a few teammates. Everyone knew who Ethan was. His name was already circulating, "That's the freshman tight end. The one from up north."

Someone handed him a drink. He didn't ask what was in it.

He sipped. Burned. Coughed. Then he smiled and sipped again.

The music shifted to a song he knew. A group of guys started a chant in the kitchen. The floor vibrated with dancing.

Then, his phone buzzed.

He pulled it out of his pocket.

Uncle George:

"Are you alright, E? Been thinking about you today. Hit me back when you can. Just checking in. Love you."

Ethan stared at it. The words blurred. The music grew louder.

Someone grabbed his arm and shouted, "Yo, they're doing shots in the back room. You in?" Ethan looked down at the message one more time. Then he turned off the screen. Slipped the phone into his pocket. And walked deeper into the party.

That night, as the lights dimmed and music pounded through his chest, Ethan finally let go of the last thread he'd been holding onto.
He didn't check the time. He didn't check his phone.
And he didn't answer the man who used to be his compass.
The silence was no longer accidental. It was chosen.

Chapter 42
Just a Little Fun

The morning light slanted through the window blinds like judgment.

Ethan groaned as he rolled over, shielding his eyes from the sudden brightness. His mouth was dry, and his head buzzed, not quite a headache, but a fog that blurred the edges of his thoughts.

His clothes from the night before were tossed on the floor. One shoe was still on. The faint smell of smoke and liquor clung to the collar of his shirt.

He sat up slowly, rubbed his temples, and looked around the room. Jamir was passed out in the other bed, snoring lightly, one arm draped over the edge.

Ethan's phone buzzed again.

He looked at three unread messages from his mom, two from Uncle George, and a church flyer someone had texted him earlier in the week about a weekend youth gathering.

He stared at the screen for a long moment.

Then, almost involuntarily, he opened his mom's last message.

"Love you always. Praying you're staying strong and focused. Call me when you can, baby."

Something twisted in his chest. Guilt. Shame.

He hadn't done anything that bad. He didn't get blackout drunk. He didn't hook up with anyone. He danced. He laughed. He drank a little. That was all.

But still… it felt like something shifted.

He sat on the edge of the bed, gripping his phone. The silence in the room was loud.

The holy scriptures were still packed at the bottom of his duffel.

His journal was untouched.

His Sunday service alarm was disabled.

His eyes drifted toward the window where the sun was beginning to warm the sky. A soft breeze nudged the edge of the curtain, like the world was waking up without him.

For a second, he thought about texting his mom back.

Just one word. "Hey."

He opened the message thread. Tapped the keyboard.

Then he stopped. Sighed. Locked the screen.

"I'm an adult now," he whispered to himself.

"I can have a little fun. It won't hurt."

He said it was like a promise.

But it felt like a lie.

He stood, stretched, and grabbed his towel. As he passed by the mirror, he caught his reflection with eyes duller, jaw clenched.

He looked… different.

Not worse. Just not the boy his mom sent off.

He pushed the thought away, brushed his teeth, and got dressed.

Later that day, as he and Jamir walked to lunch, Jamir laughed, retelling moments from the party.

"Man, you were chill though. I thought you were gonna bounce early."

Ethan smirked. "Nah, I was good. Just not used to that scene."

"You get used to it fast," Jamir said, opening the dining hall door. "One night turns into every weekend. Welcome to college."

Ethan nodded. But inside, something whispered…

You're slipping.

He didn't listen.

Weeks passed like snapshots: football drills, sweat-drenched jerseys, late-night parties, laughter, bright lights, and louder nights.

Ethan's schedule looked like success from the outside.

Team practices. Early lifts. Team meals. Film study. Walk-throughs.

Then… weekend parties. Vibe Fridays. Apartment kickbacks. Locker room dares. Red punch. Music. More names he barely remembered.

Football masked the rest.

Coach Harvell was impressed.

"You're a beast in the red zone, Phillips. Keep grinding."

His teammates hyped him up. "Yo, you're on pace to be starting by conference play. You're eating out here!"

Ethan smiled, nodded, lifted harder, and ran faster.

He was in the zone.

But outside that zone, something else was unraveling.

Text from Mom:

"Hey, baby. Just thinking of you. Love you so much. Are you eating okay?"

Ethan:

"Yeah, Mom. I'm good. Just tired. I had football practice this morning. I'll call soon. Love you."

He didn't call.

Voicemail from Uncle George:

"Ethan, just checking in, champ. Heard Greywood had a televised game last week. You played great, I'm proud of you. We miss you back home. Let's catch up."

Ethan never listened to the whole message.

Just deleted it after the first sentence.

Aunt Helen texted:

"Your cousins want to know when you're coming home. We're planning a family dinner!"

Ethan responded two days later:

"Can't come this weekend. Got a campus event and team stuff. I'll try soon."

He never looked at the calendar again.

He told himself:

"I'm just busy. This is my time to focus. They'll understand."

But deep down, he knew the truth.

He wasn't just busy. He was drifting intentionally.

Choosing the noise. Choosing the ease.

On the field, he was dialed in.

Fast. Aggressive. Dominant in scrimmage.

Off the field, he was fading.

Church services were just calendar invites, he declined.

Phone calls were background noise during pre-game music.

Scriptures were echoes of a life he no longer chased.

One Saturday night, as music blasted in an off-campus basement, Ethan stood in a haze of laughter and smoke, a drink in hand, half-listening to two girls arguing over social media fame.

His phone buzzed in his pocket.

Mom:

"Sweetheart, I know you're busy… but can you just send me a picture, or a quick voice note? I miss your voice. I'm praying for you."

He stared at the message.

His thumb hovered over the keyboard.

Then he typed:

"Sorry, Mom. I'll do better with staying in touch. Just been tired. Practice was heavy this week. Love you."

He hit send.

Then he turned back toward the room and disappeared into the crowd. Midway through the season, Greywood's football program was off to a solid start, undefeated in its division, gaining national attention, and starting to feel the pressure of conference play.

Ethan had become a key piece of the offense, dominant at tight end, making highlight-worthy catches and drawing double coverage. Reporters started calling him "The Freshman Freight Train." Local sports blogs were writing profiles. One scout even showed up to practice in a Greywood hoodie and sunglasses.

But behind the stats and the headlines, Ethan's focus was cracking.

The parties became routine. Thursday nights turned into Friday nights, and Saturday nights were now almost expected.

He kept telling himself:

"As long as I show up, I'm good."

"One mistake won't ruin me."

"I'll bounce back if I ever slip."

Then he slipped.

It was a Saturday afternoon home game, Greywood vs. Benton Hills, a key rivalry matchup.

Ethan showed up late to walk-throughs.

His eyes were red. His gait was sluggish. He'd stayed out too long the night before and overslept, missing the morning film session and team breakfast.

Coach Harvell saw him walk in halfway through warm-ups and didn't even wait until halftime.

He blew the whistle, stormed over in front of the entire team, and barked, "Phillips, OUT. Locker room. NOW."

Ethan blinked, stunned. "Coach, I…"

"I SAID NOW!"

The entire practice field went silent. Heads turned. No one moved.

Ethan dropped his helmet and walked off without another word.

After the game, a narrow win, Ethan had to watch from the sidelines. Coach Harvell called him into his office.

The room was quiet, cold, and uncomfortable. Trophies lined the shelves. A framed picture of last year's championship team hung crooked on the wall.

Coach sat behind his desk, arms crossed.

"You want to tell me what that was today?" he asked calmly, almost too calmly.

"I just… I lost track of time last night. Didn't sleep well. I…"

Coach cut him off. "You think I care about your sleep?"

Ethan went quiet.

Coach leaned forward. "You're here on scholarship, Phillips. Full ride. You're one of the most gifted athletes I've seen in the last five years. But if your head isn't in the game and your schoolwork, then you don't belong here."

Ethan swallowed hard.

"I've seen this story before," Coach continued. "Big talent. Big ego. Big distractions. You wanna be another cautionary tale? Fine. But not in my field."

He pointed to the door.

"You want to stay at this school, you get your life together. Or you go home. I don't have time for stars who burn out early."

Ethan left that meeting with his heart in his throat.

Coach's words rang in his ears the whole walk back to the dorm.

"Or you go home."

The idea hit harder than he expected.

He could see his mom's face. Uncle George. The church family. All that pride. All those prayers.

He stood in his room, staring at his Greywood jersey on the back of the chair.

He thought about the agent rumors swirling. The blog mentions the fame.

And then he said to himself,

"Alright. No more every weekend. I'll chill. Maybe every other week."

"I can still enjoy myself... but I need to focus before I lose everything."

So, he slowed down.

But he didn't turn around.

And in the distance, the echo of his coach's warning still chased him…

"You want to go home?"

Ethan didn't know it yet,

but home was something he was getting further from every day. The following week, Greywood Stadium was electric.

Under the lights, with a packed student section and camera crews lining the sidelines, Ethan was in his zone. The Freight Train was back.

He'd caught two touchdowns already, one on a corner route in the first quarter, the second on a seam pass threaded ideally between two safeties. The crowd erupted both times, and Coach Harvell pumped his fist on the sideline with a rare grin.

This was the player everyone talked about.

The one scouts whispered about.

The one the blog posts kept calling "Greywood's Future First-Rounder."

Ethan jogged off the field after his third catch of the night, chest heaving but eyes locked in. Jamir slapped him on the helmet.

"Yo, you ON one tonight!"

Ethan grinned. "Coach said, ' Get focused… I got focused."

"Focused?" Jamir laughed. "You look like a professional reel."

In the top row of the stadium, just under the press box, a group of sharply dressed men in sunglasses sat still among the crowd.

One of them scribbled notes in a leather-bound journal. Another leaned back with his arms crossed and a quiet smirk on his face.

They didn't cheer.

They didn't talk.

They just watched.

One of them nodded once after Ethan's fourth catch.

By the fourth quarter, the game was sealed. Greywood 31, East Briar 10.

Ethan walked off the field with the kind of swagger that only came from doing what he was born to do. The locker room was loud…music, celebration, helmets banging, players yelling nicknames and stats.

Coach Harvell walked in, clapping slowly.

"Enjoy it tonight," he said. "But remember this isn't the finish line. It's just the runway. One wrong move, and it all comes down faster than it went up. Stay sharp."

Ethan nodded.

He was listening now.

At least… for the moment.

Later that night, as Ethan walked back across campus alone, earbuds in, hoodie over his head, he noticed a black SUV idling at the edge of the parking lot near Reach Hall.

Its windows were tinted. A man stepped out in a long dark coat and leaned on the passenger side with a clipboard in hand.

Ethan paused for half a second, then kept walking.

He didn't think much of it. Probably just another recruiter.

They'd been coming around more lately.

His phone buzzed.

Another podcast invite. A highlight repost. A DM from someone saying, "Yo, you went OFF tonight!"

Ethan smirked.

This was what it meant to be seen, wanted, and valued.

He didn't see the man by the SUV, still watching as he disappeared inside.

The spotlight was on.

But not all attention comes without a price. Ethan had found his rhythm again.

Classes were back in order. Practices were locked in. He even started hitting the books more, slipping into the study hall with a quiet intensity that caught Coach Harvell's eye.

He wasn't partying every weekend anymore, just some. The team still threw kickbacks. The music still shook the dorm walls. But Ethan had learned how to leave before midnight. He told himself it was about balance.

"Stay sharp enough for the field… but loose enough to enjoy it all."

He didn't write in his journal. Didn't pray. Didn't text his mom back unless it was short.

But his grades were good. His stats were better. And his name was getting louder. On Tuesday afternoon, the weight room buzzed with noise plates clanging, coaches yelling form checks, music blasting from the overhead speaker.

Ethan finished his final set of squats, wiped the sweat from his neck, and stepped outside for air. The crisp fall breeze hit his face like a slap of refreshment.

He leaned against the side of the building, earbuds in, heartbeat still pounding.

That's when he noticed the car.

Another black SUV. Sleek. Clean. Parked with precision just across from the facility.

A man in a fitted navy suit and sunglasses leaned against the driver's side door.

"Ethan Phillips?"

Ethan paused and pulled out one earbud. "Yeah?"

The man smiled, slow and confident. He held out a sleek business card.

"Frank Maddox. Maddox Talent. I represent elite collegiate athletes looking to go pro. Been watching you all season."

Ethan took the card, flipping it in his fingers.

"Appreciate that."

"Don't need a decision," Frank said, voice calm and smooth. "Just want to introduce myself. You're building something. I want to help you protect it... and grow it."

Frank didn't say much else. He nodded once and returned to the SUV.

But something about his presence lingered.

Later that week, Ethan started noticing them more. At team meals. Near the stadium gates. In the shadows of media day.

Four different men. All were wearing tailored suits. All pretending to be ordinary.

The second one introduced himself on campus near the student union.

"Name's Vick. I handle international opportunities, branding, gear deals, and offshore endorsements. There's a whole world out there waiting to pay you to wear a logo."

He smiled like he knew things no one else did. His voice was slick, his energy magnetic.

The third agent came with charm and charisma.

"Call me Ellis. I don't just manage athletes…I build kings. I connect you to real estate, business ventures, and foundations. You want to build a legacy, right?"

He handed Ethan a high-gloss folder with mockups of a future "Phillips Sports Academy."

Ethan laughed. "That's kinda wild."

Ellis leaned in. "It's already in reach. You need the right doors opened."

The fourth was more relaxed.

He met Ethan outside the locker room after practice.

"Name's Darnell. I don't believe in pressure. I believe in timing. When you're ready, I'm here. Just keep doing what you're doing, young king."

He handed Ethan a black envelope.

Inside was a single card.

No logo. Just a phone number. And a gold crown.

None of them pushed.

None of them pitched contracts.

Not yet. They were planting seeds.

Each one offered something slightly different: money, status, freedom, legacy.

All promise a path to greatness. All were watching how Ethan moved.

Back in his room that night, Ethan lay the cards on his desk like a poker hand. He stared at them.

No decision. Just curiosity. He didn't think twice about it. Not yet.

But the voices were growing louder.
And his silence was growing deeper.

Chapter 43
Pulled in Every Direction

The business cards sat on Ethan's desk like trophies…perfectly spaced, untouched, but impossible to ignore.

Frank Maddox.

Vick from Global Endorsements.

Ellis is the empire builder.

Darnell with the crown.

Each one had offered something different.

Each one had planted a thought that wouldn't go away.

That Thursday morning, Ethan sat in Foundations of Leadership, pretending to take notes while his mind replayed Ellis's voice:

"I build kings. You're not just an athlete…you're a brand."

He glanced down at his notebook.

Instead of class notes, he'd drawn a rough sketch of a gym…Phillips Performance Center.

He quickly flipped the page, embarrassed.

At practice that afternoon, he crushed a red zone route and caught a one-handed pass in double coverage. The entire sideline erupted.

But as he jogged back to the huddle, he saw Frank standing near the chain-link fence…arms crossed, sunglasses on, watching.

Ethan's chest swelled a little. He stood taller. Moved cleaner.

He didn't even notice Coach Harvell's instructions for the next play.

After the film session, Jamir nudged him. "Yo, you going to the chapel tonight? Pastor Harris is speaking." Ethan hesitated.

He remembered the flyer.

Remembered the text from Kiana.

Remembered telling his mom he'd "try to check it out."

Then his phone buzzed.

Vick:

"Downtown mixer tonight. Just info. No pressure. A few athletes and reps…networking only. You've earned the right to be in that room."

Ethan stared at the message. His thumb hovered over the screen.

Then Jamir nudged him again. "What do you think?"

Ethan smirked. "I might swing through the chapel next time. I'm gonna hit this mixer and see what it's about."

Jamir raised a brow. "For real?"

"Just to listen."

The mixer was held at a rooftop bar off campus. No cameras. No contracts. Just low light, expensive appetizers, and smooth voices.

Frank was there, casually sipping sparkling water.

Ellis made eye contact and offered a firm nod.

Darnell sat in the corner, laughing with two other athletes from another school.

Vick didn't say much. Just smiled and tapped his drink against Ethan's glass like they'd known each other for years.

By the end of the night, Ethan felt different.

Not better. Not worse.

Just… wanted. Important. Like he was becoming somebody.

Back in his dorm, his phone lit up again.

Mom:

"I missed your voice today. I know you're busy, but I always feel better just hearing from you. Love you, baby. I'm praying for you."

Ethan read it twice.

Then he heard Frank's voice echoing in his mind:

"Protect your focus. You don't need distractions, not even well-meaning ones."

Ethan didn't reply.

He put the phone face down. Laid back and stared at the ceiling.

The next morning, he saw Kiana in the dining hall.

She waved. He nodded.

But it didn't stop.

One week later, the only business card left on his desk was Frank Maddox's.

The rest were in the drawer.

He told himself it didn't mean anything. But it did. He was still playing well and still showing up. Still smiling. But inside, he was beginning to shift…

Not because of one decision…

But because of four voices pulling him in every direction, except towards the holy scriptures.

A week later, the stadium lights faded behind him, but Ethan still felt the adrenaline pulsing through his veins.

Greywood had clinched another win, putting them at the top of their conference, one game away from securing a playoff spot. His name was mentioned twice on the post-game broadcast. Four receptions. One touchdown. One brutal block that made the highlight reel.

He walked out of the locker room with headphones around his neck and a bounce in his step. Students passing by nodded at him. A few girls waved. A guy from the campus radio said, "Hey, number 87! You killed it tonight!"

Ethan gave a tight smile and a chin lift in return. He was used to the attention now.

His phone buzzed in his hoodie pocket.

Lamar Jones, Incoming Call.

Ethan stopped walking.

He hadn't heard from Lamar in months, not since summer.

A flicker of a smile crossed his face. "Yo!" he answered. "What's good, man?"

"E! What's up, bro!" Lamar's voice came through loud and full of energy. "I just caught your game. You're on fire this year! Greywood's going crazy!"

Ethan chuckled. "Yeah, man… we're doing alright."

"Alright?" Lamar laughed. "Man, y'all undefeated! I saw that toe-drag in the second quarter. Straight savage."

"Appreciate it," Ethan said. His voice stayed flat.

"How's everything else? Classes, workouts, and the dorm life?"

"It's all good. I got a solid schedule now: lift, class, film, repeat."

Lamar talked a little more about his season, his stats at the university, the D2 grind, and how their team just made the conference tournament.

Ethan's expression started to shift.

His grip on the phone tightened.

His smile faded.

He looked around the campus walkway, modern buildings, athletic banners with his face on them, and students wearing Greywood hoodies.

He remembered when they used to sit in his mom's living room, talking about dominating together in college.

Now Lamar was "grinding" at a small D2 school.

Ethan? He had agents waiting. Imaging conversations were building. National coverage was rising.

"Man," Ethan said, cutting Lamar off mid-sentence. "That's cool. You know, keep doing your thing."

Lamar paused. "Yeah… I mean, it ain't Greywood, but we're getting ours."

"Right. Right." Ethan glanced down at his Greywood hoodie. "Gotta start somewhere."

Something in his tone changed.

Lamar heard it.

"Are you good, E?"

"Yeah," Ethan said quickly. "I just got a lot going on. A lot of people are pulling me in different directions."

"I get it," Lamar replied, voice quieter now. "Just wanted to say I'm proud of you, man. Still rooting for you."

"Yeah. Appreciate it."

"Let's catch up again soon?"

Ethan hesitated. "Yeah. We'll see."

The call ended.

He shoved the phone back in his pocket and kept walking.

Part of him wanted to call back.

But a bigger part said:

You've outgrown that phase. Different level now. Different circle.

He walked past a banner hanging over the dining hall doors:

"Playoffs Are Coming. Leave Your Legacy."

Ethan stared at it for a moment.

Then he kept walking. Not looking back.

He didn't notice it yet…

But pride was replacing the echo of every voice that had once kept him grounded.

The weekend came quickly, and the dorm was buzzing with music, laughter, and the smell of cheap apple cider and cinnamon-scented plug-ins. Holiday lights were strung across the ceiling, blinking red and green over loud conversations and background beats.

Ethan leaned against the hallway wall, phone to his ear, one hand in his hoodie pocket.

"Hi, baby!" Elle's voice rang out, full of warmth and joy. "Merry Christmas, my heart! Oh, I wish I could hug you right now."

Ethan smiled faintly. "Merry Christmas, Ma."

"How was your dinner? Did they serve something decent this year?"

"It was alright. They had turkey, mashed potatoes… the usual."

Uncle George's voice chimed in from the background. "E! Merry Christmas, champ!"

Ethan chuckled. "Hey, Unc. Y'all behaving back home?"

"We're trying. Your aunt made three pans of dressing like she was feeding a whole town."

Elle laughed. "I saved you a plate. Might be a little cold by the time you get it, though."

Ethan smiled again, but it didn't quite reach his eyes.

From down the hall, a few voices shouted:

"E! C'mon, man, we're waiting on you!"

"Bro, the game's starting!"

"You bringin' that punch or what?"

Ethan turned slightly, covering the speaker with his hand.

"Hey," he said into the phone, "I gotta run. We're doing a holiday thing down here."

Elle's voice softened. "Oh, I just wanted to tell you one more thing, baby…"

But he was already pulling the phone away.

"Love y'all," he mumbled. "Talk soon."

Click.

The line went dead.

Back home, the kitchen was full of smells and warmth, but Elle stood still, phone in her hand, tears slowly filling her eyes.

"I…I didn't get to tell him I prayed for him this morning… or that I found one of his old journals in the closet."

She turned to Uncle George, stunned. "He hung up. Just… like that."

Uncle George stepped forward, gently placing a hand on her shoulder. "Don't panic, Elle. Ethan's a good kid."

She wiped her cheek, silent.

George continued, steady and calm. "We raised him right. And we raised him to let God lead him. That part's still there. Even if he doesn't hear it right now."

Elle nodded, trying to smile through the ache. "He's just… never ignored me like that."

George looked toward the front window, where the snowfall had started, soft and quiet.

"He's in a storm," he said. "We just gotta keep praying that he remembers how to get home."

Back at Greywood, Ethan dropped his phone onto his bed without thinking.

Someone handed him a red plastic cup. A girl in a Santa hat wrapped a scarf around his neck playfully.

He laughed and walked toward the noise.

And never looked back.

It started with unread messages.

Kiana:

"Hey, we missed you at holy scriptures study in the library. Hope everything's okay."

Ethan glanced at the notification, then locked his screen without replying.

Campus Ministry Group Chat:

"Just a reminder, worship night is Thursday. Come hungry. Spirit & pizza provided."

He swiped it away.

Even the quiet devotionals someone used to slip under his door had stopped appearing. Maybe they got the message. Or perhaps they were praying from a distance now.

Either way, Ethan didn't miss them.

The season was nearly over. Greywood had just locked in their playoff spot.

The locker room buzzed with energy. Coaches high-fived players. Reporters circled the press table. Social media lit up with predictions and hashtags.

That's when Frank Maddox stepped into the hallway…polished, calm, smooth like always.

He pulled Ethan, Jamir, and Steven aside just outside the athletic office. They leaned against the railing, out of earshot but not out of sight.

Frank opened a sleek black folder.

"Gentlemen," he began, "let me introduce something exclusive. Klyro Gear. Performance apparel. High-end, built for champions. They want faces, young, rising talent who represent grit, discipline, and the future of the game."

He handed each of them a glossy one-sheet with their names printed at the top.

"Imaging partnership. Stipend. Merch. Media appearances. Optional content schedule. You don't even have to post every day."

Steven, the defensive end, whistled low. "Yo, this is serious."

Ethan studied the sheet. His name. His stats. His image is in mockup Klyro gear.

He liked what he saw.

Jamir frowned. "How'd they even get our names?"

Frank smiled coolly. "We've been watching. Doesn't take long to notice talent. And value."

Jamir folded his arms. "I don't know, man. It's clean and all… but something about this feels off. I don't trust it."

Frank's smile didn't fade. "That's okay. I'm not here to push. Just present."

Jamir looked at Ethan. "You taking it?"

Ethan hesitated, but only for a second.

"Yeah," he said. "It's a good deal. Why wouldn't I?"

Steven nodded. "Same here."

Jamir stepped back. "I'm out."

He handed Frank the paper and walked away, shaking his head.

Frank watched him go, then looked at Ethan with a slow, unfazed grin.

"That's alright. I can't get everybody."

Ethan didn't respond.

He looked down at the paper again, then signed the bottom line.

The wind outside the building picked up.

Later that night, as the dorm pulsed with music again, another message came in from Kiana.

"I don't know what's going on, but I hope you remember who you are."

He read it.

Then deleted it.

He did not respond. He had agreed, and agreements required adherence to specific rules, including maintaining silence. Ethan was benefiting from the perks. Greywood's campus had always paid attention to football players, but now, Ethan Phillips wasn't just a name on a roster. He was the name.

Posters with his face in sleek Klyro Gear started appearing in the athletic building. His locker had a duffel bag full of fresh merchandise: fitted joggers, insulated tech hoodies, compression sleeves with his initials embroidered in silver.

He no longer had to ask for anything.

It was given.

His first social media post in Klyro gear went viral on campus. @EthanTheTrain:

"Grind now. Reap later. #KlyroElite #GreywoodStrong"

Ethan was standing on the practice field, arms folded, wearing a custom tracksuit

Over 10,000 likes.

Hundreds of comments.

Fire emojis. Crown emojis. Muscle arms.

One girl commented, "Husband material."

He didn't reply.

But he bookmarked the comment.

When he walked into the dining hall, students moved aside.

A staff member gave him two extra cookies and whispered, "Big game coming up, I'm praying for you."

He nodded but didn't say thank you. Just kept walking.

A student reporter asked for a quote for the campus newsletter.

"Feels good," Ethan said. "All this is the result of focus and hard work. You stay ready, and everything else follows."

The reporter asked if he ever expected to be the face of the team this fast.

Ethan shrugged. "I didn't expect it, but I'm not surprised."

He started posting more: gym clips, brand tags, locker room shots, vague captions like "Don't talk, just sign."

His follower count exploded. Even Klyro's official account reposted him, calling him "A future the game will remember."

But for all the perks… something else was happening too.

Jamir stopped hanging out as much.

He said less during practice.

A few times, Ethan caught him looking his way, but not with envy, with concern.

Once, after a workout, Jamir walked by and said, "Just don't forget who was there before all this."

Ethan didn't answer. He didn't need to.

He just tossed his Klyro duffel in the back seat of the team van and put his earbuds in.

On Sunday, Kiana passed him in the quad. She smiled faintly.

He nodded but didn't stop.

Later that night, he opened a DM from a Klyro rep.

"We'll be sending a camera crew next week. They want a few interview clips before the playoffs. You're the anchor now, Phillips. Let's keep it polished."

He smiled.

He liked the sound of that.

Anchor. But anchors don't just steady ships. They weigh things down.

And Ethan…

He was sinking slowly.

Without even noticing.

Chapter 44
The Cost of Winning

The crowd at Ridgefield Stadium was electric.

Greywood University vs. Atlantic Crest. Playoff round one.

The cold night air didn't bother Ethan; he was locked in. Zoned. Sharp. A machine on the field.

First drive? 12-yard snag over the middle. Second quarter?

Touchdown in the back corner of the end zone. Coach Harvell clapped so hard his clipboard fell.

"THAT'S how we finish!" he shouted. Greywood won. Then won again. And again.

Three rounds deep into the playoffs, they punched their ticket to the National Championship. Ethan was trending on college sports channels. Commentators used words like "elite," "unstoppable," and "next level."

He walked differently now. Not cocky.

Just... elevated. And the night of the championship, it all came to a peak.

Final score: Greywood 27, West Republic 21.

Ethan caught the game-winning touchdown with 08 seconds left on the clock.

The stadium erupted. Teammates swarmed him, dumping water over Coach Harvell, screaming, chest-bumping, leaping like kids at recess.

Trophy presentation. Gold confetti. Flashbulbs. Reporters. Victory.

Elle and Uncle George stood in the bleachers, wrapped in team scarves, faces lit with both pride and hope.

"There he is!" Elle beamed, tears in her eyes. "That's my baby!"

"He did it," George said, smiling as the stadium roared.

Ethan stood on the podium, holding the MVP trophy high above his head, spotlights bouncing off his gold-trimmed Klyro gear.

After the ceremony, families filtered down to the field.

Moms hugged sons. Fathers wiped away proud tears.

But Ethan wasn't there.

Elle scanned the crowd.

"Do you see him?" she asked, stepping around families, peeking through groups of players.

Uncle George checked his phone. "Maybe he's still doing interviews?"

Just then, they saw him across the field, walking toward the parking tunnel with a group of friends, laughing, tossing his jersey over his shoulder like a towel.

"Ethan!" Elle called, waving. "Baby!"

He paused. Turned. Their eyes met. She smiled widely, waving both hands.

He raised a single hand in return and gave a quick head nod.

Then he turned back around and kept walking with his group. Elle's hand slowly lowered.

The noise of the stadium around her faded. Uncle George noticed her silence.

"He's in college now," he said softly. "He's growing up. Got friends. A whole life down here."

Elle said nothing. George continued, trying to comfort her. "As long as he stays grounded, he'll be fine. We raised him right." She nodded. But inside, something twisted.

This wasn't just growing up. It was pulling away. The drive back home was quiet.

Elle stared out the window, still wearing her Greywood scarf.

Her fingers were wrapped tightly around the MVP game pamphlet she picked up off the bleachers. Uncle George glanced over once or twice. "You okay?" She nodded, but she wasn't.

Her heart was full of joy... and grief. And she kept her thoughts to herself.

Back on campus, the Greywood Hawks arrived just after 2:00 a.m., but the energy waiting for them was wide awake.

Students lined the sidewalks, waving signs, banging on drums, and holding up their phones to record the moment the championship bus rolled in. Fireworks popped just beyond the athletic quad, and the university's fight song blared from a portable speaker someone had set up near the team dorm.

Ethan stepped off the bus first, MVP trophy in hand, and the crowd surged forward, chanting:

"E-P! E-P! E-P!"

Jamir jogged up beside him, arms raised.

"Bro, we did that." Ethan gave a tight grin and raised the trophy higher. The crowd roared louder. Klyro had already posted the clip of his game-winning touchdown. Ethan's name was trending in two states. Fans shouted for autographs. People he'd never spoken to before wanted selfies. A banner stretched across the student center balcony read:

"Welcome Home, Champions!"

President Weller met them at the stairs, shook hands, and a camera crew was there. "Ethan Phillips," she beamed. "Greywood is proud of you. The school's never seen a first-year performance like this."

He nodded, still holding the trophy. "Just doing my job."

Someone tossed him a school flag. He draped it over his shoulders like a cape.

Pictures. Hugs. Shouts. Applause.

But he never once looked toward the edge of the crowd.

He never checked whether anyone from home had waited.

Days later, the noise faded. The interviews stopped. The celebration banners came down.

But something stayed with Ethan, the feeling of being seen, celebrated, chased.

And so, when the time came to decide what to do for the summer, he thought hard.

The spring semester moved fast after the championship.

Classes wrapped. Exams were taken.

The football season was over, but the buzz around Ethan Phillips wasn't.

He was featured in Greywood's Spring Sports Magazine, photographed in full Klyro gear under the headline:

"The Freight Train: Unstoppable. Unapologetic."

His social media was now part of his daily routine: scheduled posts, gear drops, sponsored links. Even when he wasn't posting, people were tagging him.

One afternoon, Coach Harvell caught him in the hallway.

"You sticking around this summer or heading home?" the coach asked casually.

Ethan paused. "I'm staying."

"The weight room needs a few guys to help train incoming first-year students. You interested?"

Ethan nodded. "Yeah. That's perfect."

When Elle called the next day to ask about summer flights, Ethan told her over speakerphone:

"Yeah, I'm not coming home this summer. I received a job offer to join the team, assisting the Coach with upcoming recruits and possibly handling some brand-related tasks. Gonna stay sharp."

Elle hesitated on the line. "Oh… okay. I just thought you might want to come home for a bit. See your room. Go to church. We can have a little cookout or something."

Ethan chuckled lightly. "Ma, I'm good. Just trying to keep momentum. It's just the summer."

She tried not to let the hurt seep into her voice. "Well… alright. We're proud of you, baby."

"Thanks, Ma."

"I love you."

"Love you too."

He hung up before she could ask anything else.

Later that week, he signed the paperwork to become a summer strength and conditioning assistant. It came with housing, a meal stipend, and access to upgraded training equipment.

He also took a part-time brand ambassador role for Klyro's summer "Rise & Reach" campaign, filming clips at 5 AM in Greywood's weight room, holding protein shakes, and motivational hashtags.

Success doesn't rest. Neither should you."

The brand sent a videographer every Tuesday.

The clips were polished. His followers grew.

The campus was quieter now…fewer students. But for Ethan, it felt like his world was getting louder.

More focus. More control. More of him.

And less of everything else.

Kiana passed him once on the breezeway.

"You're staying all summer?" she asked.

"Yeah," Ethan said, pulling off his earbuds. "Got a few things lined up."

"You didn't want to go home at all?"

He shrugged. "Just trying to stay locked in."

She gave a faint smile. "Well… don't lock out the people who love you."

He nodded but didn't say anything.

When she walked away, he put his earbuds back in.

Ethan Phillips was officially in his world now. No curfews. No check-ins.

No church. No home. Just work. Grind. Appearances. And the voice in his head is saying:

"You're building something. Don't slow down."

The sun hit differently that summer.

Campus was mainly empty: no crowds, no noise, no distractions: just morning lifts, afternoon workouts, media appearances, and branding meetings.

And Ethan loved it that way. He wasn't a freshman anymore. He was a name, a presence, a brand.

By 6:00 a.m., he was already in the weight room, camera crew positioned in the corner, capturing every rep for Klyro's "Rise & Reach" campaign.

"Success doesn't sleep, and neither do we."

That slogan was now printed across his limited-edition gear. Athletes from other schools started tagging him in workout posts, calling it the #EthanStandard.

By noon, he was in the film room.

By 3:00, he was helping Coach run drills for incoming first-year students.

By 6:00, he was online posting product links, signing virtual autographs, and reviewing his weekly content schedule.

He was working. Grinding. Growing. And still… never calling home.

His mom texted once in June:

"Just checking in. I miss you, baby. Your room is still the same."

He read it.

Didn't respond. The Klyro team loved him. Always on time. Always camera-ready.

Never questioned the script. Never asked for more.

He filmed two podcast interviews on personal discipline.

He was flown to Atlanta for a promotional shoot in July.

He was invited to a preseason player summit, where Frank introduced him to a few "former pros turned executives."

Ethan took notes. Learned fast. He didn't smile too much. Stayed sharp.

"You're not just an athlete," Frank told him one night after a meeting. "You're a blueprint."

Ethan nodded. "I'm just getting started."

He didn't go home. Didn't check on Jamir. Didn't stop by the chapel.

Didn't reply to Kiana's last message from the spring:

"We all drift sometimes. But don't forget how to swim back."

He blocked the number the next day.

When August came, and the fall semester returned, he was ten pounds stronger, mentally sharper, and socially louder. A returning king. A quiet soul. No cracks. No questions.

Just grind. Sophomore year at Greywood didn't start; it launched.

Ethan returned leaner, louder, and more locked in than ever. His presence was no longer questioned; it was expected. First Game of the Season: Touchdown. Media mention.

Postgame interview where he called himself "more focused than ever."

By week five, he was already a front-runner for the All-Elite Conference team. Klyro dropped a custom apparel line named "The Freight Series." It sold out in 48 hours.

By midseason, another SportsCenter feature. A clip of his 37-yard one-handed touchdown was shared by a pro tight end with the caption: "Next one up." Ethan reposted it without comment.

But the smirk on his face said it all. At home, Elle watched every game, and Uncle George recorded every postgame interview. Neither of them got calls anymore.

Sometimes Ethan texted "thanks" after a big win, but never called. And never came home.

In terms of spirituality, there is no involvement with a church, prayer, or Kiana.

No, Jamir, who had quietly transferred to a smaller university in Texas after telling Coach, "Some people change when they start winning."

In Late October, Greywood beat their rival in overtime. Ethan caught the game-winning pass again. But he didn't celebrate like he used to. No jumping. No praying. No pointing to the sky.

Just a stone-faced walk back to the sideline as the cameras swarmed.

During Thanksgiving Break, Coach gave the team four days off. Most players flew home.

Ethan stayed behind and had dinner at Frank's house. They also filmed two brand commercials, went on a photoshoot for an energy drink collab, and posted a story on social media in front of a luxury car with the caption:

"No time off when you're built differently."

In December, Greywood won its second straight championship.

Ethan caught two touchdowns and was named Back-to-Back MVP. Confetti. Trophies. Applause.

But after the ceremony, he didn't call his mom. He didn't even look for the team's chaplain, who came to congratulate him. He left with Frank. The ride back to campus was quiet.

Frank was in the backseat with him and said, "Two rings. Two years. And still rising. Most people wait four years for what you're already holding." Ethan nodded, staring out the window.

"Next year's your real payday," Frank added. "Everything changes after year three."

In Ethan's mind? There was no going back. No slowing down. No room for anything that couldn't keep up. He was a star. But he was no longer the same. And somewhere deep down, he wasn't even sure when that change had happened. Once back at his dorm, Ethan sat on his bed thinking about his accomplishments. He thought to himself, "I did it."

Spring came fast.

Greywood's campus bloomed with fresh banners and freshly cut lawns, but Ethan barely noticed.

His days are a blur of film study, workouts, brand meetings, and late-night calls with marketing teams and sports reps. He wasn't just a student-athlete anymore. He was a name. A product. A business.

Final exams came and went.

Ethan passed not because he cared, but because private tutors were assigned to ensure he did.

One of them said, "You're too important to fail."

He believed them.

Coach Harvell pulled him aside after the final practice of the year.

"You good?" Ethan nodded.

"You know," the coach said, "it's not just what you do on the field. It's what lasts after it."

Ethan didn't respond. Not out of disrespect, just detachment.

The last day of the semester, Ethan stood in his dorm window, staring out over the quiet campus. Students were hugging goodbye, loading up cars, and making plans to see each other back home.

Someone shouted, "Happy summer!" He didn't reply. He didn't pack. He was staying, again. He scrolled past a missed call from his mom. Listened to part of the voicemail:

"I was just thinking about you… Praying you're staying strong, baby. Call me when you can…"

He deleted it without even finishing. That night, as most of the campus emptied, Ethan walked across the stadium field alone. Championship flags flapped from the bleachers.

He stood at the 50-yard line. He had his hands in his pockets. Head up. Alone.

He had won again but lost more than he could name. Year Two was done. And whatever was left of "home" felt miles behind him.

Chapter 45
Year Three: No Looking Back

The summer between sophomore year and junior year passed like a shadow. No beach trips. No home visits. No reconnections. Just brand deals, early morning workouts, press interviews, and whispered conversations about "what's next."

Ethan didn't even look back when the spring semester ended. He didn't pack to go home. He didn't ask about church. He didn't text his mom.

He stayed at Greywood, the same campus, a different world.

By the time fall training camp opened in August, Ethan Phillips wasn't just a college athlete anymore. He was a projected first-round draft pick. Every scout in the United Gridiron League (UGL) had his name on their list. Greywood's quarterback whispered to teammates, "If he declares this year, he's gone top 10."

Even Coach Harvell, once a source of guidance, gave him more space than ever.

"He knows what he's doing," the coach muttered to an assistant. "That kid's been living like a pro since last season."

Ethan was sharp, missed no workouts, had no attitude issues, and had no drama.

But he was colder. He barely spoke to first-year students. He stopped eating in the team dining hall.

He moved into Klyro's off-campus athlete housing. The distance wasn't just physical. It was personal. Frank Maddox was now a constant voice in his ear.

He started showing up to practice, standing quietly near the fence in his dark coat and glasses. Never disruptive. Never flashy. Just watching. One afternoon after scrimmage, he approached Ethan near the locker room. "You ready to talk next steps?" Ethan didn't hesitate. "Yeah."

"You stay healthy this season," Frank said, "and we start preparing for the EFL Draft. January. Full rollout. You'll have more endorsements than half the league before you even sign." Ethan nodded. "Let's get it done." Frank paused. "We'll talk contract soon."

As the season rolled in, Ethan's numbers exploded. First four games: seven touchdowns

National Player of the Week twice. Reposted by UGL legends' Fan pages, dubbing him "The Freight King." Social media was flooded with edited videos of him breaking tackles and high-stepping into the end zone. One post from Klyro read: "Three years. Three titles? Let's finish it right."

But not everyone cheered.

Coach Harvell noticed it in the huddle. Ethan didn't listen anymore, just executed. His eyes were elsewhere.

When a teammate tried to pray before the game, Ethan walked off early.

And when the team gathered for their traditional post-win prayer circle, Ethan was always conveniently missing.

One afternoon, the athletic department hosted a panel with past Greywood legends.

Ethan didn't show that Frank had scheduled a photo shoot at the same time for a new energy drink campaign. When Coach confronted him later, Ethan shrugged and said, "I'm focused on what comes next."

He wasn't a college student anymore. He was a brand, a business. A future the world was already fighting to own. And the boy from Elle's house in Gerry, the one who used to write a journal at night and pray before games, was buried somewhere behind the headlines.

As winter crept in and the season neared its end, Ethan's name echoed beyond Greywood's campus. Sports analysts debated his draft status daily. Frank shadowed every game from the sidelines like a silent prophet, always just close enough to be seen, never close enough to be questioned. Campus posters plastered Ethan's face with phrases like "One More Win" and "Finish the Dynasty." But while the team practiced harder, bonded tighter, and prepared to defend their reign, Ethan trained like a man alone, no more chapel. No more calls home, no more questions. The final championship game was coming, and for Ethan, it wasn't just about winning. It was about sealing a legacy… and signing away something far greater than a football future.

The championship confetti rained down harder this time…gold and silver mixed in swirling celebration.

Greywood University: 38. Bay Central: 17.

Three years.

Three rings.

Three MVPs.

And Ethan Phillips stood alone in the spotlight, holding the trophy as it had always belonged to him.

He'd dominated from the first snap…

8 receptions

136 yards

2 touchdowns

0 drops

The announcers said his performance "sealed his legacy."

Social media crowned him "The Greatest Greywood Player Ever."

What they didn't see what no one saw was how silent his spirit had become.

There were no prayers after the game. No calls to his mom. No nods to his past. Only applause. Only cameras. Only Frank was waiting at the edge of the tunnel with that same polished smile.

Academically, Ethan had done well enough to graduate early.

He wasn't just a brute athlete; he'd kept his grades up, passed every class, and carried himself with just enough discipline to be a model student in the eyes of the media.

Still, he hadn't filed to return for a fourth year. And word was spreading.

The day after the championship parade, Coach Harvell called him into his office.

The room was quiet, trophies lining the shelves, game balls stacked in a display case behind the desk. The smell of worn leather and old chalk filled the air. Ethan sat across from him, silent.

Coach cleared his throat. "You've done everything you came here to do, no doubt. On the field... and in the classroom. But I gotta ask, are you really leaving?"

Ethan leaned back in the chair. "Frank said I'm going to have enough money to live on. I believe that I have enough credits to finish early, but I need to check with my academic advisor. This is a one-time opportunity."

Coach nodded slowly, his jaw tight.

"I figured he'd say that."

Ethan raised an eyebrow. "You don't think I should take it?"

"I think you should be careful," Coach said. "I think he's showing you all the fame and wealth without telling you about the consequences."

Ethan tilted his head. "What do you mean?"

Coach leaned forward, resting his arms on the desk.

"There's always another side to a story, son. Especially when there's that much money involved. Make sure you read carefully before you sign anything."

He paused, then added, "You just might sign your life away without knowing it."

Ethan froze for a moment.

No comeback. Just stillness. Then he stood.

"I trust Frank," he said. "He's not going to steer me wrong."

The coach didn't stop him. He just nodded and watched him walk to the door.

Right before Ethan left, Coach spoke softly, barely loud enough to hear:

"Sometimes the wrong people show up dressed like the right ones."

Ethan didn't turn around. He left the room. Coach Harvell sat alone in the silence. Then slowly leaned forward, put his elbows on the desk,

and covered his face with both hands.

"God, please don't let him walk off that cliff." Outside, Ethan stood under the stadium lights one last time. Frank was already waiting near the exit. The next morning, the headlines hit like wildfire:

ETHAN PHILLIPS DECLARES FOR THE EFL DRAFT

Greywood's golden boy had made it official.

No senior season. No final lap around campus.

Just a video posted on his social media, looking sharp in a tailored grey suit, with that trademark smirk on his face.

"I want to thank God, my coaches, my teammates, and everyone at Greywood. I've decided to declare for the EFL Draft. This is a once-in-a-lifetime opportunity…and I'm ready."

The campus erupted. His followers multiplied. And Frank… was waiting. They met in a downtown office suite overlooking the city. Floor-to-ceiling windows. Marble countertops. Leather chairs. Every corner whispered success.

Frank sat behind a sleek glass desk, smiling as Ethan walked in.

"Champ," he said, rising and extending his hand. "You've arrived."

Ethan grinned. "Let's get to work."

Frank motioned for him to sit. On the desk lay a black folder, clean, embossed, and closed tight.

"I want to show you what's waiting for you," Frank said. "Once the draft's complete."

He opened the folder slowly, like a magician revealing a final trick.

Inside:

A mock-up of his EFL welcome package

A list of signing bonuses

Photos of luxury apartments in multiple cities

Sponsorship projections from fashion, sneaker, and watch companies

Estimated endorsements in the millions

Ethan's eyes darted across the glossy papers.

It didn't even feel real.

"You're looking at houses in Miami, a condo in LA, your line of gear, and a team of stylists," Frank said, his voice velvet smooth. "Jewelry. Cars. Status. Whatever you want, it's already waiting for you."

Ethan ran his fingers over the mock contract.

He hesitated. "So… when do I sign?"

Frank leaned forward, folding his hands.

"Not just yet. The draft has to happen first. This is your preview, your glimpse into what's next. But when the time comes… I'll bring the real thing."

There was a pause.

Then Frank added, almost as an afterthought:

"Just make sure you read every word… even the tiny ones."

Ethan looked up.

The sentence landed weird, but he brushed it off.

"I trust you," he said.

Frank gave a smile so wide it never reached his eyes.

"Good. That's what makes you different, Ethan. You know how to stay focused."

They stood, shook hands, and walked toward the elevator.

As the doors slid open, Frank clapped him on the back.

"Enjoy the spotlight. But remember, this is just the beginning."

Two weeks later, Ethan arrived in Michigan. Home of the EFL Combine.

Greywood's team bus wasn't needed here.

Ethan arrived in a black SUV, stepping out in designer shades with a duffel slung over his shoulder. Cameras flashed before he even reached the hotel.

The city buzzed with anticipation; scouts, sports networks, brand reps, and agents filled every hallway like sharks in suits.

Inside the stadium, the air was thick with adrenaline.

Ethan stood in a line of elite prospects, all waiting their turn to be measured, stretched, interviewed, and dissected like lab specimens.

"Phillips, Ethan, Tight End."

He stepped up.

Measured at 6'6".

Weighed in at 270 pounds.

Wingspan: elite.

Vertical: explosive.

The scouts scribbled notes. The evaluators nodded. The cameras zoomed in. Later that day, the skill drills started. His 40-yard dash? Blazing. His cone drills? Fluid. His route-running? Precise and dominant. His hands? Sticky. His interview answers? Polished, too polished. Because Ethan wasn't just here to perform, he was performing a persona. Back at the hotel suite, the distractions came full throttle. Brand reps slipped him exclusive sneakers and watches "just for being here." Influencers invited him to rooftop mixers. Cameras followed him to dinner. Models flirted with him by the elevator. Teammates partied on the 27th floor. One night, Lamar, who'd stayed local back home, texted him: "You good, bro? Been a minute." Ethan saw it. Didn't answer.

On day three, Frank appeared. He wasn't in the stadium. He was in the hallway outside the conference room, waiting like he knew precisely when Ethan would walk by. "Looking sharp," Frank said, nodding at the logo-embroidered tracksuit. Ethan smiled. "Feels like I'm already there." Frank's grin widened. "You are. But don't lose focus. The Draft is weeks away, and when the spotlight's brightest, it's easiest to trip." Ethan laughed, brushing it off. Frank pulled a sleek envelope from his coat. "Put this in your duffel. Read it when you have time."

Ethan looked at it, unmarked, slim, and black. No logo. No label. He took it anyway.

That night, the envelope sat on the hotel nightstand while the suite pulsed with music and laughter. Ethan never opened it. He didn't feel the need. Everything was already falling into place. The EFL Draft wasn't just a ceremony.

It was a coronation.

Red carpets, booming lights, thousands of cheering fans packed inside the Metropolis Dome. Banners of the top picks circled the massive stadium like Greek gods in the clouds.

Ethan sat backstage in a private green room, a crisp custom suit stretched across his broad frame. His heart pounded, but not from nerves. This was the moment.

Frank stood across the room, calm, collected, holding a leather briefcase in one hand and a glass of sparkling water in the other.

"This is it," Frank said smoothly. "Everything we talked about. Everything you worked for."

He opened the briefcase.

Inside, a thick contract with gold-edged paper.

The top read:

"Career Acquisition and Brand Agreement– EFL and Phillips Global Image"

It looked legit. Too legit. Pages and pages of promise.

Ethan sat down slowly, flipping through the packet.

"Can I… check with my mom before I sign?" he asked, fingers hovering over his phone.

Frank's tone didn't change, but his eyes locked in sharply.

"Come on, E. You know me. I've been with you the whole way. You want to call your mom in the middle of this moment?"

Ethan hesitated.

"Just sign it," Frank said. "You'll have everything you need. Homes. Jewelry. Cars. Your line. I'm talking generational wealth."

"Yeah, but…"

"But what?" Frank stepped closer. "You trust me, don't you?"

Ethan looked down. The signature page glowed under a spotlight, its edges slightly red, though he couldn't tell if it was the lighting or something else.

The fine print at the bottom blurred slightly. He blinked. It was small. Really small.

But the pen Frank handed him was warm, smooth, and black as night.

"Go ahead, champ. Step into your legacy."

Ethan didn't feel God in the room.

But he didn't feel fear either.

He signed. The crowd erupted a few minutes later when his name was called:

"With the 1st overall pick in the 2015 EFL Draft... the Monarchs select... ETHAN PHILLIPS, Tight End, Greywood University!"

He walked across the stage, smiling, waving, putting on the Monarchs' purple and gold cap.

Back in the green room, Frank watched the screen with a smirk. He folded the signed contract, slipped it back into the briefcase, and whispered: "Another one down." Then he turned and walked away.

Chapter 46
The Glare and the Quiet

The cameras flashed nonstop as Ethan stepped onto the Monarchs' stage in a tailored charcoal suit, purple-and-gold cap tilted perfectly. The backdrop was a wall of logos: Monarchs. EFL. Power Bank Energy. Elite Drip.

To his left sat Coach Vann, the Monarchs' seasoned head coach. Beside him, the sharply suited General Manager, Mr. Calder. Frank leaned against the edge of the table with a polished grin, proud like a father who had delivered a king.

"Ethan," a reporter from The Grid-Iron Post asked, "you've got the speed, the strength, and now the spotlight. How does it feel to be here finally?"

Ethan leaned toward the mic.

"It's a dream. I'm ready to give this team everything I've got."

The press clapped. Flashbulbs erupted.

But Ethan's heart thudded slower than it should have.

His voice was confident, but something inside didn't echo back. Later that afternoon, Ethan walked the glistening halls of the New Gate Performance Complex, the Monarchs' state-of-the-art training center. Turf fields stretched behind glass walls. Recovery pools steamed. Flat screens blinked with stats.

Coach Renzin, a thick-necked assistant with a buzz cut, handed Ethan a thick black binder.

"That's your life now," he said. "The Monarchs' playbook. Get used to seeing it in your dreams."

Ethan flipped a few pages. The formations blurred.

"Thanks," he said, tucking it under his arm.

As he walked down the hallway, every jersey number hanging on the wall stared back like ghosts from the future.

In Studio Room 3, bright lights bathed Ethan in white-hot light as he stood in full uniform, pads, helmet under his arm, and fresh cleats.

Photographers barked orders.

"Hold the ball like this."

"Now flex."

"Give us the 'Monarch glare'…yes, that's it!"

Ethan did what they asked.

He felt like a product.

In one corner, Frank whispered with a producer.

Ethan caught a glance, and Frank gave him a nod and a wink.

"You're gonna look good on every billboard from here to Blue Harbor," he said later. "They already love you."

A conference room full of smiling reps awaited him:

Dynex Energy. Elite Drip. Iron Haze Apparel. Storm Vault Watches.

Each had a script. Each had a vision.

"You're going to be the face of the 'Grind to Greatness' campaign," said a woman in red heels.

"We'll start with a ten-part social media series about your journey," another added.

Ethan listened. Nodded. Signed.

He was handed a silver Storm Vault Watch with his number engraved.

It ticked loudly on his wrist.

That evening, back at his luxury apartment on the 28th floor of the K Towers, his phone buzzed.

Deposit: $2,500,000.00

"Monarchs Signing Bonus: Wire Complete"

Ethan sat down on the edge of the bed.

The view outside sparkled. Downtown New Gate City pulsed with life. But inside his chest, it felt… quiet.

Frank texted:

"Enjoy it. It's only the beginning.

Ethan didn't reply. The apartment had everything from glass walls to marble countertops, and a custom welcome basket with champagne and Monarchs gear. No food. No pictures. No voices.

Ethan poured a glass of water from the bottle, sat on the leather couch, and stared out the window.

He thought about his mom. Uncle George. Coach Harvell. Even his friends from high school.

The envelope from Frank, the Career Acquisition and Brand Agreement, was now locked in the nightstand. His phone buzzed again.

Mom Calling… He saw it. Let it ring. Then, it was silenced. The phone screen dimmed. So did something else. Ethan raised the glass and whispered, "To the future." He drank. Alone.

The first day of rookie training camp began before sunrise. Ethan stood in front of the mirror in his new Monarchs-issued gear: a navy compression shirt, silver shorts with the EFL logo stitched into the hem, and brand-new cleats molded to his feet like armor. The stadium was still dark, but the parking lot buzzed with rookie hopefuls and coaching assistants.

Frank had called him twice the night before. Not to say good luck, but to confirm the media team would be on-site to capture his entrance.

"Make it iconic," Frank had said. "Don't just walk in, arrive." So, Ethan did.

He pulled up in his black sports car with the vertical doors and diamond-stitched interior. As he stepped out, sunglasses low on his nose, camera shutters flared like summer lightning. His teammates clapped and whistled.

"Man, that's cold!"

"Yo, that's the Monarch money!"

But Ethan didn't smile. He just nodded, dapped a few hands, and kept walking like a man on a mission with no room for emotion.

Camp was brutal. Two-a-days. Hydration checks. Media workshops. Playbook tests. Everything came fast, and the Monarchs didn't tolerate softness. But Ethan handled it. Executed reps. Dominated drills. He memorized the playbook and stayed up late watching film.

Off the field, his name soared across social media:

#EthanEffect

#TightEndTitan

#MonarchMode

But back home in Gerry, Ethan hadn't returned since college. He hadn't made a single call. Not for Elle's birthday. Not even when Aunt Tricia had surgery.

Then one Wednesday afternoon, two luxury vehicles pulled into Elle's driveway, both with red bows and tags addressed "To Mom" and "To Uncle George."

One was a pearl-white luxury SUV with chrome trim. The other, a matte graphite luxury pickup with trail mode and heated seats. There was no note. Just a delivery confirmation signed:

-E.P.

Elle stood in silence on the porch. She touched the key fob with trembling fingers.

"He didn't call… not even to tell us," she whispered.

Uncle George stepped forward and examined the truck.

"He's probably just busy," he said, though his voice lacked conviction.

Elle didn't reply.

By Ethan's second year in the EFL, another delivery came, but this time, it wasn't cars. It was a house. A custom-built, five-bedroom, stone-front home on the opposite side of Gerry. It was quiet, gated, and upscale. The kind of house people drove by slowly to look at.

Frank showed up in a luxury sedan, handed Elle and George the keys, drove them to their new home, and opened the front door with a flourish.

"From your boy," he said, "He wanted you to have something special."

Elle stepped in slowly.

Marble floors. Vaulted ceilings. A chandelier that caught every bit of light like glass raindrops.

She wandered from room to room, touching the counters, tracing the edges of doorframes, her hand brushing the stone fireplace.

Finally, she stood in the grand kitchen, silent, tears pooling in her eyes.

"It's beautiful…" she whispered. Then softer achingly:

"But where is he?" Frank stood by the door, smiling faintly.

"He's living his dream. Sometimes that dream moves faster than time."

Uncle George stared at him hard. Something gnawed at his gut.

As Frank turned to leave, he looked back once and whispered, barely audible…

"I have him now."

But Uncle George heard it.

"No, you don't," he said firmly. "Ethan was grounded in the holy scriptures."

Frank stopped walking for just a moment… then smiled…tight and cold.

"We'll see," he said.

And with that, he slipped into his car and drove away.

Elle stood at the kitchen window, her arms folded across her chest, watching the taillights vanish down the winding road.

"Something felt off about that man," she finally said.

Uncle George nodded.

"Because something was."

They stood there in silence, inside a beautiful home that Ethan would never set foot in. Ethan sat on the balcony of his luxury high-rise apartment overlooking the city skyline. The glow of tower lights flickered against his glass of sparkling water as his phone buzzed for the third time that evening. He didn't even look at it.

It was his mother.

Again.

He knew she would want to talk about Aunt Helen, or about coming home, or about slowing down. But Ethan had just wrapped another brand shoot, and he was flying to a gala in Miami. The next morning, he had a championship to win in less than a week. He told himself he'd call her after. After the season. After the parade. After everything had settled.

"Can't get distracted," he muttered. "Not now."

Frank walked in through the sliding door, loosening his tie. "Big week coming up. Titan Bowl's yours if you keep your head in the game."

Ethan nodded, barely reacting. "It's already mine."

Frank smirked. "That's what I like to hear."

He handed Ethan a sealed envelope. "These are the endorsement slots lined up if you win. Late-night shows, talk radio, shoe campaign, we're talking next-level exposure. Bigger than ever."

Ethan leaned back, confidence radiating. "Let's go get it, then."

As Frank walked toward the door, he paused for a second.

"Just stay focused," Frank added, slipping into the hallway. "The world's watching."

And just like that, Ethan was alone again, bathed in city lights, applauded by millions, but slowly becoming a stranger to the people who knew him before all of this began. The stadium was electric.

Confetti rained from the rafters of Valor Arena as fans roared in unison. "M-V-P! M-V-P!" The scoreboard blazed with the final: Monarchs 31 – Vultures 28. Ethan stood at the center of it all, hoisting the Titan Bowl trophy under the stadium lights. Cameras clicked. Broadcasters called it one of the greatest comebacks in EFL history.

It was his third year, and he had just won it all.

As he posed for photos, Ethan flashed his signature smile. The same grin is now plastered across magazine covers, cereal boxes, shoe ads, and digital billboards, and a lifetime of effort had landed him here, crowned champion, lauded by the world, the face of the game.

The day after the championship game, Elle received the news from Gerry Hospital. Her sister-in-law, Helen Phillips, had passed away peacefully in her sleep. The doctors said it was her heart. The funeral was scheduled a few days later.

Elle called Ethan twice.

He texted back:

"I can't make it, Mom. I've got a prior commitment. But everything's covered. Frank will handle the details. Love y'all."

True to his word, the flowers were abundant white orchids, roses, and lilies that draped the casket. The funeral was flawless. The bills were paid. But there was no Ethan.

He didn't zoom in. Didn't send a video message.

Just a silence that screamed louder than his fame.

Elle stood graveside in a charcoal coat, clutching a silk handkerchief. Uncle George held her steady.

"I don't need the money," she whispered. "I needed my son."

Two days later, Ethan stood on the stage of Chelsea Youth Excellence Center, flashing his polished grin under LED lights. Hundreds of teenagers sat in folding chairs. The backdrop read:

"The Path to Power: An Evening With Titan Bowl Champion Ethan Phillips."

Frank waited offstage, adjusting his cufflinks as Ethan began.

"Hard work. That's it," Ethan told the crowd. "You don't need a perfect background. You don't need people believing in you. You need the grind. I worked for this moment. I earned it. And you can too."

The crowd erupted in applause. Flashbulbs lit up the auditorium. But there was no mention of his mother. No reflection on his roots. No mention of God.

As the event ended, the crowd buzzed with excitement. People gathered to take selfies, get autographs, and catch one final glimpse of a small-town hero.

Ethan and Frank exited through the side door, walking into the evening air. A young boy, no more than 12, stood near the edge of the sidewalk, clutching a football. His eyes widened when he spotted Ethan.

"Mr. Phillips?" the boy called out. "Could I get your autograph?"

Ethan smiled and took the football, scribbling his name across the white stripe with a silver marker. "What's your name, champ?"

"Jaylen."

"Nice to meet you, Jaylen," Ethan said. "You need a ride home?"

Jaylen nodded. "Yeah… my friend was supposed to take me home, but I think he left early. My mom's at work. I was gonna wait on Coach Harris."

Frank immediately stepped in, smooth and composed.

"I got him," he said, placing a hand on the boy's shoulder. "You're on a schedule, Ethan. Let me take care of this. Head back to the hotel."

Ethan hesitated. "You sure?"

"Positive," Frank replied with a smile that didn't quite reach his eyes. "He'll be in good hands."

Ethan nodded, handed Jaylen back his ball, and climbed into the waiting black SUV that pulled around the curb.

Frank turned to Jaylen. "Let's go, sport. I'll drop you right at your doorstep."

Just as Jaylen was climbing into the front seat of Frank's sleek car, a rusted silver sedan screeched into the lot. The door flung open.

"Jaylen!" a woman called out, rushing toward the scene, keys jingling in her hand.

Jaylen turned, surprised. "Mom?"

"I don't know who you are," she said firmly to Frank, "but something told me to leave work early. I couldn't shake it. I was supposed to stay and close, but my spirit said, "Go now. Get your son. So, I did."

Frank straightened, hands in his pockets. "Ma'am, I'm a sports agent for Ethan Phillips. Your boy is in good hands."

She narrowed her eyes. "That may be true. But I'm his mother. And I'm here now."

Jaylen stepped away from the car and into her arms.

Frank smirked, ever so slightly. "They are always getting in the way," he muttered under his breath as he turned and got into the driver's seat.

The mother watched his car peel away into the night. A chill crawled up her spine.

Something wasn't right.

Back in Gerry, Elle sat on the living room couch, watching the interview replay on her TV. Ethan looked happy, prosperous, and untouchable.

She slowly picked up the remote and turned it off.

"I don't even recognize him anymore," she said softly.

Uncle George didn't say a word. He just sat beside her, resting a hand on her shoulder, and prayed silently.

Chapter 47
Fame

The summer sun bore down on the EFL training facility, baking the turf in waves of heat as players jogged through drills and shouted across the field. Reporters lined the fences. Drones hovered overhead. Sponsors had already begun filming content. It was Year 4 of Ethan's professional career, and everything had become louder: contracts, cameras, expectations.

But inside, Ethan was quieter.

His jokes didn't come as often. His phone rarely rang without Frank answering it first. His texts to Uncle George had slowed, and even his mother's occasional voice messages were usually left on read. To the world, he was on top. Titan Bowl Champion. The pride of the Monarchs. His face is on bus wraps and cereal boxes.

But something was dimming.

Ethan dominated the season. With over 1,200 receiving yards and a record-breaking 18 touchdowns, sports analysts called it his "glory run." But something shifted off the field. The parties weren't just post-game celebrations anymore; they were distractions, obligations, and escapes.

Frank's calendar was always packed with brand shoots, business dinners, and late-night appearances. And every time Ethan hesitated, Frank reminded him, "This is the price of greatness. The life you signed up for."

By the time the postseason came around, Ethan was running on fumes. He led the Monarchs to the conference finals, but they fell short in the fourth quarter. Ethan took the blame in front of the press with a plastic smile, but inside, he simmered.

That winter, Ethan bought a third home, this one in the mountains, but never visited it. He ghosted his old high school coach, who invited him back to speak at Gerry High. He told his mother he was "on the road" when she asked him for a quiet dinner over the holidays.

"You good?" Uncle George texted once in January.

"Just busy," Ethan replied. Then silence.

The 5th year came with a vengeance. Ethan came into training camp laser-focused, though his inner fire was harder to read. His plays were sharper than ever, but his smiles seemed rehearsed. Frank chalked it up to maturity. The media called it professionalism. But to those who knew Ethan, it looked like he was fading under the lights he once loved.

As the Monarchs barreled toward the playoffs, the spotlight grew hotter. Every touchdown Ethan scored came with more endorsements, more meet-and-greets, more staged moments.

The Titan Bowl returned with electric fanfare, this time hosted in Fire Stadium, the EFL's newest dome arena. Ethan walked through the tunnel in his customized cleats, barely flinching at the fireworks exploding overhead.

He played with precision. No drops. No hesitations. Two touchdowns. One game-winning block sealed the championship. The Monarchs won the Titan Bowl for the second time in three years.

The confetti rained again. This time, Ethan didn't look up.

He accepted the MVP trophy with a faint smile and raised it for the cameras, but when asked in the postgame interview who he wanted to thank, he said:

"My team. My agent. Myself."

After the Game, the team flooded into the locker room, laughter and victory chants echoing through the walls. Ethan slipped out early. Frank was already waiting in the car, sipping something dark from a silver flask.

"That's two, champ," Frank said as Ethan slid into the back seat. "You're becoming a legend."

Ethan leaned back, silent.

Frank grinned. "One more Titan Bowl to go. Then… the real fun begins."

The car disappeared into the city lights as the world celebrated the Titan Bowl MVP, unaware that Ethan's soul was somewhere far from the spotlight. By the time Year 6 rolled around, the roar of the crowd still followed Ethan Phillips, but it no longer reached his heart.

He showed up to training camp in peak condition, flashing the same polished smile for the cameras, but there was something hollow behind his eyes. Interviews came easily now. The right words. The media-savvy answers. He knew how to play the part of a superstar.

But off the field, things were different.

Calls from home went unanswered.

Birthday invites from cousins, holiday gatherings, church prayer requests, they all blurred together in a stack of unopened messages and voicemails. Uncle George had texted him a scripture verse on his birthday: "For what shall it profit a man, if he shall gain the whole world, and lose his own soul?" Mark 8:36, KJV. Ethan saw it but never replied.

The luxury cars, homes in multiple cities, private chefs, and red-carpet appearances kept stacking up, but so did the silence in his personal life.

Frank kept his calendar tight and his circle tighter.

"Everything's a brand now," Frank said one evening while Ethan sat in a velvet booth at an upscale lounge. "Your walk, your smile, your next endorsement, they're all part of the machine. Stay visible. Stay relevant."

Ethan nodded, sipping from a crystal glass filled with something stronger than he used to drink.

He told himself he was still grounded. Still, that kid from Gerry. He was still in control.

But he hadn't prayed in a while. The holy scriptures collected dust on a shelf and went unread. Even his old spiral notebook, the one he used to write in, the journal of plays, thoughts, and prayers, hadn't been cracked open in years.

One night after a win, Ethan was supposed to meet with a group of young fans from the local boys' club. Instead, he bailed and headed to a private yacht party. The pictures went viral with morning dancers, drinks, and diamonds. Frank spun it as a marketing win. "They love seeing you out there. Just enough access to make them envy you. That's the trick."

But deep down, Ethan felt the ache as an echo of something missing.

That year, the team didn't make it to the Titan Bowl.

They lost in the second round of the playoffs.

When Ethan walked off the field that night, he didn't hear the crowd. He didn't notice the cameras. He just walked past his teammates, past the press, straight into the locker room.

Frank met him in the tunnel. "One-off year," he said coolly. "Don't worry. Next year, we take it all."

Ethan didn't respond. He just kept walking.

And in that brief moment of silence, somewhere buried beneath the layers of pride, performance, and possessions… his soul stirred.

But just for a moment.

Then it was gone.

Next season, training camp opened with heatwaves and headlines.

"Ethan Phillips: Can He Win a Third Titan Bowl?"

"The Legacy Season Begins"

"Will This Be the Year of the Monarchs Again?"

Ethan no longer needed the media to hype him up. By now, he was the headline.

He arrived at camp in a black luxury SUV, stepped out with a crisp designer hoodie pulled low over his sunglasses, and nodded to the cameras like a king returning to his throne.

Inside the locker room, there was talk of retirement.

"You thinking of hanging it up after this season?" one rookie asked.

Ethan shrugged. "We'll see."

But he already knew.

This was it. The final lap. He'd done what most only dreamed of: established a brand, built a fortune, lived like royalty. A third Titan Bowl ring would seal the legacy.

Frank was already planning the next moves.

"We'll start the brand expansion mid-season," Frank said during a private lunch at a rooftop hotel. "Protein line. Fitness wear. A whole 'E-Philly' franchise. You'll be unstoppable."

Ethan nodded but said little.

The stadiums were still full. His fans still wore his jersey. But everything felt… routine. Empty. He couldn't put his finger on it, but the joy was gone.

Back home, Elle sent a message through Uncle George:

"If you slow down long enough to listen, you might remember who you are."

Ethan read it once. Deleted it.

Now inside the Titan Bowl LXX Valor Arena, it pulsed with energy. Flashing lights, halftime performers, celebrity sightings. It wasn't just a football game; it was a global spectacle.

Ethan's team, the Monarchs, faced the East Ridge Eagles in a clash of defensive titans and offensive fireworks. It was his toughest Titan Bowl yet.

In the third quarter, down by 14, Ethan caught a 45-yard pass over the middle and took a brutal hit. He lay on the field for a moment, gasping.

Get up, he told himself. Don't let them see you fall.

He rose to his feet, nodded to the sideline, and went back to the huddle.

Fourth quarter. One drive. Under two minutes.

Ethan caught the game-winning touchdown again.

Final score: Monarchs 34 – Eagles 31.

As confetti exploded overhead, the cameras surrounded him. Reporters pushed mics in his face. One shouted, "Ethan, how does it feel to win your third Titan Bowl?!"

Ethan grinned and said the same line he always did:

"All glory to the grind." No mention of God. No call home. No moment of reflection.

He raised the trophy. The crowd cheered. His teammates hoisted him on their shoulders.

Frank stood at the edge of the field, smiling as if he had won something more than a championship.

Later that night, back in his penthouse, Ethan removed his Monarch's polo shirt and stared at his reflection in the mirror.

The rings.

The titles.

The wealth.

And yet… something unspoken.

He walked past his Holy scriptures on the shelf without touching them. Poured a drink. Sat down and watched the game highlights on mute.

The screen flashed his face in slow motion, arms raised in victory.

But in the silence of the room, no voice congratulated him.

Only the quiet.

In the 9th year of his career, the Monarchs didn't make it to the Titan Bowl this time.

It wasn't a terrible season; Ethan still played at an elite level, but injuries, younger talent, and locker room politics began to chip away at the dominance they once had.

And for the first time in years, Ethan sat at home in February watching someone else lift the Titan Bowl trophy.

He didn't clap.

Didn't cheer.

Didn't even finish the interview clip.

Instead, he muted the TV and stared at the fireplace in his luxury high-rise. Outside, the city lights glowed like jewels, but inside, everything felt… still.

Frank stopped by that evening.

"Next season, we push harder," he said, sipping imported bourbon. "You've still got gas in the tank. These young guys aren't built like you."

Ethan nodded.

But in his chest, something tugged.

He hadn't called home in months, not since the time he sent Elle a wire transfer and a generic card.

She replied with a voice message that started with, "I love you," and ended with, "Call me when you can. I miss your voice."

He never returned the call.

That summer, the noise continued, while others relaxed in the off-season, Ethan stayed on the road. Public appearances. Brand deals. A late-night talk show circuit.

The questions were always the same:

"What's next for you?"

"How long do you plan to play?"

"Are you thinking about family, settling down?"

Ethan laughed them off.

But one question during a college panel event caught him off guard.

A young journalism student asked, "Mr. Phillips, with all the success and fame, what grounds you? Like, what keeps you anchored when the lights go off?"

Ethan paused for too long.

Frank, sitting off to the side, subtly shook his head.

Ethan finally smiled and answered, "Work ethic. Purpose. I don't look back. I keep moving forward."

The audience clapped, but his own words echoed hollowly in his ears.

Meanwhile, in Gerry, Elle prayed more these days.

Every night, she sat by the window in her luxurious living room, holy scriptures open, hoping that somehow her son would feel the pull.

"I don't care about the money, Lord," she whispered one night. "Just let him come home. Not to the house, but to You."

Uncle George added quietly, "Before it's too late."

Ethan stood in a luxury hotel suite, glass in hand, staring down at a city he no longer recognized as his own. The endorsements were still coming in, but the excitement was… gone.

He had everything he'd ever wanted.

And nothing he truly needed. As the sun set beyond the skyline, Ethan's phone buzzed.

It was a text from Jamir, the teammate who had walked away from Frank's imaging deal back in college, Jamir: "Just checking in, bro. I don't know what you're carrying these days, but if you ever want to talk, I'm here. For real." Ethan stared at the message for a while… then put the phone down without responding. Outside, the wind howled. And somewhere far off in the shadows, Frank smiled.

Chapter 48
Echo

Ethan's body didn't recover like it used to.

He took more hits this year on the field and off it.

The stats were still good, but the spark was gone. Drops that never happened before. Slower cuts. A few missed blocks left quarterbacks scrambling.

Coaches defended him publicly, but behind closed doors, the whispers started:

"He's not the same."

"Too many distractions."

"Slipping."

Off the field, things spiraled faster. Parties lasted longer. Nights blurred into mornings. He started drinking more expensive whiskey, fancy cocktails, things he once turned down in college. He stopped showing up to optional team workouts. He stopped calling home entirely. The penthouse was quieter now. His phone buzzed less only fans tagging him in old highlight reels or marketing teams requesting interviews he never confirmed. Frank rarely showed his face anymore. Instead, the once-persistent agent texted Ethan cryptic lines:

Frank: "Enjoy it while it lasts."

Frank: "Everything has a shelf life."

Frank: "You signed. I delivered. We're square."

Ethan began to wonder if it had all been a setup. But who could he trust now? Everyone either wanted something or left when the spotlight dimmed. Even the women who once clung to his arms now whispered rumors behind his back. "He's washed." "Not what he used to be."

"He's got demons."

The news came suddenly. It was cold that day: grey skies, stiff wind.

The entire Monarchs team gathered at St. James Memorial for the funeral of linebacker Chris Vaughn, a 30-year-old rising star who collapsed during practice the week before. Autopsy results were inconclusive. Some said heart failure. Others hinted at painkillers, stress, pressure, and secrets.

Ethan stood in the back of the sanctuary, dark sunglasses covering his bloodshot eyes. He hadn't slept and hadn't wanted to.

The pastor's voice echoed through the space: "Life is but a vapor. Here one moment, gone the next. Make peace while there's still time."

The words settled in Ethan's chest like bricks.

At the burial site, he watched Chris's mother throw a single white rose on the casket and collapse into her husband's arms.

That night, Ethan didn't party. He didn't eat.

He sat in his luxury penthouse alone, flipping through old photos on his phone, pictures of his high school days, family cookouts, and friends from Greywood.

One photo stopped him cold.

It was Aunt Helen, hugging him after his senior game at Gerry High.

He stared at it for a long time.

And cried.

The next morning, he stared at his reflection in the mirror.

Same face. Same fame. The same body, sculpted by years of discipline.

But inside, he felt hollow like a man being haunted by his own decisions. And yet, even in the emptiness, he couldn't bring himself to call home. He couldn't face his mother or Uncle George.

Not yet. Not while the contract still bound him.

A few months later, Ethan sat alone at the podium.

The press room inside Monarch Arena was hushed no fireworks, no fanfare, no flashing lights. Just reporters, notebooks, cameras… and silence.

He adjusted the microphone.

"Ten years ago, I walked onto this field with a dream," he began. "A dream to play at the highest level, to win championships, to make a name for myself."

He paused, his eyes glossing over the media row in front of him.

"I've done that. I've won. I've sacrificed. I've bled. I've lived this game with everything I had. But today… I'm walking away."

Murmurs rippled through the room.

"I'm officially retiring from the EFL."

Click. Click. Cameras snapped.

"I want to thank my coaches, my teammates, and… those who believed in me, even when I didn't answer their calls. I was focused. I was driven. But sometimes… I forgot the people who matter most. I hope one day they'll understand."

He didn't mention his mother or his uncle by name, but his voice cracked.

"I don't know what's next. Maybe a vacation. Maybe silence. But I know it's time."

Ethan stood slowly. There were no cheers. Just a standing silence as if everyone sensed there was more to the story than he said. He didn't take questions. He just walked off stage.

Back in his penthouse that evening, Ethan stared at his reflection in the dark glass of the window. He sat alone. The floor-to-ceiling windows framed the night skyline bright, distant, hollow. On the screen behind him, his retirement press conference played again. Reporters called it a fitting end to a legendary career. Ten years. Three Titan Bowl rings. Millions made. But there was no parade tonight, just silence. His phone buzzed beside him. Mom. For a moment, he considered ignoring it.

But something tugged.

He swiped to answer. "Hey, Mom."

There was a pause. Then Elle's voice trembled through the speaker. "Ethan, baby, I'm so glad you answered."

"Yeah," he said, suddenly quieter. "I... I've been thinking about you. About everything."

Uncle George's voice joined the call; it was on speaker. "We've been praying for you, son. You've done a lot. But your soul still matters most."

Elle inhaled. "I need to say this now, Ethan. Before it's too late."

He blinked, swallowing. "What do you mean?"

"I mean... I see what's happening. And so do you. All the lights. The noise. The praise. But your spirit's not right, Ethan. I can feel it. Repent. Please. Come home. Not just to us. Come back to God." Ethan felt a lump rise in his throat. Just as he opened his mouth to respond...

Black screen. The phone died. The line went dead.

He stared down at it, frozen. "...What?"

He shook it. Held the power button. Nothing. The battery had gone from 30% to zero.

He stood up to plug it in... his heart pounding.

That's when the door opened. And Frank stepped inside. No knock. No announcement. Just a presence. Ethan furrowed his brow. "Frank?" Frank adjusted his suit cuff, his voice smooth. "I came to collect the body." Ethan blinked, then laughed nervously. "Man, stop. You're always saying something weird." Frank just smiled. Ethan turned back toward the couch. "Whatever. I'm done with everything anyway. Time to chill and enjoy the silence." He plopped down on the sofa and turned the channels on the TV. A second later, his chest seized.

He gasped. The remote clattered to the floor. His hand gripped his heart. A sharp pain stabbed through his left side. He leaned forward, struggling to breathe.

Then, through the haze...a memory.

Chris.

His old teammate.

"The one who collapsed on the field a few months ago."

"Chris…" Ethan whispered.

"Is this what happened to Chris?" Frank was there. Suddenly.

At his side. Kneeling.

Too close…… "Of course, it did," he replied. Ethan reached for him. Frank slapped his hand aside. Still, Ethan tried.

His fingers clawed for help. His eyes found Frank's.

Black pupils. A void.

Frank leaned in. The silence cracked.

His voice, cold as ice:

"No one reads the tiny words.

No one.

Not until it's too late."

Ethan's eyes widened. A breath hitched, then broke.

The final rattle left his lungs.

Then silence.

Frank stood. Looked down at the lifeless body. No sorrow. No remorse. He walked toward the door, opened it quietly, and glanced back once more. "They never listen," he muttered. Then he disappeared into the night. The apartment door clicked shut. Three days passed.

No lights in the penthouse windows. No grocery deliveries. No car moved from the valet line. The doorman noted it first. Then the concierge. Ethan Phillips, the retired star of the EFL, hadn't been seen since Monday.

And Ethan Phillips never missed Monday workouts.

A call was placed to the team, but there was no response. Then the building's maintenance head, Mr. Russo, used the master key.

He found Ethan collapsed on the floor.

Remote on the floor. TV was still playing in the background. A half-finished bottle of water sat on the coffee table. He looked peaceful, almost asleep. But the silence was too complete.

Russo stepped back, whispering, "Oh no…"

Back at home, Elle was folding laundry in the den when the phone rang.

"This is Mrs. Phillips," she said, smiling slightly at the unknown number.

A pause.

Then: "Ma'am, this is Officer Lattimer with the local PD. I'm calling about your son, Ethan…"

Elle's world blurred. The phone dropped to the carpet. Uncle George rushed in. "Elle?! What is it?" She sank into the couch, breath gone. Tears fell freely.

A week later, the funeral was held in Gerry. The church was packed wall-to-wall. Athletes, coaches, former teammates, friends, family, and media. The same voices that used to shout "M-V-P!" now murmured, "Too soon." Ethan's casket was draped in his Monarchs jersey. Flowers towered behind the pulpit. But the real weight was in Elle's heart. She stood to speak.

"My son, 30 years old, had it all: glory, talent, wealth. But what I wanted most for him… was peace. Real peace." Her voice broke.

"I prayed every night that he would turn back to God. That he'd remember who raised him. I know he made mistakes, but I also know God is merciful." Tears fell throughout the room.

As the family stood to prepare for the burial procession…

Frank appeared. Uninvited. Unannounced. Dressed in a sharp black suit and his sunglasses on inside the sanctuary. Elle saw him. Uncle George whispered, "That's him." Frank approached slowly.

"I'm sorry for your loss," he said smoothly.

Elle's voice cracked. "Where were you when he died?"

Frank tilted his head slightly.

"I was there," he said. "But I had to collect what was mine." He lowered his sunglasses.

For a heartbeat, his pupils turned black.

Then he walked away.

Elle and Uncle George stood frozen, hearts hammering.

Tears blurred Elle's eyes.

"He didn't see it coming."
Just before the door closed, Frank whispered….
"On to the next one."

Epilogue
The Tiny Words

The news spread quickly.

Titan Bowl Champion Ethan Phillips died at 30.

Sports networks ran tributes. Highlight reels, emotional reflections from former teammates. The nation mourned a star taken too soon.

But in Gerry… there was no fanfare.

Just a mother in black, sitting quietly on a porch Ethan never returned to.

Elle didn't cry anymore. The tears had dried weeks ago. What lingered now was silence, and holy scriptures opened on her lap.

Uncle George sat beside her. He hadn't said much since the funeral. Neither had she.

Until one afternoon.

A yellow envelope arrived in the mail.

Inside, a copy of Ethan's Career Acquisition and Brand Agreement was delivered anonymously.

There, in fine print, barely legible beneath the signature line, were the words:

"Your image, likeness, voice, soul, and service are bound for the duration of your earthly influence and beyond."

Elle's hands trembled.

Uncle George read it silently. Then he bowed his head.

"No one ever reads the tiny words," he whispered.

They sat together on that porch as the wind moved through the trees like a warning… or a whisper.

"And fear not them which kill the body but are not able to kill the soul: but rather fear him which is able to destroy both soul and body in hell."

Matthew 10:28 KJV

Ethan chased glory, wealth, and praise.

He had everything except the one thing that mattered most.

And in the end, the silence of his soul was louder than the roar of any stadium. Let this story remind us:

Success can be blinding. Fame can be fatal. And the enemy rarely shows up with horns; sometimes he comes with promises and paperwork.

Always read the tiny words.

Always guard your soul.

The End.

Author's Note

Not every story ends with a second chance.

Some people spend years pursuing success, fame, or influence, believing they're in control and that they can always turn back to God "later."

However, the truth is that every heartbeat is a gift. And when we choose to glorify ourselves instead of the One who made us, we may not realize how close we are to the edge.

Matthew 10:28 KJV tells us to fear not those who can kill the body, but Him who can destroy both body and soul in hell.

This story is a wake-up call, not a scare tactic.

If the Holy Spirit is convicting you to return to Him, don't wait for your final echo.

Choose Him now while there's still time.

K. Cummings

About the Author

K. Cummings is a passionate storyteller known for blending emotional realism with powerful spiritual truth. Through her red-covered books, she explores the complexities of human choices, faith, and redemption. With a background in child development, criminal justice, and community service, her writing is deeply rooted in her commitment to inspire hope and healing through every page.

K. Cummings is the author of several impactful novels, including I'm Not Him: The Stranger in the Mirror Was Me, Cracked Glass, Love Only Me, and Table of Regrets: What Was Too Much? Her stories often reflect the battles between good and evil, the weight of silence, and the enduring power of faith.

When she's not writing, K. Cummings is actively serving her community, mentoring youth, and empowering others to find their voice through storytelling.

Follow her journey or connect at www.kimberlycummingsauthor.com or on Instagram @ScratchpadCreate.

Email: scratchpadcreate@gmail.com